FORGOT TO TELL YOU SOMETHING

M.L. BROOME

TERRACOTTA DRAGON ARTS

Forgot to Tell You Something
Copyright © J.E. Soper 2020
All rights reserved.

This book is a work of fiction. References to real people, events, establishments, organizations, or locales are intended only to provide a sense of authenticity and are used fictitiously. Names, characters, dialogue and incidents depicted in this book are products of the author's imagination and are not to be construed as real.

No part of this publication may be reproduced, downloaded, transmitted, decompiled, reverse-engineered, or stored into any information storage and retrieval system, in any form or by any means, whether electronic or mechanical, now known or hereafter invented, without the express written permission of J.E. Soper and TerraCotta Dragon Arts.

Digital Edition 978-1-7360214-0-8 NOVEMBER 2020

Print Edition ISBN: 978-1-7360214-1-5

Cover Design

Suzana Stankovic, LSDdesign

This book is dedicated to all the men and women working in the healthcare field, in an attempt to better the lives of others. Until you have worked by their side or walked in their shoes, you cannot understand the sacrifices they make and the heartaches they suffer in silence.

Thank you. I am proud to be part of the medical community, and no matter where in the world I travel, they will always be my family. My home.

ACKNOWLEDGMENTS

To my Beck, you are the living embodiment of Tally—fierce and beautiful with a heart of gold.

To my dear friend, Astrid. Your talent and capacity for kindness knows no bounds. I am truly inspired by your works and can't wait to see all the offerings you bring to the world.

To Trisha, you were one of my first friends in the indie world. You took me under your wing and showed me the ropes. Not once has your kindness faltered. I wish you so much success.

To Angie, whose words touch my soul and whose soul touches my heart. You are a gift in my life.

To Taryn, my quiet warrior. One day, I'm going to make you shout out how amazing you are so that the world can hear it—because you are.

To Grace, my unstoppable fiery friend. You are my cheerleader, shaking those pom poms and clearing away all self-doubt. I see big things in your future.

To Marissa, your enthusiasm is contagious. Never forget your strength. Or your talent.

WHO WANTS A SNEAK PEEK AT SPARK RIDGE?
JUMP INTO MY UPCOMING SMALL TOWN ROMANCE SERIES!

Lovelies, I am **beyond** excited for my upcoming small town romance series, *Spark Ridge: Scenes from a Small Town*.

Why?

Because this baby has **everything**—sexy cinnamon roll heroes, sassy heroines, sizzling banter and off-the-charts steam all set against the backdrop of a New York town where anything can—and will, happen.

And the tropes—so many luscious tropes! If you enjoy small town romance with a touch of suspense, then you're going to **love** Spark Ridge and her residents.

To sweeten the deal, I'm offering Spark Ridge's intro novella **free** to my newsletter subscribers. The original version was part of a charity anthology, but I loved Ori and Ash too much to end their story with only a HFN ending. These two deserve the big bang of HEAs.

The first full-length novel, **Catching Sparks**, centers once again around Ori and Ash. Throw in the return of an old love, a sexy commitment-phobe and some seriously devious bad guys and you've got one hell of a ride. That's not even the biggest plot twist, but you'll have to grab your copy to find out!

Catching Sparks will be out in a few months, but until then you can whet your appetite with **The First Spark**!

Remember, this updated version of the novella is solely for my **newsletter subscribers**, but trust me, with tons of giveaways and exclusives, you want an invite to this party.

Download The First Spark

Add Catching Sparks to GoodReads

CONTENTS

Chapter 1   1
Tally

Chapter 2   21
Tally

Chapter 3   33
Tally

Chapter 4   47
Owen

Chapter 5   55
Tally

Chapter 6   61
Tally

Chapter 7   73
Owen

Chapter 8   81
Tally

Chapter 9   87
Owen

Chapter 10   101
Tally

Chapter 11   113
Tally

Chapter 12   125
Tally

Chapter 13   137
Tally

Chapter 14   145
Owen

Chapter 15   153
Tally

Chapter 16   161
Owen

Chapter 17   171
Tally

Chapter 18   181
Owen

Chapter 19   193
Tally

Chapter 20   199
Owen

Chapter 21   207
Tally

Chapter 22   219
Owen

Chapter 23   229
Tally

Chapter 24   243
Owen

Chapter 25   255
Tally

Chapter 26   263
Tally

Chapter 27   273
Tally

Chapter 28   283
Tally

Chapter 29   289
Owen

Chapter 30   299
Tally

Chapter 31   313
Tally

Chapter 32   323
Owen

Chapter 33   331
Tally

Chapter 34   343
Tally

Chapter 35   355
Owen

Chapter 36   365
Tally

Chapter 37   373
Owen

Chapter 38   385
Tally

Chapter 39   399
Owen

Chapter 40   415
Tally

Chapter 41   427
Tally

Epilogue   431
Tally

Hello lovelies,   433
Also by M.L. Broome   435
Connect with M.L. Broome   437
About the Author   439
Make You Stay   441

CHAPTER ONE
TALLY

"Ugh, the floor is sticky, and what is that smell?"

I swing my gaze over to Stefani, her button nose scrunched in disgust. "That smell is smoke and sweat, and you don't want to know what's on the floor. Do yourself a favor—remain upright. There's all manner of bodily fluids down there."

I choke back a laugh at her horrified expression. To be honest, I'm not positive there is any blood or urine on the floor, but I wouldn't put it past Wicked Chucks. It's the epitome of a dive bar, but they sure know how to bring together the underground punk and rockabilly community.

"Great. Now, I need to boil all my extremities." Stefani waves her hand in the air after touching one of the black concrete walls, as if the bubonic plague is alive and well within the paint.

"Stef, correct me if I'm wrong, but weren't you the one who wanted to come here?"

"You come here all the time, Lu."

"You're not me." That is the understatement of the century. Stefani is my polar opposite—tall and lanky with huge tits and a face that makes men forget their own names. Did I mention the size of her breasts? They can double as flotation devices should the need arise. They're not God given, but ask any man tripping over their own tongue as she walks by if they care. Simple answer—not one bit.

Then there's me—the anti-Stefani. Standing next to her willowy frame, I might be mistaken for her pet chihuahua. I'm a foot shorter with enormous eyes hidden behind tortoiseshell frames and a mouth lacking any sort of filter. I guess God forgot to install one of those bad boys before I was shipped down here. Hell, sometimes I even surprise myself with the statements flowing from my lips.

But, despite the polar opposition in the looks department, I love this woman something fierce. Stefani is my ride or die. While she's more Givenchy than counterculture, she's hardcore loyalty and heart. So, the whole gorgeous supermodel vibe? Something I happily accept. Okay, not happily. There's a shred—or ten—of jealousy that she is Heidi Klum's doppelgänger, but I'm also aware that most men see nothing past her looks.

And most men don't see me at all.

"These guys are hot as hell, though." Stefani surveys the crowd, her lashes fluttering, but I'm not sure if it's a seductive flirtation or the weight of her falsies. "I understand why you like the place."

"I don't come here to pick up guys."

"You need to get laid, Lu."

I can argue her suggestion, but it's true. A painful, pathetic truth. I haven't had sex in over two years, and even then, it was hardly memorable. Actually, it was only noteworthy because it was such a lousy lay. "I don't remember what good sex feels like," I grumble, downing the last swig of my beer.

"Can I give you some advice?"

I'm shaking my head before Stefani finishes her sentence. I know exactly what she's going to say. I also know she's going to ignore me and plow ahead with her well-intentioned statement.

"Throw out the rule book."

See what I mean?

"Contrary to what you might think, Stefani, I don't

have *that* many rules. I'm just particular. Besides, my rules keep me safe. You might try getting a few of your own."

She chews her bottom lip, considering my advice. I'm not alone in the bad boyfriend department. Stefani's heart has been used as a punching bag more times than I can count. But, unlike me, she still believes in fated love.

I envy her optimism.

I shake my empty bottle in Dan's direction, and he wastes no time bringing me a refill. The man is not only a kick-ass bartender, but he's also a card-carrying member of my ride or die crew. We hit it off immediately the night I dared to enter Wicked Chucks alone, and he elected himself my personal bodyguard. The sad part? Dan earned his title that same evening, fending off a drunken buffoon who got a bit handsy. But luckily, he doesn't hold it against me.

"What's up, Strawberry Shortcake?" Dan jokes, tugging on my unicorn pink locks.

I scrunch up my face. So much for looking sultry; I apparently resemble a cartoon character.

Stefani, as always, has my back. "I like the pink. It's funky, like you," she states, pulling her hand through my hair with reassuring strokes.

I stick out my tongue in Dan's direction. "See? I'm cool."

"You don't need pink hair to be cool, Tallulah," Dan reminds me with a wink.

"This coming from electric blue boy," I retort, as I offer a pointed stare at his bright azure hair, gelled into short spikes.

"You got me there," Dan chuckles, turning away to serve another customer.

"He's beautiful," Stefani murmurs, giving me a hip check as we lounge against the bar. Her eyes track Dan from one end of the floor to the other. "He has a great laugh."

"Agreed." I love Dan's laugh—it holds nothing back, and it's fiercely genuine. The truth is, most of the people in Wicked Chucks are genuine. Oh, they can be assholes, but they own that facet of their personality. Hell, they're proud of it. It took years of training to grind their uncouth states to a fine edge.

It's a motley bunch, but I find the honesty in this group of rag-tag punk rockers highly refreshing in a world hellbent on half-truths.

"Is he single?" Stefani presses, jostling me back to the melee of the moment.

"Define single." Dan has his choice of women, a rotating harem that fulfills any of his physical desires, at a moment's notice.

But his loose tendencies aren't because of an overinflated ego. It's a mode of protection.

Keep your heart unreachable, and no one can crash in and mangle it. In that regard, Dan and I are kismet. If only I felt anything beyond friendship for him, and vice versa, our lives would be set.

No such luck.

"Don't tell me, he's one of *those* guys." Stefani fluffs her waves, releasing a huff of resignation.

"He's not one of *those* guys. He's single, but he's not celibate. However, I have it on good authority that he'd love to fall head over heels for some lucky lady."

"Are you hoping to be that lucky lady?"

I sputter my beer. "No, not at all. We are 100% platonic." I cock my chin at her, a smile coloring my lips. "You're interested, aren't you?"

Before she can answer, Dan re-enters the conversation. The man has perfect timing on lockdown. "Are you going to introduce me to your friend?"

"No, I plan on being rude the rest of the evening," I volley back, smirking at the come-hither gazes my friends are exchanging. If anyone can tame Dan, it's Stefani.

"Since Tallulah is refusing to cooperate, I'll take the reins on this one. I'm Dan, pleasure to meet you."

"I'm Stefani. I work with Lu," she coos, extending her hand in greeting, her smile showcasing perfect white teeth.

Poor Dan doesn't stand a chance.

It's funny, but the old adage that opposites attract holds true in this scenario. Dan and Stefani are a mismatched set. She looks like she sauntered off the catwalks of Milan, while Dan would sooner gouge his eyes out than sit for a fashion show. Come to think of it, so would I.

But he is terminally good-looking, from his square jaw to his piercing, dark eyes, and it's apparent from Stefani's nervous titter that his charm is working its magic.

Feedback echoes from the front of the bar, and the locals gravitate toward the stage. Time to hightail it to my hiding spot.

"Hey, Dan, is my balcony available?" I question, nodding my head toward the back of the bar. Wicked Chucks wasn't always a punk dive. In its heyday, it was a community theater, complete with velvet curtains and box seat balconies. For obvious reasons, the balconies are closed to the general public, although the staff still uses them for storage and all manner of illicit activity.

After the unfortunate manhandling incident on my inaugural visit to Wicked Chucks, Dan granted me access to one of the balconies. I left him little choice, especially when I threatened to show up solo to a show the following evening. Per him, he'd much rather seat me up there, away from the noise and hoodlums on the floor. Hell, it's also the best view in the house.

"Tallulah, would I ever deny you your balcony?" His gaze returns to Stefani. "Will you be joining your friend, or can I convince you to park it here?"

Stefani glances at me, a puppy dog expression crossing her face.

Okay, Stef, you can stay and play.

"I think I'll stay down here for a bit, so long as I'm not bothering you, Dan."

"You're never a bother. But I will ask you to move to this side of the bar. It's safer. More private."

That's Dan-speak for tucked away in a corner where other ogling men have less of a view. Well played, my friend.

Dan hands me another beer with a wicked grin. "You're on your own, young lady."

"So, like every other night, basically. Take good care of Stefani. Anything happens, I'm holding you personally responsible." With a final wink, I leave the burgeoning lovebirds and stroll upstairs.

I hope they hit it off. Someone should get laid tonight, and I know it isn't going to be me. I envy Stefani and Dan—they make the game of flirtation look easy. When I attempt flirting, I feel like a hack, a teenager who stole her mom's dress and is trying to pass for a lady.

In other words? It isn't pretty.

As I climb the stairs to the balcony, I realize that the floor's stickiness extends to the second level, and I'm thankful for the dim lighting. I really don't want to know what happened here the other night.

Using my hip, I heave the oak door with a grunt, losing my balance as the door swings open from the other side.

Large hands grab me before I tumble to the floor, and I find myself staring into the eyes of the most drop-dead gorgeous man I've ever seen.

"And here I thought I was helping. You okay?" He smiles, showing perfect white teeth nestled against a neatly trimmed beard.

"Nice catch. You must have played football in high school." I offer him my unopened beer with a chuckle. "Payment for your troubles?"

"Your timing is impeccable. I was about to head back down and fight the crowd."

I shrug and wrap my hand around the neck of the bottle. "If you prefer to wait in line, be my guest."

Another smile, his fingers firmly attached to the beer. "I'll take you up on your generous offer and buy you a replacement when we head downstairs. Fair enough?"

"Fair enough." I shoot him a glance, my nose scrunching as I examine him. This must be his first time at the club, because I've never seen him before, and he is definitely not a face you forget. "Do they know you're up here?"

He chuckles, sipping his beer. "I was planning on robbing the place, so I figured it best if I kept a low profile."

"You've got a bit of a wait. They won't have any money in the tills for another couple of hours. Until then, I suppose you can hang out in my balcony."

"Your balcony, huh? I don't see a sign. Do you have a deed handy?"

I nod, pointing at the worn velvet sofa. "Absolutely. Signed my name in blood and swore an oath on a goat."

That did it. His laugh is full-blown now, gravelly and sexy as hell. "You're *that* woman. I've heard about you."

"All bad things, I'm sure...and they're all true." I swig down a mouthful of beer, offering up a saucy grin.

"What's your name, Darlin?"

Wow, I really like his use of that pet name. Usually, I loathe cheeky nicknames, but from his lips, it's the most enticing two syllables I've ever heard.

"Tallulah."

He extends his hand in greeting. I expect to see a working man's hands—banged up with dirt under the nails and ink across the digits. Fairly standard for this scene. But his fingers are long, lean, and without a single tattoo. Unexpected. "I'm Owen. Pleasure meeting the owner of this fine establishment."

Usually, I'm spot on with a clever retort or comeback. What I lack in flirtatious ability, I make up for in wit. But this time, my mind blanks as I meet his gaze. I'm mesmerized by the feel of his hand engulfing mine and the warmth spreading through my body. "You too," I stammer, finally finding my voice.

"That's a beautiful name."

Earth to Tallulah, snap out of it. What is wrong with me tonight?

I'm the homegirl all the guys kick back with, not the fluttery eyed doe who can't add two and two.

Or at least I was until Owen wandered into my balcony.

"They named me after my grandmother."

Owen nods, his gaze focused on the crowd below. "It's an unusual moniker, but then again, so are you."

My heart sinks at his statement, but I'm not surprised. His words are par for the course. Some women are beautiful, lush, and sensuous. I'm unusual. But this time, the descriptor stings like hell. On the plus side, at least now I can relax. The man isn't interested.

"I'm also geeky and klutzy. You wouldn't want to forget those adjectives," I shrug, trying to play off Owen's unintentional kick to my ego.

Owen chuckles. "I agree with the klutzy part, but how are you geeky?"

I point at the tortoiseshell rims on my face. "Glasses."

"I think a woman in glasses is sexy...particularly one who's got a kick-ass sense of humor."

"You're just saying that, so I don't kick you out of my balcony." Although I'm sure his compliment was an offhanded offering, my ego appreciates the bolster. Sexy siren, I am not.

"You got me pegged." There's that laugh again, and once more, it sends tingles up my spine. It's as if each note dances along my nerve-endings, short-circuiting my body.

While he observes the increasingly raucous crowd, I take the opportunity to steal glances in his direction. Owen is gorgeous. Drop-dead delectable. He's tall and broad, with sleeves of tattoos covering both arms, the ink traveling up to what I surmise is a firm and sculpted chest. His dark hair is buzzed close to his head, and a neatly trimmed beard adorns his face. But it's his eyes, dark gray like a sky right before a storm, that hold me captive.

"They all tell a story," he murmurs, his gaze swinging back in my direction.

"What?" Crap, he caught me looking at him.

"You were checking out my ink, right?"

Sure, we'll go with that answer. "I'm a fan of tats. I have several of my own."

"You know you have to show me now."

CHAPTER ONE

If there's one thing I'm not shy about, it's my body art. I've spent years—and thousands of dollars—decorating my skin with designs from some of the country's top tattoo artists. I'm not covered like Owen, but my pieces are anything but flash.

I lift the cuff of my jean to show him the artwork on my calf, but Owen has other ideas as his fingers slide along my upper arm.

"This is a beautiful piece. The linework is exquisite." He lifts my shirt, examining the half-sleeve design of flowers and fairies.

"Thanks," I laugh, shaking my head. "I don't know why I said thank you. I didn't design it."

"You selected a terrific artist, and that's half the battle."

"Munoz, out of Miami." My eyes travel down to his fingers, still pressing against my skin. "It's one of my favorite pieces."

"I've read about Munoz, but now I know he does quality work."

I startle when his fingers creep under the hem on my t-shirt, exposing my side piece.

"Ticklish?"

"Yes," I mumble. I *am* ticklish, but that's not the issue. My body is quickly overheating from this man's caresses. The worst part? They're not caresses; he's just examining my ink. Now tell that to my sex-starved body, all fired up and ready for action.

Stefani is right. I need to get laid.

The feedback sounding from one of the amps rattles me from my Owen-induced stupor. Enough fuzziness and feels, it's time for a bit of rage-filled anarchy.

"Game time." I perch on the back of the sofa, fully expecting this gorgeous demagogue to disappear downstairs for a close-up view of the band.

Instead, Owen settles next to me with a wink. Surprising. I glance toward the bar, ensuring that Stefani is still in one piece and not an unwitting crowd surfer. I find her tucked into the far corner, chatting up some dude with a mohawk. Even here, totally out of her element, my friend draws men to her like bees to nectar.

"You're staying?" I inquire, taking another swallow of beer. At the rate I'm drinking, I'll need a refill before they finish the first song.

"Are you kicking me out, Tally?"

I cock my head at the nickname. "Everyone calls me Lu. My Dad is the only person who calls me Tally."

"I prefer it to Lu. So, is it cool for me to stay?"

I tap my finger against my chin. "Hmm, maybe."

"What if I show you a kick-ass card trick? One you won't be able to figure out."

"You carry around a deck of cards?"

"Just for this occasion," Owen volleys back.

"Fine. If—and *only* if—it's a really good trick, I'll let you share my balcony."

"How magnanimous, Tally."

I've seen plenty of card tricks in my years, some better than most. But his trick puts all the others to shame. I'm not certain if it's the dexterity with which Owen shuffles the cards or his smooth, gravelly voice serving as a distraction, but he selects my card. Every. Single. Time.

"That is the coolest thing I've ever seen." I'm fully aware that my grin matches the Cheshire Cat's, but the trick blew my mind.

Actually, Owen is blowing my mind.

"Told you. So, now we're partners." He extends his hand to seal the deal.

My eyes narrow in confusion. "Partners?"

"Co-owners of the balcony, and this uncomfortable as hell couch."

"Hey, leave my couch alone. Don't you enjoy a spring in your ass?"

"Not at all. Are you going to leave me hanging?" he inquires, motioning to his still outstretched hand.

I throw back my head, laughing. "Fair is fair. I never renege on a deal."

A sexy smirk breaks across Owen's mouth as his tongue glides along his lower lip, and my body clenches. Again.

Calm your tits, hormones. It wasn't an overt gesture.

"You're really beautiful when you smile, Tally."

His compliment catches me off-guard. "Thanks."

"You look surprised that I said that."

"I'm the cool, fun, funky chick. It's nice to be beautiful for a change."

He reaches up, tugging at my pink locks. "I have a feeling you're always beautiful. You're one of those women that wakes up looking like you did when you went to sleep."

I snort my sip of beer. "Sorry to disappoint, but I'm like everyone else in the morning—a hot mess."

"I'll be the judge of that," he replies, breaking his gaze from mine to focus on the people below.

I take a second to process his words. Owen did *not* just intimate a sleepover. Did he? Well, wouldn't that be a hundred shades of deliciousness?

I release a slow exhale, trying in vain to calm my nerves. "I might have to go rescue my friend."

Owen follows my hand as I point out Stefani, still huddled at the bar. "The blonde?"

Yes, with the knockout body and perfect profile.

"She's a looker, isn't she?"

But Owen doesn't commiserate with my statement. Hell, he doesn't even acknowledge it. "She doesn't appear in desperate need of a rescue."

"If you can't tell, she's not a regular, so I want to keep my eye on her. Jump in should the need arise."

Owen bites back a laugh, shaking his head as he clinks my beer bottle with his own.

"What's so funny?" I demand.

"You are."

"How so?" What did I say now?

"How tall are you, Tally? No offense, but you're not exactly intimidating."

I cross my arms over my chest, sending him my best fake glare. "You forget that you're talking to the blood oath goat girl. I'm scary as hell."

"Clearly." And clearly, he doesn't believe a word I say. Granted, he is at least a foot taller than me, but that's hardly difficult. I barely tip the scales at five feet.

"Look. It's my mantra." I direct his attention to my top, noting the irony that I wore it this evening. It proclaims, '*I'm too short for this shit (me, with almost everything)*'.

His eyes skate over my shirt, and I swear he lingers a few extra seconds on my tits. Boys will be boys.

"Apropos, indeed." Despite Owen's unmistakable bad-boy exterior, he doesn't behave—or speak—like the typical punk rocker. He possesses a quiet grace and power, exuding an air of importance without the usual cockiness or bravado.

I want to know more about this man. Much, much more. Even if he thinks I'm klutzy and a poor excuse for a guard dog.

"It's a good crowd tonight. Surprising for a Wednesday."

"Wicked Chuck's may be part of the underground scene, but it's well known in the area." I take in the ever-growing sea of humans below us, wondering how long we have until one, or several, break into some form of violence. "It will be off the chain crowded tomorrow."

"That's right. Hedgecore plays tomorrow night." Owen shifts his attention to my face, those gray eyes studying me. "Are you a fan?"

He's kidding, right? "Am I a fan of Hedgecore? They're only one of the greatest rockabilly bands in the history of the world."

He chuckles, taking a pull from his bottle. "I'll take that as a yes?"

I hold up my fingers. "Just a bit."

"I'll be seeing you tomorrow night, then, too."

I scrunch up my face in confusion, even as my insides flash with warmth at the idea of seeing this man again. "Huh?"

"At the concert."

My ego deflates to its standard size as I deduce his statement. "I wasn't able to get a ticket. They sold out before I got one."

He taps the beer bottle against his boot, clearing his throat. "That's a shame."

"It is. I guess you're a lucky bastard with a ticket?"

Owen nods, chuckling. "I am definitely a lucky bastard. I'm also in need of a refill. You ready for another?" He motions to my empty beer bottle, which I gladly hand over.

"Thanks. I'll hold down the fort."

With a grin, Owen ducks out the door, and I release a breath I wasn't aware I'd been holding. Holy God, where did that man come from?

Owen is, without a doubt, the sexiest slice of heaven I've ever met, and if his nimble fingers are anything to go on, he's talented in other areas, as well. Several other areas. Wouldn't I love to test that theory...over and over again.

I don't get all tongue-tied and fluttery over men, but Owen is not most men. Even better, he's hanging out here with me, when there's a bar full of eager recipients for anything he might be offering.

I peer over the railing, hoping to catch a glimpse of Owen. Even with the crowd, he's easy to spot. Especially since he's talking to Stefani.

I remind my crushed hopes that this is not unexpected. Stefani is gorgeous. Owen is gorgeous. Besides, I did mention that she's my friend. Like a jealous voyeur, I study their interactions as Owen accepts a couple of beer bottles and points to the balcony. Stefani nods, flashing him a brilliant smile.

Any glitter from my flirtation with Owen drifts to the ground. Time to slip back into my tried-and-true role—the cool chick, the buddy, the friend.

With a huffed sigh, I flop back against the sofa cushion. For once, I'd like to be the beauty queen, let someone else play my role for the evening.

"Here you go, Darlin." A beer bottle wags under my nose, and I accept the offering with a smile.

"Thanks. I appreciate it, but you didn't have to get me a beer."

"I owed you one."

I nod, picking at the label on the bottle. "I see you met Stefani."

"You saw that? Wow, you do have eyes everywhere."

"I wasn't snooping. I was just—"

"Checking up on her. I get it. I introduced myself and let her know where we were."

"So she could join us?"

"No, so she wouldn't worry." Owen shifts on the cushion, pivoting to face me. "How much do you really like Hedgecore?"

"Is that a trick question? I like them more than Santa and the Easter Bunny combined."

"What about the Tooth Fairy?"

"Nah, she and I aren't on speaking terms."

"What would you say if I told you that I got you a ticket for the concert tomorrow?"

My eyes widen as my fingers clutch my beer. He's joking. He must be joking. "I would say you're full of crap. It's sold out."

"I got you a ticket, Tally, but there is one catch."

I groan, taking a swig of the cold brew. "I knew it! I have to ride in your backpack, don't I?"

There's that smile again. Each time, it's more vivid than the last. "How did you guess? I don't doubt that you would."

My grin matches his. "I totally would."

His fingers reach out, tracing along my knee in an unexpected tingle fest. "The catch is that you have to go with me."

I'm hearing things. Yep, it finally happened—that unfortunate LSD incident when I was a teenager has caught up to me. "You want to go to Hedgecore with me?"

Instead of moving away, he slides his hand under my thigh, his fingers tightening around my leg. "Very much so. What do you say?"

I'm an affectionate person, but I'm also highly selective with whom gets that attention. Owen has earned it in spades, whether or not he wants it.

Throwing my hands around his neck, I let out a squeal of excitement. "Oh my God, how fabulous!"

If I thought it was tricky sitting next to the man, it's damn near impossible to calm my hormones when our bodies press together. Add in his arms wrapping around my frame, and the situation turns downright electric.

"I like you excited," he murmurs, that gorgeous mouth dangerously close to my own.

My gaze travels down his face. Bad idea. His lips are full and soft and look like they could do all manner of naughty things to my body.

The clang of guitars sounds from the stage, ending our moment. I push myself off Owen and reclaim my perch on the back of the couch, trying not to read into the fact that instead of releasing me, his fingers tightened when I pulled away.

As if he didn't want to let go, either.

Just this once, I wish I could flirt. Bat my eyes and play the role of the damsel in distress, desperately in need of male attention. Men eat up that shit.

I suck at flirting. That's why I'm the cool chick. I can discuss any manner of topics—from music to politics to sports—but feminine wiles? God neglected to install those on the same day he forgot my filter.

So, instead of pretending to be someone I am not, I let down my guard. I banter with Owen about the musicians of today and how they lack any real depth. Musically, the man is my twin. We adore the same genres, albums, and songs. An added bonus? The more I drink, the more my awkwardness falls away. Or the less I notice it, anyway.

When the band plays their cover of 'Girlfriend in a Coma', I let out a squeal of excitement. I adore The Smiths, and this song puts me in my happy place. As the music washes over me, I fall into the beat, forgetting that tonight, I'm not alone.

As the song plays, my gaze slides over to Owen. He's not even subtle as he watches me dance, his eyes moving over my body, a heated expression on his features.

I'm grateful for the dim lighting as a flush rushes over my cheeks. "I love that song."

"I can tell." Now those dark gray eyes lock onto mine, but the smoldering expression remains. "After seeing you dance, I'll have to add that song to my playlist."

I know it's harmless flirting, but my sex-deprived body lights up like New Orleans in February.

Once again, I lack a comeback. So much for the cool chick persona. With a sigh, I pop off the couch. I need a refill and now seems as good a time as any to regain my emotional footing. "I'm headed to the bar. Can you move your legs?" I request, sending his outstretched, booted legs a pointed look.

"Maybe."

"Maybe?"

Owen nods, putting his hands behind his head. "What's the magic word?"

"If you think I won't climb over you to get to another beer, you are sadly mistaken."

"Is that so? This, I might have to see."

"Are you really going to make me climb?" *Please say yes.*

"It depends. How badly do you want the beer?"

I've never had this much fun bantering with a man. Owen is in a class by himself. "Suit yourself, but don't say I didn't warn you." I hoist my leg over his, wishing in this scenario that I was a few inches taller. As it stands, I'm practically grinding against him. I lift my other leg to cross over him, but Owen widens his stance, and I collapse on his lap.

The beer bottle slips from my fingers, but Owen catches it in a move that would make Joe Montana weep. His other hand wraps around my hip, his fingers dancing ever so slightly across my back. "Sorry about that."

Judging by the smirk on his face, the man isn't sorry, but neither am I. In fact, I'm tempted to wrap my legs around his waist and lock him in my grasp, never to escape. Instead, I focus my gaze on the serpent wrapped around his bicep. Without thinking, my finger reaches out, tracing the lines of the tattoo. "Is this the creation story?"

Owen's breath hitches as my nails drift along his skin. Good to know our proximity is having an equally unnerving effect on him. "It's my adaptation of it."

"Where else are you inked?"

Another catch in his breathing, his fingers sliding up my spine and pulling my body tight against him. His lips hover at my ear, his beard causing all manner of tingles. "Everywhere, Tally. My best work is in places reserved for very few people to see."

"That's a shame. I'd like to see them." Holy shit, did that brazen remark fall out of my mouth?

His hands slide from my hips to cup my ass, and this time, I know it's not an accidental slip. "You will, Darlin."

Everything—the noise, the lights, the din, fall away as I hold his stare. I'm pressed against him, and it's impossible not to feel the erection straining his jeans. I shift ever so slightly against him, biting my lip to hold back the grin when a low moan falls from his mouth. "Little girl, you'd better behave."

"Or what?" Another shift earns a second moan, his fingers tightening around my ass cheeks.

"I'm going to do what I've wanted to do since the first moment I laid eyes on you."

I'm not sure if it's the alcohol or overactive hormones, but my bravery suddenly knows no bounds. My hand strokes the back of Owen's neck and along his scalp, feeling the smoothness of his skin. "What would that be?"

Owen doesn't get a chance to answer my question as Stefani's lilting voice cuts into the moment. "Lu, are you up here? Where are you?"

Owen's hands drop to his side, his head falling forward. "Perfect timing," he mutters, but I catch his smile.

Perfect timing is right. Perfectly awful.

"That would be Stefani," I mumble, forcing myself to a standing position.

My friend's eyes widen when she catches sight of me in the middle of climbing off Owen. "Oh shit, am I interrupting something? I can leave, it was just getting scary down there."

Sometimes, I hate being a good friend, but I promised to keep an eye on Stefani, and the drunken crowd is turning rowdy.

"You're fine, Stefani," Owen assures her. "Tally was proving a point."

My buzz from Owen's caresses fades into the din of the music. Was that what I was doing?

"What point was that?" Stefani's gaze moves to me, curious for my explanation.

"How my determination to get a beer is unmatched. Owen wouldn't move his legs, so I was climbing him. What's a thirsty girl to do?"

My friend's eyes rove over Owen, drinking in every sexy morsel. "You wouldn't let her through?"

"I thought I'd make it more interesting," Owen replies, stretching his legs out to rest on the edge of the balcony as his gray eyes hold mine. "Tally isn't one to back down, but I do love a challenge."

"She's a tough one," Stefani concurs, smiling at Owen. Crap. I know that smile. I've seen it a million times. It doesn't help that my friend has consumed at least three or four drinks. The more she imbibes, the better her flirting tactics. I've never seen anything like it. "Lu, would you get me another beer, too?"

"You were just downstairs," I argue, desperate *not* to leave Stefani alone with Owen.

"I know, but these shoes are killing my feet," Stefani pouts, plopping onto the couch and slipping off one of her stilettos. "I'll keep Owen company while you're gone."

"Tally, I can go get the beers," Owen offers, but I wave away his suggestion.

"You got the last one, remember?" I don't wait for his reply, turning on my heel and yanking open the door. I can't read Owen's expression, but I know what Stefani has in mind for my sexy balcony cohort.

The worst part? If Owen is like any other man on the planet, he doesn't stand a chance.

But just this once, I hope Owen is immune.

CHAPTER TWO
TALLY

I trudge down the stairs. A more apt description is that I stomp down the stairs in the midst of a temper tantrum. Either way, I don't draw any attention in a place like Wicked Chucks. As far as the patrons are concerned, I'm feeling the vibe.

I push my way to the bar, daring to cast a look up at the balcony. Stefani's head is bent close to Owen, huge grins decorating both of their faces.

"Changing it up or keeping it the same?" Dan inquires, jolting me from my voyeuristic nightmare.

"Same. Three, please."

"Who's your new friend? You two seemed to hit it off."

I shrug, not sure what, if anything, Owen is to me. "I guess."

"Uh-oh. What happened?"

"Stefani happened," I mumble under my breath.

"I wouldn't worry about Stefani. She's been flirting with everyone down here. That's her thing, right?" Dan's eyes widen. "Hold on a minute. Are you interested in this guy?"

Dan knows that I don't date. He also knows the details of my pitiful sexual history, so the concept of me liking a guy shocks the hell out of him. I fiddle with my hair before shaking my head. What does it matter anyway? Stefani has her sights—and hooks—set on Owen. I don't stand a chance.

"Have I ever told you what a shit liar you are, Tallulah?"

I flip him off as he hands me the bottles. Screw him for being right. I turn with a huff, mentally preparing myself to be the third wheel in my own love life.

Thank God for beer and rage music. I'd go bat shit crazy, otherwise.

I jump when a hand reaches out, grabbing two of the beers. "Hey, Darlin, I was coming down to help you."

Color me surprised.

Then I notice Stefani only a few inches from Owen's side.

Eraser, please.

"I would have brought them to you." I ignore Stefani, cocking her head in Owen's direction, her eyes widening at me. Instead, I focus on Owen's ridiculously sexy smile. A smile aimed at me.

Owen leans down, that glorious scruff brushing against my skin. "It's getting a bit wild down here. You're too tiny to walk around without a bodyguard."

I appreciate his concern. Truly, I do. But, as per usual, it fires up my short woman indignation. "Are you my bodyguard now?"

"I can be a lot of things, Tally. Just name it."

Meanwhile, Stefani is becoming more brazen with her non-verbal cues. Leaning against Owen for support, she pretends to adjust the strap on her heel while clearing her throat and sending me a side-eye glance.

It's her signal—a signal for me to hit the highway, giving her some time alone with the man of the evening. Usually, that slight hint is enough. I'm a good wing woman, and most men don't arouse my curiosity.

Owen is not most men. I'm so far beyond curious it's ridiculous. In my mind, I've already stripped him down and licked every inch of him. Repeatedly.

I'm not willing to give him up without a fight. I walk the few steps to the bar, feeling Stefani as she sidles up next to me.

"Do you have dibs?"

"I'm assuming you mean Owen?"

"Obviously."

"I thought you liked Dan," I mutter.

"I do, but so does every other woman in here."

"So, you're interested in Owen as a fallback?"

"Jeez, Lu, you make me sound like an evil bitch!" she scoffs, downing another swig of her beer. "I'd like to get to know Owen better, but you saw him first. You can call dibs if you want."

If only it were that simple.

"That isn't how it works, Stefani." I rub my brow, offering a mirthless laugh.

"You know I would never impede on your territory."

I can lay claim to Owen right now, and my friend will be good to her word. She will back off. But that's not fair to any of us. "You make him sound like a country to be conquered."

"I wouldn't mind conquering him," she whispers, giving me a nudge.

Stomach contents, please stay where you are.

I need to end this conversation. Fast. "We're going to a concert tomorrow night."

"Why didn't you say that you and Owen have a date?"

Because I have no idea if it is a date or not. Better to err on the side of caution.

I shrug, swigging back some beer. "It's not a date."

"Are you cool with me pursuing Owen?"

Another shrug. I can't believe how disappointed I am about the whole scenario. "Is he interested in you?"

One thing about being gorgeous is that you don't hear the word no very often. Stefani giggles, downing the rest of her drink. "If he isn't, he will be by the time I'm through with him."

I hate that she's right.

She draws me into a drunken embrace. "I love you, Lu."

I grumble out a reply because I'm not feeling the love. But in true masochistic fashion, I turn to watch Stefani home in on the first man I've found interesting in years. The woman has a PhD in flirtation, complete with hair flips, bicep caresses, and lash batting.

But even masochists have their limits.

I focus my gaze on the far wall. Maybe if I ignore them both, they'll disappear, and I can retreat to the safety of my balcony. Alone.

"Hey Dan, can I get another shot?" Stefani requests with a giggle, throwing an arm around my shoulders. "Have I told you I like the pink?"

Oh, lovely, she's flat out hammered. "You mentioned it."

"It's so hard to talk with all this noise. So, I drink." Another shot poured and down Stefani's gullet before I can blink.

Lord, have mercy.

"You might want to slow down, Stef. You didn't eat dinner, remember?"

She waves off my warning, motioning for a refill. "I'll be fine. Owen says you two have plans tomorrow night."

I roll my eyes. So much for Stefani's short-term memory. "I told you. He was able to get me a ticket to—"

"Hedgecore." Owen finishes the statement, his broad body standing in front of us like a linebacker. The man is gigantic—easily 6'2" or more.

He's way too tall for me, and I'll keep telling myself that fib until I believe it.

Stefani's eyes widen in fake surprise. "I love Hedgecore."

"You do?" Owen and I ask in unison.

What a crock. The woman doesn't love Hedgecore. She's never heard of them.

"I would give anything to go to that concert tomorrow." Stefani bats her lashes at Owen.

Talk about laying it on thick. But this, I have to see.

Owen crosses his arms over his barrel chest. "What's your favorite song?"

"Oh...it's so hard to choose one." Stefani begins a long, bumbling explanation, while I try to decide if I should let her hang herself with her own lie.

Judging from the smirk on Owen's face, he knows Stefani is lying, too. But he'll play along. Maybe we are kindred spirits. "You must have a favorite album."

"Um...well..."

I could be a bitch. I should be a bitch. But karma is a worse bitch.

I groan before entering the conversation. "Stefani and I have a disagreement. She claims *Green Sneakers* is the catchiest album while I think their best work is on *Rapid Cycle*."

A smile flashes across Owen's face. I know my shit, and now he knows it, too. "*Rapid Cycle*? Brave choice. I'm with Stefani on the *Green Sneakers* album."

"Of course you are," I mutter, unable to hold back the eye roll. Queen Snarky, at your service.

Stefani jumps at her chance. "See? Yet another reason to take me tomorrow night. I love punk music."

She was doing so well, right until that lie dripped from her lips. Anyone who knows Hedgecore knows that they are *not* a punk band. They're rockabilly.

Owen, for his part, remains a gentleman. "I only have two tickets, and I already invited Tally. But you might be able to scalp one tomorrow night."

I chew the inside of my lip, watching my friend's face fall. At this moment, being her wing woman is the worst job in the world. "You can take Stefani. No need to feel obligated."

Owen's gray gaze probes me. "I'm taking you."

"I'm just saying," I flounder, but Owen raises his hand, cutting me off.

"Suddenly, you don't want to go? Did you develop alternate plans in the last thirty seconds? I recall how excited you were when I told you about the extra ticket." He leans closer, his next words meant only for me. "I also remember how it felt to have your body pressed against mine." He straightens, those stormy eyes daring me to lie to him. "Have you changed your mind?"

Am I insane? What am I doing? I want to go to this concert. I want to see Owen again. Why am I throwing up roadblocks and giving Stefani an opening? "I want to go."

Owen smiles, letting his fingers slide through the ends of my hair. "Then it's settled. Sorry, Stefani."

My friend pooches out her lower lip, but we aren't caving to her wishes.

The truth is, I'm not entirely sure if Owen wants me to go because he's interested in me, or because he feels obligated that he asked me first. Possibly, it's because, unlike Stefani, I actually know —and love—their music. But regardless of his reasoning, I know mine.

I want to see Hedgecore. Seeing them with Owen is a beautiful bonus. Stefani will just have to sit this one out.

"There will be other shows, Stef." I offer her a smile, and she gives me a halfhearted hug.

"I'm glad you get to see them, Lu." Even if she's disappointed, I know she means those words.

"Thank you. I'll be right back."

I don't make it two steps when Owen wraps his hand around my upper arm. "Where are you going?"

"Bathroom." I offer up a cheeky grin. "Do I need a permission slip?"

"Might need a bodyguard." Even with all the other smells in the bar, I pick up Owen's scent. He's wearing cologne, but it's not over-done, and holy hell, it mixes well with his body chemistry. Yummi-ness squared.

"What could happen between here and the toilet?"

Famous last words.

In the bar patron's defense, he wasn't aiming for me. He likely didn't even see me until after he knocked me off my feet, himself a casualty of the boisterous mosh pit.

But before my ass hits the ground, inflicting any number of colorful bruises, I'm in Owen's arms. His hands tighten around my body as he sidesteps the would-be assailant, now lying face down on the ground next to my smashed beer bottle. "What the fuck is wrong with you? She could have cracked her head against the bar."

The man staggers to his feet, muttering an apology as the blood drips from his mouth and nose. "I didn't see her."

"Pinch your nose and hold your head back," I order from my perch in Owen's arms. Catching my savior's inquisitive look, I shrug. "I'm a nurse. I think he broke his nose."

"Likely cracked a few teeth, too. Either way, he's not my problem. I'm just glad you're not hurt."

My face splits into a grin at his concern. "We can now add hero to your resume."

"I don't know if I'd go that far."

Even though the danger is long past, Owen is still holding me, and my body is awash with handy-dandy sensations. Everywhere his fingers touch me, rivulets of heat flow into my body, and my core temperature is nearing nuclear levels.

A meltdown is imminent.

Finally, finding my voice—and my snarky facade—I push my glasses up with one hand and point to the ground with the other. "Not that I don't appreciate the view from way up here, but can you put me down? I must be getting heavy."

It's a cue to set me back on my feet, but Owen ignores the hint. Instead, he tightens his grip, his fingers tracing ever so softly along my body. The man knows exactly what he's doing to me, and he's enjoying every second. "You're tiny, so holding you is not an issue. Besides, I'm not quite ready to let you go, Tally."

A shiver rushes up my spine. I like the way my name sounds dripping off his tongue. Actually, I like everything about Owen's mouth. *Focus, damn it.* "Do I get a say in this decision?"

With a chuckle, Owen sets me back to rights, and I'm loath to admit I miss the warmth of his skin. "Although you'd sooner die than admit it, I think you enjoyed every second in my arms."

Cocky bastard. Accurate, but cocky as hell. I plant my hands on my hips, a vision of righteous indignation. Or so I tell myself. "Is that what you think? You know what I think?"

"Tallulah, I get the impression you think *way* too much. You've been doing nothing but thinking since your friend showed up in the balcony." He plops down on a bar stool, offering me a dimpled smile beneath the coiffed beard.

"You two seem to hit it off," I argue, hating that he can see right through my front.

His brows raise as he chuckles, accepting a fresh beer from Dan. "I think *we* hit it off, Tally."

"Obviously. You need me. I own the balcony."

"Part owner."

"No, that's a one-night deal. You did not swear on a goat."

"I'll bring one the next time." His fingers slide along my jaw, such an intimate gesture from an almost stranger. "Glad to see you back."

Before I can retort, Stefani, ever the concerned friend, cuts into the moment. Again. Judging by her dilated pupils, the alcohol has finally made its mark. "Lu, are you okay? I saw that moron slam into you."

"Almost slam. But I'm right as rain, thanks to this big lug here." I smile up at Owen, giving him a light punch in the bicep. "He's my new bodyguard."

"The guy bled the entire way outside. I think he broke his nose," Stefani adds, motioning to the door.

"Are you a nurse, too?" Owen inquires.

"Yep. Lu and I work together. She's technically my boss." She flashes Owen a sultry smile. "What do you do, besides saving damsels in distress?"

"I'm not exactly a damsel in distress," I mutter, but my friend only has ears—and eyes—for Owen.

"I'm in between jobs at the moment," Owen states, taking another swig of his beer.

I clear my throat and glance away. Well, that's what's wrong with him—he's unemployed and likely broke.

Owen must be a mind reader. "That sounded terrible, didn't it? I'm not some vagrant. I just moved here from San Francisco, sewing up some loose ends with work."

Whew. Thank God.

"Big move," I comment, my gaze traveling up his body. It's funny. Owen is over a foot taller and likely a hundred pounds heavier than me, but all I feel is safe around him.

Owen guffaws, nodding in agreement. "That's an understatement."

"How do you like Florida?" Stefani presses, her words becoming progressively more slurred.

"I love the ocean, but it's hot as hell down here. I'm still looking for a place." The smile falls from his face, replaced with a look of concern. "Stefani, are you alright?"

Lovely, my friend is green about the gills. "Time for some fresh air, beautiful."

I offer Stefani my arm, but Owen stops me. "Remember what happened last time, Rocky? I'll take her outside. We'll be right back." With his hand on her lower back, they disappear into the crowd.

I bet money they won't return.

"Is she going to hurl?" Dan questions, nodding in their direction.

"Probably. Owen went with her, so I guess he'll take care of her." I bite my lip, swallowing back my disappointment. Over the years, Stefani has had her pick of all the eligible men that floated our way, and I never begrudged her one. This is the first time I've wanted to keep the man all for myself. And maybe, just maybe, Owen feels nothing for Stefani beyond sober concern.

"Stefani doesn't feel like coming back inside," Owen states to my left, making me jump. For such a Goliath, the man sure is nimble.

"That's my cue. Hey Dan, what do I owe you?" I ask, pulling out my wallet.

Owen places his hand over mine. "I'm going to take her home."

Well, fuck my life. So much for the sober concern theory. "You don't have to do that—"

"She asked if I would. She said that you love this band, and didn't want to ruin your evening."

Quite the stench coming off that load of crap.

Stefani ruined my night when she set her sights on Owen. There's no salvaging it now. Besides, I'm not one to get into a catfight over a man. Particularly not when I'm certain to lose.

I huff out a sigh and force a grin. "Are you okay to drive?"

He nods, that dimpled smile once again upending my ability to think. "I'm fine."

"Okay. Get home safe."

"No deal. You may like this band, but I came in to get you. I'm giving you a ride home, too."

Nothing beats being a third wheel. "I have my car. But I appreciate you getting Stefani home safely."

That is Owen's cue to leave. I've offered the white flag of surrender. He's free to go.

Only he doesn't. "I don't want to leave you here alone."

Ah, there's the sober concern. "I'll be fine. Wicked Chucks is my second home. Besides, Dan will keep an eye on me."

My bartender buddy nods. "Always. She's safe with me."

"Are you sure?" Owen presses, his hand rubbing my back.

Of nothing. "I'm positive. Thank you for the offer. It was nice meeting you."

He leans in, his breath hot against my ear. "I need your number, Tally."

"My number? Oh, sure, in case something happens."

Owen pulls out his phone, a lopsided grin decorating his face. "I need it for tomorrow night, Darlin."

For a second, my mind blanks, and then I remember. The Hedgecore concert. "I can meet you here if that's easier."

"It's not easier. Do you not want to give me your number?"

I chuckle and rattle off the digits. I'm being silly. It makes sense that Owen needs my number. What if he decides he'd rather take a tall, willowy blonde to the show? "I'm really looking forward to seeing Hedgecore. Thank you." I stand up, holding out my arms for a hug.

Hey, friends hug.

Owen pulls me against him, but in an unexpected move, he tips up my chin, pressing his lips against mine. It's short and sweet and yet lights up every nerve ending in my body. "I'm really looking forward to seeing you. Goodnight, Tally."

I watch him leave before spinning around to face Dan, releasing a loud groan as I settle my head on the bar.

"What's your issue?"

"Another one bites the dust," I mutter from the cocoon of my hands.

"He seems interested."

"Yeah, in Stefani. He's driving her home, remember?"

Dan knocks the bar in front of me, making me raise my head to meet his gaze. "Tallulah, he's interested in you. In fact, he was blatantly obvious about it."

"Just because a man is friendly doesn't mean he's interested."

Dan shrugs, shaking his head. "Maybe not, but uninterested men generally don't offer up a ticket to a sold-out concert, either."

"He left with Stefani. Trust me, there's no way they're not screwing tonight."

"Whatever you say, Lu. I think this guy might surprise you." He motions to my head. "Enough of the Strawberry Shortcake. Lose the pink."

I smirk at Dan as I slide off the wig, letting my dark hair cascade down my back. "Better?"

"Much. I prefer you natural. You want another drink?"

I shake my head. What I want is Owen in my bed, but that's not happening. "I have to get home. Hecate is waiting."

"She is the coolest cat in the world."

"You know it." I stand up, giving Dan a kiss over the bar. "Thanks for being my ride or die."

Dan ruffles my hair. "I have a feeling I'm going to be replaced soon."

"Dream on," I mutter, giving a wave as I walk out the door, but I can't help but hope that my buddy is right.

CHAPTER THREE
TALLY

"Stop judging me, Hecate," I order as I try on a fifth outfit. It might seem pointless, since the man I'm trying to impress drove my friend home last night, but a girl has pride. I want to look good.

Who knows? Even if Owen is off the table, maybe he has an equally hot friend, just for me.

"A snowball's chance in hell of that one," I mutter, watching my cat curl up on my discarded clothing pile, stretching her black paws in front of her. Apparently, my social life isn't exciting for her, either.

No matter what, Owen is a gentleman. The man texted last night, informing me that both he and Stefani arrived home safely and inquiring if I'd done the same. I assured him I had, complete with a smiley face and a thumbs-up emoji.

I didn't ask where he spent the evening. First, it's not my business, and second, I don't relish acute nausea at the idea of him nailing my friend. Repeatedly.

My phone rings, and I glance at the caller ID. It's Stefani. I hesitate, uncertain if I'm up for an all-access pass to her escapades with Owen.

Finally, morbid curiosity wins. "Good afternoon."

"There's a marching band in my head," Stefani groans. "Sorry about last night, Lu."

"It's fine," I lie. "Are you okay?"

"I will be. I'm definitely not twenty-five anymore."

"Preaching to the choir," I chortle. Stef and I are only six months apart in age, and we passed the quarter-century mark over a decade earlier. In summary, hangovers hurt.

"What are you wearing tonight?"

Odd segue.

"To the concert?"

"No. To the dentist. Of course, to the concert."

I don't want to admit that I've tried on several outfits, particularly not when she may have spent the night with Owen. "I was going to wear jeans and a t-shirt." Actually, that's not a bad idea. I can still accessorize, so I fit the scene. Plus, I won't look like I'm trying too hard. Or at all.

"No dice. Wear a dress and show off that body. You need to look smoking hot tonight, Lu."

I shoot the phone a curious glance. Why in the world is Stefani upping my sex appeal for a man she likes? "Do you know something I don't?"

"Wear your red dress. You look amazing in it," Stefani prattles on, ignoring my question.

I stifle a laugh as I catch a glimpse of my reflection in the full-length mirror. My friend knows me well, and she's right. I love the way the lipstick red swing dress hugs my curves. Besides, it's fun, flirty, and short enough that it doesn't hide my leg ink. "I actually have it on now."

"Keep it on! Wear some sexy underwear, too."

What the hell? "Why?"

"Just in case you have a Marilyn moment, and your skirt flies up...or someone makes your skirt fly up."

My friend is still drunk. Either that, or she's high on something. "The pink wig doesn't go with the dress."

"Ditch the wig. You want to showcase your natural beauty."

"What if Owen thinks it's too much?"

"He won't. Trust me."

She's right. This outing is strictly platonic. Besides, I'll hardly look out of place dressed in rockabilly gear at a rockabilly concert. "I'll take your word for it. Will I see you tonight?"

"Hell, no. I couldn't care less about Hedgecore. Besides, tonight is about you, Lu. Have fun. Don't do anything I wouldn't do." She ends the call with a kiss into the receiver, as I shake my head in confusion.

"I'm nervous, Hecate."

My cat, for her part, yawns, looking mildly amused at my plight.

"I shouldn't be nervous, but I am. I like this guy, and I'm not sure how cool I can play it tonight."

Hecate lifts her hind leg and begins grooming, a sure sign she's signed off this conversation.

"Thanks for your help, cat," I mutter.

Owen is on my doorstep at eight o'clock sharp. Talk about punctuality. He must be former military because most men run on a timeline of their own design.

With a deep breath, I pull open the door, my heart catching in my throat.

I was mistaken last night when I thought Owen was gorgeous. He's so far beyond that, I don't think they've invented a word to describe his appeal. A tight black shirt hugs every inch of muscle, his lower half encased in a pair of dark denim. His head is freshly shaved and his beard newly trimmed, and I want to jump him and rip every stitch of clothing from his body. In his hands is a bouquet of lilies, the most impressive blend of pinks and oranges I've ever seen.

"Hi," I manage, leaning against the door frame as I gape up at him.

I swear his eyes light up when he sees me. I must be imagining things. "Wow. I like the dark."

"Huh? Oh, my hair. That was a wig last night."

"This," he motions up and down my body, "is beautiful. Wow, Tally."

He's repeating himself. Maybe he's nervous, too. Likely afraid I'll give him an inquisition about his escapades the night before.

I hold open the door, waving him inside. "Come in. Make yourself comfortable. I hope you didn't have any trouble finding the apartment."

"A little, but I finally figured out how to open the gate. I thought I might have to jump the damn thing."

"My landlord, she worries about vagrants. The area has changed over the years." I'm babbling about my landlord. God help me, I'll never survive the evening.

Hecate approaches Owen, arching her back as he strokes her sleek, black fur. "Who's this?"

"That's Hecate."

"Guardian of the Crossroads. She looks fierce enough."

I laugh, tossing a toy in her direction. "Yeah, right, fierce if you're a catnip cigar. I'm surprised she's letting you pet her. She doesn't warm to most people."

"Maybe she knows I'm not most people." Owen holds out the bouquet. "I know it's not much, but I got you these. I tried to find the most vibrant colors, to match the most vibrant woman." His gaze returns to my cat, but I swear he flushes under his tan.

"They're beautiful. I never get flowers."

"We'll have to change that." Now his eyes meet mine, and I'm so screwed. The things this man does to my body with only a simple glance.

I snap my fingers in a vain attempt to regain my emotional balance. "I actually got you something, too."

Owen's eyes widen with surprise when I hand him the book. "I've never gotten a gift on a first date before."

"I guess it's time to change that," I blurt, feeling my cheeks redden with embarrassment. God, can't I rent a filter for just one night? "I mean, I know it's not a date, but I thought you might like this."

Owen pages through the book, a smile crossing his features. "This is wonderful. Thank you."

I focus on the book, flipping through to a section, aware of his gaze on me. "It's like a Zagat for the underground, listing all the cool spots in the area. There's even a section on tattoo artists and the punk scene. I thought since you're new to Florida, this might be helpful."

I'm not sure how much longer I can flip through pages while his gaze heats my body to scalding. "Anyway, enough of that. Let me grab my bag—"

Owen grabs my wrist, pulling me against him and tipping my chin up. "I forgot to tell you something, Tally."

Great. Here it comes—the unwelcome but expected disclosure of last night.

"What's that?" I inquire, plastering a smile that I pray isn't too artificial on my face.

"This is most definitely a date." Owen takes advantage of my slightly parted lips, possessing my mouth without permission, and setting off an internal inferno.

Some kisses are pleasant. Pretty much all the kisses I've ever experienced land in that category. I never felt sparks or butterflies or any other variety of insect, but they were nice.

This is not one of those kisses. The moment Owen's lips brush mine, my body lights up like Mardi gras.

I push up on tiptoe, my hands circling his neck as I surrender to the weight of his mouth crushing mine. There is nothing easygoing about the way he lays claim. No, this kiss is a firestorm, his body daring me to disobey his commands.

Owen hoists me into his arms as my legs lock around his waist. We aren't 0-60, we're 0-1,000. My back hits the wall as Owen cradles my head from impact, his mouth refusing to release me.

I slide my hands along the lines of his chest, desperate for the feel of his skin against mine. I'm tempted to rip the shirt from his body and judging from the way his hands knead my ass, pulling me flush against his erection, Owen is just as desperate.

With a strangled huff, Owen breaks the kiss, burrowing his face against my neck. "We have to stop, Tally."

"Okay," I manage, willing my heart—and hormones—to settle.

He lifts his head, those stormy eyes hooded with lust. His lips graze mine as he thrusts his hips forward, trapping my body between the wall and his broad frame. "Because if we don't stop now, I'm going to carry you to the bedroom, and we aren't making the concert."

My hands slide down his pecs, across his chiseled abdomen. "I really want you to do that."

He smiles before nipping my lower lip, earning another moan from my sexually overheated mouth. "So do I. But first, I want to show you an amazing evening, with our clothes on."

I smooth my dress—and embarrassed ego—as Owen sets me back on the floor, my cheeks burning from my impetuous behavior.

Way to make the man work for it, Tally.

Should I be pleasantly surprised that the man wants to get to know me before shagging me, or mortified that he turned down a definitive green light?

One look into his silver eyes ends any negative self-talk. Owen radiates heat from every pore, all aimed in my direction. That, and the man has yet to stop touching me.

Not that I'm complaining.

That gaze of his is unnerving. It's almost paralyzing in its power. "What are you thinking?" I question, my hands unwilling to behave. They're drawn to his body like a moth to a flame.

"Now that I know how good your lips taste, I can't wait to savor the rest of you."

Holy hell, this man is basically a stranger, but his words aren't a turnoff. Not. Even. Close. No, his words heat me from the inside out. "Too bad, we have to behave tonight."

He rests his forearms against the wall, caging me in his embrace. Not that I'm itching for release. "What I said is that I want to show you an amazing evening." His fingers trace the skin underneath my collarbone, dipping slightly into the cleft of my cleavage.

"With our clothes on," I remind him.

"Me and my big mouth." He captures my lower lip between his teeth, tugging lightly before tangling his tongue with mine. "What if I make you come without removing a stitch of clothing?"

That brazen question would have earned any other man a slap. But not Owen. Perhaps I'm the queen of naivety, but there's something achingly honest in his touch. It might be part of his repertoire, but something tells me he hasn't ever taken to a stranger in this manner before, either.

That brutal honesty spurs me on. "Is that a promise or a threat?"

He smiles against my mouth as his fingers trail up my thigh, playing along the edge of my g-string. "It's a promise I'm dying to keep."

Owen's gaze meets mine. He's waiting. He won't do anything further without my consent.

Do I want to allow a stranger this level of intimacy? In a word—yes. Two words, actually. Hell, yes.

"Can I keep my promise, Tally?"

Two can play this game. I slide my hand down the front of Owen's jeans, gulping at his sheer size. The man is a mutant. No one can be that large and be human. It's just not possible. I lightly scratch my nails over his bulge, biting my lip in pleasure as a low groan escapes his throat. "Therein lies the issue. I'll want to return the favor, and that will require you to lose some clothing."

Our gazes catch and hold as the energy between us tingles. Changes.

I suck in a breath as his fingers glide across my clit. Only a thin scrap of lace separates his fingers from my skin, and I wish to Christ that I'd forgone underwear. His thumb circles my nub, and I close my eyes, resting my head against the wall, releasing a moan when his tongue slides along my pulse point.

But before my hormones run off with all vestiges of common sense, my mind barges into the moment. Always the party pooper, it reminds me that A) I hardly know this man and B) there's a high probability he screwed Stefani against a similar wall in her home not even twenty-four hours ago.

My muscles tense as I try to shove my mind back into its cage, but Owen senses the change.

Tipping up my chin, he searches my face for answers. "Something happened just now."

I tongue my upper lip, a nervous habit. "Sorry."

"Don't be sorry. Did I do something to make you uncomfortable? I never want to hurt you, Tally."

"You didn't. I'm...fine."

"I hate that word."

"Which word?"

"Fine. It means you are anything but fine." The corners of his luscious mouth curl upwards, offering a knowing—and smoldering—smirk. "Come on, talk to me. I can't fix it if I don't know what I did."

Damn him for being so endearing. "You didn't do anything. It's me."

I hope the answer will appease him.

It doesn't.

I change the subject with a sigh, praying I don't wind up a solo act tonight with my vacillating emotions. "We should go. Don't want to be late."

"Not until you talk. I can stay here all night, breathing you in."

Owen twists a strand of my long, dark hair around his finger. "You have beautiful hair."

"Jealous?" I smirk, running my hand over his bald scalp.

"This," he retorts, pointing as his head, "is a choice. I actually had hair up until last week."

"Hard to picture."

"Want me to grow it out and show you?"

"No," I blurt. Way too quickly, I might add. "It's actually my kryptonite." I giggle when his eyes narrow in confusion. "Beard, shaved head, tons of tattoos. It's my weakness."

"You're like this with all bald, bearded men, huh?" He's teasing, but I catch a hint of uncertainty flash in his eyes. It's a pleasant reminder that I'm as unknown to him as he is to me.

"Oh, yeah. I hump their legs and everything." His gaze widens, and I smile. Even the most beautiful need some reassurance from time to time. "Never. Most men don't interest me. Stefani says I have ridiculously high standards."

"But I fit the bill?"

"You created the bill. They broke the mold after you." *Way to go, Tally. Just vomit your unmitigated yearning all over him. He should be leaving in 3-2-*

"I need to kiss that luscious mouth again."

What a sexy, unexpected response. "What's stopping you?"

"You still haven't fessed up." A grin splits his face, and he nips my neck. "I know what it is."

"Do you really?"

"You think something happened last night between Stefani and me."

Well, shit. "How the hell did you know?"

"I love that you actually answered me honestly."

"That doesn't clear up any confusion, Owen."

"I dropped Stefani at home and drove back to Wicked Chucks looking for you."

"You did?"

"I told you that I didn't want to leave you last night. I meant it."

"Stefani thought you were gorgeous. I'm shocked she didn't proposition you."

Owen's grin widens. "It took about four blocks of me asking incessant questions about you for her to figure it out. She was the one who told me to go back to the bar and find you."

That explains her insistence on my looks tonight. I'll have to buy that woman a drink the next time I see her. Ride or die, for sure.

I'm Owen's first choice, not the fallback, and that knowledge brings all my raging hormones racing to the forefront again.

"I love that you did that." Standing on tiptoe, I press my lips against his. It's a chaste kiss, or it's supposed to be. It stays that way for about two seconds until Owen pushes his full length against my body, wedging me between the wall and his iron chest.

His hands knit in my hair as the kiss deepens. The intimacy is off the charts, and for once, I don't run from it. I crave it. I crave him.

I break the kiss, my breathing heavy. "At this rate, we'll never leave the apartment."

"I love that idea." He drops tiny kisses along my jaw, his hands wrapping around my hips. "Do you know how much I wanted to kiss you last night? How much I want to strip you naked and spend the rest of the night buried inside you?"

My last vestiges of resolve weaken at his heated words. Let's be honest, it's nonexistent around this man. "Owen—"

"How much I need you to know that this isn't some play for sex? I've never reacted to another human being this way." His forehead rests against mine, his fingers skating along my body.

We're on the same page, because I've never felt anything remotely like what I feel with Owen. Hedgecore be damned, I'd rather spend the evening with him. Sans clothing, of course.

Then I feel it. The gentle vibration is unmistakable. "Someone's trying to reach you."

"Talk about terrible timing." He pulls out his phone, glancing at the caller ID. "I'm so sorry. I really need to take this call. It's about work."

"Of course, go," I reply, shooing him out of the room.

In a way, I'm glad the moment was broken before we wound up naked and sweaty on my bedroom floor. Okay, fine. I'm glad the moment was broken before I wound up *alone* the morning after a night on the bedroom floor.

I powder my nose in the bathroom, returning to find Owen once again petting Hecate, a confident smile on his face. "Good news, I take it."

"Great news," he replies, grasping my hand and twirling me around. "You're my good luck charm, Tally."

"Better keep me close, then," I reply, grabbing my purse from the chair and pressing a kiss to his lips with my finger.

"Darlin, I don't plan on ever letting you go."

I flush as he leads me out of the apartment, but I can't keep the smile from my lips.

Good, Owen. I don't plan on letting you.

WICKED CHUCKS IS FAR MORE SEDATE THAN LAST NIGHT, ALTHOUGH IT could be that the air is imbued with a festive spirit instead of anarchy and melodrama.

Owen links his fingers with mine, weaving us through the crowd to grab a seat at the bar.

Dan offers a knowing wink when he spots us. "Hey, Tallulah, aren't you gorgeous tonight?"

"I don't know about all that."

"I do," Owen answers for me. "You're absolutely stunning."

Dan nods at Owen's statement, a nonverbal cue that he approves of his response. "Owen, right?"

"Good man. Nice to see you again, Dan," Owen replies, shaking hands with my friend and ordering us a couple of drinks. He then turns to me, his hands skating under my skirt to press on my thighs. "Look at you, Tally."

"What about me?"

"You're the sexiest woman I've ever laid eyes on. Is it wrong that I'm praying for a freak cancelation, so I can take you home?"

I've never encountered a man so blatantly sexual toward me. Okay, never one where I actually returned the affection, and all I can say is keep it coming. "What would you do to me?"

He crowds into my space, and the surrounding noise falls away, as his hands grasp my ass, pulling me against him. "To start, tie you up and kiss every single inch of you. I want to watch you come again and again…from my fingers…my tongue…and my cock. I wonder, how many times can I make you come tonight?"

"Can I play, too? You're not the only one with a talented tongue." Lord have mercy, my mother would roll over in her grave, hearing me say such delightfully dirty things.

Owen's eyes blaze, his fingers digging into the meat of my thighs. "Is that a promise, little girl?"

I pull his mouth to mine, tracing the outline of those lips with the tip of my tongue. "Only if you're interested."

Dan sets down our drinks with a flourish. "Am I going to have to turn the hose on you two? I can feel the heat from here."

My cheeks flame as I shoot him the bird, sipping my whiskey sour.

"Actually, I have a nursing question for you." Dan snickers at my intense stare. He knows better than to be a cock block. "I don't mean right now. Later. Once you two have cooled down." He ducks away from the napkin I lob at his head, walking to the opposite side of the bar.

"Jackass," I mutter, swinging my gaze back to Owen, who is studying me intently. "Do I have something on my face?"

"Talk to me, Darlin."

"About?"

"What are your rules?" Owen asks, leaning his forearm on the bar, his other hand stroking my knee.

"Excuse me?" What in the world is this man talking about?

"Every woman has rules, that unspoken code they'll never break."

"I think *everyone* has rules. It's not gender specific."

"Fair enough. What are yours?"

The man is nothing if not direct. "No one's ever asked me to state my rules upfront."

"I'm not everyone."

"Don't be an asshole."

"Trying not to be," he chuckles, his gaze never leaving mine as he sips his drink.

"I didn't mean *you*. That's a rule."

"Agreed. Seems fairly simple."

"Not as simple as you might expect. Don't hit."

That got his attention. "Not in a million years."

I fiddle with the hem of my dress, as the conversation veers into unexpected territory. "That's good because, with biceps the size of tree trunks, you could inflict some damage on a woman my size."

His hand cups my face, forcing me to look at him, those gray eyes soft as a foggy morning. "I will never raise a hand to you, Tally. Unless it's to spank that delicious ass of yours."

I giggle, thankful for the segue back into banter. "Well, that's an entirely different chapter of the rule book."

"Glad to know it's not off the table."

"Only if you kiss it afterward."

"Every. Single. Inch."

There goes my pussy again, all aflutter with this man's overt sexual teasing. Granted, I'm hardly holding back on my end. "Hmm, sounds enticing."

"I'll be sure to demonstrate for you later, unless you want to lock the door in the bathroom here."

The nurse in me breaks into the moment. "Have you seen their bathroom?"

Owen laughs, finishing off his drink. "Good point. We can wait. So far, your rules are cake, Darlin. Anything else I should know?"

I stare into his light gray eyes. Such a unique color. Sometimes with a shadow of blue, other times with a hint of purple. Mesmerizing. Much like the rest of him.

"Not that it matters, but I don't date doctors." I shrug, sliding off the bar stool. "That's it, the extent of my rules. I'll be right back. Going to analyze the bathroom for cleanliness."

Owen nods, giving my hand a squeeze before I walk off, but he seems preoccupied. Distant, all of a sudden.

Shit. Did I say the wrong thing? Before my mind can replay every word in our conversation, I shake off the doldrums. *For once, Tallulah, do not read too much into it.*

CHAPTER FOUR
OWEN

I watch that tasty morsel disappear into the crowd, confident that I heard her wrong.

Tally doesn't date doctors?

"On the house." Dan sets a refill in front of me, but I can tell by his intense gaze that he wants to have *the* discussion.

I get it. He's friends with Tally and wants to ensure she's safe. I admire anyone who wants to protect that adorable woman, although I plan to take over the position full-time.

"Appreciate it."

"Did you tell Tallulah that you came back here last night?"

I nod, glancing in the direction of the bathroom. I know Dan wants to interrogate me, but I have a question of my own. "Can I ask you something?"

Dan nods, filling a glass from the tap. "Yes, she really is that kick-ass of a woman."

I smile. That much he didn't need to tell me. "I knew that the second I saw Tally."

"What's your story? Tallulah said you just moved here from San Francisco. That's a big change."

"I needed a big change. Besides, they offered me a position at Memorial."

Dan pauses, the pint glass only half-filled. "You work at the hospital?"

"Well, not yet. I start in a couple of weeks."

"What are you doing?"

"I'm an interventional cardiologist."

"You're a doctor?"

Okay, buddy. You can pick your jaw up off the floor. Just because I'm inked doesn't mean I'm a moron. "Don't look so surprised."

"Sorry, man. I didn't mean it that way, but does Tallulah know?"

I do not like his tone with that question. "That I'm a physician? No, it hasn't come up. I was about to tell her, celebrate my new gig."

"Shit," Dan huffs, grasping the edge of the bar.

That's never a good response. "Let me guess. Tally doesn't date cardiologists." It's a ridiculous statement, one I expect Dan to rebuke.

Only...he doesn't.

"Tally doesn't date any doctor. *Ever*. That's her one unbreakable, unshakable rule."

My stomach flips at Dan's statement. I did hear her correctly. *Focus, Owen, there has to be a reasonable explanation.* "She's sworn off all doctors? Forever? That doesn't make any sense. Nurses date doctors all the time."

Dan nods, wiping an invisible spot on the bar. Again and again. Apparently, he doesn't like this conversation any more than I do. "I'm not saying that it's fair, I'm just telling you the way it is with Tallulah. She had a real traumatic experience dating a doctor several years ago, and now, she won't touch them with a ten-foot pole."

"Great. So, I'm fucked, basically."

Dan shrugs, topping off my drink. *Keep them coming, please.* "I don't know. I know she doesn't date doctors, but then again, she also doesn't date. The way she's opened up to you is surprising."

I'll cling to that sliver of hope with both hands. "So, there's a chance?"

"I hope so. You seem like a nice guy, but Tallulah is a tough nut to crack. She's stubborn as hell."

Actually, she's soft as hell, I bemuse, recalling the feel of her ass beneath my palms. "Can we keep quiet about my job, just until I figure out how to broach it? I've never encountered this scenario before."

"You've never encountered someone like Tallulah before."

Understatement of a lifetime. "She's amazing, which is why I don't want to mess this up."

"The woman is gold. Seriously." Dan rubs his chin, his gaze bouncing between me and the bar. "I'll keep quiet. For now. But understand that my loyalty lies with her. If she asks, I won't lie. And don't make me be the one to tell her."

I hold up my hands in mock surrender. "Understood. Let me earn Tally's trust, and hopefully, I can convince her to give one more doctor a chance."

"It's a big hospital, so there's a possibility you'll never see her. What kind of doctor are you again?"

"Interventional cardiologist." I smile at his confused expression. "I work in the cath lab." More confusion. "I work with heart patients."

"Ah, why didn't you say so?" Dan smirks before his face clouds. "Shit, I'm pretty sure Tallulah works in the cardiac unit."

Well, shit. I release a groan, downing another swallow of my drink. What are the chances? "That figures."

Dan leans on the bar, his face earnest. "Since you're a heart doc, can I ask your opinion?"

I chuckle, although it's tinged with nerves at Dan's revelation. "You can ask, but I'm not sure I can answer it." I'm used to being questioned on all manner of medical topics—everything from dermatology to brain surgery. You would think it would act as a deterrent when I mention my area of expertise. It doesn't.

"My mom, she needs her valve replaced. I'm not sure which one. Begins with an A, I think—"

"Aortic valve?"

Dan snaps his fingers, smiling at me. "Yes. But she is terrified of open-heart surgery. Her friend died on the table, and no amount of prodding on my part can change her mind. So, she's refusing the procedure, which Tallulah highly advised against. But Tally also mentioned that Memorial is expanding, creating some hybrid operating room for high-risk heart patients. Hell, she mentioned that there will even be robots involved. It sounds like science fiction to me, but since you're a heart doctor, I thought you might have heard of it."

It's uncanny. I've never felt both pride and nausea in the same breath. The robotic procedure and hybrid lab to which Dan is referring, I helped to spearhead. I'm damn proud of my works, and it's a big reason Memorial was champing at the bit to hire me. The downside? If Tally is keen on the details of the hybrid lab, she's not only a cardiac nurse, she's a cath lab nurse. She works in the same unit I'm about to head up.

Life is so damn unfair.

"So...have you heard of it?" Dan presses, and I clear my throat, downing the rest of my drink.

"Actually, that robot is why I'm here." At his narrowed stare, I explain. "I was part of the original team of interventionists who brought the idea to life."

"Holy shit. You're a genius."

"No, far from. I work my ass off, and I love what I do."

Dan hands me another drink, waving away my credit card. "No way. You're a hero, man. Your money is no good here."

"Tally, as a nurse, is a far bigger hero than I could ever be." I lay the card on the bar. "Take the money."

He relents with a sigh, chewing my ear for the next few minutes with questions about the procedure's side effects and efficacy. From his viewpoint, I'm a godsend. "You're a wealth of information. Now I can talk to my mother about the damn surgery."

I jump when a hand settles on my arm, turning to see Tally behind me, a curious look on her face. "Shit. You startled me, Darlin,"

I slide an arm around her waist, pulling her close and tucking my head against her neck. She's got the most intoxicating scent on the planet. God, I could eat her for days.

"I didn't mean to scare you," Tally states, putting a bit of space between us. "I overheard your conversation with Dan. That's some impressive medical knowledge."

Crap, here we go. "Yes, I guess it is."

Her lower lip trembles, her gaze focused on the far wall. "Please tell me you're not a doctor."

And there it is. I catch Dan's eye over Tally's head, his expression sympathetic. He knows I'm screwed. We both do. Maybe, just maybe, if I play it off with a wink and smile, we can move past this topic of conversation. At least for the present. "I don't think I've ever heard someone hope I'm *not* a doctor. I thought doctors were quite the catch."

The smile slides from Tally's face. "Are you?"

I chuckle, determined to get to the bottom of her rule. I run my fingers along her jaw, trailing them down her neck, willing the tension down. "What if I am? What if I'm a doctor at your hospital? What then?"

But Tally is more than happy to hold on to every ounce of tension in her body. She stays my hand, her eyes hardening. "It would suck."

"You were serious about that rule?"

"I don't date doctors. Or co-workers."

Christ, I hope my poker face doesn't fail me now. "Never?" I press, unwilling to let the topic drop. "I would think a doctor would be a natural fit for a nurse."

"Maybe some nurses, but not me. I dated a doctor—once—and he burned me. Burned is an understatement. Torched is more accurate a term. He got me fired, out of spite, from a job I worked my ass off for... among other things." Tally focuses those big eyes on me, but her gaze is unflinching. She's not kidding. "I only have three rules, Owen, and I'm more willing to overlook the other two than this one. So, if you're a doctor, you might as well tell me now. Why prolong the torture?"

I have two choices, and I can't believe the one I'm about to make.

I stare into those deep pools and lie. "You've got nothing to worry about, Darlin."

"You're not a doctor?"

I shake my head, ignoring Dan's incredulous stare. I get it, man; I get it.

"How do you have so much medical knowledge?" Tally is like a bloodhound, sensing my falsehood.

"Same way that you have so much musical knowledge. It's a topic that interests me."

"You probably think I'm crazy, huh? I know it might not make sense to you, but my rules keep me safe."

At that moment, I see it flash in her eyes. Fear. Not toward me, but the memory of what that son-of-a-bitch did to her. It was far beyond the loss of a job. One thing is certain, I never want to see that look cross her face again. But it gives me hope, too. I just have to prove I'm not the monster who hurt her.

I reach over, grasping her fingertips. "You don't have to explain wanting to be safe."

She giggles, taking a sip of her drink. "Don't you wish you'd never asked that question now? My rules likely would never have come up, and we wouldn't have wound up down this rabbit hole."

You have no idea, Darlin. "I want to know everything about you. Besides, I asked."

"I want to know everything about you, too."

That's the problem. She can't, at least not right now.

Tally steps closer and palms my cheek, before pressing her lips to mine. I want to resist her—I *should* resist her—especially since she wants nothing to do with doctors, but it's a lost cause. The moment her tongue teases my mouth, it's all over. I pull her against me, tangling my hands in her hair and taking control of the kiss.

I hate that I lied to Tally, and I'm sure Dan wants to kick my ass straight to the street corner. But he has to understand. Desperate times call for desperate measures.

If Tally was like every other woman, she would have squealed with excitement at the idea of dating a doctor. Spilling the beans would have earned me a blowjob, not a blow-off. But Tally is unlike any other woman I've ever met—in every way.

I've waited my entire life for this woman. Thirty-eight years for her to cross my path. Now, she's here, and I refuse to release her just because she doesn't date doctors.

Instead, I withhold the full truth because I know that truth will make her run away. I want to know this woman. I need to know this woman.

I only pray that she's as crazy about me as I am about her by the time she learns about my profession.

It's a chance I'm willing to take.

CHAPTER FIVE

TALLY

I breathe out a sated sigh when Owen releases me from the kiss. I say release, because there is a power and dominance now. A claim—over me, my body, and if I'm not careful, my heart.

But as I read his features, I can't help but sense that he's not entirely forthcoming. I know some people find my rules odd, but no one has ever called me on them the way Owen did.

Then there is his intimate knowledge of cardiac surgery. I realize you can learn it from a textbook—hell, felons earn their law degrees behind bars—but something is off. But, I asked him, and he said, in no uncertain terms, that he was *not* a doctor. I'm taking him at his word.

"I don't want to know how many women you kissed to have a mouth that talented," I purr, running my thumb along his lower lip.

"I had to be perfect for you." Owen clears his throat, that low, gravelly chuckle rising up from his chest. He steps in between my legs, hiking my skirt up to very unladylike heights. Not that I'm complaining. "Enough about the type of men you *won't* date. Tell me about the men you will."

I tap my finger against my chin as I bite back a smile. "Let's see. Well, he has to be smart."

"Two plus two is four."

I giggle, gliding my hands along the planes of his chest. "Genius level, sir. He also has to be kind."

"I helped an old lady just last night."

I guffaw, my eyes widening. "You'd better not be referring to when you picked my ass up off the ground, buddy."

He's got the most endearing smile. Some smiles are too perfect—the teeth sculpted and whitened to a neon glow—but his are straight and white without dipping into social media influencer territory. The dimples sure aren't hurting his cause, either, or the way he catches his lower lip with his teeth. "Definitely not referring to you, although having you in my arms was the highlight of the evening."

I'm tempted to look away from his intense stare, but opt to meet it head-on. My fingers slide down his torso, hooking in his jeans, and I feel his breath hitch. "Most importantly, he needs to know how to touch me."

Oblivious to the crowd, Owen cups my ass, bringing me against him. His mouth drips kisses along my jaw as his fingers run the length of my spine. "I could spend years touching you and never get bored. Just say the word, and I'll take you back to my hotel where I'll spend the rest of the night exploring every inch of this delicious body."

"Interesting proposition."

"I told you earlier, Tally. It's a promise I'm dying to keep." His hands frame my face and everything—all preconceived notions, past events, and broken hearts—fly out the window. "Tell me what you want, Tally."

I curl my fingers into his belt loops, pulling him flush against me. I feel his erection straining, and it takes everything in my power to not slide my hand along him. "Kiss me like you can't hold back a second longer."

"I can't." He winds one hand into my hair, forcing my head back, as he nuzzles my neck, dropping kisses along my collarbone. His free hand fingers the zipper of my dress, tantalizing me with promises of all the places he'll kiss if I only say the word.

He tongues a path up my neck, nipping at my earlobe, his breath hot against my skin. All the while, I feel his fingers lowering my zipper, pushing my limits, seeing how far I'll let him travel in such a public space.

"Owen," I murmur, my nails scratching along his arms as every nerve cell fires at once. He tightens his grip in my hair before capturing my lips. His tongue traces along the roof of my mouth at an achingly slow pace. Teasing me. Priming me. When I slide my tongue against his, eager to take part, he pulls my hair.

He wants complete control, and I want to give it to him. He delivers his delicious brand of torture until I'm heady with lust.

A drunken bar patron jostles us, jolting us from our moment. I run my tongue along my upper lip, holding Owen's stormy gaze. "What am I going to do with you, Owen?" I manage to whisper.

He slides his hand under my dress, his thumb circling my clit, and I whimper in surprise. I'm never this forward, but with Owen, I don't want him to stop.

Screw public indecency. Owen is so worth the ticket.

His mouth settles against my lips, while his fingers slide inside me, and I writhe against his hand, desperate for more. "Everything, Tally."

"THAT WAS *AMAZING*," I EXCLAIM, SKIPPING OUT OF WICKED CHUCKS INTO the balmy evening.

Hey, I'm not lying. Hedgecore was incredible. Granted, I missed half of the show, but I blame Owen and his incredible mouth. A mouth that stayed in all PG locations. Mostly.

We behaved for the second half of the show, focusing on dancing instead of heavy petting. Well, Owen danced, and I attempted to keep up. I'm beginning to think the man is perfect, or at least perfect for me.

It's uncanny how much we have in common. Besides music, we share the same taste in movies, superheroes, hell, our sarcasm runs in the same vein. He even claims to skate, although he hasn't been on a board in years. I might have to put that theory to the test.

So, even if there wasn't this insane, undeniable attraction between us, we would undoubtedly be best friends.

Owen slides his arm around my waist, pulling me against his side as we stroll to the car. "It was a hell of a concert."

"Made better because you know the lead singer," I mention with a wink, smiling as Owen opens my car door. A gentleman. That's a rare treat.

"I've known him for years. How do you think I managed an extra ticket last minute?"

"You are friends with one of my all-time favorite bands. I don't know whether to be more jealous of that or this car."

"Don't be jealous of the car. It's a rental."

I pivot in my seat, facing him. "You really are living out of a suitcase, aren't you?"

"For the time being. I didn't have a car in San Francisco. I didn't need one."

"Definitely a necessity in Fort Lauderdale."

"Exactly. So, I rented this beauty to see if I like her before I buy."

I run my hand along the dash of the Audi A8. Owen is right; she's a gorgeous car. An expensive, gorgeous car. "This is a pricey vehicle."

"About $85,000 new."

My jaw drops at his blasé mention of the price. "My entire life isn't worth $85,000. So, you can afford a wickedly expensive car, and you left your life in San Francisco. You're a bank robber on the lam, aren't you?"

Owen chuckles, pulling away from the curb. "I told that last night. I'm a thief, but you caught me. Now the question is, what are you going to do with me?"

Oh, my gorgeous man, the possibilities are endless.

My apartment—and old as crap vehicle—are only a few miles from Wicked Chucks, so the ride is over far too soon.

"Stay right there," Owen orders, popping out of the car to open my door.

We stroll up the walkway, and my brain flips into overdrive. I'm wearing my sexy lingerie, and God knows I want this man's hands all over my body. But, despite our necking session at Wicked Chucks, I don't want Owen thinking I'm the type of woman to jump into bed with a stranger.

Even if that stranger is the most handsome and charming man I've ever met.

Owen stops on the doorstep, pulling me against him. But this time, the kiss is less demanding. It's as if he's savoring every second of me for the future. His tongue melds with mine as his hands frame my face, holding me in the moment.

His mouth teases me with restrained passion while demolishing my last vestiges of self-restraint.

I never stood a chance.

"Do you want to come in?" I breathe, breaking from the kiss.

His fingers caress my jaw, those eyes catching the moonlit glow. "You have no idea how much."

"I'm pretty positive if you come in that we'll wind up sleeping together."

"Is that so bad?"

"I'm fairly certain it will be spectacular."

"Agreed."

My hormones are going to kill me later.

"But," I sigh, grasping his forearms, "I don't believe in one-night stands. At least not for me. I'm not judging you or anyone who does—"

"Shh," Owen whispers, lifting my hand and pressing a gentle kiss to the palm. "You don't have to explain."

"I feel like I should, and I really *want* you to come inside."

"I will, when you're ready." He kisses my forehead, smiling against my skin. "How about this? Goodnight, Darlin. I would love to see you tomorrow, or whenever you're available."

Okay, that was not how I expected him to respond. Totally unlike all the men I ever dated, and sexy as all get out. "Wow. Don't men usually play it cool? The whole 'call you in seventy-two hours' line?"

Owen chuckles before nodding. "Most of the time. But you're not a 'most of the time' type woman."

"What am I?"

That delectable mouth captures mine, nipping at my lower lip. "Hold on for dear life and never let go type woman. I'll call you in the morning."

The man just paid me the greatest compliment of my life. The best part? I think he means every word. "Thank you for tonight. It was…there are no words to describe our evening."

"Yes, there is. Perfect."

With a last kiss, I step into my apartment and watch as Owen heads toward his car.

I'm inside all of five seconds when I fling open the door and sprint after him, wrapping my arms around his waist.

Owen chuckles, surprised by my sneak attack. "Hey, beautiful. Everything okay?"

"Not yet, but it will be."

"What riddles are you spinning, little Sphinx?"

I prop my chin on his chest and offer him a smile. "I'm holding on for dear life."

A look of understanding crosses over his features as he bites back a grin. Then the grin slides away, replaced by a hungry gaze as he lifts me into his arms. "Do I get to keep my promise now?"

"You damn well better," I reply.

CHAPTER SIX

TALLY

Owen is still sleeping.

I try to maintain my focus on the coffeepot, ignoring the delicious hunk of a man crashed out in my bed. I say try because my gaze keeps slipping to his snoozing form like high heels on ice. I grab a mug and stroll back into the bedroom. My hope? He's still asleep, and I can bask in his perfect form without him thinking I'm a level nine creeper.

But those gray eyes are wide open when I cross the threshold. "Good morning."

"Morning. Sorry if I woke you. I needed my morning java fix. Nursing hazard." Holy hell, I'm babbling. It's been a hot minute since there's been a man in my bed, and I know there's never been one of Owen's caliber before. His appeal is off the charts.

"Come here." He pats the bed, a smile playing on that luscious mouth. The mouth that was all over me last night.

I pad to the bedside with barely enough time to set down the steaming mug before Owen grabs me about the waist, trapping me underneath him. "I was wrong."

Oh, crap. "About?"

"You're more beautiful in the morning." His fingers push my hair from my face as his lips claim me.

I'm gasping when his mouth breaks from mine, traveling down the column of my neck. I saw one bite in the mirror already, but I have a feeling he's planning to add to the collection.

"You taste so good."

"I can fix you breakfast. Are you hungry?" I manage, but judging from his erection pushing against me, it's not food he's after.

"Only for you."

Who can argue that statement? Not me, as I slide my nails along his scalp, feeling his quiver of excitement.

"Too many damn clothes." Owen paws at my shirt and panties until I'm as naked as him.

He nuzzles my breasts, nipping and sucking at the tips. "Your body is perfection."

The man is ravenous, all hands and tongue, as if he can't get his fill of me. Let me tell you, it doesn't get any sexier than that.

My hand closes around his shaft as he grunts into my mouth. I run my thumb over the tip, moving my hand along his length, and guiding him into me.

"Fuck me, Tally. You're so tight. Christ, you feel so good."

I scratch my nails down his back, my legs wrapping around his waist. "Show me how good I feel."

Owen slides his hands under my ass, tipping up my hips as he buries himself inside me. I cry out, but he's relentless—pulling almost all the way out before driving into me again. So slow, so calculated, so delicious. I squeeze around him, my body thrashing against the mattress as he owns every inch of me.

Just like he promised.

His grip on my hips tightens, his fingers digging into my flesh until the blistering pleasure tears me in two. Owen releases a rough cry as he comes, and I feel him erupt inside me. He collapses on top of me, both of us covered in a sheen of sweat.

I stroke his scalp and back, reveling in the weight of him on top of me. He lifts his head, peppering my face with kisses.

"You're amazing," he whispers, his voice hoarse.

I run my tongue along his lower lip, a smile breaking across my face. "Ready for round two?"

"Little girl, you are going to kill me."

"Is that a yes?"

His mouth claims mine, and he starts moving inside me again with slow, undulating pumps that perfectly match my rhythm. "What do you think?"

"I think I'm the luckiest girl in the whole damn world."

"Are you working today?" Owen inquires, his fingers running along my body. "You work three twelve-hour shifts, right?"

"I'm not a staff nurse."

He props up on one elbow, his free hand getting more devious by the second. Glad to know I'm not the only one with an addiction. "What do you do?"

"I'm the nurse manager of the Cardiac Cath Unit at Memorial. Sorry, medical terminology. Heart unit. What do you do?"

A cloud flickers over Owen's features, but it's gone in an instant. "I told you, I'm a thief."

"Are you seriously not going to tell me what you do for a living?"

"I think I just did."

I send him a fake glare, but I enjoy our ribbing. I feel like I've known Owen my entire life. "Fine, don't tell me," I mutter, turning my focus to the suit of ink covering his body. The man is decorated from the chest down, except for his hands. The work is breathtaking.

Who am I kidding? Owen is breathtaking. My fingers trace along his rib cage when I notice it.

A caduceus—the symbol of doctors and medicine.

"Huh."

Owen tips his head to the side. "What?"

"I'm admiring your ink. I hadn't noticed this one before."

"Tally, I'm pretty sure there's several you haven't seen yet."

"I don't know. I examined every inch of you last night...and this morning."

He props himself up, his gaze flitting to where my fingers trail along his ribs. "Oh, that one."

"The symbol of doctors. An odd choice for someone not in the medical field."

Owen rolls onto his back, putting his hands behind his head. "Well, to be honest, it was my lifelong dream to be a doctor."

For some reason, this piece of information doesn't surprise me. Or freak me out like I expect. I prop my chin on his chest as my fingers trace yet another piece of skin art. "I think you would have been an excellent doctor."

His eyes widen at my words. "I thought you hated doctors."

"Not at all. Some of my closest friends are doctors. Just because I won't date them, doesn't mean I don't respect and admire them."

"Interesting," Owen murmurs.

"Let me guess? You wanted to be a cardiologist? I can't blame you. I adore the field." I pepper kisses to his chest, taking his nipple between my teeth. "It's not too late."

"For what?"

"Go to school. Become a doctor. We need good doctors."

His fingers slide along the length of my hair, and I lean into his caress. Christ, I'm as bad as Hecate. "But if I was a doctor, you wouldn't be here right now."

"In bed after a night out? Sure, I would," I joke, but Owen doesn't return my smile.

"But I wouldn't be here, would I, Tally?" He doesn't let me answer, choosing instead to pull me into another heated kiss, his bulk rolling over me. "There's nowhere I'd rather be than next to you."

I release a heated cry as he buries himself inside me, capturing my moans in his mouth.

At the rate we're going, we'll never need clothes.

"You can't stop smiling, can you?" Stefani asks, popping her head into my office.

"Go away, I'm doing important things," I volley back, but my friend plops into the vacant chair, a knowing grin on her face.

"So? Did you get your skirt blown up?"

I shake my head as a flush crosses my cheeks. If she only knew. "I'm not entertaining that question."

"How was he?"

I don't normally kiss and tell. Let's be honest, in the last two years, there has been nothing *to* tell. But Owen is too delicious not to share. "He's fantastic. Seriously. Our chemistry is off the charts, but it's more than that. He's become one of my closest friends."

Stefani mouth falls open. "In a week?"

I nod, biting my lip. "It's crazy, right? Tell me I'm crazy. Make me snap out of it."

"No chance in hell. I like this version of you—all giddy and sexually satisfied. Good for you, Lu. Owen is quite the catch. What does he do, anyway?"

And that's the million-dollar question. The one crimp in my groove is Owen's continued evasiveness about his occupation. "I'm not sure. He's very vague about work, aside from joking that he's a bank robber."

"If he is, he can steal my money anytime." She grins at my heated glare. "Stop it. I know Owen is your man. He made his desires real obvious that first night."

I prop my chin on my hand, tapping my pen against the desk. "Should I worry that I don't know what he does for a living?"

"Do you think it's illegal?" When I shrug, she continues. "Some people are weird about their work. They don't like to talk about upcoming deals in case they fall through. Maybe he's superstitious."

"Or maybe he's a doctor," I blurt, finally giving voice to the nagging feeling in my gut.

"Why do you think that?"

I shake my head, trying to clear it. "He's evasive about his job."

Stefani's brows draw together. "Why would he be evasive about being a doctor? That's bragging rights central."

"I don't date doctors, remember?"

"Does he know that?"

I nod. "I told him on the first date."

"Did it faze him?"

I shake my head, recalling the memory. "Faze isn't the right word, although he seemed shocked that a nurse wouldn't consider dating a doctor. It was more like he wanted to know the reason behind my decision. That, and he has caduceus tattoo on his ribs."

Stefani shoots me an exasperated glare. "You have a unicorn on your thigh, but I don't see a horn sticking out of your head."

I snicker, picturing myself with a horn and hooves. "This is also true."

"Don't invent problems, Lu. For once, believe something good has fallen into your lap. Lord knows you deserve it."

She's not lying. I've been through the wringer with men, most notably with the doctor I dated. I know it isn't healthy to dwell on the past, but even the thought of that piece of crap makes me seethe with anger.

My friend senses the tension, opting to change topics. "Did you hear they filled Dr. Levinson's spot?"

"Dr. Watts sent me an email this morning. She didn't mention his name, but she claims he is brilliant, and we are beyond lucky to have snagged him." I shrug, shoving the remains of my lunch into the fridge. "I just hope he's nice to the staff. Levinson was a tool."

"He was great in the cath lab, though. A total turd of a man, but expert-level interventionist."

I can't disagree. "But for once, can't we have a brilliant doctor who is also an agreeable person?"

"And hot as hell."

I smirk. "Can't forget that."

"You can. You have a hot as hell man already. It's my turn."

"I thought you liked Dan," I murmur, watching my friend's face flush.

"I do, but he doesn't reciprocate."

My eyes narrow. "He thinks you're gorgeous."

"He also thinks I have the depth of a mud puddle since my musical tastes run more toward Taylor Swift than the Sex Pistols. Don't give me that look, Lu. You know it's true."

"Is that even a competition? I can't say I like Taylor Swift, but she's more musically inclined than the Sex Pistols."

"You missed the point."

I lean across the desk, squeezing my friend's forearm. "No, I didn't. My advice? Prove Dan wrong. I think he's more concerned that you're only looking to warm his bed for a night, and he's got a full roster there."

"Gee, that was a lovely visual."

"Stef, you have a full roster, too. If you like Dan, let him know you're willing to cut your roster. Significantly. I'm not the only one who deserves some long-term happiness."

OWEN IS ON THE PORCH, CHATTING WITH MY LANDLORD WHEN I ARRIVE home. With anyone else, I would feel suffocated. But I want Owen near me all the time. The man warms my soul and judging from the smile on Mrs. Small's face, he's charmed the pants off her, too.

"Hey folks," I throw up a hand in greeting, giggling when Owen jumps down the couple steps and swoops me into his arms.

There is something delicious about a man who is unafraid to

show affection. Particularly when said affection is aimed solely at me.

"Hey Darlin," he coos, as his lips waste no time finding mine.

I fall into the kiss, not caring that Mrs. Small is privy to our intimate moment. "You're a pleasant surprise."

"I made plans for this evening. Come on, let's get you clean, so I can dirty you up again."

Thirty minutes later, we are in Owen's car, heading toward the ocean. I say Owen's car because he's now the proud owner of his very own Audi A8, complete with every upgrade imaginable, and I still don't know where the money is coming from.

"We aren't swimming, are we? I didn't bring a bathing suit."

Owen pulls into the parking lot of a luxury condo complex, right on the Intracoastal Waterway. "I have an appointment with a realtor to look at a few places. I wanted you to come with me."

I nod, as my stomach rumbles. "One condition."

"What's that, Darlin?"

"Feed me afterward."

Owen smiles, leaning across the seat to kiss me. "I made reservations at La Dolce Vita."

"You thought of everything," I reply with a smirk as he helps me out of the car. The man insists on treating me like a lady, and for the first time in my life, I'm allowing it.

I gaze around at the luxury accommodations. I've driven past this part of town, but I can't afford a mailbox in one of these buildings, much less a condo. "This is the high-rent district."

Owen shrugs, an embarrassed smile on his face. "It's not *that* expensive." He holds out his hand to me. "Come on, let's see if we like it."

I slide my fingers into his hand, but his words repeat in my mind.

Let's see if we like it.

Ninety minutes and four condos later, Owen and I are seated in La Dolce Vita, tucked into a private booth at the rear of the restaurant. In the short time I've known Owen, he's treated me like a kid on Christmas. I've had more five-star meals in the last couple of weeks than I have in the three years prior. Even then, those were medical dinners, riding on a pharmaceutical company's tab.

But this, this is divine. Just me and the man I'm swiftly falling head over heels for...fine, the man I've already fallen head over heels for. But I keep that handy dandy fact to myself. Those words are sure to send him screaming in the opposite direction.

I prefer him right here, next to me.

"Talk to me, Darlin. Did you like any of the condos?" Owen inquires, popping a shrimp in his mouth.

I take a bite of my bruschetta, catching the stray piece of tomato that falls from the bread. I'm the definition of grace. "They're all beautiful."

"You can do better than that."

"I like the third one the best. I love the rooftop garden and the kitchen. But that's just me, and my opinion doesn't matter."

His eyes narrow in my direction. "Of course it matters. I like that one, too. Plus, it has three bedrooms."

"It's a lot of room for one guy. You could save money by buying a one-bedroom."

His stormy gaze holds mine as he slides his hand across the table, grasping my fingers. "I hope I'll need the room in the future."

My mouth goes dry at his statement. *Brain, slow down. Don't start playing the wedding march just yet. Gather your facts first. You probably heard him wrong.* "Home gym?"

Owen laughs, releasing my hand as our entrees arrive. "Not exactly."

By the end of dinner, Owen has narrowed down the condo choices to two, and I'm choking over the price. I know that San Francisco is much more expensive than Fort Lauderdale. Still, three-quarters of a million dollars is way above my pay grade—in either city.

I try to snatch the bill, but Owen smacks my hand away. "No chance in hell, Darlin."

He scribbles in the tip, and I giggle.

"What's so funny?"

"If you decided to become a doctor, you'd blend right in with that almost illegible penmanship."

He chuckles, offering me his hand. "I'll keep that in mind."

"It was a wonderful dinner. Thank you, Clark."

Owen's face scrunches in confusion. "Are you forgetting my name now?"

"No. Clark Kent. You're so mysterious, but you're also my definition of perfection, so I can only assume that you're Superman."

His arms wrap around me, his mouth nipping my exposed shoulder. "I thought you were a Marvel girl."

"I am," I declare, twirling in his arms. "But for you, I'll make an exception."

He presses his forehead to mine, and I breathe in the delicious scent that is all Owen. "I really want to be your exception, Darlin."

That makes two of us. I really want him to be the exception, too—the one who holds my heart without breaking it. A woman can dream, right?

"I have another surprise."

"Let me guess. You're buying a yacht, or perhaps a private island in the Caribbean. Am I close?"

"Not today. Maybe next week."

The temperature is finally dropping when we pull up to the skate park. My jaw slackens when he pulls two boards from the trunk, along with a bag of clothes. "Go change, and then, Ms. Big Talker, I want to see what you've got."

I place my hands on my hips, offering up a fake glare. "I'm not a big talker, I'm a truth talker."

"You think you're pretty badass, don't you, Tally?"

"I *know* I'm pretty badass. And this badass is about to show you how it's done."

Owen is damn near doubled over as I accept the bag of clothing.

Let him laugh. I'll simply have to wipe his sweet cheeks all over the pavement.

Granted, it's been years, but how hard can it be? Like riding a bike, right?

So very, very wrong.

Never ask rhetorical questions that involve bodily injury. Karma loves to quiet your mouthy ass for that level of stupidity. Suffice it to say, I'm not the skater I once was, and my ankle has paid the price.

"Ouch," I grumble, grabbing my injured extremity. That's what I get for attempting a kickflip after a decade away from the skate park.

Owen races over, his long fingers palpating my foot. He maneuvers it with gentle pressure to the left and right, and I can't help but notice how professional he is in his examination. "Can you wiggle your toes? I don't think it's broken, but we need an X-ray to rule out a fracture."

"Okay then, Dr. Stevens," I retort, his eyes bulging at my nickname. "What? You sounded like a doctor just now. Even the whole examination part. Something you want to tell me?"

Owen settles on his haunches, his gaze focused on the beach beyond the park. "I told you, I always wanted to be a doctor."

"Maybe you should go back to school for medicine," I suggest, surprised how calm I am at the idea. "In between your robberies, of course."

It's a joke. He should smile, but a worry line creases Owen's brow. Apparently, this whole doctor discussion is a bigger deal than I thought. "If I did that, I'd lose you. Right?"

My mouth goes dry at his direct question. What if he is considering a career in medicine? What then? "I...I don't—"

"Exactly. I'm not willing to give you up, Tally."

I wrap my arms around his waist, giving him a squeeze. "I don't want you giving up on your dreams, Owen."

He drops a kiss to my forehead before hoisting me off the ground. "Why can't we have it all? Your dreams, my dreams, and our dreams?"

Something flickers in the back of my brain, like a tiny beacon flashing out a warning. A warning that, for the time being, I'm choosing to ignore. Owen has something to tell me, and when he's ready, he will. Until then, I'm enjoying every second.

CHAPTER SEVEN
OWEN

"Let me get this straight. You don't want me to mention that you're a doctor?"

I nod at my mother, unsure why this is so difficult for her to comprehend. "Just don't say anything about my work. There are tons of topics we can discuss."

My mother scoffs, shaking her head in dismay. She is not a proponent of half-truths. Come to think of it, neither am I, but Tally is a special case. "Darling, Tally is going to find out, eventually. You said you're working in the same hospital."

"In the same unit," I mutter, running a hand over my brow.

The clock is near zero on the big reveal, and my stomach has been tied in knots for days. Every time Tally mentions the new interventionist at Memorial, I slide on my poker face. Dr. Watts, the chief of staff, is keeping my identity under wraps. She wants to surprise the employees.

Let's just say one of them will be more shocked than most.

On the bright side, Tally seems to be softening to the whole idea of dating a doctor. She's mentioned me attending medical school a few times, insistent that I follow my dreams. Maybe, just maybe, the fact that I completed medical school twelve years ago won't be unwelcome news.

I admit that I'm a chickenshit. But I'm also in love with her, and I think she's in love with me.

Yes, it's fast. No, I don't give a crap. I dated Charlotte for years and never felt one iota of what I felt for Tally within the first hour.

Now, if I can just drum up the courage to let the woman I love know my full truth, I'll be set.

Provided Tally doesn't run screaming in the opposite direction.

"You've fallen hard for Tally, haven't you?" My mother gives my arm a reassuring squeeze.

"That's an understatement. What Tally and I have together is so good. I don't want to mess it up."

"Then don't. But might I suggest you start by telling Tally the truth before any more time passes? Sweetie, you start work tomorrow. Tick tock."

I get it, Mom. No need to twist the knife, even if she's spot-on accurate with her statement.

TALLY OPTS TO MEET US AT THE RESTAURANT, AND I SEE THE TREPIDATION ON her face as she approaches the table. I sprung this dinner on her only a few hours earlier, which I know was a dick move, but I need my mother to meet the woman who has turned my world upside down.

Besides, Tally is a rock star. My mother is going to adore her as much as I do.

"Hi, Mrs. Stevens. It's a pleasure to meet you." Tally extends her hand in greeting, but my mother pops up, pulling her into a hug.

I melt when I see my tiny vixen relax into the embrace. Her own mother died several years earlier, but she still feels the loss acutely.

The first few minutes sail by, exchanging pleasantries about the weather, beach, and restaurant. Just as I'm relaxing, my mother decides to dive into the deep end of the conversation pool.

I had one request—don't mention that I'm a doctor. Well, she doesn't. She does one worse.

"Owen tells me you have an interesting rule."

Tally's eyes widen as they swing between us. "I do?"

"You don't date doctors."

I put my head in my hands, the muscle in my jaw jumping. What part of my simple request was too difficult for my mother to follow?

"How in the world did that come up in your conversation?" Tally chokes back a nervous chuckle, sipping from her water glass. No doubt she wishes it was vodka. I know I do. "I guess it is weird, considering I work with doctors every day. But I have my reasons."

My mother waves her hand, dismissing Tally's anxiety. "I understand that, dear. In fact, I dated a doctor when I was in college. The man ripped my heart apart."

"I'm sorry that happened to you. I had more than my heart ripped apart, hence, my rule."

"It's never easy to overcome a broken heart or will. But, as luck would have it, I met a delightful man only a few weeks later. Owen's father."

Tally smiles, reaching across the table to squeeze my mother's hand. "It all worked out, just as it was meant to. You didn't need that silly old doctor, anyway. His loss."

Christ. Mom, for the love of everything, please stop.

"It was his loss, but the man I married was also a doctor."

Now those huge, luminous eyes focus squarely on me. "Your father was a doctor?"

Oh, boy, this is going to get interesting.

"He was a pediatrician for thirty-five years," I reply, guzzling down my drink and motioning for a refill.

I'm glad my tiny vixen is sitting. She might fall down otherwise. "No wonder you dreamed of being a doctor. It makes sense now."

She's not wrong. My father instilled his love of medicine in me from the time I could walk, but I never had the slightest interest in pediatrics. For me, it was always cardiac medicine. I'm glad that my father got to see my dream come true, even if he'd kick my ass right now if he heard the half-truths I'm spouting to the woman I love.

"My point," my mother continues, accepting her own wine refill, "is that if I had sworn off all doctors forever, then I would have missed out on the man of my dreams. A man who treated me like a queen until the day he died."

Tally laughs, but it's tinged with nerves. "What am I missing here? Are you two trying to set me up with a doctor?"

That is my segue. My mother, intent on getting the truth onto the proverbial and literal table, set it all up.

Now it's my turn. With a deep breath, I grasp Tally's hand. "Funny you should mention that—"

I don't get any further, as our server interrupts the conversation. Honestly? I've never been more grateful. I know I have to tell Tally, but I have my own set-up in mind. One with far less clothing.

I don't know if it's the darts I'm shooting at my mother or her own desire to ease any brewing discord, but she steers clear of medical conversations. The three of us fall into an easy banter, and it's clear that Tally has earned my mother's seal of approval by the end of the night.

It took my tiny vixen two hours for my mother to love her; Charlotte never managed it in several years of dating. Hell, it's hard to warm to an iceberg.

But now it's time—the big discussion with Tally.

God help me. I'm going to need it.

"I LIKE YOUR MOM, EVEN IF SHE IS TRYING TO SET ME UP WITH A DOCTOR." Tally shimmies out of her dress, and my dick springs to life. I'd be happy being inside her 24/7. It's insatiable, my appetite for this woman.

"She's crazy about you."

CHAPTER SEVEN • 77

"I'm surprised you wanted me to meet her. We've only known each other for a couple of weeks."

"When you know, you know." And just like that, I say it.

I stand there as the words hover between the two of us. I pray Tally doesn't run screaming from the apartment. Granted, it is her place. She'll likely chase me out with a paring knife and a rolling pin.

Lucky for me, she does neither. Tally pushes me back on the bed, her luscious curves straddling my waist. Her dark eyes hold my gaze, daring me to look away. "Why won't you tell me anything about your work? Is it illegal? Are you an assassin?"

I know she's joking, but I see the hesitancy lining her face. At this point, she doesn't know what to think.

I stroke my hands along her legs. The woman has the smoothest damn skin. "No, it's definitely not illegal."

"You are a doctor, aren't you, Owen?"

I want to tell her. The searching look on her face is killing me. "If I was a doctor, you wouldn't be here. Remember?"

"Two weeks ago, that would be true. But the way I feel is making it harder and harder to stand by that statement."

What is wrong with me? She's given me an in, I just have to tell her...followed up with the fact that I'll be heading up her unit tomorrow.

Therein lies the issue. If I was working in a hospital across town, I could tell her. If she worked labor and delivery and I worked in the cath lab, I could spill the beans.

I'm not only in the one field she claims to *never* date, but I'll also be her boss...in a loose manner of speaking.

Can it get any more complicated?

Instead of coming clean, I play ostrich. I'm not even a chickenshit anymore. I'm an ostrich shit. And I hate myself for it.

"I'll show you something hard," I murmur against her lips, sliding my tongue along the roof of her mouth, teasing her. Her mouth—like the rest of her body—fits mine perfectly. It's as if she was created with me in mind.

I break the kiss, running my finger along her lower lip, my gaze locked with hers. "I'm in love with you, Tally. You know that, don't you, Darlin?"

I want to freeze the smile that lights up her face. "You are?"

"Without a doubt."

She nuzzles my nose, that husky chuckle firing up my insides. "That's good, because I'm in love with you, too."

WE LAY CURLED TOGETHER, BUT MY HANDS CAN'T KEEP STILL. IT'S TALLY, for God's sake. This woman's body was created for my pleasure. I don't want anything to break this moment.

Can't we stay here forever and forget reality?

My fingers play along her side and lower back. One of her larger pieces decorates the area, but I know scar tissue when I feel it. Tracing the line, I can only surmise it was from a car accident or from the piece of shit that turned her against doctors. "What happened here?"

"Accident," Tally stumbles out a bit too quickly.

Okay, she's not telling the whole truth.

"Car accident or some other type of accident?"

"An 'I don't want to talk about it right now' type accident."

I press a kiss to her shoulder, squeezing her tighter. "You'll tell me one day?"

"One day," she murmurs, stretching as a tiny moan escapes her lips. I love that I wear her out, although she gives me a run for my money, too. "I need to sleep tonight. It's a big day tomorrow. The new interventionist arrives."

Those words tank my high as reality creeps in. I'm on empty, without a gas station in sight. "Should I worry?"

"Why would you worry?"

"What if he steals you away from me?"

Tally giggles, burrowing her face in my chest. "Not a chance. I don't date doctors, remember?"

I run my fingers through her hair, my heart racing. "What if you meet the perfect man, and he happens to be a doctor?"

She props her chin on my chest, offering me a smile. "That won't happen. I've already met the perfect man. You."

"You mean that, Darlin?"

"I do. I love you, Owen."

With a deep breath, I fling open the door to my soul. "Move in with me. I know that it's fast, but I don't care. I know what I want. I want you. I want us."

Tally's eyes widen like saucers, and I'm not sure if I should keep going or start backpedaling.

"I'm not saying we have to get married right away, although I want marriage and kids and the whole white picket fence scenario. But I don't want to wait six months or a year to move forward with you. I already know. I knew it the second I laid eyes on you."

Her jaw slackens, but she has yet to utter a single word.

"Can you say something, please?"

With an excited squeal, my tiny vixen flings her arms around my neck and presses her lips against mine.

I roll on top of her, never breaking contact with that delicious mouth. "Is that a yes?"

"Yes, to all of it. In whatever order it comes."

My Tally is always beautiful. But at that moment, she radiates an ethereal glow.

My initial plan was to spill the truth about my occupation after I spilled my heart. But, as I look down at her, joy emanating from her entire being, I can't do it. I can't douse that happiness.

Call me a bastard, but I'm basking in the glow from our love. I only pray that come tomorrow morning, it will be enough.

CHAPTER
EIGHT
TALLY

There's only one downside about being in love. It usurps your soul, making it impossible to think of anything else.

I've been walking around like a lovesick fool since the day I met Owen, but after last night, I'm on cloud nine.

"Lu, you got a minute?" Stefani joins me at the coffee counter, giving me a gentle nudge.

"He loves me," I mumble, my gaze on the creamer as I mix my coffee.

"What?"

I snap from my reverie with a guilty smile. "Sorry. Actually, I'm not sorry. Owen asked me to move in with him last night, after he told me he was in love with me."

Note to self, have your friend sit before you drop a bombshell. I swear, Stefani staggers for a moment before regaining her composure. "You're moving in with Owen? Are you getting married, too?"

"Not yet."

She grabs my arms, giving them a squeeze. "Lu, this is amazing news. Wow." She takes a step back, a radiant smile crossing her face. "How do you feel?"

"I want to pinch myself. It has to be a dream. Happiness like this cannot exist in the real world."

"Yes, it can. It does, and you're proof of that. I call dibs on being maid of honor." Her phone sounds in her pocket. "Time to get back. Dr. Watts will be rounding with our new cardiac savior soon."

"Let's hope he is all that, and more."

I can hope, right? I'm not sure why the idea of meeting the new interventional cardiologist has me tied up in knots. I get on wonderfully with most of the doctors here at Memorial. I respect their talent, and they—some more grudgingly than others—respect mine. Hell, some of my constant companions in the happy hour department are cardiologists. Let's hope this new addition is ready to jump in and get his hands dirty, instead of preening in his ivory tower.

It takes all kinds to run a hospital.

I glance at the clock. Fifteen minutes until showtime, but my punctual ass is always early. That, and Dr. Watts wants me to meet the man of the hour before the rest of the staff.

My phone buzzes in my hand. It's Owen.

Tally, I need to speak with you. Please. Call me as soon as you can.

I dial his number, strolling down the back hallway to the conference room. I hear a cellphone ringing as I near the door, but it's the ringtone that stops me.

It's 'Girlfriend in a Coma' by the Smiths, Owen's ringtone for me.

Yes, I'm well aware that some might consider it morbid, but it's our inside joke, and besides, the song kicks ass. But that isn't what concerns me right now.

I push open the door and see Owen standing there, a cup of coffee in his hand.

"Owen? What in the world are you doing here?" How in the hell did he get back here? It's only accessible with a badge. Maybe he really is a world-class burglar.

"Tally, can we talk?" My man looks positively stricken, and all I can deduce is that something happened to his mother.

"Is your mom okay?"

CHAPTER EIGHT • 83

Owen nods, but he doesn't get to say anything more.

"Lu, there you are." Our medical director, Dr. Watts, strolls into the conference room. "I see you've met the surprise."

"What?" I ask, scrunching my nose in confusion.

Dr. Watts motions toward Owen, a smile on her face. "My surprise to Memorial. This is Dr. Stevens."

I'm a nurse. I'm prepared for all manner of emergency. I juggle stress and the fine line of life and death every day.

I'm not prepared for this. My knees buckle, but I catch myself on the edge of the table. I'm quick, but not quick enough. Owen is by my side, his gray eyes wide and terrified.

"Dr. Stevens?" I choke out, praying I heard our illustrious leader wrong.

"Yes," Dr. Watts confirms, destroying my world with one syllable. "Dr. Stevens is a top-notch interventional cardiologist. Remember the robotic procedure you and I discussed at the last function? He helped spearhead the development of that robot. We are beyond blessed to have him working with us at Memorial."

"Dr. Stevens?" It's all I can say, my mind swirling along with the coffee in my stomach.

"Lu, are you feeling alright?" Dr. Watts places her hand on my arm, shooting me a look of concern.

"I'm a bit lightheaded. I need some water." What I really need is an escape. I need to run far away from this place—and this man—and never return.

"I'll get it." Owen dashes to the water cooler, pressing the cup into my hands. How chivalrous of him. The lying lech.

Dr. Watts's pager sounds, and she glances at it. Crap, I know that look. She's got an emergency. As the chief of staff, her working life is nothing *but* emergencies. "Dr. Stevens, I apologize. I have to deal with a situation in the emergency department. Perhaps, after Lu is back to rights, she'll take you on the tour. She knows the hospital like the back of her hand."

"I don't think..." It's all I can manage.

"Be a pal, Lu," Dr. Watts beseeches. She's lucky I love her. Granted, her new cardiology addition might not make his first procedure. I'd rather kill him first.

"Fine," I mutter, sipping the water and taking long, slow breaths.

"Keep an eye on Lu, will you? She works too hard." With a squeeze to my shoulder, Dr. Watts walks out, leaving me alone with the man who spent last night buried inside me.

The man who spent the last two weeks feeding me one lie after another.

The fury overtakes the anger, particularly when Owen sits next to me, placing his hand on my knee.

"Tally—"

"Don't touch me," I snap, jerking my knee from his grasp.

I'm a professional. It's time to act like one.

Pushing myself to a standing position, I adjust my glasses, avoiding Owen's—I mean *Dr. Stevens's*—gaze. "If you'll come this way...Dr. Stevens." I don't wait for him as I walk out the door, turning left toward the cath lab.

"Tally, please. Let me explain." He's at my side, and I hear the panic in his voice.

I, on the other hand, am cold as ice. At least, externally. Internally, I'm suffering a nervous breakdown, temper tantrum, and crying fit all at the same time. But Owen will never know. "The doctor's lounge is at the end of the hall."

"Tally."

"There is an employee gym down there, as well. I don't go there often, but I'm sure some other medical staff can give you the lowdown."

He grabs my shoulders, backing me against the wall. "Tally. Stop."

For the first time since this liar upended my happiness, I meet his gaze. His eyes are wild, and I feel the fear washing off him.

His hands massage my shoulders, but I shirk his touch, tensing. "Darlin, please talk to me."

"I don't appreciate pet names, Dr. Stevens."

But he isn't listening, intent on making me hear him. Fat chance of that. His forehead presses against mine, and I smell his minty breath. I'm mere inches from his lips—lips that loved every inch of my body while spouting countless lies.

No. No more. I lift my hands to Owen's chest and push against him.

"Tally—"

"What?" I snap, shoving at his muscled torso. "What do you have to say, Dr. Stevens? I have a job to do here. I'd appreciate it if you'd let me finish, so I can continue my day."

"I wanted to tell you. So many times."

"But you didn't. Instead, you lied—*so many times*—and here we are." I suck in a lungful of air when he backs off me, rolling my shoulders and willing up my last vestiges of courage. "I'd like to finish the tour. Beyond that, we have nothing to say to each other." I turn, taking a few steps down the hallway.

"So that's it, then? Less than twelve hours ago, we were discussing marriage, Tally. While we were making love. Now you're going to act like you don't know me?"

This man did *not* just try to turn this situation on me. Not again. Never again.

I whirl on him, my eyes blazing. "No, Dr. Stevens. I don't know you at all. The man I knew doesn't exist. You made him up. I'm not sure why. To fuck with my head? My heart? Bravo, doctor. You win. You sick bastard, you involved your mother in your game. Is it something you two do for kicks?" I take in another deep, shaky breath before setting off down the hallway. "It doesn't matter. It's over and done with, so if you follow me, I'll show you the cath lab."

I'm not sure how I manage the rest of the tour. I give myself credit that I didn't impale the good doctor with something. Lord knows there is all variety of sharp instruments in a hospital. The place is a veritable treasure trove of torture devices—just ask our patients.

I purposely avert my gaze from Owen during the rest of the tour, but I feel him burning holes into my visage.

Look all you want, doctor, that's as close as you'll ever get to me again.

Rounding the corner, I make a beeline for the nurses station, catching Stefani's wide-eyed gaze when she sees Owen.

"Owen? What the hell are you doing here?"

"That's Dr. Stevens. He's our new interventional cardiologist," I hiss, spitting out his name as if it tasted bitter. Come to think of it, it does.

"Wow, you're the new genius doctor? At least I know we'll get along. Lu, you certainly kept quiet about this news!"

"That would be because I didn't know until this morning."

"But I thought you two were—"

"Nothing. We're nothing." For the first time, I look directly at Owen, driving the point home. "Absolutely *nothing*."

Owen clenches his fists and looks away, a muscle jumping in his jaw.

I hope my words hurt him as badly as he's hurt me, but I have my doubts. It's likely all a game he plays, and everything was a lie. Why, I don't know. But the why doesn't matter anymore.

"That tour only covers the highlights, but I don't like to overwhelm people on their first day. If you don't have any questions, I'll be in my office. Good day, Dr. Stevens."

CHAPTER NINE

OWEN

My blood boils at the severity in Tally's tone. I know she's furious, and she has every right to be. But to claim that we're nothing?

I resist the urge to kiss that rigid line in her mouth until she softens. I want to tongue that spot at the base of her neck and feel her pulse quicken. I want to tell her I love her even more than I thought possible.

But she cast me aside. Treated me like a leper. Or worse.

And that makes me furious.

"We have a meeting at three, Tally. Don't forget." It's the first words I've uttered in the last fifteen minutes.

Tally stops but doesn't look at me. "I'm well aware. You can trust me on *my* word. Unfortunately, I can't say the same for you."

I watch her stalk into her office, every word from her gorgeous mouth a bullet that leaves me bleeding profusely.

"Ouch," Stefani mumbles.

I should maintain some professional decorum, but Tally just ripped me to shreds. "Well, that fucking sucked."

Stefani crosses her arms over her chest, narrowing her gaze in my direction. "Perhaps I'm Captain Obvious here, Owen—Dr. Stevens—but why didn't Lu know about your job until this morning?"

"I didn't tell her."

"Yeah, I got that." This time, Stefani isn't bothering to disguise the disgust in her words.

I'm going to have to provide a better explanation, or Stefani will hate me, too. At the rate I'm going, the entire staff will despise me by the end of the morning. "I sound like a total prick, don't I?"

"Pretty much. I just hope—for *your* sake—that you have a good reason for lying to my friend."

I lean against the nurses station, feeling more desperate with each passing minute. Talk about hindsight being 20/20.

"You know Tally's rule, right? She doesn't date doctors. She made that very clear on our first date."

"She was badly burned by a doctor."

"I get that, but I'm not *that* doctor." I lift my hand toward her office, feeling sick to my stomach. "I've been crazy about Tally since the moment we met, and I figured that…fuck, I don't know what I figured." This is a disaster.

"That she would understand and accept it because she was in love with you?"

"Yeah."

"Are you in love with her?"

I force a smile, but my face feels like it will crack from the effort. "Would I be this messed up if I wasn't?"

"Well, if it's any consolation, if Tally didn't love you back, she wouldn't be this messed up, either."

"She won't even look at me, Stefani."

"She's angry. You lied to her and broke her trust."

I run my hand over my scalp. If I'm not totally honest with Tally's best friend, I don't stand a chance in getting back my tiny vixen. "I want to love her. Hell, I want to marry her."

Thankfully, my words hit home. Stefani reaches out her hand, squeezing my forearm. "Look, she's angry, but I know my Lu. She's a big softie, hiding behind that tough as nails exterior. Give her time to calm down and then talk to her. If you want, I'll put in a kind word."

"You would do that?"

"I've known Lu for a decade, and I've never seen her so happy as she was these past few weeks. I'll do anything to bring that back to her"—her gaze hardens—"on one condition."

"Name it."

"Don't make me regret this, Dr. Stevens. Don't you hurt her again."

Dr. Watts interrupts our chat, fetching me for the first of several meetings. Before I leave, I lean over, catching Stefani's ear. "I swear."

MEMORIAL HAS A TON OF PROMISE.

Who the hell am I kidding? I don't remember a damn thing they told me today. My mind is fixated on Tally, locked in her office, likely with a voodoo doll of me in her hand.

Stefani offered to speak with her, but I can't wait that long. It's only been a few hours, but maybe, just maybe, Tally will let me plead my case.

Either that, or she'll ship my ass straight to the executioner.

My heart quickens as I knock on the door to Tally's office. Much more of this stress, and I'll be in the cath lab as a patient.

"Come in."

I'm not sure what I expect when her gaze rises to meet mine. The warmth and softness I found there is gone, replaced with a wrought iron ferocity.

"Are you lost, Dr. Stevens?"

I swear if it gets any frostier between us, icicles will form at the end of my nose. "May I have five minutes, and then I'll go? Please, Tally."

"Contrary to popular belief, I don't work for you. Find yourself another beck and call girl."

I lack a retort, so I keep silent, my gaze intent on her form.

Tally sucks in a breath, her eyes staring at some distant point on the wall, her foot tapping against the floor. "What do you need?"

I sink into the chair, leaning across her desk and catching a faint whiff of her scent. I'm drawn to her like a dog in heat, and it doesn't matter if she's mad as hell or riding my cock; some things don't change. "*We* need to talk, Tally. I understand you're angry, and you have every right, but I don't want this to come between us."

She scoffs, shaking her head. "You're funny."

"I'm not trying to be."

"There is no us, Dr. Stevens. Not now. Not ever." Her dark eyes peer at me through her lenses. "Is there anything else?"

The finality of her statements hit like bullets, but I plow ahead. Hey, desperate times call for desperate measures, and I've never been more determined. "What has changed besides the fact that you know my job title? I'm still the same guy, Tally. The guy who loves you."

"Everything has changed."

"That's just it. Nothing has to change, unless you want it to."

"You lied to me."

"About my job! Tally, I never lied about how I feel about you. Did you forget what we discussed last night? Living together? Getting married? Having a family? I meant every word. I've never discussed those things with anyone before. I've never wanted them with anyone before. I want them all...with you."

She still won't look at me, but I see her jaw wobble. Maybe I'm getting through. "It's so stupid, really. Who knows they want to marry someone after a couple of weeks?"

"You're right."

"See? At least on that, we're on the same page. Something in common."

"I knew I wanted you after the first night. It didn't take two weeks to feel it. It only took two weeks to gather the courage to speak the words."

"I need you to leave. Please." The words are harsh, but her tone is uneven.

I'm not going anywhere. Tally is about to break, and I'm going to catch her when she does. "If you want me to go, look me in the eye and tell me that the last two weeks meant nothing to you. Tell me you lied when you said you loved me, when you claimed to want the same things I did. Do that, and I'll walk out that door. I won't bother you again."

Those large, dark eyes meet mine, but I see the tears brimming. "The last two weeks...the last two weeks—" Tally's voice cracks, and she buries her head in her hands. "Why did you do this to me? Why did you have to break my heart?"

That does it. I'm at her side, kneeling by the chair and forcing her to look at me. "Why are you breaking mine? I want to love you. Let me love you, Tally."

"I can't."

"Why?"

She doesn't reply. Instead, she slides a new piece of emotional armor into place. With a sniffle, she wipes her eyes. "I can't have this conversation, Dr. Stevens. You may think what you did is acceptable, but it's not. You asked for my rules, then you played them against me."

"I had to prove I wasn't like the rest of them."

"Instead, you proved that you are *exactly* like them. Please, leave me alone."

"I won't leave you alone, Tally." The desperation is kicking into high gear. I can't let her shut me out. She's everything I've ever wanted. "You told me you wouldn't date a doctor or someone you worked with—and I was both. I wanted to get to know you, Tally, and have you know me. So, it wouldn't matter when you found out."

"It wouldn't? The fact that our time together was based on lies?"

"I lied because I was terrified you would push me away when you found out."

"What did you think would happen?"

"I thought when I told you I loved you and you said it back, that our love would carry us through this."

"Do you even know what love is, Dr. Stevens?"

I wipe her tears with my thumb. Her sadness rips at my soul, especially when I know I'm the cause. "I didn't until I met you."

Tally pushes my hand away, pulling a tissue from the drawer. "I asked you so many times. I gave you so many chances to come clean. But you never did."

"I was scared shitless."

"Of me," Tally barks out a laugh. "That's the most ridiculous thing I've ever heard. Well, right up there with all the crap you spouted last night."

"I meant every word." I'll stay crouched next to her, repeating myself for the next year, until she believes me. "I planned on telling you this morning, but you were gone when I woke up."

"So, it's my fault."

"No, Darlin, none of this is your fault. It's my fault. I—"

Her phone rings, cutting into our conversation. "I have to take this. If you'll excuse me."

"Tally—"

"I said, *excuse me*." She points at the door, and I have no choice but to abide by her wishes.

Just like that, the door closes, and I'm stuck standing on the wrong side of it. I'm locked out of Tally's life and heart, and I don't know when she'll let me back in. Even worse is the idea that she won't ever consider the possibility.

I can't even blame her. She's hurt and angry because of me.

"One hell of a first day. You okay?" Stefani inquires, giving me a gentle jab in the ribs.

"I save lives. I'm good at it. I know my shit. I've had some really tricky cases, but I always believed I could power through them." I put my hand against the door, willing Tally to feel me. "I feel completely powerless right now."

The door swings open, startling us both. Tally stands on the other side of the threshold, her eyes brimming with tears. Her gaze swings between the two of us before settling on Stefani. "I have to leave for the day."

"Lu, are you okay?"

She shakes her head, and I see her fighting back the sobs.

Jesus, please don't tell me I wounded her this deeply. I'll never forgive myself.

She grabs her friend into a quick hug. "I'll call you later, Stef."

"Tally, Darlin, what's going on?" I move to embrace her, but she holds up her hand, dismissing my concerns—and me.

Without another word, she hurries down the hallway, disappearing into the elevator.

I PRAY THERE ISN'T A TEST ON WHAT I LEARNED TODAY. CORRECTION, WHAT I *should* have learned. I muddle through the remainder of the afternoon, images of Tally running from me burned into my brain.

I meet with the realtor after work, leaving an earnest money deposit on the condo. Tally's choice won out, of course, but it isn't just a ploy to win back her love. It really is the nicest of the four, although it doesn't hurt that there's a rooftop garden for Hecate.

My phone rings, but it isn't my tiny vixen. Damn. "Hey, Stefani."

"Hi, there. I wanted to give you an update."

"You spoke to Tally?"

"I did. She's furious with you, but right now, Lu has bigger problems."

"What in the world is going on? Hang on, Stefani." I set down the phone and sign a final document for the realtor before heading to my car.

"If I'm interrupting, you can call me back."

"No, I'm just finishing up with the realtor. I bought a condo. Tally's favorite."

"Congratulations."

"Hold off on any celebrating until she agrees to live with me." I shake my head. The condo is not the damn issue. "Is Tally okay?"

"Her father took a turn for the worse. That's why she left in such a hurry this afternoon."

My heart smashes to the ground. "I didn't know he was sick."

"Mr. Knowles has dementia. Tally took care of him for several years, but then his condition worsened. She pays for his treatment in a memory care facility."

I know the price of those facilities—thousands of dollars per month. That explains her modest apartment and beat-up car. "What happened to him?"

"He fell and hit his head. They don't know—"

"I'm driving to her apartment now."

"Owen, I don't think you should do that. Tally is very private, especially in her grief. She doesn't want me around tonight. I highly doubt she'll want to see you."

Too damn bad. She needs me, and I've got a ton of making up to do. It starts now. "Well, I'm going to find out. Thank you for letting me know."

I pull up to her apartment fifteen minutes later. Thank God, she's here. For the first time, I inspect her vehicle, noting the wear and age. It's over fifteen years old.

Decision made—Tally is getting a new car.

I knock on the door, but there's no answer. I try the handle. Unlocked. I'm going to spank her sweet ass for not protecting herself and then kiss every inch for granting me easy access.

The bathroom door is closed, and I hear the shower. I order in some food because I know my little minx. She hasn't eaten. Then I uncork a bottle of wine and pour us each a glass. God knows we both need one.

"What are you doing here?"

Showtime.

I turn, handing her a glass as I try not to ogle her towel-wrapped frame. That I know what the towel is covering is not helping my hormones.

Down boy, this is not a good time.

"I know you haven't eaten, so I ordered Chinese."

Her eyes widen, darting between me, the floor, and the wine glass. Best guess? She's deciding if the broken glass is worth it when she hurls it at my head. "What are you doing here, Dr. Stevens?" she repeats, her voice thin and strangulated.

Screw this distance. I'm ready to bust through every wall Tally has erected between us.

I pull her to me, feeling her stiffen in my arms. "Stefani told me about your Dad. I know that you hate me, but I'm here to take care of you."

She pushes away from me, her towel loosening in the process. Sweet Jesus, let me get another glimpse of paradise. "I don't need your help. I'm fine."

"No, Darlin, you're not fine. You're anything but fine."

She whirls on me, her eyes blazing. "You're right. I'm not fine. I'm having a terrible day. My life is turning upside down, and I don't know what to think. I don't know what to do—" Her words end as the sobs overtake her.

As a doctor, I've watched many family members weep. I saw my mother break down after my father passed. But none affected me as much as watching the woman I love crack under the strain of heartache. I scoop her into my arms, ignoring her huffs of protest.

She can hate me later. Right now, she needs me. I carry her into the bedroom, setting her on the bed. My dick, always at attention around Tally, thinks it's game time.

Sorry to disappoint you, big guy. Not tonight.

I pull sweats and a tank from her dresser and stand in front of her, my best doctor's stance at the ready. "Come on. Let's get you dressed and fed."

"You shouldn't be here."

"Actually, this is exactly where I should be, so good luck in scaring me away."

"Can you give me some privacy?"

"No."

"No?"

"Darlin, my tongue has explored every inch of you. On multiple occasions."

She crosses her arms, frustration taking over the sadness. "That was before."

"That was *last* night."

"Like I said. Before." Her words are clipped, but I see a slight flush crawl over her cheeks. She's not immune. "I'm not changing until you leave."

"Well, I'm not leaving."

Now we're in a standoff. Both of us, glaring at the other, arms crossed, the energy between us thick and hot.

I move first. I admit it, I'm weak as hell where this woman is concerned. I tangle my fingers in her hair, pulling enough to reaffirm that I'm the boss, and then I stake my claim.

She struggles, but I pin her wrists to the bed as my mouth reminds Tally of what she's missing. My tongue pushes past her lips —possessing her, owning her.

After a few seconds, I hear her low moan as her mouth gets in on the action. Hell yes, this woman is trapped fire.

Her teeth sink into my lower lip, much harder than usual, and I pull back, licking my wounded skin. "Fuck, Darlin."

"That," she hisses, "is for lying to me." She shoves against my chest. "Get off."

"No."

"Get off now, Owen."

"I can bite too, Tally." She knows I'm good to my word. I've covered her body in love bites. I nuzzle her neck, breathing deeply of her scent. Christ, she's addicting. "How would you explain wearing a turtleneck in Florida?"

"Don't even think about it."

"I'm so far past thinking about it," I murmur as I nip her skin, my hands stilling her halfhearted attempts to push me away.

"Do *not* mark me," Tally warns.

But what good is an idle threat? Holding her wrists firm, I travel south to the top of her breast, sucking the soft skin into my mouth.

When her body arches against me, I release the grip on her wrists to pull open the towel and expose every inch of her deliciousness.

The doorbell rings, and we both startle. Figures. For once, the delivery guy is on time. With a hooded glance and a cock straining for release, I push off her. "Chinese."

"Right," she breathes, her entire body flushed from my exploration. "Let me get dressed, and I'll be right out."

"Feel free to eat naked. Hell, let me grab the food, and I'll come back and eat you."

She opens her mouth to retort as the doorbell peals again.

Patience, dude. It's only been thirty seconds.

I adjust myself and open the door, shooting the guy a forced smile. I'm starving, but it's not for Chinese. I pay the bill and bring the food into her small living room, catching sight of her worn furnishings, threadbare in spots. I'm not sure how I missed it before.

Tally never spoke about financial difficulties, but judging by her modest life, she's suffering from them. She won't admit it, but she needs help. I'm just the man for the job.

"Come on, let's get some food in you," I call into the bedroom.

I hear Tally's mumbled voice and realize she's on the phone. Glancing at my watch, I know it's the hospital. Please let it be good news.

She joins me on the couch a few minutes later, tucking her legs under her as she grabs a pint off the table. "Thank you for dinner. I love lo mein."

"I know, Darlin. How's your Dad?"

She pokes at the noodles with chopsticks, her eyes averted. "He's the same. The nurse was giving me an update before change of shift."

"What's his prognosis?" No point in hiding my medical expertise now, thank Christ.

"He has Lewy body dementia, so there's no positive outcome. But," Tally pauses, a tear rolling down her cheek, "I think he still remembered me? The neurologists can't say what the fall will do to any remaining cognitive function. I meant to go there two nights ago, but I didn't. I was selfish."

"Why didn't you say anything? I would have gone with you."

She shrugs, wiping a stray tear. "People are weird about dementia, or illness in general. I didn't want to saddle you with that. Too much reality for the first couple of weeks."

"Not for me, especially not when it's for you."

Tally sighs, and I see her erecting the emotional wall again, brick by brick. "If I'd known you were a doctor...actually, I knew. There were too many signs. I just didn't want to believe it. I guess some people aren't meant to have the fairy tale ending."

"I want to give you the fairy tale ending. I'm planning on it, actually. I'm planning so many things for us, but it only works if you're there."

She averts her gaze, nibbling her bottom lip as she pulls at a thread from the throw pillow.

"I signed the paperwork for the condo," I offer, trailing my fingers down her arm. "The one you like, with the rooftop garden for Hecate. The one with an extra bedroom, just in case."

Funny thing. My ex, Charlotte, is all about the material pleasures. That condo, and the idea that I bought it with her in mind, would have sent her into squeals of delight. But for Tally, it's not even remotely impressive. I wounded her soul, and an oceanfront view will not change that fact.

Maybe honesty will. "I want to tell you everything, Tally."

"There's more?" she inquires, fumbling to get the noodles into her mouth. Tally is the least graceful woman in the world with chopsticks. God, I love her.

"No, but I'd like you to know me. All of me. You'll see that I'm not that guy, that I'd sooner walk through fire than hurt you."

"You'd better get to stepping, then"—she grits out—"because you did more than hurt me."

"Can we talk about it? Let me tell you my reasons. Please, Darlin."

"Not tonight. I'm too tired." She rolls her shoulders, wincing in pain. "I thought the shower would help."

"Let me give you a massage." Her mouth opens to argue, but I silence her. "Don't say no. This is therapeutic. You're in pain, you need to rest, and I can help."

"Can you write me for some Valium?"

I chuckle. "I can, but I'm not going to."

She snaps her fingers. "What good is a doctor if he won't write you scripts?" As usual, her delivery is dry and sarcastic, but I see the small smile playing along her mouth.

"I have complementary techniques I can employ. I guarantee it will relax you."

She shakes her head. "No, we better not. My pussy has no control when it comes to you."

As if on cue, Hecate jumps into my lap, demanding attention.

"Either one," she jokes, her smile the first genuine one I've seen today.

I put her to bed an hour later, after she passed out watching old reruns on television. My body aches to curl up next to her and hold her the entire night, but I can't push too hard.

Not right now.

Right now, she needs my support. I scribble a note, recalling how Tally mentioned my doctor's scrawl. She knew. Almost the entire time, she had me pegged. If only I had the guts to come clean then, maybe I'd be sleeping next to the woman I love, instead of leaving her for a cold hotel room.

Sleep, my beautiful Darlin. I'm going to make this right. I love you, Tally—every single, delectable inch of you.

I leave the note on her nightstand, pressing a final kiss to her head before letting myself out. I have a long night ahead of me.

CHAPTER
TEN
TALLY

TALLY

Stefani slides the basket of bread across the table, offering me a rueful smile.

"Beautiful carbs, how I've missed you." I grab a roll and slather it with butter. Screw dieting. My heart hurts in too many places for a salad to heal.

"You don't need to diet. You're tiny, Lu."

"It's because I diet. I'm five feet tall. If I ate what I wanted, I'd blow up like a beluga."

"I highly doubt it," Stefani snickers. We're across the street from the hospital in a pub-style eatery, frequented by medical staff. She's working today, but I haven't drummed up the courage to walk into the unit yet.

I took a few days off to handle my father's injury, but I'm mostly avoiding Owen. It's safer for my heart this way. My hormones aren't speaking to me at the moment, but no matter. My brain is riding shotgun, and it knows that Owen and I are too cosmically connected when we're in the same room.

Hence, avoidance.

"How's your Dad?"

"He has to go to rehab for a few weeks, but they don't think there's any permanent physical damage."

"Did he know you?"

I shake my head, tears filling my eyes. "He didn't seem to."

"Lu, he might be having a bad day."

I nod, but we both know the truth. The fall knocked any remaining remnants of my father's personality from his body.

Stefani toys with her napkin. Oh, I know what she's about to ask. Joy of joys. "So…Owen. What's happening there?"

I shrug, grabbing another roll. Diet, sit down, and shut up. "Nothing."

"Just nothing? He told me he's called you countless times, but you don't answer. He texts, but you don't respond. He stopped by your apartment last night and the night before, but you weren't home."

None of this is news. Okay, the visits are a surprise, but my phone is fully aware of how many times Owen called. "I fell asleep at the hospital, so I got home late. Besides, it's better if I don't see Owen. Seeing him only muddies an already precarious situation."

Stefani swigs down her soda, tapping her fingers on the table. "We've been friends for years. Best friends."

"Ride or die."

"But I have no idea why you won't date doctors." She holds up her hand, preventing my interruption. "I know, you dated one, and he screwed you out of a job. Lu, that doesn't even make sense. Doctors don't hire nurses, and nurses don't directly report to doctors. You're not telling me the entire story. So, if you want me to have sympathy for your plight, spill it, girl."

But I can't spill it. Not today, possibly not ever. The only person who knows the truth of the situation is Beth, the manager at the women's shelter where I volunteer, and it only spilled out during a drunken crying fit.

I run my hand along my right side, feeling the raised areas, now covered by ink. No, Stefani doesn't need to know this ugliness.

No one does.

"I have rules, Stefani. Those rules, however ridiculous they may seem to you, have kept me safe. I've been taking care of myself for as long as I can remember. My parents did the best they could, but Mom was fragile, and Dad was always working. When you grow up alone, you learn to walk the straight and narrow, because when you don't, should you fall, there's no one to catch you."

Her hand reaches across the table, squeezing mine, her eyes bright. "But if you never leave that path, you won't see all the people there waiting to help you. I'm always here, Lu. That bastard deserves no more of your time or energy."

"Owen? You're right, so he's not getting any of either." Am I deflecting? Absolutely. Am I lying? Oh, hell yes.

"Sure. That hot, tattooed body hasn't been running through your dreams the last few nights? I know a load of crap when I hear one."

"He's gorgeous. Delicious, in fact. But he's off-limits. It's in the rule book."

"It's your life—and your rules, Lu, but the man is crazy about you. Maybe you should reconsider those rules as they apply to Owen?"

That's the problem. I have considered it, but I can't get over the crux of the issue. "He lied, Stefani."

"I get it. Owen knows it was a shit thing to do. So do I. But you love him."

"I'll get over it."

"So, you two are friends now?"

"We're work colleagues. Nothing more."

"Liar."

I flip her the bird as we stroll back to the hospital. I won't admit it to Stefani, but I took extra time getting ready this morning, donning a navy-blue dress that Owen damn near ripped off me during our brief courtship.

Maybe I'll get the same reaction today, sans any public indecency. I would love to make the bastard drool, though.

We round the corner of the unit, and my heart jumps into my throat.

Standing directly in our line of sight is Nicole Hedges, aka Hot Doc. I'm serious, that's what they call her on the units. Everyone with a penis, and many without, lust over the woman. Right now, she's lusting all over Owen.

She isn't even trying to be discreet. Her hand rests on his arm as she bats her lashes in his direction, her high-pitched giggle carrying throughout the unit. It's all systems go for Hot Doc.

But it's Owen's reaction to her advances that make me see red. He's grinning down at her with that wide, dimpled smile that is an equal mix of flirtation and sex god.

Stefani shoots me a pointed look. She knows my fiery temper firsthand and is likely placing bets on how long it takes for my feelings surrounding our new cardiologist to become public knowledge.

Sorry to disappoint, Stef. I will maintain my outward facade of calm, even if I'm seething on the inside.

I stalk into my office and riffle through papers, my ears keen to the conversation between our two most eligible doctors.

"Did Ken mention that dinner with Sanofi? You must come. It will be a wonderful introduction for you, and they're holding it at this five-star seafood restaurant that just opened. Their food is divine. Besides, we can get to know each other better."

I glance up, catching Owen's gaze. He knows I'm hearing every word. If he values his life, or his balls, he'll tread lightly.

"Sounds like a plan. Thank you for the invitation, Nicole."

"It is black-tie, but I'm certain you can fill out a suit."

Is she fucking serious right now? I hold back a gag, pretending to be terribly interested in a staff newsletter. God, I hate women like her—all pretty and confident and sexually brazen.

"I have one just for this type of occasion."

Wow. If I thought I could hit him from here, I'd pitch my stapler right at his handsome shaved head. The son of a bitch made plans with another woman.

CHAPTER TEN • 105

In front of me.

How typical.

I feel Owen looking at me, but this time, I don't give him the benefit of eye contact. Screw him. Actually, I'll leave that for Nicole, who likely will be before too long.

"Lu, I have a proposition for you. One that will set your panties on fire."

My head flies up, smiling at Eric, one of the surgical techs. Behind him, I notice Owen hovering, his jaw tense, our roles reversed from only moments ago.

The banter between Eric and me is innocent—we are strictly work buddies. The man is happily married to Jeff in the Emergency Department. And I mean *happily*. Romance film level happy.

But Owen doesn't know that fact. All he knows is some good-looking young guy wants to set my panties on fire.

Eric, I love your timing. Owen, eat your heart out. Not so much fun on the receiving end.

"A statement like that will certainly get my attention. What's up, Eric?"

"I have someone for you to meet. Get this, he loves punk music, he's inked, he's cool as fuck, and sexy as hell. He's also off tonight and looking very forward to meeting you."

I clear my throat, chancing another glance in Owen's direction. The man is borderline furious. I can continue poking the bear, or I can dead the situation.

As tempting as poking one handsome hunk doctor sounds, I'm not in the mood for a mid-unit tussle. "I don't know, Eric."

"I showed him your picture. He thinks you're beautiful."

That did it. "Tally, can I speak to you for a minute?" I swear Owen is puffing his chest out, as if he needs to look any bigger. He already towers over Eric.

"Hey," Eric grins at Owen, earning a forced smile in return, before swinging his gaze back to me with a shrug. "Just think about it, Lu.

You need a good man in your life. Unless you're dating someone. It's been a while since we talked."

Of all the questions he had to ask, he chose that one. Right in front of Owen.

I mumble the only two words that describe my current situation. "It's complicated."

"Isn't everything?" Eric retorts with a wink. "Well, back to the dungeons. See you later, Lu. Call me if you change your mind."

Owen closes my office door, flipping the latch to the locked position. "What the hell was that?"

"By all means, make yourself comfortable."

"I'm not kidding. I'm about to lose my shit."

He cannot be serious. This man just made plans with another woman in front of me. Now he's giving me crap? Oh, hell no. "If you're having issues, contact HR."

His fist hits against my desk, making me look up. "Oh good, we're back here. I wasn't sure which Tally I'd get today."

"Which Tally? No doctor, unlike you, I only have one version. And *unlike* you, I don't make dates in front of the staff or former relations. But then again, I don't lie, either. So, you and I have very little in common."

Owen huffs as he plops into a chair. "You went MIA on the man you're dating. So much for taking the high road."

I want to hit him. Hard. It wouldn't hurt him, but it would shock him into silence. "What the hell are you talking about?"

Owen turns on his phone, scrolling through his call log. "Twenty phone calls and forty texts over the last few days, all unanswered. Not to mention, I stopped by your place the last two nights, but you were conveniently out. Me? I look like an obsessed psychopath."

I hate how much my heart warms, hearing how desperate he was to see me. Then, my brain reminds my naïve heart that this man made plans with another woman.

Heart, return to icy exterior immediately.

"I didn't think we had anything to discuss." I speak the words without emotion, but they elicit one from Owen. I swear, the man winces at my statement, and me, being a marshmallow in armor, feels immediate guilt over his reaction. "I turned my phone off last night. I stayed in the hospital with my Dad. I didn't want to leave him."

He's on his feet, his bulk pinning me against the filing cabinet. "Is there any improvement?"

I nod. "He's going to rehab tomorrow or the next day." That's his cue to back up. A cue that Owen ignores as his fingers trace along my collarbone, and I bite back a whimper. This is the trouble with amazing, mind-blowing sex. When it ceases to occur, your brain and body go on strike, and the slightest touch can hurtle you over the cliffs of madness.

I'm clinging to a bare root on the edge of that cliff.

"I've been so worried about you, Tally. I haven't heard from you since the other night."

The night he gave me a hickey, fed me Chinese, and put me to bed. But when I awoke, he was gone. It's funny how, after only a couple weeks, I'm used to his presence.

"You snuck out."

"I didn't sneak out. You fell asleep. I had an early call and didn't want to wake you."

The truth of our reality seeps back in. He's off-limits, and the sooner my heart gets with the program, the better. "Look, I have a ton of backlog here. It's been a rough few days."

He presses his forehead to mine. "I'm sorry."

"For what?" It's an honest question. There are multiple things he can apologize for right now.

"Anything that hurt you."

"You hurt me."

"Not intentionally."

My anger flares at his qualifier. "Yes, intentionally. I don't know what, if anything, I should believe from the last few weeks."

A muscle ticks in his jaw. "What is that supposed to mean? How do you think I feel, Tally? The woman I'm dating won't talk to me. For days. Then she waltzes in, looking so good I can barely contain myself, and agrees to be set up with another man!"

I love how he remembers a totally different version of events than the one I took part in. "That is rich, Dr. Stevens," I scoff, pushing my hands against his chest. "I didn't agree to anything. You, on the other hand, simpered all over Dr. Hedges. I have a tux just for the occasion."

He captures my wrists, holding them captive. "That's different. It's a work event, Tally."

"It's not different. Not for her. It's a segue. You're too smart not to know that, so spare me whatever bullshit excuse you have for making plans with another woman in front of me."

"I want to take *you* to the dinner."

"Sure you do. I heard you inquire about that part real clearly."

"I was going to—" Owen takes a step back, running his hand over his beard. "Fuck, Tally. Can we please stop fighting?"

"Sure. You came into my office, yelling at me and making demands. If you're quite done, there's the door."

But Owen is an immovable mountain. He's not going anywhere.

I have to get back to work. I pull open the filing cabinet, bending over to grab a file. Yes, it's a cheap party trick, but I never claimed to play fair. Work with what you've got, right? "Since you won't leave, what do you want?"

"To rip off your underwear, bend you over this desk and lick every inch of your pussy until you're screaming my name."

I whirl around, my jaw slack, but my body overheating at his words.

"You asked," he responds with a wink.

I've never met a man with such an obsession for my lady parts. Oh, sure, I've met men addicted to sex, but they were more concerned with getting themselves off. Owen loves getting me off. And I love letting him.

The trouble is, sex can't fix our issues.

"It's all about sex, isn't it? Men are so typical," I sneer, acting as if his statement didn't send my hormones into an uproar.

"That's a load of crap. Why haven't you returned my calls? We're never going to work through this if you don't spend time with me."

A knock sounds at my door, and Owen unlatches it, pulling it open a few inches. Oh, joy. It's Hot Doc, come to collect her new man. "Hi, Lu. Owen, a few of us are grabbing a drink later. Did you want to join us?"

"Not today, Nicole. Thanks," Owen replies, his tone clipped, his gaze intent on me.

"Are you sure? Well, here's my card, if you change your mind." She slips him her digits, sending me a pearly smile before ducking out of the office.

I've got to hand it to the woman, she's persistent.

Owen taps the card against his shoe before shoving it in his pocket. "You know, I have an answer for all of our issues."

"Hold my head underwater until the voices stop talking?" I'm kidding. Mostly.

"You'd better not."

"I'd totally haunt your ass," I reply with a smirk. This time, I'm not joking. I would be his worst phantasmic nightmare.

"I might spend more time with you that way." At my scowl, he chuckles. "I'm kidding."

"What's your answer to all our problems?"

Owen pulls me into his arms, his lips capturing mine without warning. Sneaky bastard. Lucky for him, he tastes delicious. "We tell people that we're in love and moving in together. That puts all interested parties on notice."

Just like that, the glitter fades, and the truth rears its ugly head once again. "Not an option."

"Why?"

"You know why. I don't date doctors."

Owen throws his head back with a groan. "Yeah. I heard you the last hundred times. But I don't want you to date some random doctor. I want you to date *me*. I want you to move in with me. I miss you, Darlin."

See? That's where he gets me, because I miss him, too. I ache for Owen. But this time, I have to protect my heart, a heart that got wounded watching the man I love make dinner plans with another woman.

In. Front. Of. Me.

Love looks better from a distance. It's like an impressionist painting. Close up, it's sticky and messy and riddled with uncertainty. Far safer to keep it at arms' length.

"Owen, even if I threw out my rule, which I'm not saying I will, we aren't allowed to be together."

His eyes narrow at my words. "Why the hell not?"

He told me a lie. Now it's my turn to spout one. "We work together. In the same unit. There are rules against that sort of thing."

Owen shakes his head, chuckling. "They never enforce those rules, and you know it. But, just in case, I plan on reading the employee handbook."

"Why?"

"Because I don't believe you, Tally."

What a smug bastard, being all...right and everything. "Well, now we're on equal footing. I don't believe you, either."

Another knock at the door. Like I said, the bitch is persistent.

"Sorry to interrupt—"

"Again," I mutter, forcing a grin in her direction.

"The rep from Sanofi is here and would love to meet you. Do you have a minute, Owen?" Her face is so eager.

Damn girl, play a little hard to get. Truth be told, I understand. I fell into Owen's lap that first night. Literally.

"I'll be right out." Now it's Owen's turn to force a smile. What a banner day we're having at Memorial.

I cross my arms over my chest, motioning toward the door. "Nicole is waiting."

"Tally, so am I. I'm not going anywhere."

"Except to dinner and drinks with Dr. Hedges."

He rubs his hand over his brow. "Not that I was going to do anything, but I won't go for drinks or to the dinner—on one condition. You agree to give us a chance."

Oh, good. An ultimatum. Either I renege on my morals, or I can watch Owen saunter into the sunset with another woman. "Wow," I manage. Truthfully, it's about all I *can* manage as my anger careens into the red. "You have some nerve."

"I don't mean it like that, Tally. I'm desperate to spend time with you."

"I told you, we aren't allowed—"

"Bullshit. That's complete garbage, and you know it. You're so unwilling to bend your own rules that you would rather let me walk away? I know you love me, Tally. God knows that I adore you. Why isn't that enough?"

"You lied to me. You betrayed me, Owen." I blink back tears. "My faith in people is all I have, and you broke it. Then you make plans with a beautiful woman in front of me. What did you think would happen? Did you think that would make me cave? You hurt me, and then you hurt me again, and now I'm the bad guy? No way."

"It's not a date, Tally. But you're right. I will speak to Nicole and let her know I'm involved."

I shrug, chewing my lip. "But you're not. You're a free man, and you've already made plans with her. On multiple occasions, and in front of me, I might add. Have fun." The words fall like acid from my mouth, destroying everything the sound waves touch.

His eyes blaze at me, and I swear he's going to throw something. "Fucking great. Thanks for that, Tally."

He storms out of the office, and for once, I don't care who's watching.

CHAPTER ELEVEN
TALLY

Life sucks. Life without Owen really sucks. I know some people will say I've only known him a few weeks, and it can't be that hard. Those people can kiss my ass.

Those same well-intentioned idiots claim being friends is better than nothing. Another lie. Being friends with a man I'm so insanely, ridiculously attracted to is torture in its purest form.

Thankfully, and I'm lying when I say this, I've been occupied the last few nights. Okay, I've been creating crap to keep busy. Still, anything is better than thinking about the amazing sex I'm *not* having with Owen. Or the amazing sex he might be having with some other hot commodity at the hospital.

I'd have to be deaf, dumb, and blind to not hear the women gushing over his good looks and easygoing bedside manner. They have no idea how hot his bedside manner truly is.

Crap, what if they do know?

"Ugh, I can't do this." I toss down my pen in frustration, earning a side-eye glance from Stefani. The woman is a saint because I've been insufferable the last week.

"What's up, Lu?"

"I'm stressed." It's not a lie.

"I'm surprised you're not on cloud nine today."

"Why would I be on cloud nine?" Does she know something I don't? Have I won the lottery, and everyone failed to mention it?

"Where did that man take you last night? He looked divine."

"What man?" I'm not sure why I'm asking this question. I know exactly what man. What I don't know is where he went the night before. Looking divine, apparently.

"You're funny. I know you don't kiss and tell but come on, give me something. A man doesn't wear a tux every day."

My heart sinks as I collapse into the chair. So much for Owen's declaration of love and fidelity the other day. He really showed Nicole how involved his heart was with someone else as he escorted her to the dinner.

He claimed he wasn't going to the dinner. Another lie. Hell, the paint is still wet on the casket of our relationship.

Easy come, easy go—a perfect motto for Owen.

"Where did you two go?"

"I didn't go anywhere. He had a date."

"A date?"

"Yes, Dr. Hedges invited him to some fancy-schmancy dinner at a five-star restaurant."

"Well, that's not a date." Stefani drums the desk with her fingers. "That's a work function."

I shoot her a look. We know Nicole's reputation—in and out of the emergency department. "It wasn't just dinner, either."

"Are you sure?" When I nod, she rolls her chair over, giving me a fierce hug. "I'm sorry, Lu. I shouldn't have said anything."

I shrug, determined to present a brave face. "I'm glad you did. You're my ride or die, remember? The one who tells me I have broccoli in my teeth or that the man I dated briefly has moved on."

"What man is that?"

I swear Owen moonlights as a ninja. His timing is impeccable.

CHAPTER ELEVEN • 115

"Good morning, Dr. Stevens. How are you today? Late night, I'm assuming?" Stefani is cordial, but her tone carries an arctic chill.

Thank you, sweets. You always have my back.

"In need of a vat of coffee," Owen chuckles, swigging back the last of his cup. "Tally, would you like to join me for breakfast?"

"I'm busy," I mutter as I stalk into my office and shut the door. It's a universal signal that I'm off-limits, otherwise engaged.

A 'stay the hell away from me,' sign.

It's also one which Owen blatantly ignores as he pokes his head in the door. "Tally?"

I hate how appealing this man is on every level. Why can't I be immune to him?

"Yes, Dr. Stevens."

"I found this great restaurant. They have an amazing mahi-mahi dish. It's supposed to be the best seafood in the area. I'd like to take you."

"I'm busy." I don't even raise my head from my paperwork. If I look at him, every emotion will show on my face.

"I didn't say a day."

I remain silent. It's my best defense at the moment.

"Tally, can we talk?"

"I'm busy. Is there something I can help you with, Dr. Stevens? I don't have the time nor the inclination to discuss mahi-mahi right now."

"Darlin, what's going on?"

I stand up, bracing myself as I meet his gaze. I open my mouth to repeat my former statement, but Owen isn't having it. He crosses the small space, pressing his fingers to my lips.

I'm tempted to bite them, but I surmise he'll enjoy it too much. Come to think of it, I will, too.

"I wouldn't if I were you."

"Or what?"

He kicks the door closed, turning the latch in one deft move. Then he comes for me. Damn my tiny office.

His hulking frame backs me into a corner, as he wastes no time pressing his length to mine. "Or I'll be forced to find other ways to get the truth out of you." His hands are like homing devices as they skate under my skirt, sliding along my thighs.

But his talented digits are not welcome anymore. Not in my office and not on my body. "I'm not in the mood for your games, Owen."

The teasing grin slides from his face when he realizes—finally—that I'm not kidding. "Are you still mad at me?"

Why can't I lie? God didn't gift me with a filter; why couldn't he have given me a damn poker face? "No."

"Okay, that's a yes."

"Did you have an enjoyable time last night?"

A knowing look crosses his features. "I'm assuming you mean the dinner?"

"Yes. I'm assuming that's how you know how delicious the mahi-mahi is there. I know who you escorted to the dinner. You must think me very foolish, Dr. Stevens. And until now, I suppose I have been. But I won't be sloppy seconds for anyone. Not even you."

A muscle ticks in his jaw.

Come at me, Dr. Stevens. I'm locked and loaded.

"Wow. First," he barks, holding up one finger, "I didn't escort anyone to the dinner. I recall asking you to be my date, but you refused. Oh, yes, because, two," a second finger joins the first, "you claimed that we couldn't be together, because of *your* rules. A decision I was adamantly against. So, don't give me crap now because you're jealous."

The bastard. "You're right. I was jealous. *Was.* But then I realized, you're just like every other guy. Not. Worth. My. Time."

My words are untrue, but harsh zingers are my only defense against the ache in my heart. I don't fool myself into believing I'm irreplaceable, but I didn't plan on being optioned out this quickly.

Owen's breathing is harried and uneven. My words have found their target. "I'm glad to know I'm not the only liar, then."

"What the hell is that supposed to mean?"

"You told me you loved me. You were on board with marriage and kids and the whole nine yards. Whatever order it comes, right, Darlin?" Owen seethes, but there's no warmth in the pet name, only pain. "But at the first obstacle, you cut and run."

"This is not my fault."

Owen throws up his hands, looking skyward. "I lied to you about my job. You're right, and I'm sorry. I took a chance because I never felt this way before. So, I lied about what I do for a living, not because I'm ashamed of it. I'm damn proud of being a doctor. I worked my ass off to get here. But I lied because you informed me I didn't stand a chance in hell if I was a doctor. Not a drug addict, not an adulterer, not an abuser—a doctor! So, I kept quiet to see if you would fall in love with me." He leans in, his face inches from mine. "And you did. You fell as hard and as fast as I did. But in the end, my job title was more important than the fact that I love you."

"Have you once, in all of this, stopped to consider how I feel?"

"Tally, that's pretty much all I've done."

I stand up, glaring down at him as he slouches into the chair. "No, you haven't. Not once. You keep insisting that I should overlook this indiscretion, but your apologies are half-assed, at best. You didn't come clean, Owen. I found out your identity from our chief-of-staff. In the weeks we were together, you had so many opportunities to sit me down and have a serious conversation, but you never did."

"Would it have mattered?"

The truth? I would have been terrified and angry, likely punched a wall, and then spent a few hours in the ED getting my injured paw wrapped. But I would have caved. For Owen. For us.

But now, it's too late. He's moved on, or is in the process, no matter how much he argues that fact.

I shrug, wiping away a few more tears. "I can't answer that because you never gave me a chance, but now you're angry that I won't give you one. I don't abide by secrets and lies, Owen. Besides, you've already moved on. I don't see what else there is to discuss."

He needs to leave. Now. My bravado is as thin as rice paper, ready to crumble from one more blow.

Owen ignores my statement about Nicole, but he seizes on another part. "You want to talk about secrets, Tally? I didn't know your father had dementia."

"It wasn't a secret. I didn't tell you, because some people can't handle the stress of chronic illness, particularly when their new girlfriend is the caregiver."

Owen taps the desk with his thumb while his foot drums out a rhythm on the floor. I've seen him angry before, but this is a whole new level of agitation. "Here's the problem with that statement. I'm not some people. When are you going to realize that?" He stands, pacing the small space. "I want to know about your scars."

I freeze, externally and internally. I know Owen is aware of them, but I won't dive headfirst into the shallow end of the pool. "I don't want to talk about them, Owen."

"Well, I do! I want to know what that son-of-a-bitch did to you because I'm paying the price for his actions. But you won't tell me a thing, because that would involve letting someone in. Christ, even Stefani doesn't know what happened with that man."

My heart beats like a freight train, threatening to derail and explode into a million shattered pieces. "How dare you dig into my past without my permission. You have no right—"

Owen grabs my arms, forcing me to look at him. "Oh, I dare. I hoped your best friend might have some insight, but you're a vault, Tally. Look at you, mad because I'm trying to find out *what* happened to you, instead of realizing *why* I'm trying to find out."

My office line rings, and I'm thankful for the distraction. It's the emergency department. I'm needed—one of my many hats at Memorial. I hang up the phone, taking a sip of water. "I have to go to the ED."

"I would say we can talk later, but you never pick up the phone." He shrugs, both of us searching for some way to fix this mess.

He follows me out of the office, and who, but Dr. Nicole Hedges is waiting at the nurses station. It would be funny if she weren't trying to bag the man I love. Before Owen's arrival, I saw her maybe once a month for a patient consult. The Emergency Department is her usual haunt. But lucky me has seen her a few times already this week.

Joy of joys.

"Owen, there you are! Always hiding in Lu's office, aren't you?" She gives his arm a playful punch. "Are we still on for drinks tonight?"

Game. Set. Match.

I'm done.

I gather my paperwork and storm to the elevator, pushing the button and trying to maintain some semblance of calm.

"I can explain," Owen states, his eyes apologetic, his expression rueful.

"It's not my business. But please, stop acting like you want us back when it's blatantly apparent that she's more than a work colleague."

"Tally—" Owen begins, but the doors slide open. Thank the Gods, there's only room for one of us.

Time for me to go.

I NEED TO PUT ON MY GAME FACE. ANYTHING HAPPENING BETWEEN OWEN and me must remain at the door.

The woman inside is tiny. According to the medical report, her name is Marla. She's twenty-six, one hundred pounds soaking wet, and covered in all manner of lacerations and contusions.

I hate that I know how she feels.

Her story is like so many other women, but equally heart-wrenching.

He was a nice guy in the beginning.

Then things changed.

Maybe it's her fault. If she had dinner ready when he got home, he wouldn't have started drinking.

It's all bullshit. She's a victim, even if her abuser won't let her admit that fact. This case differs slightly from so many others that roll through the emergency department. Namely, because Marla is ready to leave Earl, the monster who gifted her with this colorful collage of bruises.

She's afraid for her son because Earl thinks he's weak and needs toughening up. Marla knows his discipline all too well—she's felt it countless times.

As the Sexual Assault Nurse Examiner, I have a process. Once my examination is complete, and the paperwork filed, we can address the elephant in the room. Where can we discharge Marla that is safe for her and her son?

That's where Beth comes in. She's one of my best friends and the director at the local women's shelter. She's also the only one who knows the full story behind my scars because she bears scars of her own.

Beth works as a victim advocate, and she's bar none at giving the extra nudge necessary for an abused woman to seek safety. Thankfully, Marla reached that conclusion on her own. Now, with Beth's help, they will move into the shelter and away from Earl.

"Code gray, emergency. Code gray, emergency."

We reserve the term code gray for a violent altercation. My ears perk up as the voice sounds over the intercom, and I intrinsically know that Earl has arrived at the hospital.

"Stay in here," I warn Marla, leaving her in the exam room with Beth. I turn into the hall and come face to face with a crazed man, swinging his arms wildly.

Lovely. He's a live wire.

"Sir, you need to calm down." A nurse tries unsuccessfully to deescalate the situation.

"I need to speak to my wife." Then his gaze swings to me.

I haven't uttered a word, but he knows I hold the information he's seeking.

"You," he sneers. "You know where my wife is, don't you? I want to talk to her."

"What is your name?" I inquire, swallowing my fear and moving toward him.

"My name is Earl, and I know that bitch is here. Our neighbor told me she was leaving, spouting some lies about me hitting her."

That's the other thing. Marla has agreed to press charges. Earl made it significantly easier for the police to track him down. In fact, here they are now.

Like I said, timing is everything.

Earl is read his rights and handcuffed, hurling obscenities in my direction. One, in particular, shakes me to the core. "Just wait, you filthy whore, until I get out. I'll find you. I'll finish what he started."

As far as I know, Earl doesn't know the monster I dated, the demon who left the scars along my side. But even the smallest kernel of fear is enough for my knees to wobble.

I return to the exam room and promise Beth and Marla, in a shaky voice, that Earl is headed for the station house, and they are safe to leave, complete with a police escort.

Beth pulls me out of the exam room, grabbing my arm. "What is it, Lu? I see it in your face."

I shake my head, not letting the seeds of hate Earl tossed about take hold. "Nothing, just another asshole."

"What did he say? Did he threaten Marla? Her son?"

"No. He threatened me. Said he would finish what my ex started."

Beth pulls me to her, squeezing me tight. She says nothing. What is there to say? She knows, as well as I do that as long as your abuser is on this side of the dirt, you're never truly safe. Hell, even when they are behind bars, there's still a danger.

"Tally? Are you okay?" Great. Owen, who's never in the ED, just happens to be here.

I pull back from Beth, offering him a stiff smile. "I'm fine." It may be rude, but I don't plan on introducing Owen and Beth. Why complicate matters?

Owen takes that job upon himself. "Hi, I'm Owen Stevens."

How odd. He didn't introduce himself as a doctor.

Beth shakes his hand, smiling up at him. No woman is immune to the man's charm. "Beth Smith."

"How do you know Tally?"

Okay, time for me to jump in. "Dr. Stevens is our new interventional cardiologist. He's a brilliant addition to Memorial."

Beth's eyes widen with recognition. No surprise, since I talked about him non-stop during our brief courtship. To her credit, she hides it well. "You're a doctor?" Beth inquires. "Well, I suppose the white coat and scrubs are a dead giveaway."

It's unfair. Most people are shapeless in scrubs, but Owen? He fills them out to the point of bursting. No wonder he's on the top of every woman's eye candy list.

Time to steer the conversation to neutral territory. "Beth runs the women's shelter downtown. She helps patients who need a safe haven."

"We'd be lost without Lu. This woman is tireless in her work and dedication." Beth wraps an arm around me in an embrace. "I'm going to head out."

"I'll check in tomorrow. Call me if you need anything," I remind her, watching as she guides Marla to a new life, free from abuse.

"Ken told me you're the Sexual Assault Nurse Examiner." Figures Owen would glean info off one of my closest cardiology buddies, the talented and big-mouthed Dr. Jessop.

I meet Owen's gaze, not emotionally ready for another round. Thankfully, I find only compassion in his eyes. "They need a voice. I understand—" I break off, realizing this is the first time I've intimated to Owen that I'm an assault survivor.

He pulls me to a quiet alcove, cupping my face with his hands. "My God, Darlin, what did he do to you?"

I blink back tears. Time to come clean. "Bad things."

Pressing his forehead to mine, I feel the emotion in his voice. "I'm not him, Tally. Please let me in. Let me protect you."

"What are you doing down here?" I inquire, wiping the tears from my eyes. "Were you looking for me?"

Uh-oh. I know avoidance when I see it, and Owen is looking everywhere *but* at me right now. "I didn't know you were still here."

I'm about to ask why he's here. It's on the tip of my tongue, but then I spot Nicole, and I have my answer. To think, I almost caved. I must be stronger, which means more distance between me and the man who will shred my heart when he falls in love with another woman.

"Ah, I see." I step away, nodding in Nicole's direction.

Owen's eyes widen. "It's not just us for drinks. I swear, Tally. Come with us. Or, let me cancel this evening, and you and I can go somewhere."

Just like the first night, I feel like a third wheel. A flat third wheel. In other words? Totally useless. "I have some work to finish. Have a good time."

"Tally," Owen calls after me, but I'm not waiting around for him. He's made his choice.

CHAPTER
TWELVE
TALLY

TALLY

There's a reason I don't date people at work. When it goes south, it's painful.

With Owen, it's the seventh circle of hell.

He's been at Memorial a little over two weeks, but his reputation as a miracle worker is already secured. Even without robotics, his work in the cardiac cath lab is quickly becoming the stuff of legends.

No surprise there. I know firsthand how talented his digits are.

He also sets every tongue wagging when he strolls through the hospital with his confident swagger. There are rumors that Nicole is close to landing her prey, but I don't investigate.

I don't want to know.

I haven't spoken to Owen since that evening in the emergency department when I watched him leave for drinks with another woman.

He has a new trick, sliding notes under my office door. I was tempted to toss them, but like everything else with the man, they're endearing as hell.

Note, Day 1: *Knock, knock.*

Note, Day 2: *The joke only works if you actually respond.*

Note, Day 3: *I'm much better at card tricks, but for you, I'll attempt comedy.*

Note, Day 4: *I can't believe I have to write out the entire joke. You'd better laugh. Knock, knock. Who's there? (that's your line). Sherwood. Sherwood who? (another one of your lines). Sherwood like to be your valentine!*

Note, Day 5: *Did you laugh? If you did, I have another one. If you didn't, I have another ten. I'm going to assume you laughed because it was the epitome of comedic genius. So, here's another one: What do squirrels give each other for Valentine's Day? Wait for it...forget me nuts.*

I chuckle, dropping the note with its counterparts into my desk drawer. If this whole interventional cardiology gig doesn't work out, Owen definitely *doesn't* have a future in stand-up.

I'm not sure how to interpret the notes. They're cute and funny. Friendly, but with no overt romantic tones or sexual innuendos. I don't know if this is what friendship with Dr. Stevens looks like, but I guess it could be worse.

However, the mental reel in my head of Owen screwing Nicole is the stuff of nightmares, and lucky me, I have it on permanent playback.

"Come on, Lu, we don't want to miss the first round." Stefani plops into my office chair, swiveling back and forth with an air of impatience.

Tonight is the unofficial welcome party for Owen. In other words, it's the cool doctors and nurses on the unit hanging out, coupled with copious amounts of liquor and laughs. Normally, it's right up my alley.

Not tonight. It's bad enough that Owen and Nicole may or may not be involved. I don't need a front-row seat. "You go ahead. Have a good time."

"Don't tell me you're not coming."

"Okay, I won't tell you."

"You always go to these get-togethers. How's it going to look if you suddenly don't attend?"

"It might look like I have work to do."

"Which you don't."

I tap my pen against the desk, glaring at Stefani over my glasses. "*They* don't know that."

Stefani shoots me a knowing look. "This wouldn't have anything to do with Dr. Nicole Hedges and her obvious infatuation with the man of the hour? I overheard her say she wants to carry his babies."

"That bitch," I mutter under my breath. I'm loath to admit how much I detest anyone looking at my man. Former man. I hate my life. "He's probably eating up all the attention."

"Owen isn't interested in Dr. Hedges, and you know it."

"I don't know a damn thing anymore. Wait, that's not true. I know he and Nicole had dinner and drinks together after he said he wouldn't. I also know he claimed he wasn't a doctor when he was. So, I know he's a liar."

"Have you asked Owen if anything is going on between them?"

I shake my head at Stefani's idea. "Are you insane? It's not my business."

"Only because you won't let him anywhere near you. Yes, he lied about being a top-notch cardiologist, but he did it because he didn't want you walking away. He's an amazing man, Lu."

"Go for him. He's newly single. Actually, I don't know that. He and Nicole are likely screwing at this point. It has been almost a week."

Stefani leans across the desk, grasping my forearms. "Stop that. You didn't hear how Owen spoke about you that first night. You don't see how looks at you."

"Looked at me," I correct.

"No, looks at you. Trust me, I've seen it numerous times. On the car ride home, he kept asking questions, wanting to know everything about you. He was so nervous about coming on too strong or scaring you away. It was the most real I've ever seen a man behave. And it was all for you. Doesn't that mean anything?"

I collapse my head into my hands. Her words are cutting serious chinks into my armor. "I believed him. Every word, I believed. When Owen told me he loved me and wanted a life with me, I knew it was the truth. I saw it in his eyes." I toss my pen down, groaning at the ceiling. "Deep down, I knew he was a doctor. There were too many coincidences, and honestly, if he'd come clean when I asked him, I would have accepted it. I gave that man every chance to tell the truth, but he still lied."

"Look at the reason why Owen lied. It's actually adorable."

"He's an adorable liar. Now I've heard everything."

"He lied because he's in love. I think that's pretty damn adorable. Come on, everyone is waiting for you. I know you want to see Owen, even if you won't admit it."

"That's just it, Stefani. I don't want to see him because it's too painful right now. It's too raw." I shoot her a smile. It's fake, but this once, I hope it will suffice. "Go have double the amount of fun for me."

"Buzzkill," she whispers, dropping a kiss on my head before heading out the door.

I sit at my desk for another fifteen minutes, waging an internal war with my psyche. I'm desperate to see Owen. But what if Nicole is there? There's no way I can sit through a dinner of them canoodling, but I also can't storm out if they're dining together.

That would make me feel more foolish than I already do, and trust me, I have straight A's in that department.

My phone buzzes. It's Dr. Jessop, my resident drinking buddy. *'Lu, get your ass over here right now. I'm not above coming to fetch you. Come on, kid, drinks are on me.'*

I huff out a groan, earning a quizzical look from one of the night nurses.

Trust me, sweetheart, I don't get me either.

I can ignore Dr. Jessop, but he's not lying. He will drive all the way to my house and drag me, kicking and screaming, to whatever pub they're frequenting. I don't stand a chance when I'm right across the street from the group.

With a sigh, I head for the locker room to change into my street clothes—a fitted t-shirt, jeans, and chucks. Aren't I the picture of glamour? A fedora and my tortoiseshell glasses finish the look. While I won't be winning any beauty pageants, I'm at least rocking my element.

Hey, I'll take what I can get.

I cross the street as the dread and anticipation battle for control of my brain. But, as I pull open the door to the bar, the anxiety wins out. I don't know if I can do this.

My false bravado works with everyone *but* Owen. He can, and will, see right through any mask.

Damn him for knowing me so well.

"Look who decided to show up," Ken Jessop exclaims with a wink.

"Who turns down free alcohol?" I counter, avoiding any glances in Owen's direction. "Will you order me a whiskey? I'm running to the ladies' room."

Not two minutes after arriving, I dash into the bathroom. I must look like a maniac. On a positive note, Nicole is nowhere to be found. On a negative note, I'm so nervous, I can't breathe.

I will my heart rate down, taking deep breaths, and examining my reflection for clues. Why can't they install wine coolers in bar bathrooms? There's a need for that sort of thing.

After realizing I will eventually have to face the crowd of my co-workers, I push open the bathroom door, my heart leaping in my chest. Owen leans against the corridor wall, arms crossed over his chest, those thundering gray eyes daring me to avoid him again.

"Hi." Aren't I the eloquent one this evening?

"I like the hat."

It hurts to look at him. Every cell in my body screams out for this man, but I remain rooted to the spot. "Thanks."

Owen caves first, scrubbing his face with his hands. "Can we take down the damn wall, Tally? I hate this distance."

I drop my gaze from those stormy eyes to the floor. "I hate it, too."

"Can we stop?"

I still don't know if Owen is dating/sleeping/screwing the lights out of Nicole. But in the grand scheme of things—and excluding the status of my heart—it doesn't matter. Work colleagues need to get along. Our jobs are hard enough.

I offer him a small smile and nod. "Sure." I take a step toward the main restaurant, but Owen isn't moving. Wonderful. Don't tell me he's about to drop a Nicole Hedges bombshell. There isn't enough booze in the entire bar to soothe that level of pain. "Anything else I can do for you, Dr. Stevens?"

He rolls his eyes. "Tally, if you call me Dr. Stevens one more time."

"You'll what?" At least my sarcasm is on-point.

He crosses the small space, caging me between the wall and his body. "Either spank your sweet ass or kiss every inch of you. Likely both. Actually, please call me Dr. Stevens again."

So much for presenting a strong front. His words, coupled with the heat radiating between us, light me up like a fireworks display, and the man isn't even touching me. Time to segue to safer topics, before I rip his clothes off in the middle of the pub. "I wasn't sure if you'd want me to come. It is your welcome party."

Owen slides his fingers through my hair, setting off a shower of sparks. "Tally, you'd better believe I want you to come. Several times to make up for all the nights I've been without you."

Is it legal to have sex in a bar? Asking for a friend.

"I got your notes." I'm determined to stay on neutral topics, no matter how much this hot hunk of a doctor is trying to lure me into a night of sin.

Owen chuckles. "I wondered how many terrible jokes I'd have to tell before you broke."

"Ten. You were halfway there."

"You caved?"

CHAPTER TWELVE • 131

"I told you. My pussy has no control around you." So much for a platonic conversation. In my defense, Owen started it. Now, I just pray he makes good on his promise.

"It won't later. I'm tying your sweet ass up and taking back what's mine."

Stefani rounds the corner, her face lighting up when she spots us. "I knew I'd find you two together. You know, they make bedrooms for this sort of thing."

I flip my friend the bird as my face flames. Owen, for his part, hasn't moved an inch. He's still pinning me to the wall in a very unprofessional and hot as hell manner.

"I'm giving you fair warning that Jessop has made it his personal mission to eat all the artichoke dip. The man is shoveling it into his gullet. But it seems like you two are otherwise engaged. Hey, there's an idea." With a wink, Stefani squeezes past us into the bathroom.

My face *was* flaming. After my best friend's observation, it's at volcanic temperatures. "We'd better get back," I mumble, adjusting my glasses.

"What happens when we go back out there?"

I shoot him a curious look. "Eating. Drinking. Normal dinner type stuff. Surely they do this in San Francisco."

"I mean with us." Suddenly the joking manner is gone, replaced by uncertainty. He holds out his hand.

I want to take it so badly, slide my fingers against his, and let the world know that he's mine. But his betrayal, and most importantly, his time with Nicole, stops me. "What about Dr. Hedges?"

Owen's eyes widen in surprise. "What about her? You don't think—"

He doesn't finish the statement. He doesn't have to. We both know exactly what I'm thinking. Now, the question is whether I'm right.

"Wow. You *do* think something is going on."

I focus on the carpet, worn in the middle from countless steps.

"To be honest, I don't want to know. I'd like to enjoy a dinner with my friends. Can we do that?"

Owen runs his hand over his scalp, finally relenting with a smile. "We can enjoy dinner, so long as you remember that I'm so much more than your friend." He holds up his hand in the direction of the table, and we stroll back to the party.

"Where am I sitting?" I ask, looking around the table for an empty seat.

"Sit here, Lu," Jessop pats the seat next to him, directly across the table from Owen.

I plop down, accepting my whiskey and some chips with a grateful smile. I need this release, far more than I'm willing to admit.

When you work in a high-stress environment, you develop a dark and twisted sense of humor. That, and alcohol loosens the lips. Within twenty minutes, our band of merry medical workers is regaling Owen with all types of tales.

The best part? I'm having fun. That, and every time I glance across the table, Owen is watching me, the corners of his mouth pulled up in a smile, reminding me that his focus is on something far more carnal.

Maybe we aren't a lost cause.

"So, Owen, what's going on with you and the illustrious Dr. Hedges?" Dr. Jessop inquires.

Mayday, mayday, this ship is sinking.

Owen's brows shoot skyward. "Me and Nicole?"

"Yes. She's a hot ticket," my colleague adds. What a pal. I'd like to punch him, but he speaks the truth.

"She's not that great," Stefani interjects. I'm hugging that woman something fierce later.

"Nothing is going on. Nicole isn't my type." Owen catches my gaze, nodding at the plate of shrimp in front of me. "Tally, can you pass me the shrimp, Darlin?"

My body warms at his pet name, but then I wonder how many

other women have earned that personal moniker. "Sure," I reply, passing over the tray, his fingers sliding against mine.

"Thank you."

"Someone better let Nicole know nothing is going on," Jessop persists, grabbing the plate of shrimp from Owen.

"Turn a fire hose on her if she can't take the hint." Stefani sends me a smirk. God, I love this woman.

"You know, you could sleep with her, and let us know."

I pivot in my seat, scalding my cardiology friend with my glare. *Jessop, either you shut up, or I'm lacing your coffee with a laxative.*

Owen chokes on his food, earning a pat on the back from Stefani. "I have no interest in sleeping with her, Ken. But thanks for making me the sacrificial lamb."

"Wait," Dr. Jessop wags his finger in Owen's direction. "There's a reason you're not keen to Dr. Hedges's offer. You're dating someone, aren't you?"

Those gray eyes connect with mine, holding my gaze for a few moments. "I was, but I fucked it up. Now, I'm paying the price. I'm fighting to get her back, though."

Oh, my heart, you don't stand a chance.

Thankfully, for both of us, the conversation veers into medical territory. Blood and guts are a far safer environment than love. For the first time since Owen's arrival, I listen to him discuss the latest cath lab procedures and treatments. He's a genius, that much is apparent, but he lacks the bravado typical of a man with such an illustrious work history.

His humility only makes him that much more delicious.

I raise my glass, nodding in Owen's direction. "I know it's a couple of weeks late, but welcome to Memorial. We are damn lucky to have you amongst our ranks. Few people can do what you do."

A tender heat lines his face. "I think we toast you, instead, Tally. Not only are you a top-notch cardiac nurse and manager, but you're an assault nurse examiner and a victim advocate. For such a tiny woman, you have more strength than all us men combined. To you."

There are several other people at the table, but I only see Owen. Everything, and everyone else, falls away.

Stefani cuts into our moment, raising her glass between the two of us. Unlike me, Stefani has a working filter. She knows how to keep her mouth shut and toe the line—unless she's drinking. Then, all bets are off as to what might flow from her lips.

Right now, she's three drinks in. This should be interesting.

"You know, you two are both absolutely adorable."

Oh, Christ, she's still hung up on that word from earlier. The best part? She's not done.

"I think you two should get together, have a baby or something." She shrugs at my astonished expression. "What? I said it."

I bury my face in my hands. I'll never live down the ribbing from my co-workers. That, and Owen will probably never speak to me again. "I'm going to the bathroom," I mumble, sliding out of my seat.

"Again?" Stefani asks, and I flip her the bird. Is it childish? Yes, but it's all I can manage.

This time, Owen is not waiting for me outside the door. Yep, that comment pushed his ass right over the edge.

I return to the table to find the doctors splitting the bill and dig into my purse to contribute. I know they earn six times my meager salary. That's not the point. I've always paid my own way.

But this time, I'm going to have to fight Owen on the subject.

"Here, let me give you some cash." I open my wallet, but his hand descends on mine.

"Don't even try it."

"Come on, Lu. Party is just starting." Dr. Jessop divorced his wife six months ago when he discovered she was having an affair with their maid. She took him for half of everything they owned, even though she never worked a day in her life. Before the ink was dry on the paperwork, Ken made it his personal mission to bag as many eligible beauties as possible. With his good looks and pedigree, it's easy.

Usually, I'm up for a bit of fun with my friends. Not tonight. I have somewhere else to be. "You guys go ahead. I'll bail you out, should the need arise again." It's a joke, although I damn near had to post their bail a few years back. Even doctors aren't immune to the dark side of alcohol.

"Suit yourself. You ready, Owen?"

Owen shakes his head, his focus on me. "I'm walking Tally to her car."

"Right," Dr. Jessop drawls, a knowing look on his face. "Now I know the situation you're trying to repair. I approve." He waves us off, stumbling to the bar down the street.

Owen and I step out into the night air. It's clear and cool, with a hint of the ocean on the breeze. I'm so glad the relentless Florida heat is finally backing off.

"You don't have to walk me back, Owen. You can catch up with them."

"I don't want to catch up with them," he replies, intertwining his fingers with mine. "I want to catch up with you."

CHAPTER
THIRTEEN
TALLY

I struggle to breathe as the tingles running through my body reach nuclear proportions. I'm behaving like a sex-starved addict, and it's only been a couple of weeks.

"Tonight is the meteor shower," I blurt, earning a surprised look from Owen.

"We should watch it."

"I was actually headed to my favorite spot to do just that."

He presses my palm to his lips, that sultry smile on full blast. "Am I special enough to join you in your favorite spot?"

I consider his question, before returning his grin. "Hmm, I suppose I can make an exception and allow a visitor. Come on."

This is where knowing people comes in handy. I became buddies with the head of maintenance years ago, and he gave me an access key to the roof of the hospital. It was for when I needed to cool down and not making out with a handsome doctor, but my friend will have to understand.

To some, the meteor shower might seem a dull way to spend an evening, but I'm a total geek. I've been an avid stargazer since I was a child and my father would lie with me under the stars, telling me the myths surrounding the constellations.

"Ta-da," I exclaim as we step onto the roof.

"This is seriously cool, Tally."

"I got the hookup."

His hand cups my ass, his fingers sliding along my inner thighs. "You've got more than that."

I swat his hands away. "Behave."

"No way in hell," he volleys back, settling down against a brick column. "Come here."

I sit next to him, but apparently, that's not close enough for Owen. He picks me up, setting me in between his legs, his arm locked across my chest. I try to keep my breathing even, but it's a lost cause. I'm all fireworks and fairy dust where this man is concerned.

"Do you come up here often?"

"Not enough, but I love it here." I lean back against him, melting into his embrace. So much for willpower. "Do you have a favorite spot?"

He smiles against my ear. "I do."

"Where is it? The mountains in North Carolina?"

"Inside you is my favorite place in the world." Owen presses a kiss to my pulse point, which is now racing from his words.

I'm losing all grasp on reality, not that I stand a chance with Owen in my vicinity.

A bright streak catches my eye, and I raise my hand to the sky. "Did you see that?"

"No, I was watching you." His talented hands push my hair from my neck, every graze leaving sparks in his wake.

"I'm not nearly as interesting as a meteor shower."

"I beg to differ. You're intoxicating, actually. I want to kiss every inch of you." His hands slide to my thighs, those talented fingers wrapping around my legs.

As another star streaks across the sky, Owen creates his own brand of fireworks inside my body.

"Are you keeping track of your wishes?"

"Absolutely." It's true, although I'm not sure what to wish for anymore. Then it hits me.

A love bigger than the oceans, wider than the starlit sky, and stronger than a hurricane. One that can survive anything God or man throws its way.

"What did you wish for?" His breath is hot at my ear, firing up every nerve ending.

"I can't tell you, or it won't come true." I hope it's a good enough answer. I should know better.

Owen grazes his mouth along my neck, delivering a series of small nips. "How can I make any of your dreams come true if you don't tell me?"

I feel the tears back up in my eyes. "That's the funny thing about dreams."

"What, Darlin?"

"You always wake up."

He rests his chin on my shoulder, his grip tightening around me. "I'm going to make your waking life better than any dream. Just you wait and see. But first, I need to take you home."

That's an abrupt topic change. "Take me home?"

"I'm going to make love to you for the rest of the night."

"Was that your wish?"

"You're my wish, Darlin. Every facet of you. You're it for me. The first shooting star? For you to forgive me. The second one? Your heart."

We spend the next thirty minutes holding each other, basking in the comfort we always find together. I could stay here forever, but eventually someone will find us. "We better get going."

Owen nods before helping me to my feet. "Can we stop by my office first?"

Since I've never been there, curiosity wins. "Sure."

We step into the elevator, his hand still clasping mine. There's not really anyone walking the halls at this hour, but it's certainly not a friendly gesture. "It's down here."

He unlocks the door, flipping on a small table lamp. It resembles an English study, complete with a leather couch and a huge wooden desk. Compared to his office, mine looks like a closet. Come to think of it, my office *is* a closet.

I hear the door lock and turn to him, eyes wide. "What did you need in here?"

I don't get the opportunity to say more as his lips crash against mine and he hoists me into his arms. I could fight the kiss, but who the hell am I kidding?

I moan into his mouth, his hands tightening around my ass as I wrap my legs around his waist. He knocks the hat off my head as my fingers dig into his shoulders. I can't get close enough. Even if I rip every shred of clothing from his body, we're still too far apart.

It's fairly apparent, as Owen paws off my shirt, that he feels the same way. He deposits me on the large table, wasting no time in pulling off my sneakers and jeans.

"Owen, we can't—"

"Bullshit," Owen hisses, ripping my underwear from my body and burying his face between my legs. He bites my thigh with enough force that I jerk my eyes open, meeting his gaze. "Do not stop me, Tally. If you do, I'll tie your sweet ass up. Understood?"

I love when Owen takes control.

A sound, somewhere between a moan and purr, escapes my mouth as his tongue teases me open. I've never known a man so talented at touching me, or relentless in his pursuit.

My hands grip his scalp as his tongue lashes my clit, his hands holding my legs open. There's a roughness in his touch, as if he's warning me not to leave him again.

It's the most beautiful form of punishment.

"Tell me who this body belongs to, Tally. Say my name," Owen demands, his fingers digging into my soft flesh.

"Owen," I murmur as my hips arch up toward his talented tongue.

"Louder." He takes my clit between his teeth, torturing it with gentle nips.

I'm writhing on the table, holding his head in place as he brings my body to boiling point. "Fuck, Owen."

His thumb teases me open, pushing inside me. It's too much. The array of feelings is dizzying, and my body explodes, bucking against him while I scream his name.

I'm a quivering mess, my body still convulsing, as Owen fetches a damp towel from the private bathroom. He cleans me up, depositing kisses along my lower abdomen and thighs.

"I'll replace the underwear."

"So worth it," I mumble, barely able to form a coherent sentence. With a grunt, I push myself to a sitting position, my legs dangling off the edge of the table. "What am I going to do with you?"

"Love me." Owen sinks to the ground, peppering my calves with kisses. "I'll gladly stay on my knees until you forgive me."

I skate a finger down his nose and across his lips. "You can't solve things with sex. Even our mind-blowing sex."

"I'll make you a million promises, but you have to be willing to believe them."

"What promises do you plan to make?"

"To love you. Not just on good days, but on the really tough days. On those days when you question why you're with me, or how we were ever a good idea. I promise to always put you first—before any job, career, friend, or family. It will always be you before anything else. I promise—"

I press my fingers against his lips, sinking onto the carpet next to him. "Those are really big promises."

"It's a really big love, Tally. I told you, I've never felt this way before. I won't give up on you. On us."

He's right. It's the biggest damn love I've ever known.

I move my lips over his, tracing the outline of his full mouth, and earning Owen's grunt of approval. "Shall I take you home and have my way with you?"

"I've been praying for that all night."

OWEN DOESN'T LEAVE IN THE MIDDLE OF THE NIGHT. I WAKE UP TANGLED IN his arms, his lips pressing against my hair.

"Good morning," I murmur against his chest as he stretches beneath me.

"It is when I wake up next to you."

It's uncanny. Last night, he ravished every inch of me. This morning, he's a teddy bear, snuggling against my curves.

He's my perfect. There's no other explanation.

"You want coffee?"

Owen nods, running his fingers through my hair. "What are you doing today?"

"I'm assisting Beth at the shelter for a couple of hours. There's a new resident, and she's having some issues adjusting. I thought I could help."

"I'll go with you."

"You don't want to spend your day off at a shelter. Although it's a terribly sweet offer."

"You can make it up to me." There's Owen's infamous smile, his Cheshire cat, my dick is hard, grin.

I love that grin.

"Race you to the shower," I giggle, jumping from the bed and making it four steps before his arms grab me, tossing me over his shoulder in a fireman's hold. "Hey, no fair. You're so much taller."

He smacks my ass before dumping me onto the bed, his form descending over me. "Too bad you didn't establish any rules."

"You'd only break them anyway," I murmur as his mouth begins its southerly descent.

"Which is why you need to forget your rules. Make some new ones with me."

He makes a damn good point. But for now, I have more pressing topics on my mind.

CHAPTER FOURTEEN
OWEN

"I'll wait for you in the car," I mutter, pulling the keys from my pocket and storming out the front door.

It's not the friendliest gesture, but it's the best I can manage.

To think the day started on such a promising note.

Tally and I spent the last couple of hours at the women's shelter, sans Beth, who was at the hospital, functioning as a victim advocate.

Marla, the newest resident, is skittish as a beaten dog. The bruises covering her slight frame prove that my assessment is on target. Her son, Brad, is in better shape physically, although I can't fathom what the boy has witnessed in his young life.

But they're no match for Tally. My tiny vixen exudes a quiet power. She knows firsthand what it's like to live in fear, and although she won't disclose the details, I see the terror living in her eyes. The son-of-a-bitch better pray I never meet him. He won't make it three steps. I'll make damn sure he pays for what he did to Tally.

"Do you like card tricks?" Tally asks Brad, winking at me over his head.

"I love them! Can you show me a card trick?"

"No, but I can," I interject, settling down next to the boy. At first, he shirks away, his natural fear of men coming into play.

But Tally is smart. She knows that Brad—and Marla—need to learn that not all men are evil. Not all men hurt. Not all men hit.

Hopefully, my darling girl can figure that out right along with them.

I flip through the cards, showing Brad the trick I've performed countless times. His eyes widen, and he chuckles, a genuine belly laugh that is the most incredible sound I've heard in ages.

I spend the next fifteen minutes showing Brad the sleight of hand behind the trick, before gifting him the deck of cards. It's the best five dollars I've ever spent.

I find Tally in one of the bedrooms, her arms wrapped around Marla as the woman weeps. It's impossible to know if they are tears of anger, frustration, sadness, or denial. Likely all of those emotions.

"I didn't mean to interrupt. I'll wait in the kitchen."

Tally shoots me a grateful smile before returning to her unofficial counseling session.

"May I help you?"

I turn to see Beth standing in the kitchen doorway, a guarded expression on her face. I suppose men aren't a welcome sight in this house. Can't say that I blame them. "Sorry to startle you. We met the other day. I'm here with Tally."

Her eyes widen in recognition. "Hello, Dr. Stevens. I apologize, I didn't recognize you from behind."

"No worries, sorry I crept up on you."

"It's fine. We're happy to have you here. Where is Lu?"

I smile at my girl's nickname. Everyone in the world calls her Lu. "In the back with Marla. How did she get the nickname Lu?"

Beth contemplates the question for a moment before shrugging. "I'm not sure. You don't call her Lu, do you?"

"I call her Tally, but it seems only her father and I do that."

She snaps her fingers as if a lightbulb of realization sparked in her brain. "Forgive me for being forward, but didn't you and Tally date? I didn't realize you were still friends. That's nice."

"Figures you two would hole up in here," Tally interjects, joining us in the kitchen. "Beth, you remember Dr. Stevens."

"I do. We were just touching on your dating history."

Tally's eyes widen, her gaze swinging between us. "Why were you discussing that?"

"Well, it's nice when two people remain close after a break-up," Beth states, pulling groceries from the bags.

"Right," Tally sighs, nodding in agreement. "Dr. Stevens is a wonderful man. It would be an enormous loss if we weren't friends."

I hope she can feel me burning holes into her, waiting for her to admit that although we did break up, we are very much together again.

I'll be waiting for a long time.

Instead of confessing the actual status of our relationship, Tally changes the subject. My blood runs hot as I realize she's not going to divulge anything. Not today, possibly not ever.

Once again, I'm a dirty secret. The details are different, but this is a repeat of the situation with my ex, Charlotte. She came from money—oodles of it, and her Daddy disapproved of her slumming it with a student—a tatted, hardcore student, to boot.

Charlotte didn't want to anger her father, so she never brought me around to any public place. God forbid anyone saw us together. But her father was no fool. Mr. Auerback met me outside my university one evening, with a bribe to stop seeing his daughter. I should have accepted the offer—it was ten grand, and I was broke—but I tore up the check and tossed it in his face.

It wasn't until I started working as a cardiologist that he even deigned me worth speaking to; it wasn't until I helped spearhead the robotic cath lab that he approved of my relationship with his daughter.

I thought, when I left San Francisco, that I'd escaped that feeling. A gnawing in the pit of my stomach that I'm not enough. At least not to be seen in the light.

Such bullshit. I'm a good-looking, smart guy with a wicked talent in cardiology. I know this. But sometimes, when I look in the mirror, all I see is the man who doesn't fit the bill.

Tally's behavior just proved my reflection right.

But this time, I'm not sticking around to be shoved into a corner. Fuck that.

Tally opens the car door not five minutes later, but I'm no calmer. If anything, my aggravation has reached new heights.

"Everything okay?" she questions, sending me a quizzical look as she fastens her seatbelt.

I have two options. I can pretend that everything is fine, or I can let her have it. With both barrels. I understand that option one is a safer route, but my emotions are too twisted to care.

"Everything is fucking great. Can't you tell?" I jerk the car out of the parking spot, my foot leaden on the gas pedal.

"Owen, what the hell is going on? Did something happen at the shelter?"

I swerve to the side of the road, throwing the car into park, before turning my glare on her. "No, something *didn't* happen at the shelter, thanks to you."

"I'm trying to decipher what you're talking about, but you're not making any sense."

Running a hand over my scalp, I release an agitated huff. "Are you ashamed of me?"

Her eyes widen with shock. "Absolutely not. I think you're way out of my league." Her hand touches my forearm, but I jerk it away. "Why would you ever think that?"

"I guess we're fuck buddies, huh? Good to know," I mutter, gritting my teeth. "Are we exclusive, or do I get to whore myself all over town?"

That did it. Now Tally is as pissed off as I am.

Good.

"What the hell is your problem? Do you *want* to whore yourself all over town? Go ahead, don't let me stop you. I'm sure you have an open-ended invitation with Nicole."

"Leave her out of it."

"Aww," she hisses, her eyes narrowing, "did I upset you when I dissed your girlfriend?" Tally throws open the car door. "Screw this shit. I'm out of here. Go live your life, however you choose. I'm done."

I reach across the interior of the car and grasp her arm, preventing her exit.

"Let me go, Owen."

"No," I reply, tightening my grip.

She swings her gaze to me, as those soft, dark eyes fill with tears. "Why would you say something like that? Why would you ruin a beautiful day?"

"Why would *you*, Tally?"

"What did I do?" she screams, throwing her hands up in frustration.

I scrub my face with my hands. I have to calm down. The two of us are combustible when we're both heated. Especially when that heat is fueled by insecurities. "Why didn't you tell Beth that we were together?"

Everything freezes at that moment, and for the first time, I'm not confident that we can overcome our differences. Tally might make me pay for my deception forever.

When she finally speaks, her voice is low. Uncertain. "I'm not sure what we are, Owen."

"You're not? I thought we patched up everything last night."

"Because we had sex?" Tally scoffs. "Is that why you think everything is hunky-dory? That the lie you told and the fact that you've been hanging out with Dr. Hedges would magically disappear when you gave me an orgasm? Please, tell me that isn't what you're saying."

How did I end up in the hot seat again? "So, last night—and this morning—meant nothing?"

She grabs my hand, giving it a squeeze. "It always means something with you, Owen. I'm the woman who didn't have sex for two years, remember? I'm hardly the type to fall into bed with people. Until you, anyway."

It's her attempt at levity, but I'm not in a jovial mood. I'm angry and hurt and beginning to realize that I have little right to be.

"I don't want to do this halfway, Tally. I'm not looking for a no-strings fuck buddy. Not with you."

"You're turning down every man's dream," she snorts. "I'm joking. Please smile."

"Not in the mood for smiling right now."

She fiddles with her long braid, her nerves apparent. "I'm scared, Owen."

I grasp her chin, forcing her to look at me. "Of what? Me? Us? A future together? What scares you? I told you that first night, I can't fix it if I don't know what you're thinking."

"I was furious that you lied to me and more furious with myself that I didn't figure it out sooner. But then, it seemed like the moment you walked into the hospital, you were surrounded by all sorts of women, begging for attention."

"Tally, I don't want those women."

"Then why did you spend time with Nicole? You knew she was after you, but you did it anyway. Hell, you gave me an ultimatum—forgive you or you'd shack up with another woman."

What the hell? I didn't say that...did I? "That is *not* how I meant it, Tally."

"You sure about that? I think it's exactly how you meant it. Now you're angry because I'm not jumping straight into the relationship ring with you again. Our situation is complicated—"

"No," I cut her off, shaking my head, "it's not. I want to know where I fit into your life. Do you want to be with me or not?"

She wipes away a few stray tears. "I do, Owen. But we work

together, and after what happened to me before, I'm terrified of enduring that again. I don't think I could survive it twice."

I slam the steering wheel, making Tally jump. I cringe from my action, placing a reassuring hand on her shoulder. "I'm sorry, I didn't mean to scare you. I would never hurt you, Tally. *Never*. I would take a bullet for you."

"You better not," she warns, clasping my hand again.

"How long will I be chasing ghosts, Darlin? I'm sorry that scumbag hurt you. I'm not him, but you need to figure that out because I can tell you until I'm blue in the face, and you won't believe me. And until you believe me, you won't let me anywhere near your heart. I worship more than your body, Tally. I want the entire package. I'm not willing to settle for having pieces of you."

Tally chews her lip, her gaze averted. Well, the ball is in her court. I've laid out what I want, but she has to decide if she's on board with that decision. "Can we keep it quiet?" At my frustrated groan, she squeezes my hand. "Only at work, and only for the time being. Let me wrap my head around everything. I'm sorry, but with our situation and my father getting injured, I'm a bit out of sorts. Can you please compromise with me on that?"

I want to hold out, but when her lips press to my hand, I cave. I'm such a pussy for this woman. "We aren't dating anyone else, right?"

I expect a sigh of relief, but her eyes darken until they shine black. "Is that something you want?"

"No, I'm just asking. Christ, Tally." How do I keep managing to step in it? Every. Damn. Time. "Do you think I'd be jumping through hoops if I wanted anyone else? Come on, give me some credit."

A smile splits her face. "Sorry, I got a bit defensive."

"I take the cake on that one, Darlin. Today, at least. Just don't push me away. I'll play by your rules, but I really hope you'll want to play by our rules soon."

"Fair enough," she whispers, leaning across the car to offer a chaste kiss.

Screw that. I need passion, and I need it now. I grasp both sides of her face, pushing my tongue into the sweet recesses of her mouth. My fingers twist in her dark locks, and a low groan sounds from us both when her hand settles on my cock. "I need inside you."

She laughs, that husky, 'I want to rip your clothes off,' chuckle that is my own personal Viagra. "Thankfully, we're only a few minutes from the apartment. Think you'll make it?"

"I don't know," I mutter, pulling back onto the highway, bucking my hips when she scratches her nails over my bulge. "You keep doing that, and we won't make it another ten feet."

But my tiny vixen doesn't listen. All Tally hears is a challenge. Get me as hot as she can, while I can't do anything about it. By the time I pull into her driveway, I've damn near busted a nut. But once I shut off the car, she knows.

I'll torture her with orgasms the rest of the night.

CHAPTER FIFTEEN
TALLY

I'm halfway through a patient's dressing change when Owen pokes his head around the privacy curtain. I meet his gaze expectantly while trying to control my hormones whenever he's in my space.

I know it was my idea to keep our dating on the down-low. I didn't say that it wouldn't suck. It's awful, but I'm still working through my own demons. My ghosts, as Owen calls them.

I get it. He's *not* that guy, but he also doesn't know how close I came to losing everything. It doesn't help that Nicole is not taking the hint, although part of me doubts that Owen has actually tempered her advances. I don't think he's messing around with her. But she's a gorgeous woman, and he's basking in the adoration.

He is a man, after all.

So, at work, we are colleagues. Outside of work, behind closed doors, we are passion personified. Unfortunately, that passion has been shelved for the last few nights. I've been with my father and Owen...well, I'm not entirely sure where he's been. All I know is that he wasn't with me.

"Can I help you, Dr. Stevens?" I inquire, pushing a stubborn strand of hair from my face with my forearm. Why is that whenever your hands are unavailable, your face itches? Seriously, what kind of next level hell is that?

"You're working bedside today, Tally?"

"I do it a few times per month. Keep my hand in."

"That's smart," he remarks, flashing a hint of that dimple beneath his neatly trimmed beard. Have I mentioned how much I adore that dimple?

"I have my moments." I gaze down at the patient, her eyes widening with worry that I might not be an experienced handler. "Don't worry, Mrs. Hobbs. I'm the nurse manager for the unit."

Owen looks past me to the patient. "You're lucky. Tally is an amazing nurse. She's an amazing soul."

My heart catches. "Thank you. I appreciate that."

"I mean it. Can you come to my office?"

I lift my gloved hands, giving him a shrug. "I'm a little busy at the moment. Can it wait?"

Owen chuckles. "I meant later."

"Okay." Our exchange is innocent, but it's the way he looks at me, the fire burning in those gray depths, that sets my body humming. How in the hell am I supposed to claim we're just friends when I drool every time I see him?

The good doctor knows the effect he's having on me, and he's enjoying every second. Owen leans in, his lips brushing against my ear, his voice low so that only I can hear. "I miss that gorgeous mouth. I need a refill."

AN HOUR LATER, I STROLL DOWN THE VIP CORRIDOR, HEADING FOR OWEN'S office. No, it's not the technical name, but with all the big-wig doctors down this hallway, it might as well be.

I wonder how often Dr. Nicole Hedges finds a reason to be in this same hallway, with the same destination.

Bitch had better back off. Just saying. I know it might be a 'having my cake and eating it too' scenario, but I'll break every finger on her pretty hand if she touches Owen again.

Ugh, I really hope he isn't lying when he says they haven't done anything together.

I bite back some nausea. Another fun addition over the last week. No doubt it's because of the stress I'm putting myself under by over-analyzing everything. As per usual.

I knock on his door and immediately hear his gravelly timbre. "Come in." Even those two simple words drip with appeal, but hell, Owen is appealing to everyone. It makes his comment last week so confusing. He asked me if I was ashamed of him as if that was a scenario he encountered before.

I can't imagine any woman anywhere, being anything but proud of Owen Stevens. Hell, I'm in awe of the man, even if I can't admit publicly the number of his body parts on my worship list.

Discretion is a dying art. I don't need our co-workers poking their noses into our business. Besides, should it go south, I don't want those sympathetic glances or whispers about another one biting the dust. Yep, it's my good old self-esteem issues. Back in action. I need a shrink. Or a drink. Likely both.

I walk into Owen's office, jolting when I spot Dr. Empreso standing by Owen's desk. I break out in hives whenever I'm near him. He is one of Memorial's top surgeons and an absolute sleaze. Literally, that's his nickname, and I didn't invent it. I certainly use it enough, though.

Owen smiles at me from across the room. "Hi, Tally. It'll just be a second."

"Should I wait outside?"

Upon hearing my voice, Dr. Sleaze pivots, offering me a slow, shark-like smile. "Oh, it's *you*, Lu. What's shaking?" The question is innocent, but his openly ogling gaze is anything but.

"Why does everyone call you Lu?" Owen questions. "Why not Tally? It's softer."

I shrug, aware that Dr. Sleaze is still ogling me, and Owen is blissfully unaware. "Everyone always called me Lu. I can't remember how it started."

I really wish this surgeon would look *anywhere* but my tits. Hell, could he at least pretend to be interested in the conversation? "A good question. Lu is such a masculine name for such a wisp of a woman."

"Your Dad calls you Tally. I call you Tally. But then again, I'm not everyone. Am I, Darlin?"

My jaw slackens at Owen's brazen use of my pet name, showing just how well he knows me. Then I meet his gaze and realize he is blissfully unaware of nothing. Owen is rigid in his seat, and I bet money his fists are clenched under the desk as he observes Dr. Empreso's blatant eye fuck.

The surgeon swings his beady-eyed gaze to Owen. "You sly devil. It appears you know *Lu* better than I do. Well, I won't keep you two. I'm sure you have tons to discuss." With a final wink, he walks out, ensuring his body brushes against mine. "See you soon, *Darlin*."

I close my eyes and grimace at his unwelcome touch. When I hear the door latch, I release an audible shudder. "I want to go take a bath in bleach."

Owen is on his feet, striding with purposeful anger toward the door. "That smug son of a bitch—"

My hands raise to his chest, halting any further forward movement. "No. Go sit down."

Owen grabs my upper arms, his eyes flashing. "The way that man looks at you. The way he *touched* you. No, just no. It's not happening."

"Stop it. He's not worth it. Dr. Sleaze does that to several women. He thinks he's God's gift."

"I'll take him down a few pegs. He won't do that to you again."

There's nothing quite as endearing—and sexy—as Owen's quest to save my virtue. But he's also very determined in said quest, and if I don't distract him fast, there will be a heated exchange for the hospital to see. Not the best way to end a week.

Looping my arms around his waist, I lay my head on his chest and squeeze. Holy hell, I love this man. He's my home. "Thank you."

As soon as my body connects with Owen's, I feel the fight leave him. His tense muscles relax as he returns the hug, squeezing me so tight it almost hurts to breathe. "I know what you're doing."

I giggle. Of course he does. The man knows every facet of me. "Is it working?"

"You have the magic touch. But I'm still going to speak to him."

My gut clenches. Dr. Empreso is a sleaze, no doubt, but in Memorial's eyes, he's irreplaceable. Me? Not so much. I don't want to lose another job because of a jealous and vindictive man, and I certainly don't want Owen coming under scrutiny for defending me. "And say what? He's a pig, Owen. That's what he does."

"I've seen the way he ogles you, and not just today." He runs his fingers across his beard, letting out a huff. "The way most men here ogle you. It drives me crazy."

I laugh, gazing up into that gorgeous face. "Don't even get me started. The entire hospital is in love with you, one doctor in particular." I don't say her name. He knows who I'm talking about.

"I'm in love with you."

I burrow my head deeper against his chest, willing back the tears. God, I love him too. I just can't say the words. When I said them the last time, everything went to crap. Call me superstitious, but I'm being careful. "Owen—"

"I read the employee handbook. Cover to cover."

I narrow my eyes at him. "That's likely a first for anyone, even those working in HR. Cure for insomnia?"

"Yes, but that's beside the point. The insomnia is your fault."

"Mine?"

"Yes. Anyway, the handbook doesn't say anything about employees dating."

Holy shit, the man really did read the book. "It doesn't?"

"You know it doesn't, Tally."

"What are you saying?"

"The same thing I've been saying since we met. I want to be with you—publicly with you—like we were those first two weeks. It's hard to defend my rage when I'm your co-worker, and a guy hits on you. But if they know we're dating, they'll keep their mouths shut and their hands to themselves."

I consider his statement, not because I'm worried about the ogling philanderers at Memorial, but because I'm finding it exceedingly tricky to not stake my public claim on Owen. "You really think that would stop them?"

"If it doesn't, a punch in the mouth will," Owen mutters. "Although I have another idea."

My ears perk up. Hopefully, Owen hasn't decided that an open relationship is the best option. I'll vomit all over his shoes. "What's your brilliant idea, Dr. Stevens?"

His eyes are silver with intensity. "We make you Mrs. Stevens."

My jaw slackens as my gaze flies up to meet his. *He did not intimate what I think he intimated...did he?* "What are you talking about?"

Owen grins, and I know I'd be happy staring at that smile for the rest of my days. "We get you an enormous diamond. You can pick out the ring, or I'll design it for you. I've considered a few styles."

I open my mouth to retort, but I've got nothing.

He sends me a knowing wink. "No, I want to design it."

Words. I need words. I'm fluent in English, so why can't I figure out anything to say? All I can do is gape up at him, certain he'll burst out laughing, claiming it's a joke.

The question is if he is kidding, would I be relieved or disappointed? I'm leaning toward disappointment, making this utterly untrodden ground.

"I'll make sure that the ring represents you."

"All this to ensure Dr. Sleaze stays in his own lane?"

Owen shakes his head, dipping down to steal a kiss. "Hey, it is a solution," he replies, chuckling at my glare. "Darlin, I'm going to marry you because I love you."

I bite back a smile. Damn him for getting me so excited. "Do I have a say in any of this?"

"Sure. Emerald cut or round?"

That Owen knows the cuts of stones stops me in my tracks. Could he mean what he's saying?

"You didn't think I was serious, did you?"

"Damn mind reader," I grumble, tucking my head back against him.

We pass the next few minutes like this, existing in the warmth of one another. My hands stay firmly planted against his lower back, maintaining a relatively PG posture. Not Owen. His hands are totally misbehaving. Within moments, they're traveling along the curve of my ass, causing his erection—and my desire—to grow by the second.

At this rate, we'll be naked and screwing on the table. Again. Time to shift back to our regularly scheduled work personas. "You wanted to see me?"

"Shh." He presses my head back against his chest while his free hand slips beneath the waistband of my scrubs, tracing along my skin.

"Hey, hands, mister."

"It's your fault. Your skin is like silk, Tally. I want to peel off your clothes and devour every inch of you."

"Right here?"

"Right now."

It's suddenly a thousand degrees in here. Placing my chin on his chest, since he isn't letting me break the embrace, I meet that glacial gaze. "Dr. Stevens, are you trying to seduce me?"

A half-smile decorates his lips as he moves his hands up to frame my face. "That's called love, Darlin. If I wanted to seduce you, you'd be sprawled across my table, and I'd be replacing a second pair of underwear."

Two thousand degrees and rising. Maybe I can skip my daily rounds. This is far more important for my mental and emotional well-being.

"My Mom is in town," Owen states.

Random subject change, but at least it throws water on my overheated hormones. "Really?"

"She never actually left Florida, just traveled to Tampa to visit a friend. She's taking full advantage since she only saw me once a year when I lived in San Fran."

"I get it. You're her baby boy, and she's spent enough time away from you."

"I'm having dinner with her tonight at that restaurant. The one you refused to dine at with me. She wants you to come."

I arch my brow. "She does?"

"Yes, and so do I."

"Are you sure it's a good idea? How do we explain being together if someone sees us?"

Owen clears his throat, a muscle twitching in his jaw. He's aggravated as hell with our arrangement. "Is there something you need to tell me? Are you secretly married, Tally?"

"No, what a ridiculous question!"

"Then who cares is someone sees us. In fact, I hope the entire staff sees us tonight."

"But—"

His fingers press to my mouth, and I reward them with a kiss. "Stop arguing, Tally, or I'll announce right now, over the hospital loudspeaker, that you and I are getting married."

That's such a tempting idea, maybe I should keep arguing.

"Just say yes, Darlin."

With a smile and nod, I concede. "What time should I meet you two?"

CHAPTER SIXTEEN
OWEN

"How in the world did you close so fast?" my mother inquires, pouring herself a glass of water. "It takes months in North Carolina."

"The condo was vacant, with a motivated seller. I already had my pre-approval, so smooth sailing." On something, at least.

My mother leans over, squeezing my hand. "I'm so proud of you. You've done so well for yourself."

"Thanks, Mom. My folks were pretty supportive," I reply with a wink.

"I wish you could build a time machine and travel back to tell your teenage self those words." She taps the butcher block counter, sending me a pointed glance. "I'm thrilled Tally is still part of your life. I told you it wouldn't be a big deal when she found out you're a doctor."

Oh, Mom, if you only knew.

My mother, being my mother, has inspected every inch of the condo, and it's garnered her seal of approval. "Three bedrooms. Plenty of room, should you need it."

It's no secret that my mother wants grandchildren, and as her only son, she's champing at the bit. "That's what I was thinking."

"Is there something you want to tell me?"

"Mom, I can't even get Tally to live here, and trust me, it's a step *way* up." I grimace at my words, offering a sheepish smile. "That sounded terrible. Her apartment isn't bad, and her landlord is a lovely woman, but the neighborhood has gone downhill over the years. It's not the safest location, and I want her safe."

My mother cocks her head. "Don't nurses make a good living down here?"

"The pay is decent, but that's not the issue. She spends $3500 per month on a memory care facility for her father. There's not a ton left over after she pays his bills. I can help foot those expenses."

"Don't be a savior—" she raises her hand, halting my argument. "Tally doesn't seem to be a woman who's looking for charity."

"It's not charity. It's love."

She sighs, a grin playing on her mouth. "What have you done with my son? I never thought I'd live long enough for you to want to settle down."

"I was engaged, Mom," I remind her.

"Yes, but you never made it down the aisle."

"Thank God. It's different with Tally, though. Everything is different with her."

My mother pulls out an envelope, sliding it in my direction. "Speaking of your ex-fiancée, Charlotte sent this to me. She claimed she didn't have your address in Florida."

Christ, another headache I don't need. "What does she want?"

"I don't know, dear. I may be a mother, but I'm not that nosey."

"Yeah, right," I laugh, tearing open the envelope. The letter is written in Charlotte's elegant penmanship. That, like everything else about the woman, has been curated to perfection.

Owen,

After so many years, I find it sad that I have no clue where in the world you are. I know that our lives were drifting apart, but I hate that it ended on such an abrupt note. One moment you were there, and the next, you were gone.

There are some things I need to say, and I would like the opportunity to do so. I've tried calling and left numerous messages, but I have a suspicion that you've blocked my number.

At this point, nothing would surprise me.

At the very least, you should want the ring back. I know that it's tradition for the jilted bride to keep the diamond when the groom breaks off the engagement, but I've no need for such a reminder.

I'll be in Florida soon, for an undetermined duration. I hope we might get together and chat.

Regards,
Charlotte

"Cold as ever," I mutter, tossing the letter on the counter.

"She always was the ice queen," my mother adds.

She's not wrong. Charlotte is a gorgeous and wealthy socialite, but years of training in the social graces have left her hard and unfeeling. There's nothing behind the mask.

"Are you going to call her? I doubt she'll relent until you do."

I release a resigned sigh. "Charlotte is used to getting what she wants in life."

"And now, she wants you back." It's my mother's turn to sigh. "You aren't considering reconciliation, are you? It's your life, but—"

I pull my mother into a hug, chuckling at her horrified expression. "Don't worry, Mom. No such intentions."

"Good. I like Tally."

"I love her."

Her hand cups my face as she kisses my cheek. "I know. It's written all over you."

~

TALLY INSISTS ON MEETING US AT THE RESTAURANT. SHE CLAIMS SHE HAS TO run by the women's shelter, but I know it's a load of crap. She's still hesitant about the idea of us together in public. I have no idea what her ex did to her, but it certainly screwed with her head.

Now, I'm paying the price. Not that it matters. She's worth it.

Despite our shaky relationship status, this dinner is far more relaxed than the first one—at least for me. Tally looks as if she's about to lose her lunch.

"Darlin, are you okay?" I lean over, giving her a reassuring back rub.

Tally offers a small smile. "I'm sorry. My stomach hasn't been great for the last few days."

"I think I have something for that." My mother digs into her suitcase of a purse, pulling out some antacid. "Here you are, my dear. I know you don't feel well, but you look beautiful. You're glowing."

My mother's words hit like a fist as my gaze returns to Tally.

She *is* glowing. The woman is always beautiful, but lately, she's had this ethereal quality about her.

She's pregnant.

The thought hits hard and fast. I wait for the internal freakout, but it never arrives. Instead, I smile at the idea of my tiny vixen carrying my child.

"Hey, try not to look so happy about my nausea," Tally teases, grabbing a roll from the basket.

I surprise her with a kiss to that gorgeous mouth. "I'm smiling because my mother is right; you look beautiful."

She chuckles, waving her hand—and the compliment—off, but I see the slight bloom across her cheeks.

"Tally, I noticed that you haven't moved into the condo yet."

Thanks, Mom. Nothing like prodding an already agitated woman.

"There was a change of plans," Tally murmurs, her eyes focused on the butter dish.

"You mean my son neglecting to tell you he's a doctor?" She pats

Tally's hand, sending her a reassuring smile. "I disapproved of Owen keeping the truth from you. I knew it was a bad idea, but he is a good man, and I'm glad you forgave him."

Not so certain about that, Mom.

Why do I take part in these dinners? Without fail, they veer into uncomfortable territory before the appetizers hit the table.

Tally sets down her roll and butter knife, her smile wavering. I'm not sure if it's her nausea or anger at my mother's assumptions, but I'm praying it's the first. The last thing I need is Tally mad at me. Again. "I guess to most people, it makes little sense. Owen is the complete package. I told him on our first date that they broke the mold after him. I still stand by that assertion." She rubs her brow, and I clasp her free hand, trying to offer whatever reassurance I can. "My reasoning sounds so silly when I say it aloud. Doesn't it?"

"No, dear. He betrayed your trust, and trust is a valuable commodity. I know you have issues trusting people, and his betrayal only cemented that concept. But, in Owen's defense, I need to say one thing. This man loves you more than I've ever seen him love anyone."

Usually, I would be mortified at my mother's public declaration. This time, I hope that her statement resonates with Tally, driving my words home to her heart.

I miss her, the Tally I met that night at Wicked Chucks. I fell immediately. She was everything—beautiful, smart, sarcastic, funny as hell. Crazy about me, too. This version of Tally is hesitant, uncertain, her heart surrounded by a thick wall to prevent any additional pain.

This Tally won't let me in, and I've no one to blame but myself.

She doesn't respond to the declaration about my love. I guess she's not ready for that yet, but I note the smile crossing her face. At least her heart hasn't canceled out the option.

"I'm sure I don't have to tell you this, but your son is a genius. Honestly, he's the best doctor I've ever worked alongside, and I've worked with my share. He's brilliant in his diagnostics, calm in his approach, he thinks outside the box, and he's unflappable under pressure. Not to mention that he's exceedingly kind to patients and staff." She sends me a wink. "Doesn't hurt that he's damn easy on the eyes, either."

Tally may be unsure about any public displays, but at that moment, I don't give a rat's ass. I lean over, wrapping my hand around her nape and pulling those delicious lips to mine. I don't care that my mother is watching; I don't care if the pope is watching. I slide my tongue along her lower lip, begging entrance to the most talented mouth I've ever known.

After a second's tension, her lips part, and I feel her shiver beneath my palm. I maintain an easy rhythm, caressing her tongue with my own. For a few moments, I forget that anyone exists beyond the two of us. I melt into her, begging without words for her to return to me.

Tally didn't state outright that she's in love with me. Her declaration was so much more than that, and she needs to know I feel the same way about her. She's my perfection.

Pulling back, I chuckle as Tally wipes a bit of her gloss off my lips. Her cheeks flame pink, and she's the epitome of everything adorable in this world, wrapped up in a sexy, edible package.

"So much for keeping it on the down-low," she mumbles, but I don't detect any hostility in her voice.

"I told you I wasn't in favor of that approach," I volley back, earning a full-fledged grin from my tiny vixen.

"Your mother—" Tally argues.

"Is fine, with everything." My mom takes another bite of her salad, a bemused smile on her lips. I guarantee the woman is planning table arrangements for our wedding. In her book, we can't march down the aisle fast enough.

The rest of dinner passes in jovial conversation, complete with a few tales about my first few weeks at Memorial. My head won't fit through the door to the restaurant, thanks to all the accolades the two women shower on me, but I'd be lying if I said I didn't love every second.

I'm used to my mother bragging on me. Hell, she's a mom. That's what they do. But to hear Tally sing my praises? That's sexy as fuck.

Just saying, if Tally told me to go down on her at the table, I wouldn't say no. Hell, licking her pussy is tempting without her saying a word. I'm addicted to that woman's body, something else I don't think she's used to experiencing.

"Nightcap at the condo?" I ask, shooting Tally a warning look as she pulls out her wallet to pay the bill. "Your money is no good here. I'm treating my two favorite ladies to dinner."

"Let me leave a tip," Tally insists, pulling out far more than the standard twenty percent.

I cover her hand. "I've got it, Darlin. You keep your money." A few moments pass before Tally concedes, slipping her wallet back into her purse.

It's ironic. Charlotte has scads of money. She has millions in trust funds, but never once opened her wallet. On those rare occasions we spent together in public, she expected me to pick up every tab. Every single time. Meanwhile, Tally has little—if anything—saved, but offers to pay without hesitation.

My tiny vixen is a class act. "Come on. You can help me select some furniture. The condo is eerily empty. It needs your touch."

Tally shakes her head. "As much fun as it sounds to spend your money, I have to get home. I'm working tomorrow."

I narrow my eyes in confusion. "You are?"

"Yes, I have some reports to file, implementing ideas that a certain recent addition to our staff mentioned."

"Darlin, it can wait until Monday. Enjoy your time off."

"I want to do it. Your ideas are brilliant, and I want the staff and patients to feel the ramifications of the changes as soon as possible."

God, I adore her. She's as dedicated to her work as I am. "Can't you come by for a little while? You haven't even seen the condo since I moved in."

Tally presses her lips to my cheek. "I'll see it soon. Promise." She stands, but hesitates, her fingers gripping the edge of the table as she wobbles.

I'm on my feet, my arm around her waist. "Are you okay?"

She nods, waving off my concern. "I'm fine. I stood up too fast, got a bit dizzy." She swings her smile between my mother and me. "I promise, I'm okay."

I help my mother into my car before walking Tally across the lot. After seeing her old car again, I blurt, "We're taking you car shopping."

"I can't afford a new car, Owen. She looks ragged, but she's reliable." She pats the roof of the old sedan, not meeting my gaze, and my stomach flips. I embarrassed her, which is the last thing I want to do.

Time to make it right. "I can afford one. You deserve a new car, and this old gal deserves a well-earned retirement."

"I'm not letting you buy me a car."

"I'll buy you one, anyway." I expect a smile, but she scowls, instead. Wonderful, I've stepped in it again. "Did I say something wrong?"

"*He* offered to buy me a car, after everything he did to me. What did he call it? Oh yes, a parting gift." She pulls her keys from her purse, her hands trembling. "I told him where he could shove his parting gift."

"Tally, I'm not him."

"I know, but—"

"But what?"

She throws up her hands, her eyes bright. "Why do you want this? You know my situation now, just as I know yours. I'm broke. My money goes to care for my Dad. I can't afford the lifestyle you're used to. Hell, I ordered a salad because I couldn't afford the meal."

I grab her to me, anger flashing through my brain. I'm tempted to march her ass back inside and order one of everything on the menu for her. "Don't you *ever* do that again, Tally. You order whatever you want."

"It's not fair. I can't contribute at places like this. Hell, I'm barely able to cover an extra round of brews at Wicked Chucks."

"Let's make a deal, Darlin. We take care of each other. I ensure that you are happy and healthy and loved. You, in turn, grant me unlimited access to this body."

I push her back against the car, my dick springing to attention as it nestles against her curves. If she had parked the car in a dark corner, I'd hike this little black skirt up to her waist and slide inside her, showing her just how much she contributes. It would be worth a night in jail to hear her scream my name.

"I knew it was going to come back around to sex," she jokes as I claim her mouth.

"Had to happen eventually." I press kisses against her throat, knowing I'll have one hell of a hard-on by the time I'm through.

"Who's going to ensure that you're happy and loved, Owen?"

I slide my hands up her thighs, palming her delectable peach. "It's a guarantee when I'm with you."

"Good answer," she laughs, rewarding my statement by pressing her body closer.

I stage a one-sided internal argument before asking the next question, but I need to vocalize it. "Tally, can I ask you something?"

"No, we cannot have sex in the parking lot."

"Damn." I press my forehead to hers, feeling that inner fire smoldering beneath her skin. "If you're pregnant, you'll tell me, right? You wouldn't hide that from me, would you?"

She pulls back, her eyes wide. "It's just a stomach bug."

She's trying to reassure me, now it's my turn to reassure her. "Likely, but we weren't very careful, Darlin."

Tally snorts. "You mean *never* careful? Is that what you mean? I blame you. Totally your fault. You shouldn't be this good-looking. I can't be held responsible for my actions, such as ripping off your clothes or dry-humping your leg."

"I'll take the blame," I reply with a grin.

"We'll be careful from now on," she offers, pressing her mouth to mine.

Like hell we will.

I get it. Some will say it's not the smartest route. But I'm clean, she's clean, and I'm not a twenty-year-old delinquent. That, and I'm obsessed with Tally. Knocking her up is not my definition of hardship.

"We'll see." That's as close to a concession as she'll get. Besides, all this sex talk is sending my dick screaming into overdrive.

"If we don't take precautions, then you'll keep worrying about it."

"I'm not worried about it." It's the truth.

"Okay." With a last kiss, she shoos me back, sliding into the driver's seat.

Good to her word, she texts when she arrives home.

I'm not pregnant. Stop worrying.

I chuckle to myself, tossing the phone on my nightstand. "I'm not worried, Darlin. Just some wishful thinking."

CHAPTER SEVENTEEN

TALLY

Owen and I don't see each other for the next few days, although we speak multiple times on the phone. He isn't happy about the separation, but this time, it's not out of anger, but necessity.

His mother is only in town for a short time. They need to spend quality time together.

Me? I'm busy helping Beth at the shelter, in between visiting my father and throwing up at least twice a day.

Owen's inquiry about me being pregnant is never far from my mind, and now that I'm a week late, I have the sneaking suspicion he's right. Granted, with the upheaval of the last month, anything is possible. All my body systems may be on hiatus, or strike, or whatever.

It's probably nothing.
You should take a test.
Brain, sit down, and shut up. You're not helping the situation.

The ongoing debate in my head continues, as it has for the last seventy-two hours. My brain will win, but my delusional self isn't going down without a fight.

But that's an argument for another day. Today is about staff call-outs and uncooperative patients—the joys of nursing.

Yay, me.

Owen's muttered curse floats over to my seat at the nurses station, and I swivel in my chair. We offer pleasantries at work, but it's getting increasingly difficult. Hey, I deserve some credit. It's damn near impossible to act nonchalant around the man I want to jump 24/7. I think our ruse is working, too. Unless Dr. Empreso, aka Dr. Sleaze, starts flapping his gums.

"Stupid thing."

I bite back a laugh before strolling over to Owen's chair. I lean over, taking control of the mouse. "We have an ongoing joke that this computer is possessed by the ghosts of patients past. It's not just you."

"Is that a fact?" Owen catches my gaze, his finger sliding along mine in the slightest of caresses. "You smell good."

The man is becoming more brazen at work, but I don't mind the affection. I think it's time to call us what we are—in love.

"I'm not wearing anything, Owen."

"On the contrary, you're wearing *way* too much."

I try to play it off, but he knows me too well. "Behave."

"I'm sick of behaving. I want to see you tonight."

With a final click, the computer is once again cooperating. "There you go, handsome." I wink at him, throwing in an extra hip shake for kicks. I know he's watching me walk away. My only hope? I'm making him as hot and bothered as he makes me.

All's fair in love.

I'm not two minutes into my coffee break, hoping that Owen will sneak in for some playtime when I hear the dreaded announcement.

There are two words that every nurse and doctor know—and hate.

"Code Blue, room 410. Code Blue, room 410," the voice sounds over the loudspeaker.

CHAPTER SEVENTEEN • 173

Fuck. My floor, my unit. I tear out of the break room, grabbing the code cart as I race down the hallway.

Owen is already at the bedside, while another seasoned nurse administers compressions.

I fly into reactionary mode. It's a gift and a curse. A gift because I've seen enough codes in my life to know the steps by heart. A curse for the same reason.

But today is a good day. Today, we get the patient back, with a few cracked ribs after some zealous compressions. Hey, a small price to pay for life. There's a ton of activity during a code, but you get tunnel vision, focusing on the task at hand. The noise is a low roar in the background, existing in the periphery.

But once it's finished, reality swoops back in, in vivid color. There's also generally one hell of a mess to clean up, but again, a small price to pay. I send the opened code cart downstairs with a staff nurse and reorganize the patient's room.

Owen left a few minutes after the patient stabilized, to write some new orders. At this point, he's likely back in his office or rounding.

Or...visiting with Hot Doc, who is on this unit. Again.

"Some fancy work this afternoon," Nicole coos, and I resist the urge to take a swing at her perfect button nose.

"It's a team effort, Nicole." Owen is cordial, but he doesn't seem fixated by the gorgeous doctor's ministrations. Lucky for him.

I, on the other hand, am captivated. I am also plotting her demise, but she's far too involved with my boyfriend to notice.

Wait, did I just refer to Owen as my boyfriend?

Owen and I need to have a talk. I'm ready for our relationship to become public. That way, I can break Nicole's neck if she looks at him again.

I'm joking. Kind of.

"You're a natural leader and the way you sprang into action. Such talented hands."

"Thank you," Owen replies, his gaze focused on his phone.

So far, so good.

"I remember how talented they were the other evening."

Oh, now the bitch has my attention. What other evening?

Owen shoots a look in my direction, and I'm sure he's scalding under the intensity of my gaze. So, that's what he's been doing these last few days.

The lying, sorry son-of-a-bitch.

"Do you have plans tonight? Let's get dinner." Nicole edges closer to Owen's side, but I'm not sure whose neck I want to wring more—his, hers, or my own for believing the man.

I don't know what variety of dining Dr. Hedges is offering Owen tonight. A co-worker soiree or a 'fuck me in the car' dinner, but my stomach won't let me stick around to find out. A wave of nausea overtakes me, and I turn, sprinting for the bathroom.

I splash water on my face, as my delusional side tries to convince my head that I have food poisoning or a stomach bug. Maybe it's the concept that Nicole may be sleeping with the man I love. That's it. We'll use that logic.

I groan and head for the changing room. I'm beyond ready for this day to be over. Stick a fork in me, Memorial. I'm done.

I hear the door open behind me but pay it no mind. There are always people in and out of the locker room. Privacy is at a premium in a hospital.

"That was great work today, Tally."

Inwardly, my body heats hearing Owen's voice. Externally, I'm far more composed. At least, I hope I am. Likely not. "What are you doing in the women's locker room?" I ask, not bothering to turn around.

"Trying to catch you alone for a few minutes."

"Why is that?"

"Maybe because I miss you, and I want to talk to you."

"About what?" I hate feeling jealous. My only saving grace is that Owen might not know that I am.

There's a chance, right?

"So," he hedges, stepping closer to my spot near the bench, "would this sudden frostiness have anything to do with Nicole?"

"I have no idea what you're talking about," I mutter, shoving on my Converse.

"I always said you were a terrible liar. Just admit that you're jealous." He's baiting me. The conceited prick.

It doesn't matter that he's correct. I'm not giving him the damn satisfaction. That, and I'm furious that he hung out with another woman after we agreed to be exclusive.

"Not my business who you're fucking, although I'd be careful. She's got a reputation on her. Then again, apparently, so do you." Damn. I have to say, I have a wicked tongue sometimes.

Owen's eyes widen as the smile slides from his face. "Jesus, Tally! I was joking. Nothing is happening between Nicole and me. *Nothing*. You know that, don't you?"

I finish fixing my ponytail, hoping the slight shrug will suffice as an answer, and he'll leave. It doesn't.

I turn to face him, and my heart catches at his easy manner as he leans against the door. He's so beautiful, even if he is a closet man whore. "Whatever you say, Dr. Stevens."

He rolls his eyes at my formal reply. "Remember what I said the last time you called me Dr. Stevens?"

"It's your title. It's appropriate."

"Well, the things I want to do to you are highly inappropriate." He jostles my arm, trying to make me smile.

Fat chance of that.

He opts for another tact, realizing he gained zero yards with the last play. "Are you hungry? I know an incredible pizza place that this sexual dynamo showed me."

"I thought you and Nicole were having dinner."

"You *are* jealous."

I flip him the bird because I lack an intelligent response. That, and my stomach is threatening to upend itself. Again.

"You're a brilliant woman, Tally. But you're an idiot if you think, for one second, that I want anything to do with that woman." He nods toward the exit, offering his famous sex on a stick smile. "Come on, grumpy girl, let's go get pizza. You can glare at me the whole time. Even douse my slice with crushed red pepper."

I shake my head and push my glasses up my nose. Usually, I find him impossible to resist. But the whole Nicole situation stinks. Worst part? It's my own damn fault. I wanted to keep our relationship on the down-low. Nicole has no such hang-ups. "I'm heading home, but thank you. Enjoy your dinner."

His large, talented hands grasp my shoulders. "Am I going to have to pull rank here, Tally?"

"For pizza?"

"To spend time with you." He frames my face, his thumbs dancing across my cheeks. "I miss you. I know it's only been four days, but I feel you putting distance between us again."

"Apparently, you were busy with Nicole," I grumble, my little green monster getting angrier by the second.

"First, it was a group of doctors grabbing a drink. I showed them that card trick. That's why she claims my hands are talented." His brows raise, waiting for me to admit that he's not a cheating scoundrel. He's lucky his tongue is so talented. It would be far easier to remain angry if it weren't. "Second, I'm never too busy for you. It's not healthy for me to be away from you. I think about you way more than I should. And by that, I mean all the damn time."

"It can't be that bad. You're busy settling in, with Nicole's help."

"Tally," Owen warns, sending me a scathing glare.

I guess I have to let the Nicole situation drop. For now. "The rumor is you've been here until after ten the last few nights."

"Yeah, working out until I'm too exhausted to do anything other than sleep. Otherwise, I'd go nuts from sexual frustration."

"It's been less than a week, Owen."

He pushes me against the bay of lockers, his hands curving around my hips. "Are you saying that you don't miss the feeling of my cock inside you? My tongue on your pussy?"

This man and his dirty talk. It's sexual lighter fluid. One sentence, and I'm a flaming torch. I move my gaze upwards, devouring every inch of him. I know it's a blatant eye fuck, but hey, Dr. Stevens is hot as hell. "I'm not having this conversation."

He smiles, winding his hand in my hair. "Why not? You're the cause of my frustration."

"You know where I live."

"I know where I *want* you to live, but you're a stubborn, gorgeous pain in my ass, and you won't do it." He shakes his head. "You've been distant since the other night. Remember, I can't fix it if I don't know what's wrong."

I bite my lip, staring at the ground. I know that I've been distant, although I hoped I wasn't obvious. But I'm having issues feeling relevant in this golden god's world.

There, I admit it. Sue me. Granted, I'll only say it to myself because I'm not voicing those words aloud.

Owen strokes his finger along my cheek. "I'm sorry I embarrassed you the other night. It wasn't my intention. I just want to help you."

A flush washes over me as he hits the nail on the head. "I don't need your charity."

"It's not charity. It's love, Tally. Hasn't anyone ever spoiled you?"

The sad fact? Never. I shake my head, nausea mixing with tears. "I took care of them."

"And now you take care of your Dad. You've spent your life taking care of other people."

"It's what I do."

His fingers curl around my nape, offering a subtle caress. "And what *I* want to do is take care of you."

Okay, I suck at emotional moments. I cover them with sarcasm and jokes, which are far less painful than showing my true vulnerability. "How many sexual favors will be involved in your assistance?" I inquire, giving him a wink.

Owen huffs out a laugh, shaking his head. In exasperation, likely.

"I'm about to turn you over my knee, Tally; spank the sass out of you."

"Don't tempt me with your promises, Owen. I'll bend over right here."

His hand smacks against my ass, and I startle as the sound echoes off the walls. It's unexpected and hot as hell, firing up every nerve cell. "Please do. I've got several days of pent-up energy, all aiming for you."

I roll my eyes, but his words flame me to the core. I ache for Owen. Never mind that the image of sweat dropping off his tattooed muscles is enough to make me swoon.

"Don't roll those gorgeous eyes at me. You remember what happened the last time you did that, don't you?"

Do I ever. It started with Owen tossing me over his shoulder in a fireman's hold and ended with him buried inside me. A delectable experience, but my ever-present nausea interrupts my trip down memory lane.

"Tally, you okay?"

Not even close. With a strangled whimper, I push past him and sprint for the bathroom, losing the contents of my stomach for the second time today. How is there anything left?

I think I'd better give up on eating. It's hazardous to my health.

Get a test, Tallulah.

Shut up, brain.

I dally in the bathroom, hoping Owen will grant me some privacy. Even better, I'll circumvent those inevitable questions if he's gone.

I emerge a few minutes later, my insides settling after my latest round with the toilet. "Stupid stomach virus."

"Are you still sick?"

Shit. He's still here. "I've got that bug that's going around."

Owen presses his hand presses against my cheek. "You're not feverish. What bug?"

"The stomach virus that's making the rounds."

"No one has a stomach virus."

Just this one time, can my poker face be on point? Please?

"Food poisoning, maybe?"

Owen crosses his arms, cocking his head as he smirks. So much for the poker face. "Ms. Tally, are you pregnant?"

"Of course not!"

"You sure?"

Yes. No. Who the hell knows?

"I'm fine." Time to move this conversation train to the next station. This stop is *way* too uncomfortable. "I'll see you later, I guess."

"You're having dinner with me." It isn't a question, and I can tell by the set of his jaw it isn't open for debate. "We'll get you some soup instead of pizza. Something easy on your stomach."

"No, pizza sounds good," I blurt, feeling my stomach rumble. Seriously, what the hell is wrong with me?

You're pregnant.

Once again, quiet in the back, brain.

Owen's eyes widen as he grins. "Does it? Is that you or the baby talking?"

"I'm not pregnant."

He wraps his arms around me. A surprise move. "Guess we'll find out, won't we?"

"Yeah, can't wait to see how fast you'd head for the hills if I'm knocked up."

His grip tightens as his hand tangles in my hair, forcing me to meet his gaze. "I'd be by your side every minute. I wouldn't run anywhere but to you, Tally."

Kerplunk. There goes my heart again. All pitter-patter for this muscled, tattooed, gray-eyed god. "Doesn't matter anyway, because I'm not pregnant."

Owen's low chuckle confirms that he doesn't believe me, either. Hell, he is a doctor. He's familiar with the 'birds and bees' concept, even alluding to our less than careful sexual history the other night.

Okay, we were never careful. We were hot and heavy and immersed in each other.

"I just want to ensure that you know you can't scare me off with any baby talk."

My heart flips again. Owen always says the right thing. The only trouble is, do I believe him this time? I smile up at him, grabbing my fedora from the bench. "Noted. Now, how about that pizza? I'm starving."

He drops a kiss of my forehead and wraps an arm around my shoulder. "Your wish is my command, Darlin."

CHAPTER EIGHTEEN
OWEN

Tally, being her usual stubborn self, refuses to leave her car in the parking garage, so I follow her to the pizzeria. I swear, that woman *never* makes it easy.

I'm in the turning lane when my phone rings. It's my ex-fiancée. Again. She's called more in the last four days than she did in the last year of our relationship.

With a resigned sigh, I answer the call. "Hello, Charlotte."

"You answered." I hear the surprise in her voice, likely because of my radio silence after the last dozen messages.

"You're persistent. What can I do for you?"

"So much for pleasantries. Can we start with a hello, first? It is tradition."

"I already said hello, Charlotte." The truth is, I have nothing to say to the woman. I never really did, but I wasted too many years figuring out that fact.

"Your mother says you're doing well, adjusting to your new role." Charlotte, for her part, is always polite. It wouldn't do to be anything else, at least in public. In private, she'll stab you while you sleep.

A light knock on my window brings me back to the moment, and my gaze swings to Tally standing outside the car, a perplexed look on her face. "Hang on a moment, Charlotte." I roll down the window, giving my tiny vixen a smile. "Sorry, it's a work call."

"Do you have to go?"

"No," I chuckle. "You're not getting rid of me that easy. Can you get us a seat? I'll be right in."

She nods, and I grab her hand, brushing my lips across her fingers. I'm no fool. Tally needs reassurance, even if she'd rather tar and feather herself than ask for it.

I also need to broach the topic of my ex-fiancée. I need total transparency with Tally, everything out on the table. Any more lies and my beauty will never forgive me.

"Owen," Charlotte's high-pitched voice calls out from the phone.

I'm so wrapped up watching Tally's sexy ass walk inside I forget Charlotte is on the phone. "Sorry about the interruption. What can I do for you?"

"No need to be short, Owen."

I run my hand over my beard, willing my heart rate down. I know Charlotte. She doesn't call people to catch up, or because she misses them. There is always an agenda. I just need to figure out what that agenda is and what role I'm playing in it. "I'm not trying to be rude, but I have someone waiting for me."

"I'll be in Fort Lauderdale next week."

My blood turns to ice in my veins. "Why? You hate Florida."

"Daddy has some business down there."

"Since when does Mr. Auerback have business in Florida?"

I hear the clicking of Charlotte's heels against the floor. She's pacing, which is never a good sign. "Since one of his largest investments relocated to Florida."

There it is.

I knew I'd have this conversation one day, but I expected it with Mr. Auerback, not his daughter. Looks like it really is a family business.

I'm grateful to the man, even if he detests me. He invested enormous sums of start-up capital into the robotic cath lab. He also made a windfall when the venture proved itself successful.

"Your father earned back four times his initial investment. They paid him off almost a year ago."

Apparently, that's not good enough. I grip the phone, awaiting a response. I'm not getting one.

I clench my jaw, beyond tired of the games played by the uber-wealthy. "Why isn't your father conducting this business? Why are you the one making contact?"

"He's not doing well. The whole stress of our broken engagement weighs heavily on Daddy."

I roll my eyes, stifling a groan. "Charlotte, our entire relationship was more of a business transaction than a love affair."

"Aren't most marriages?"

I feel sorry for Charlotte because she's serious with that question. In her world, they arrange marriages for alliance, not love. She defied her father's demands when we started dating, but it wasn't until I helped spearhead the robotics cath lab that I became a worthy contender for her hand. "No, Charlotte, not in the real world."

Silence. The woman is so closed off, it's impossible to gauge if my words have any effect.

"Be that as it may, I'll be in town. I need to see you while I'm in Florida."

I glance at my watch. This conversation has already dragged on far longer than I expected. I want to be inside, next to Tally, trying to tame my ever-present erection while I convince her that loving me is still a good idea.

"I don't think that's smart, Charlotte. We said everything we had to say in San Francisco."

"Owen, this is not about us. This is business. I believe you'll be very keen to hear the idea Daddy came up with a couple of weeks ago. After all, you are in the business of saving people, aren't you? He wants to further that cause."

I hate that Charlotte plays that card because she knows I'll cave. If there's a chance to save more lives through technology or training, I'm on board. Every time. And she knows it.

"Call me when you arrive. We'll arrange something."

"Thank you. I appreciate it."

More silence. Holy shit, this conversation is painful.

"Right, well, I'm going to have dinner. Have a nice day."

"You, too." I can tell from Charlotte's voice that she has more to say, but I don't have the wherewithal to listen.

Charlotte had her chance. I spent years trying to love her, searching for ways to heat that iceberg she calls a heart. Don't get me wrong, Charlotte is gorgeous, and she ensures the world is aware. She's smart, too, and can work a deal even better than her Dad. But she's an ice queen. Cool, collected, and without a speck of emotion.

Tally is fire. So full of vibrancy and life that she'll burn you if you get too close. But I've never wanted to be scorched so much in my life. I felt her energy from across the room that night at Wicked Chucks. I spent the better part of an hour watching her, trying to drum up the courage to approach her. Lucky for me, I stole her seat on the balcony. Fair enough, though, considering she stole my heart.

∽

"Everything okay?" Tally inquires as I slide into the booth opposite her.

"It is now. So, what are you getting?"

"I'm starving, so I ordered a supreme pizza, with extra supremeness." She smiles and giggles.

I love that Tally eats, except for that dinner, where she ordered a salad. I guarantee she scarfed down some pasta the minute she got home. I never understood women subsisting on lettuce.

"You're eating a whole pizza?" I joke, grabbing her hand.

"No, big shot, I planned on giving you a couple slices, but if you want to be huffy, I'll eat it all myself." Tally sticks out her tongue, and my dick twitches in response. I swear, the woman doesn't have to do a damn thing overtly sexual, but with Tally, my mind tuns the most innocent gesture dirty.

The pizza arrives, and my girl jumps right in. For someone with a supposed stomach bug, she is wolfing down her food.

"Glad to see your stomach has calmed down."

Tally shrugs, blotting her lips with a napkin. "Something we should all be thankful for."

"Maybe you should see a doctor," I suggest.

"I am. I'm having dinner with one right now."

"Smart ass."

"Better than being a dumb one."

I love our banter. There's never a dull moment with Tally. Like I said, she's fire, and I'll go down in flames just to be near her.

"I think I'll go skating this weekend," she says, pushing her glasses back up her nose.

Be careful of the baby. "You sure that's a good idea?"

"Why wouldn't it be? Lord knows I need the practice."

I shrug, trying to appear noncommittal. "You haven't been feeling well. You should take it easy, Darlin."

"Fine. I'll just shovel pizza into my gullet and leave the festivities for other people." She sets down her piece, her gaze on the table. "I have to ask you something."

"Anything." I mean it, too. No more secrets.

"Nicole really has a thing for you."

I nod. No point in denying it. "I know. She's obvious about it."

"Have you two slept together?"

My mouth falls open. Talk about a surprise detour. "Never."

"Everything but sex?"

I grab her hand, pressing it to my mouth. I didn't realize that Nicole's flirtations were bothering her that much. I assumed Tally knew the woman wasn't a threat. "I'm a one-woman kind of guy, and that woman has been you since the night we met. Even if you refuse to believe me."

She has yet to meet my gaze, focusing her eyes on her lap. "I believe you."

"That's a good start, but do you forgive me, Tally?"

She releases a long exhale. That's never a good sign. "It doesn't do me much good to stay angry, even if I'm entitled to my rightful indignation." The words are harsh, but her wink assures me she's joking.

"Is that a yes?"

"That's a 'you owe me amazing oral for the next month' yes," she volleys back.

I can't hold back the shit-eating grin crossing my face. My punishment is her pussy? Yes, please. "Can I start now?"

"Right now?"

"Right here." I'm serious, too. And Tally knows it.

"No," she starts, holding up her hand to prevent me from arguing, "and it's not because I won't do it in a public place. But I want to return to this pizzeria. I don't want one of those most wanted photos of me hanging behind the counter."

"There is another option, then."

"I'm not doing it in their bathroom, either," she retorts, squashing my plan.

"Buzzkill. How about this?" I take a deep breath, preparing to lay all my cards out on the table. "After we eat, I think we should go get Hecate and head back to the condo. I want you to live there with me."

She chews her lip as she considers my offer. "Why don't we stay at my place tonight, since it's closer, and head back to your—our—condo tomorrow?"

I grasp her hands. She's not the only one needing reassurance. "Are you back? Do I have my Tally back? I'm talking one hundred percent, Darlin. No more hiding or pretending that we aren't together."

After a moment, she nods. "I don't know how we're going to do this—"

"We love each other. That's all. It's pretty simple."

"You won't lie to me again?" I see the apprehension in her eyes. Tally is risking her heart by giving me another chance. I'm sure as hell not blowing it this time.

"I swear. Never again. Hey, I'm a pretty good catch. I'm a doctor, not a derelict. You say I'm hot, and I think I'm damn good in bed."

"You have a few redeeming qualities, I suppose."

"That, and if you say no, you won't have my tongue at your beck and call for the next month." It's a total bullshit statement, and Tally knows it, too.

"Yes, I will," she smiles, leaning across the table and planting a hard kiss on my mouth, solidifying our deal.

We barely make it to her apartment. Okay, I barely make it. I need my hands and mouth on this woman. Now.

I jump out of my car, grabbing the keys from her hand and tossing her over my shoulder. It's becoming a bit of a thing with us. She whoops in surprise, but I ignore any protests.

Without a word, I carry her into the bathroom, setting her down on the tile floor. I let the water heat in the shower as I turn my attention back to Tally. She opens her mouth to speak, but I press my fingers to her lips.

Sometimes, words get in the way. We'll let our bodies do the talking. I waste no time stripping her down, letting my hands skim along her skin. The woman's curves are every man's wet dream, but it's the feel of her pussy milking my cock, which sends my body into overdrive.

Shedding my own clothes, I grasp her waist, backing her against the shower wall. I wrap my hand into her hair as I claim her mouth. The woman always tastes so damn good and now is no exception.

She's ready for me, her tongue sliding against mine as she scratches her nails along my arms. My hand drifts down between her thighs, feeling her writhe against me as I stroke her. I love how wet she is; every time I touch her, she holds nothing back.

I push a second finger into her, curving around to tease her from the inside.

"Owen." It's the way she says my name, huffed out on a heated breath, that spurs me further.

My teeth scrape against the soft skin of her neck, delivering a small nip. She's so pale, I know it will leave a mark. Now ask me if I care. "What did I tell you about talking?"

A ragged moan breaks from her lips as a third finger joins the party, and she pulsates around me. She's so close, but I'm not letting her come just yet.

Flipping Tally to face the wall, I bury myself inside her warmth. Every time I sink into her, it's better than the last. Her body shivers around me, and I struggle to maintain. But when a moan of ecstasy slips past her lips, it's all over.

Fire. Pure fire.

～

I WATCH HER SLEEPING, A SATED SMILE ON HER MOUTH—NOTHING LIKE three orgasms to knock Tally out. I swear, she's so tight, she's going to snap my dick in two. But I love every second, and I love every inch of her.

Tally is terrified about giving us another chance, but I'll prove what a good gamble I am. I'm not playing around. I shocked the hell out of her when I mentioned buying an engagement ring last week. What she doesn't know is that it's already a done deal. I'm putting a ring on her finger as soon as possible.

CHAPTER EIGHTEEN • 189

How someone hasn't snatched Tally up yet is beyond comprehension. Maybe, like she said, she was waiting for me. God knows I was searching for her.

My tiny vixen turns on her side, mumbling in her sleep. I wrap my arm around her, pulling her to my chest.

This woman is everything, including a damn liar.

She's the most adorable liar on the planet, but she's a liar, nonetheless.

My darling Tally doesn't have a stomach virus. She knows it, and as I run my hand along her abdomen, I know it, too.

I've been dropping hints that I'm aware of situation, hoping she'll fess up, but as I've said before, the woman is a vault.

How many more obstacles is she going to make me dodge before she lets me back in?

I reach my free hand down to pet Hecate, curled against my leg. "You know she's lying, don't you?" I inquire, earning an affirmative purr in response.

My phone buzzes, and I stretch to reach it, careful not to wake Tally. When you're an interventional cardiologist, you're never off duty.

Only problem? It isn't work.

It's Charlotte. Again.

Five missed phone calls. I swear, if someone isn't dead, they will be after this conversation. I slip from the bed and throw on my pants before strolling onto the deck. This had better be good.

"Good evening, Owen."

Oh, hell, no. We will not exchange pleasantries like she didn't just rouse me from bed next to a gorgeous, naked woman. "Do you know what time it is, Charlotte?"

"It's eight o'clock."

"On the west coast," I snap, tapping my fist against the deck railing. "It's eleven here, and I was in bed."

I never know how to interpret silence from Charlotte. She shows no emotions, so it's a guess, at best. "I'm sorry. I forgot."

Doubtful. She is a jet setter, with friends around the globe. Time zones are nothing new for her. My guess? She was trying to catch me with another woman.

Mission accomplished.

"What do you want?"

"I'll be landing tomorrow morning, around noon. I thought we might meet for a late lunch."

My fingers tighten around the railing as my stomach churns. "You said you weren't arriving until next week."

"Change of plans. I looked online, and there's a lovely French bistro just a few blocks from your home."

"How do you know where I live?"

Charlotte, ever the elusive businesswoman, evades my question. "It will be nice to catch up. Two-thirty?"

"Does it matter if I have plans?"

She releases an irritated huff. Huh, a genuine emotion. Who knew? "If you can't have lunch tomorrow, please say so. I figured that the sooner we meet, the sooner you can be in the loop about the latest developments."

"Now they're developments? Is this a business proposition, or are we overthrowing a government?"

"Owen, please. I know you're angry, but this is a windfall opportunity for you."

"Says the woman who stands to gain even more from this opportunity."

"Why are you so hateful?"

"I'm not"—I stop myself, aware that my volume is increasing—"being hateful. I'm being real. We hardly ended on good terms, Charlotte. Forgive me for having reservations."

More silence. At this rate, the conversation won't be over until tomorrow.

It's easier to suffer through one lunch and be done—as much as I hate the idea. "Fine. Two-thirty, but it's just lunch."

"I'll text you the address of the bistro. I look forward to seeing you." There's that cheery tone again. Why wouldn't it be back? I'm caving to her whims.

"Right. Goodbye." I stalk back into the apartment, feeling the weight of my decision settle over me. I still haven't told Tally about Charlotte or our relationship. The woman knows that I've dated others, but she has no idea how close I was to the altar. When I came to Florida, it was to escape from a life that didn't fit. The last thing I expected when I arrived here was another relationship. I wasn't looking for love, but it found me.

Isn't that the way it happens?

I slide into bed, but I can tell that Tally is awake. I only pray my conversation didn't rouse her. "Sorry about that, Darlin."

Tally snuggles against me, dripping kisses along my chest. "Do you have to go?"

"No. But I have a business lunch tomorrow. It shouldn't take too long."

"They phoned at eleven at night to set up a luncheon? Sounds like a booty call, mister." She scoffs, but I hear the uncertainty in her voice. "You sure it wasn't Nicole?"

Oh, no, Nicole would be way easier.

"It wasn't Nicole. It's a business associate from the west coast. They forgot about the time difference."

"Ah, I see." She nibbles my lower lip, pulling it between her teeth. "Too bad for you. If it was a booty call, you might have gotten lucky again."

I roll on top of her, pinning her body against the mattress. "Don't you worry your pretty little head, Darlin. I'm going to get lucky again. Right now."

CHAPTER NINETEEN
TALLY

It's been one hell of a morning, and I've yet to have coffee.

My father had another rough night. I received the message first thing, minutes after Owen left. I was tempted to call and beg him to come with me, but he has a business lunch that I don't want to interrupt. So, I dial my ride or die, and as always, Stefani is by my side within the hour.

Thankfully, my father has rallied by the time we arrive, so we enjoy a quick visit and then head for a late breakfast. My stomach isn't on board with this decision, but my brain convinces the other organ that eating is a necessity and not a luxury.

"Are you going to look at it or eat it?" Stefani asks, pointing her fork toward my plate.

"I'm working on it."

"You know you're not sick, right?"

"There is the possibility that it's a stomach virus." I stare at my omelet in a futile attempt to rein in my swirling gut.

"Unlikely, considering no one else has this pernicious virus." Stefani shoots me a knowing glance. That's the third one since the start of breakfast. "What does Owen say?"

"About a stomach virus?" At her glare, I release a resigned huff. "I haven't told him. I don't know if there's anything *to* tell him."

"Lu, you're going to have to get a test. Eventually, the world will know if you're pregnant. You can't hide eight months of baby."

"Sure you can. Look at some of the people on Jerry Springer—went to the bathroom, popped out a kid."

"I wouldn't use that as my control group."

She's right. I know she's right. But I'm also scared shitless. I've known Owen for two months, and even though our relationship is back on track, I doubt he planned on becoming a father when he moved to Florida.

"I think he'll be fine with the news. Honestly, give the guy a little credit."

I narrow my gaze at my friend. "This is the same man who lied about being a doctor. I'm taking it slowly this time."

Stefani nods, but she knows it's total crap. With Owen, I lack willpower. Of any variety. He's also beseeching me to move into his oceanfront condo. I don't know how many more times I can use Hecate as an excuse, particularly when he's got the rooftop garden all set up for her arrival. The cat is going to have such a life—totally deserved, of course.

"Does that mean you've shelved the idea of moving in with Owen? No offense, Lu, your landlord is lovely, but I'm certain Owen's digs are far superior."

"I can't just up and leave Mrs. Smalls. She counts on my rent money. My lease is up in a month, so I figured I'll discuss it with her, and then move in with Owen…if we haven't killed each other first."

It's a good plan. A solid, well-thought-out plan. Owen and I rushed headlong into loving each other and look where that got us. Correction. Look where that got me.

Stefani drops some cash on the table before grabbing my hand and hustling me back to her SUV. "Let's get this over with. I need to know if you can go out drinking tonight."

I stop dead in my tracks, digging in my heels like a mountain goat. "What are you talking about?"

"Don't be dense. You know what I mean."

"I'm not ready yet."

She turns to me, grasping my shoulders. "My sweet friend, no one is ever ready for a baby. But I guarantee you will be the coolest mother on the block."

"I'll be the most single mother on the block," I mutter, climbing into the passenger seat, my shoulders hunched.

"No, you won't. That hot hunk of a doctor is going to put a ring on it so fast, your head will spin."

I grunt in response. It's the best comeback I've got at the moment.

I trudge through the drugstore, spending almost a hundred bucks on a basketful of tests. I don't think I have that much urine in my damn body.

Okay, I likely do. Peeing has become my new favorite pastime, aside from chronic vomiting.

I am the definition of a hot mess.

Stefani pulls up to her house, handing me the bag. I love her home. It's an old Craftsman-style bungalow, and I hope one day to afford a similar place with a stained-glass entry window.

Unless Owen and I *do* get married.

Stop with the overactive imagination. One hurdle at a time, Tallulah. One massive, scary as hell hurdle.

I pause by the bathroom door, my fingers tightening around the bag.

"Open the boxes, Lu. They don't work via osmosis." Stefani is so helpful. And impatient. I get it. She wants to know if her best friend is having a baby. Her best friend, on the other hand, isn't sure *what* to feel.

I flip her the bird, grab the menagerie of pregnancy tests and shut myself in the bathroom. Turns out, I have no issue using all those tests. Hey, no one can call me a quitter.

I stand over the sink, uncertain what the hell I'm supposed to be hoping for.

Do I want a baby? Do I want a baby with Owen? Do I want a baby now on top of everything else I'm juggling?

The instructions state that the tests take three to five minutes. In my case, it takes less than sixty seconds. There are blue lines and plus signs everywhere. Even a couple that scream out pregnant, in case my feeble brain can't figure out how to read the other ones.

Stefani pops her head into the bathroom. "Did you take all the tests?" she inquires.

At least, I think that's what she said. I'm so lost in my thoughts that all I hear is garbled noise.

I maintain my focus on the tests, gripping the edge of the sink so tight I'm shocked the ceramic hasn't cracked.

"Are you listening to a word I've said?"

Nope, Stefani, not one word.

"Tallulah!"

I jerk my head up to meet her piercing gaze, forcing my thoughts away from the little blue line that's forever changed life as I know it. "What?"

"Did you take the—" The question dies in her throat as she sees the collection of tests. "Knew it. Okay, it's going to be fine."

I don't know that it's going to be fine. In truth, I'm not sure what the hell to do now. Even though I knew I was pregnant before, this validates every fear. I gaze at my belly. It's still flat, no signs of life anywhere, save for the omelet that will soon vacate the premises. "I'm pregnant."

Stefani hugs my shoulders, but it offers little comfort. "You're pregnant. I guess I have to find someone else to hang out with at Wicked Chucks."

"Why would you hang at Wicked Chucks without me? Oh..." I grin, gathering up the tests and chucking them in the trash. "You miss Dan."

I always know when Stefani is avoiding a topic. She looks everywhere but my direction. "Believe it or not, I like Wicked Chucks."

"I don't believe it."

"Why not?"

I smirk. "Because *I* don't like Wicked Chucks. It's a total dive. I just love the music. That and Dan is easy on the eyes. Didn't think he'd be your type, though. At least not for anything long-term."

"He's not my type. He treats women with respect. I find that very enticing."

"Dan is a hell of a guy." I try to bite back my smile. Time to mess with my best friend—just a bit. "If I were you, I wouldn't wait to scoop him up. Tons of women have a thing for him."

I'm not lying. Dan is very popular with the ladies, but I also know that he's had eyes for Stefani since they met. But what kind of friend would I be if I didn't up the ante a bit? Her look of horror tells me all I need to know. She'll be stopping by to visit the comely bartender soon.

Stefani shakes her head in disgust. Jealousy is rare with my friend, but when it strikes, it's potent. "Enough about Dan. When are you going to talk to Owen?"

I shrug. That's an answer, right?

Apparently, not a good enough answer for my ride or die. "Lu, you need to tell him."

"Those pregnancy tests aren't 100% effective."

"Sure, all of them malfunctioned. All *eight* of them."

She's got a point, and I don't have a leg to stand on in this argument. "I'm seeing Owen tonight. He promised me this delicious dinner and a bubble bath."

"God, I hate you," Stefani huffs, but she doesn't mean it. She's thrilled that I've found someone. Now, the trick is keeping him after he discovers he has some potent swimmers.

"He said he had to talk to me about something."

Stefani claps her hands. "He's going to propose!"

I shake my head. "Owen is not proposing. I'm not sure what it's about, but now, we have two topics to discuss."

"Someone's getting married," Stefani sings in an off-key voice, as I lob a hand towel at her head.

I want to ignore her banter, but part of me wonders if he might ask me to marry him. He has been bugging me to move in, so marriage is the next logical step. Right?

Maybe then, the baby wouldn't be an unwelcome surprise. Resting my hand on my stomach, I realize that for me, this baby is a gift, even if that isn't the case for Owen.

He swore he wouldn't run in the opposite direction if I was pregnant. Let's see if he's a man of his word.

I WANDER AROUND MY APARTMENT FOR THE BETTER PART OF THE afternoon, trying to figure out how to tell Owen about the baby.

Should I act all cutesy, buying a ton of baby vegetables to go with dinner? Pick up a t-shirt that says, World's Best Dad? Just once, I wish I could pull off sappy, but it's not in my wheelhouse.

I glance at the clock. It's just after four. I know he said seven, but I can't wait any longer. I grab my keys, drop a kiss on Hecate's head, and bound out the door.

Next stop—Owen.

I send off a quick text, just in case his business meeting ran late.

I hope you're having a wonderful lunch. I'm coming by early. I need to discuss something with you. It's important.

CHAPTER
TWENTY
OWEN

I pull into the bistro parking lot, steering between the Mercedes and Porsche, both idling in the middle of the lane. They've decided they need not obey traffic laws.

Rich pricks.

I take a few deep breaths before shutting off the engine. I have no idea what kind of car Charlotte rented, so I can't be sure if she's here yet. All I know is that I'm dreading this reunion.

Please let it be short and painless.

I knew this meeting was unavoidable because when my ex-fiancée wants something, she's used to getting it. But now, the stakes are higher. Charlotte is local, not 3,000 miles across the country. Worse, I haven't spoken to Tally about my ex yet, a fact I plan on rectifying tonight.

I have the evening all planned for my tiny vixen. I even forced myself to leave her naked body at six this morning to get a head start on cooking. I'm Italian, and a good sauce takes all day. Besides, Tally deserves the best.

Underneath my armor of confidence, I'm scared. After plying Tally with food, I'm telling her that her gorgeous ass is moving in with me. I'm done with her flimsy excuses. Then, I'm dropping to one knee and begging her to marry me, preferably before she starts showing.

Maybe then, she'll fess up, or at least take a damn test.

But first, I have to pay the piper and settle whatever score Charlotte believes I owe her family.

I saunter into the cafe with far more bravado than I actually possess, and spot her at an outside table, her dark head bent over her phone. The woman is never without that device. When they offer implantable versions, she'll be the first in line.

She's garnering looks from all the men in the restaurant, but that's nothing new. Charlotte's beauty is exquisite, but it's only skin-deep. Hell, that was what first drew me to her when we met. I was in the middle of medical residency, and she was a grad student, majoring in political science. She didn't have any political aspirations. She did it to piss off her father. It didn't take me long to learn she was a petulant, spoiled, and pedantic woman—to everyone, including me.

"Charlotte," I offer as a greeting, standing over the bistro table.

She glances up, her green eyes widening as she takes in my unfamiliar look. "What the hell did you do?"

"I shaved my head and grew a beard," I respond, sliding into the seat opposite her.

"Embracing your punk roots, I see." She clicks her tongue against her teeth, a sure sign she disapproves of my current style.

I couldn't care less. Tally adores this look, and she is the one that matters. "I know you didn't call me to discuss fashion choices, so why don't we cut to the chase?"

The server interrupts, and I order a coffee. Black. It's quick and sends a signal that this will not be some drawn-out mid-afternoon date. I can't be sure if she misses my hint or ignores it, as she orders an egg white omelet and tea.

"This is a change from San Francisco," she states, fingering the cloth napkin and looking everywhere but in my direction.

I get it. I don't fit her mold anymore. I never did. I tried to please her during our courtship, covering my tattoos and attending the ballet, but it was total crap. I wore the clothes she selected, hung out with her tedious friends, and acted like any of it mattered.

When I left San Francisco, I broke that mold, and I'll never let another person put me in one again.

"I needed a change."

"We could have discussed things."

I scoff, biting back a laugh. "What was there to discuss? Your infidelity? I knew about Marco, Charlotte."

"It was just sex." I have to give it to the woman. She doesn't lie. She's cold as ice but honest to a fault.

"Hopefully, it was good sex," I announce, a bit too loudly, as the server returns with our beverages. The waitress bites back a grin, while Charlotte blushes under her caramel skin.

"Not really," she admits, opening a package of sweetener. I don't know why she bothers. There isn't enough sugar in the world to sweeten her up. "That's not why I'm here."

"Good. I didn't care to discuss Marco."

"Why did you bring him up?"

"To drive home the reason I left San Francisco,"—I pause, taking a sip of my coffee—"and why I'm happy here."

"Memorial is a reputable hospital, although they're behind cardiac wise. I'm assuming you're the only robotics certified interventionist?"

"At the moment. Certification costs money—lots of it—and there are no training facilities in the southeast."

"I'm so glad you mentioned it because that's why I'm here. With the high incidence of mortality associated with cardiac arrests in this area, Daddy believes it a travesty to not offer top-notch technology to the patients. Besides, it would behoove you both."

She didn't waste any time getting to the point. Perhaps she wants to finish this lunch as quick as I do. "While I can't argue your father's opinion, he's no longer an active investor, Charlotte. They paid him off, remember?"

"He wants to change that."

I groan, leaning back in the chair. "I figured as much. Just tell me what you two want."

"He will build a training facility here in South Florida. You will act as the trainer for the first class of students. When they are certified and dispatched back to their prospective hospitals, you will earn a handsome payday for your trouble."

To the outside world, it sounds like one hell of a sweet deal. But I know this family. This is a bribe. "What's your involvement in this plan?"

"Since Daddy is on the other coast, I will remain here to set up the facility and ensure the operations are running smoothly."

"You're moving here?" I thunder, my heart racing like a greyhound.

"Don't get so excited, Owen. It's only for the next several weeks. Then, I'll return to San Francisco. Perhaps you might join me at that point."

"Charlotte, we are not reconciling,"

"We'll see, I suppose. We have a lot of years together, Owen. An awful lot of time invested."

"Does this payday hinge on our reconciliation? Because if it does, I'm not interested."

She fiddles with her fork, and I wonder if I'm about to witness a meltdown. I've never seen her fiddle before. I sure as hell have never seen Charlotte melt down. "Daddy is a businessman, and this is strictly business."

Bullshit, and we both know it.

"I'm not with Marco any longer."

I shrug, finishing the last of my coffee. "It's not my business if you are."

"It was difficult being with you, Owen. You were always working."

"So were you. Different capacities, but you were wheeling and dealing 24/7. You never turned off."

"I guess we're both to blame."

Not really, considering I didn't screw Marco, but there's no point in arguing. "Absolutely."

She cracks a smile, motioning to my head. "It suits you."

"You hate it," I reply with a grin.

"I do, but you're handsome, regardless."

"Thank you. I appreciate that pseudo compliment."

"It's a start," she volleys back. Hell, it's the closest thing to banter I've experienced with Charlotte in years. Sarcasm is not a school that she ever attended. "Would you like a refill? We can discuss the specifics of the deal, and you can decide if you'd like to participate."

"Sure, let me go to the bathroom first." I stand, colliding with the server. For a brief second, a half-empty mug teeters on top of the plate, right before it tumbles down, dousing the front of my shirt and pants.

"Sir, I'm so sorry," the server exclaims, fumbling to set down the dishes. She grabs napkins from a neighboring table and hands them to me. A nice gesture, but it's going to take more than that.

"You need to watch where you're going," Charlotte hisses, her eyes narrowing at the young waitress.

"It's fine. I ran into her." I shoot Charlotte a warning look. Growing up in a world of privilege, she believes the world works for her. In some sick way, they likely do, considering the vast number of companies owned by her family.

"I'm so sorry, sir. I'll pay for the dry cleaning." Poor kid, she can't be over nineteen and now thinks she's about to lose her job.

"No need. It was my fault."

"It was *not*—"

"Charlotte, I said leave it," I reply, giving her one last warning.

With a huff, she waves her black Amex under the server's nose. "Settle our bill immediately."

The waitress scurries off, her eyes downcast and shoulders

slumped. I may be covered in coffee, but I feel for that poor kid. Her day is ruined because of my ex-fiancée's arrogance.

The moment she returns with the bill, Charlotte signs the document, snatching back her card. I'm shocked for two reasons: Charlotte's behavior and that she actually picked up the tab. It's the first time since we met that she paid her own way.

We walk outside, and Charlotte points to a sleek white Mercedes convertible. In a lot of high-priced vehicles, it's near the top of the dollar list. "That's me."

"Nice choice."

"I love convertibles."

"I know. Well, seeing as how I'm drenched in coffee, we'll pick this up another time?"

"I'll follow you back to your condo," Charlotte offers.

"That's not a good idea."

"Why not? You have to change, and then we can discuss the details." Her eyes narrow knowingly. "Don't worry, I won't impede on any late-night dinner plans."

I don't want Charlotte to come back to my condo. Not now, not ever. But, I'm also covered in coffee, and we need to hash out the details of this plan to ensure I don't spend every waking moment with the woman. Hell, I don't even know if the project is feasible or desirable. The sooner I know, the sooner I can send her packing or set parameters.

"I have important plans tonight."

"I can tell. Don't worry, Owen. It's only four. We'll be done by six."

Tally isn't due to arrive until seven. It's cutting it close, but it should give me enough time. "Fine," I concede.

"Who is she?"

"Her name is Tally."

"You're quite taken with her." It's not a question, and I have no intention of hedging my feelings.

"That's an understatement."

If my words bother Charlotte, she doesn't let it show. Typical. "Does she come from a good family?"

I bristle at her inquiry. "Her mother is dead, and her father has dementia. He lives in a facility."

"You know what I mean."

"Yes, I do, Charlotte, and no, Tally doesn't come from money. But I couldn't care less how much her family is worth. I know what *she's* worth."

"Without my family's money and connections, your robotic cath lab would still be in its testing phase."

"I'm forever grateful for your father's belief in me. His payout reflected that gratitude."

"But—" Charlotte wants to continue bickering, and the reason is two-fold. First, it's eating away the minutes, now that she knows I have plans. Second, she's chipping away at my Tally to make her less attractive. Not possible.

"I'm not discussing Tally any further. My personal life is none of your business. Not anymore. This isn't a good idea, you coming back to the condo. Thanks for the coffee. I'll call you within the week."

I don't wait to hear her argument. I'm done with the conversation.

I PULL INTO MY PARKING SPOT, MY BRAIN FOCUSED ON THIS EVENING. I'm preparing a collection of Italian dishes, all Tally's favorites. I'm so glad my mother taught me how to cook. Yes, I'm buttering up my tiny beauty. I want her to say yes.

Pushing open my car door, I release a heated groan. Charlotte is parking across the lot in the visitor's spot. "What are you doing here?"

She sends me an exasperated look. "I know you have a date, but I need to get certain details sorted before I can complete the business plan. It won't take long. I promise."

"You never listen, do you? You only hear what you want to hear."

"Give me thirty minutes, and I'll be out of your hair." She chuckles. "Might take less than that, now."

I want to maintain the cold facade, but I have to admit her timing was damn good. I smile, running a hand over my head. "Likely will."

I open the door to the condo, waving her inside. "I need to take a shower."

Charlotte nods, her gaze on the view of the ocean from the living room window. "This is a nice place. Bigger than I expected."

"Dollar goes further down here. It's way smaller than our apartment in San Francisco. Granted, you owned the building."

"True, but this is nice. You chose well."

I smile. "Tally chose it."

"Does she live here?"

Hopefully, after tonight, she will.

I'm not in the mood to poke the bear. It will lead to more questions, and that will suck up more time. "No, but she came with me to look at the condos. She likes the rooftop garden."

Charlotte seems to ease after learning Tally doesn't reside in the condo. She even manages a second smile. "Smart choice. She must be a smart girl."

"Very." I wave around the kitchen. "Make yourself comfortable, and I'll be out in a few minutes." I pause in the hallway, turning back to face my ex. "I do have very important plans tonight. This can't take long."

"Owen, I heard you the first, second, and third time. I'll bring up all the details on my laptop, and they'll be ready for your perusal once you're done in the shower."

"Fair enough," I mutter, hoping she will stick to her word.

CHAPTER
TWENTY-ONE
TALLY

Why is it that when you're in a hurry, the elevator moves at a snail's pace? I saw Owen's car in his parking space. He's home, and hopefully he won't have a meltdown when I share my news.

I ride to the top floor, a small smile playing on my lips. Now that I've had a few hours to get used to the idea, I'm excited. Who knew that one day I would become a mom?

I knock on the door, my curiosity piqued when I hear the familiar clacking of high heels across the floor inside. When the door opens, every sense goes on high alert.

Breathe, Tally. Maybe this woman—this drop-dead beautiful woman—is a realtor or doctor or cleaning lady.

Judging by her finely tailored duds, she's definitely not the latter. In fact, I wager her outfit is worth more than my entire wardrobe.

The woman possesses an exotic beauty that is breathtaking. She's already tall, made taller by her four-inch designer shoes, and willowy as a sapling. Her dark hair falls in waves around a picture perfect face, with bright green eyes and caramel hued skin that I would kill to have.

I shift uncomfortably as she peers down at me, acutely aware of my ripped jeans, Iggy Pop t-shirt, glasses and fedora.

"Can I help you?" she inquires, her hand resting on the door, her eyes narrowing in my direction.

"I'm here to see Owen."

"And you are?"

Who the hell is this? His new bodyguard? "I'm Tally. I saw his car in the lot, so I know he's here."

Her pupils dilate, but beyond that, her features are unreadable. "Tally, huh?" She gestures into the apartment. "Come in. Owen will be right out. He's in the shower."

I spin on my heel, my eyes bulging at her statement. "He's in the shower?"

"Yes, a server spilled coffee on him."

I release the breath I'm holding, willing my heart to settle.

See, Tally? Totally innocent.

"It happened during lunch."

Heart rate speeding up again. "I'm sorry, who are you?"

She extends her hand. Her perfectly manicured hand, dripping with all manner of gemstone jewelry. "I'm Charlotte Auerback, Owen's fiancée."

My heart is pounding so loudly in my ears that I must have heard this woman wrong. "His what?"

"Fiancée. Well, until a couple of months ago. We've been on a break."

I open my mouth to speak, but all I can manage is gasping like a fish out of water.

His fiancée?

A couple months ago?

They've been on a break?

"Charlotte, who are you talking to—" Owen strolls into the room, wearing only a pair of shorts, a towel slung around his shoulder. His face pales when he sees me, his hands dropping by his side. "Tally. You're early."

I'm the woman who knows what to say. A witty comeback or a biting remark, I'm always on point. But not this time. All I feel are the walls closing in as the reality of the situation slaps me in the face.

"Yeah," I manage, my gaze on the ground, my stomach contents threatening to emerge all over Charlotte's Louboutin heels.

"I see you've met Charlotte."

"Yes. I've met your fiancée," I spit out, my gaze finally rising to meet Owen's. I will the tears to stay in my skull, but the sons of bitches don't listen.

Owen's jaw slackens. "No, she's my ex-fiancée. Darlin, let me explain."

He takes a step toward me, and I leap back. "Don't touch me."

"Charlotte, you need to go," Owen bellows, throwing open the door.

"What about our arrangement? We need to discuss this project, Owen. It's a tremendous opportunity for you."

"Go. Now," Owen repeats, the veins bulging in his neck.

My stomach can't take any more. I push between them and dash into the bathroom, losing my lunch along with the last vestiges of my hope and sanity. I sink to the floor, leaning against the vanity as the tears stream down my face.

I'm such an idiot. A naïve fool.

Love doesn't exist, at least not for me, and the gorgeous woman outside is proof of that fact.

"Tally, Darlin, are you okay?" Owen knocks at the door and I hear the panic in his voice.

Part of me wants to remain locked in the bathroom forever, until I cease to exist, never having to face the devastation of my reality. But, I also know that piece of shit owes me some answers and this time, I'm going to get them. I won't let him walk on me like the last bastard I trusted.

I stand up, sucking in a lungful of oxygen as I stare at my reflection. I have to keep it together. I have a baby to consider now. A baby that Owen will never know about.

I splash water on my face, my hand pausing on the doorknob. With a last sigh, I throw open the door, pushing past Owen as I storm into the living room.

Screw explanations. Right now, I can't handle being in the same vicinity as Owen.

Besides, do the reasons even matter? He betrayed me.

My trust.

My heart.

My God, my heart hurts.

Owen grabs me around the waist as I reach for the front door, pulling me against him. Wrong move. I'm in no mood for coddling, and certainly not by him. I push at his hands, locked around me, squirming like an insane patient.

"Let me go," I wail, feeling his grip tighten around me.

Owen buries his head in the crook of my neck, as I desperately try to shirk his touch. "Please, Tally. You don't know—"

"You're right. I don't anything about you. But I don't have the energy to wade through your menagerie of stories, searching for the pearl of truth in your lies. My father is sick, and I need to focus my energy on him."

"Did something happen with your Dad?"

I whirl in his arms, my eyes flashing with fury. "He had a rough night. I was going to call you to come with me, but I didn't want to disturb your *business* lunch."

"Tally, you should have called me. I'm always here for you."

It's bizarre when the emotions become so overwhelming that you shut down, and a strange, detached sense of calm drifts over you like a wet blanket. You know you're suffocating, but you cease to care.

"That's just another line, isn't it? You're never here for me. Hell, today, you were busy tending to the needs of the fiancée I didn't know you had."

"Ex-fiancée, Tally."

"That's not what she said."

He grunts, shaking his head. "Fucking bitch. She's a liar."

"So are you." I push out of his grasp, standing there with defiant rage.

Owen smacks the door frame, his aggravation mounting.

About time you join the club, asshole.

"I'm not lying! Charlotte is not my fiancée. Not anymore."

"That's temporary, I'm sure. A business lunch. What a crock. Let's just call it what it is—she wants you back, and she doesn't seem like a woman who takes no for an answer. Nice outfit she had on, probably worth more than my entire apartment. Who says money can't buy love?"

"I walked away from her. I left San Francisco because I was miserable."

"Not so miserable that you would refuse lunch with her. If it was really over, you wouldn't have seen her."

"It's about the robotics cath lab. That's it."

"Sure it is, Owen. Have you meant *anything* you've ever said to me?"

"I meant *everything*, Tally."

I stamp my foot, releasing a howl of rage. To the outsider, I look like a crazy person, but Owen should thank his lucky stars. I'm holding back. "What is it about me that is so unapproachable you have to lie repeatedly?"

"That statement is so unfair."

"That statement is dead-on balls accurate. I asked you why you left San Francisco, and you made up some bullshit answer that you were searching for your why. Your reason for everything."

"I was, Tally. And I found it when I met you. Believe me."

"You lied about being a doctor, even after I asked. You lied about your reasons for moving to Florida. You neglected to mention Charlotte, or your impending wedding. Why, for one second, should I believe anything else that you've said?"

"It's the truth." Owen takes a step toward me, but I sidestep him, shooting him a warning look to not come any closer. "Christ, I know how bad this looks, and I wanted to tell you everything, right from the beginning. But I figured if I told you I'd just broken off an engagement, and that I was in the one profession you won't date, that you'd run screaming in the opposite direction."

"You never gave me a chance. And now, I won't give you another one. We have to work together, but beyond that, I don't want to speak to you again."

So much for personal space. Owen invades mine, grabbing my upper arms. "I won't let you do this, Tally. I won't let you throw us away. I was going to tell you about Charlotte at dinner."

To think, Stefani believed Owen was going to ask me to marry him. Oh no, sweet friend, he was going to tell me about the woman to whom he already proposed. Talk about a knife in the heart.

"Really?" It's all I can manage.

"Yes. I didn't talk about her because I never thought I'd see her again. Charlotte means nothing to me."

"I find that impossible to believe. You were engaged. *Two months ago.*"

"Charlotte and I haven't had an actual relationship in years. I stayed because I felt—shit, this is going to sound even worse."

I release a strangled laugh. "I doubt that."

"I left Charlotte two years ago."

"Two months, you mean."

Owen shakes his head, his lips pursed into a thin line. "Two years. I told you, it was not a happy relationship. When her father found out my plan, he called me. He's a powerful man with deep pockets. He knew that I needed an investor for the robotics lab, someone with connections within the government. Otherwise, it could take a decade for all the clearances."

I shrug, uncertain of where he's headed with this story, and whether I even want to hear more. "What's the point, Owen?"

"He offered to front the investment money—all of it—if I would reconsider leaving Charlotte." Owen rubs his brow, looking as

CHAPTER TWENTY-ONE • 213

nauseous as I feel. "I knew how many people we could save. I accepted his offer."

If Owen expects me to thank him for his martyrdom, he's got another thing coming. "I repeat, money can buy happiness."

"I wasn't happy, not with her. Charlotte was sleeping with another man. We slept in separate rooms. But her father wanted bragging rights, saying that his future son-in-law helped to spearhead the robotic cath lab. I was his prize pony. The funny thing is, the man hated me until the day he learned about the project."

"Aww, you poor little millionaire," I hiss, venom dripping from my lips. "Am I supposed to feel sorry for you?"

I know I'm being evil.

He deserves it.

Every last drop of it.

"No, Darlin, I only want you to understand. Charlotte and I have been nothing more than a paper tiger for years." He runs his hand over his scalp, the muscle in his jaw twitching. "I never knew I could feel the way I feel about you."

I hold up my hand. "Just stop with the lies—"

"No, you need to hear this. All my life, I assumed that relationships and marriage were more of an agreement. Crazy, passionate love didn't exist. Then I meet you, and within seconds, I knew you were meant for me. You can be mad at me, but I swear on my life, there is nothing between me and Charlotte."

"You act as if your life means something to me." My voice is so calm, monotone. It's as if all my feelings have packed up and vacated the premises. Good idea, actually.

"I know it does, because you don't have a vicious bone in your body." He picks up his phone. "I was in the shower when you texted. You said you had to speak to me, and that it's important. Talk to me, tell me what's going on, Darlin."

I suck at lying. Always have, always will. *Poker face, don't fail me now.* "Perfect timing, actually. I came by to tell you I can't see you anymore. But you apparently already made that decision. Beat me to the punch."

"I did *not* make that decision. Tally, please stop. You're throwing up another wall, but I'll bash through this one, too."

"Why bother?"

"Because I love you more than I ever thought I could love another person. Tally, you *know* that."

I hate that I love him, too.

He has one last chance and his answer hinges on it. "Are you going to see her again?"

"Fuck," he mutters under his breath. "I don't want to, but she flew out here to discuss this business proposition—"

I wave my hand, stopping him mid-sentence. I'm finished with this conversation. And him. "No more. I've heard enough."

There's that flash of desperation in his face again. "I told Charlotte about you. About us. Here," he grabs his phone, "call her and ask her."

I laugh at the ridiculousness of his statement. "Wow, you never cease and desist, do you? Put your phone down, Owen. I have no intention of calling the woman who not thirty minutes ago claimed she was your fiancée. Not your ex-fiancée. Your fiancée. But Charlotte doesn't have to worry her beautiful little head about us. There is no us. Not anymore."

"Tally—"

My fury unleashes on him, every cell spewing rage in his direction. "You promised me you wouldn't lie anymore. You *promised*. Owen, I'm not an unreasonable person. You're thirty-eight years old, I know you had a life before me. I don't hold that—or Charlotte—against you. I understand if you two have unfinished business. But you don't tell me *anything* about her, or your past. You want me to trust you, but you withhold vital information. You can't play both sides of the coin! I don't know how life operates in your ivory tower, but that's not how the real world works."

His eyes fill with panic as he steps toward me, beseeching me to understand his predicament. Not happening. Not anymore. "I'm not lying, Tally."

"You failed to tell me the whole truth, Owen. That's the same thing." I pull open the door to his condo, my tears making an encore appearance. "You're a fucking bastard for doing this to me, after I was willing to give you another chance."

"Please don't leave, Tally. Let's talk about this. I'm begging you."

"You don't have that right any longer. It's over."

~

I FEEL SORRY FOR THE COP IF I GET PULLED OVER. HE'LL BE STUCK LISTENING to my story, as I sob in the driver's seat, my shoulders hunched from the weight of another betrayal.

Stefani's house isn't far from Owen's condo, which is a good thing because I'm not safe on the roads at the moment. I pull into the driveway and pound on my friend's door. I'm not sure how many more rescue missions she'll abide within a twenty-four-hour period.

"Lu? What in the world happened?" Stefani pulls me into a hug, rubbing a soothing hand along my back. "Is it your Dad?"

I shake my head and open my mouth to speak. Trouble is, every time I do, sobs fall out instead of words. I never realized how many tears one human could hold.

"Shh," she whispers, leading me to the couch. "Sit down. You want some tea?"

I shake my head. It's the only communication I seem capable of, beyond the ever-present crying.

She sits next to me; her face lined with worry. "I thought you'd be at Owen's by now for that big romantic dinner."

Nothing like turning the faucet on full blast. My sobs turn into wails, and I'm thankful her neighbors aren't home. I sound like a damn banshee.

"What did the bastard do? I'm going to kill him." See? That's a ride or die. She doesn't ask questions, just shows up with a shovel to bury the body. She grabs her phone, shaking it in my direction. "Do I need to have a chat with Owen? Because I will. That son of a bitch. Did he tell you to get rid of the baby? Don't you listen to him, Lu. That sorry sack of—"

"He doesn't know about the baby."

Her worry lines deepen into confusion. "Wait, what am I missing?"

"I stopped by Owen's condo earlier. I couldn't wait. I wanted to tell him," I snuffle, wiping my nose with the back of my hand. "You can imagine my surprise when his fiancée answered the door."

My best friend blanches white under her golden spray tan. "His what?" she shrieks.

"His fiancée. She's gorgeous and horribly wealthy and important. Her father financed Owen's robotics cath lab. Single-handedly."

Stefani claps her hand over her mouth, her entire body trembling with anger.

Have I mentioned how much I love this woman?

"Holy shit, Lu. Where the fuck has she been?"

I shrug, because I've no idea. Does it even matter *where* she's been? That she exists is what threw me for a loop. "San Francisco, I suppose."

"I'd love to know how that piece of crap tried to weasel out of this one."

"Owen told me he broke it off when he left San Francisco. But she informed me they were only on a break."

"Which is it?"

"Does it matter?"

"Lu, it *does* matter. If Owen broke up with her, then it's not a big deal."

"Not a big deal?" I shriek, deafening everyone within a quarter-mile vicinity. "He neglected to mention he was engaged! Eight weeks ago."

"They broke up right before he moved here? Damn."

I flop back against the couch cushion. "Yeah. Hi, I'm Tallulah, the rebound girl, who is also pregnant with the bastard's baby."

Stefani strokes my hair, her face awash in sympathy. "What are you going to do?"

"About the baby?" I croak.

"Yeah."

"I'm not telling Owen about the baby. Chances are, he'll be leaving for the west coast soon anyway, since his fiancée has come to fetch him. Did I mention she's gorgeous?"

"You're gorgeous, too, Lu."

I shake my head so hard I'm shocked my brain doesn't rattle. "Not like her. She's pretty like you. She's movie star elegant. I can't imagine what he thought when he was fucking me."

I admit that I'm hosting a pity party, but considering the week I've had, I think I've earned some wallowing time in my sea of sadness.

"Lu, you're beautiful, and Owen is a tool for not telling you about his—whatever she is now. But he still deserves to know he's going to be a father."

"No, he doesn't. Don't you tell him, Stefani."

"Sweetie, you're furious with him for being dishonest, but now you're lying."

"Different scenario."

"Not really. Look," she adds, blotting my eyes with a tissue, "let's just watch a chick flick and camp out on the couch with junk food. Sound good?"

I nod, but in truth, it sounds terrible. I want to be curled up in Owen's arms, feeling him smile against my hair when I tell him he's going to be a Dad.

But, like Mick Jagger said, you can't always get what you want.

CHAPTER
TWENTY-TWO
OWEN

"Mr. Knowles, there's someone here to see you." The aide opens the door to his room, smiling in my direction. "He's not real talkative anymore. Not since the fall. But he can hear you."

I nod, pulling a chair next to Tally's elderly father. He smiles when I say hello, but immediately returns his attention to some distant point.

I know Tally will kill me if she finds me here, but I've driven all over this damn city, and I can't find her anywhere. Somehow, I believe that if the woman I love won't listen to me, perhaps I can get through to her father.

I reach into my pocket, pulling out my trusty deck of cards.

Mr. Knowles' eyes focus on my hands as I walk through the motions of the trick. At the end, his face splits into a grin, and I feel like I've won a damn war.

But the high is short-lived, as his eyes take on that faraway look again.

I lean back in the chair, letting out a loud exhale. "We haven't met, Mr. Knowles. My name is Owen Stevens. I'm ridiculously in love with your daughter." I shift in my seat as I feel his dark eyes on me again. "But I messed up, and she won't speak to me. She's really hard-headed," I chuckle, "but that's part of what I love about Tally. I love everything about her."

I look up, meeting the gaze that is so much like his daughter's. "I was hoping she was here. She loves you so much and judging by the photos,"—I motion at the myriad of pictures surrounding his bed—"you love her, too. I want to marry her, Mr. Knowles, but I'd like your permission first. Then comes the hard part, convincing Tally that I'm not the biggest mistake she's ever made."

I dig into my pocket, pulling out the ring. It hasn't been sized yet, but that can come later. I'll worry about sizing it when I'm certain she won't pitch it across the room. I show Mr. Knowles the ring, smiling as he takes the box and tilts it this way and that, the light reflecting off the stone.

"My wildflower loves pink."

I startle at his voice, shocked that he's speaking to me. "I know. That's why I got her a pink diamond. Do you think Tally will like it?"

He motions to a photo. "Do you know my wildflower?"

I nod, unsure what he can comprehend. "I do. I didn't know that's what you called her."

"After a song," he mumbles, tapping his fingers together, as if scanning his tattered memories for the name.

"I'll look it up. Thank you. Mr. Knowles, I don't know if Tally told you—hell, she hasn't told me—but she's pregnant. We're going to have a baby, and you're going to be a grandpa."

Mr. Knowles struggles to his feet and I grab his arm, worried he might take another fall if I'm not there to catch him. He pulls a piece of paper from the drawer, pressing it into my hands. "Wildflower," he states, nodding at me, begging me to understand.

I look at the drawing, and it's suddenly clear. He understood every word.

CHAPTER TWENTY-TWO

I NEED A DRINK. HELL, I NEED A BOTTLE, BUT I'LL SETTLE FOR ANYTHING alcoholic at the moment. I park my car and head into Wicked Chucks. Maybe, just maybe, Tally is plotting my demise with her friends.

There's a good chance I'll get jumped walking through the door. It's a chance I'm willing to take.

Dan's eyes narrow when he catches sight of me. There's no music tonight, so it's quiet, save for a smattering of locals. "Tell me why I shouldn't wipe the floor with your ass?"

I hold up my hands in surrender. Apparently he's heard the good news. "Give me five minutes to explain and if you still want to kick my ass, I'll give you a free shot."

Dan passes the bar towel from one hand to the other, weighing his options, before barking one word in my direction. "Talk."

I slide onto the seat, running a hand over my face. Here goes nothing. "We got past the whole doctor debacle. I apologized and swore I'd never lie to her again."

"That worked out well."

"I didn't lie—"

"What the hell are you doing here?" I turn my head to see Stefani next to me, a pissed off pout on her lips. "You've got some nerve."

"I've been all over Fort Lauderdale, anywhere I thought Tally might be. This was my last hope." I widen my eyes at Stefani in a non-verbal plea for information.

Not happening. Not even close.

"No way am I telling you where she is. Do you know how badly you hurt Lu today? You are *such* a bastard."

"While I agree with your take, Stef, Owen is trying to explain," Dan interjects, setting two beers down in front of us. "I told him I'd listen."

"Fine," Stefani huffs, settling into the seat next to me. "I can't wait to hear the latest bullshit."

Nothing like playing to a hostile crowd.

I pull out the ring box, sliding it across the bar. "I planned to ask Tally to marry me tonight."

"You believe in bigamy, I see," Stefani snaps, her gaze falling to the velvet box. "Aren't you already engaged?"

"I was until a few months ago. But even then, it was a relationship in name only. There were no emotions involved. I didn't even ask Charlotte to marry me."

"That's her name? Charlotte?"

I nod. "Yes. She demanded a ring, and I was so indebted to her father at the time, I agreed. Besides, I thought that's what you did. You date for a few years and get engaged."

"Didn't you want to get married?"

"Not until I met Tally." I swig back the rest of my beer, motioning for another. Dan can keep them coming. "I designed this ring for her. He only finished it a couple of nights ago."

Curiosity finally wins out. "May I see?"

I flip open the box, watching Stefani's eyes light up.

"Holy shit. Well done, you. That is a huge rock."

"It's not that big," I argue.

"How many carats is this?"

"Four total. That's not the point. Tally is worth every penny. She's worth far more than what I spent on this diamond. I just want to put it on her hand."

"You men never make it easy." Stefani sighs, rubbing her neck, her gaze volleying between the ring, the bar, and me. "Let me get this straight. When you and Lu met, you were not engaged."

"No."

Stefani and Dan exchange looks, and I know they're trying to determine if they should forgive me or hang me. After what feels like an eternity, Dan holds out his hand.

"I can't speak for Stef, but I believe you. Getting Lu to believe you is a different story."

"I'm not that quick to forgive," Stefani cuts in. "You weren't the one holding her while she wept, after being told by your *ex-fiancée* that you two were merely on a break."

That Tally cried—again—over my actions is enough to make me sick. "We are on a break—a permanent one. The worst part is that I told Charlotte about Tally. I said how important she was to me, and how I needed to get done with this business crap because I had a very important dinner. Then Charlotte answered the door while I'm in the shower, and by the time I'm done, all hell had broken loose."

Oh shit, not a good random statement to throw out. Time to fill in the blanks. "That sounded terrible, but it was innocent. Charlotte requested that I meet her for lunch to discuss a business opportunity on behalf of her father."

"I call bullshit," Stefani cuts in, her lips narrowing.

I'm headed straight to the executioner if I don't clear things up fast. "You'd be right. Anyway, the server and I bumped into each other and she dropped coffee on me. Thankfully, it was cold. But I went home to shower, and Charlotte followed me."

"Really?"

Crap, now Stefani doesn't believe me.

"I swear. I wouldn't have dropped all this money on a ring for Tally if I wanted to be with Charlotte. I left San Francisco because I realized how wrong Charlotte and I were together. We made no sense. We had nothing in common. I tired of existing in her world, more like an ornament than a fiancée. Trust me, I don't want Charlotte here. But she's a very spoiled and pampered woman. She's not used to hearing the word no."

"Women can be persistent, Stef," Dan interjects. Thank God for brotherly camaraderie.

Stefani grumbles before nodding. "You're right. Hell hath no fury like a woman scorned. But," she wags her finger at me, "that doesn't make this situation any less screwy. I don't want my friend hurt because your ex can't handle the truth."

Didn't the woman hear a single word I've said? "I don't want to hurt Tally. I fucking adore that woman. And I certainly don't want her upset. She doesn't need the stress."

Another look shifts between Dan and Stefani. Figures. They both know, but my gorgeous vixen won't tell me a word.

"What? You two have something to say?"

They shake their heads. In unison. Pack of liars.

"She's very stressed because of her Dad," Stefani offers.

"She said work has been tough lately," Dan adds.

Now I know they're covering for Tally. "Can't forget that tenacious stomach virus. I've never seen one last for weeks before."

Stefani's pupils dilate, but her face remains impassive. She will not yield. Tally calls the woman her ride or die. Apparently, she's living up to that reputation. "It is bad, but she's under so much stress, I'm not surprised her body is acting out."

I bite my tongue so hard I taste blood. Time to get out of here, before I hold one of them down and make them talk. I toss a fifty on the bar, nodding at Dan. "Cover Stefani for the night, too."

"Thanks."

I gulp down the last of my beer before turning to Stefani. "I'm not going anywhere. I'm not running away, and I'm sure as hell not mad. I love her, and I'll be there for every single moment. You make certain to tell Tally that message."

What I really want to scream is that I know Tally is pregnant, but I also don't want to be wrong. Again. God knows, I suck at reading people lately.

For now, I'll let it slide.

∽

I DRIVE PAST TALLY'S APARTMENT AGAIN, BUT HER CAR IS NOWHERE TO BE found. I'm out of options.

Time to call it a night.

I notice a car parked in the visitor's spot when I pull into the

CHAPTER TWENTY-TWO • 225

parking garage, but it isn't Tally. It's a sparkling white Mercedes convertible.

I'm done playing nice. Storming over to the car, I knock on the window with the force of a police officer.

Charlotte jumps, the phone dropping into her lap as her head jerks up. "You scared the hell out of me. Was that necessary?"

"Is *this* necessary?" I counter, drumming my fingers on the roof of her car. "What are you doing here?"

"I wanted to check on you. Tally seemed very upset earlier."

"Wouldn't have anything to do with you mentioning how we are on a break, would it?"

"Aren't we?"

I bang on the roof of the car, not giving a shit if I leave a dent. "You know damn well we are done."

"I do now. But, despite any pain that might cause me, I still think this business proposition can behoove you. And Tally."

"Because of this *business* proposition, I have no idea where Tally is, Charlotte. I highly doubt you're doing anything with Tally's best interests at heart."

"May I come up and explain?"

I shake my head, leaning against the concrete column. "No. You can tell me right here."

"You're not making this easy, Owen." She huffs out a sigh when she realizes I'm not caving. I'm being difficult. Obstinate. Both things that Charlotte can't stand.

Get used to it, sweetheart.

"I've done a bit of research on your girlfriend."

"You're checking up on her?" My blood boils in my veins. Fucking with me is one thing. But *no one* messes with my tiny vixen.

"Despite what you might believe, I wish her no ill will. But Daddy and I have a vested interest in you. You have an interest in Tally. You see the connection."

"Get to the point," I grit out, unsure how much longer I can hold my tongue.

"Since you're behaving like a barbarian, I'll give you the lowdown in a parking garage," Charlotte snaps, waving her hand at the cars surrounding us. "You and I both know that a robotics cath lab is the way of the future. It enables an entirely new playing field for patients and the medical team. But they cost money. A veritable fortune for the facility, the equipment, and the training."

I nod. This is not new information. The costs are prohibitive, and most hospitals can't budget tens of millions of dollars for a cardiac cath lab that only one or two doctors can operate. The hospitals that need them the most—inner city and rural—aren't even in contention. "What does your father suggest?"

"You and I work together to establish another training facility. The first one will open in South Florida. We rustle up funds from the wealthy here and in the West Palm area, network them with our San Francisco connections, and open up avenues for several future locations across the country."

I hate how good this sounds. The concept of the ultra-rich, all with their eyes on the same prize, is the ultimate aphrodisiac. "What are you going to offer? Naming the facilities after the largest donors?"

"Obviously. I'm not stupid. I have to pet their over-inflated egos. But do you care? Honestly, Owen, with everyone working together, we might open a dozen robotics cath labs within the next two years. But it was you who spearheaded the original project. We need you as the face of the company. Besides, we both remember when I tried to discuss a cholecystectomy with the orthopedic surgeon."

I bite back a laugh. It was one of the few times that Charlotte ever appeared flustered. Or human. "I recall that dinner. However, in your defense, you held it together beautifully."

Charlotte smiles. She needs to do that more. Real, genuine smiles, not the fake crap she flashes for the camera. "Thank you, even though I know you're lying. We have to target the top cardiologists and surgeons in this area. You not only speak their language, you can empathize with them, get them on our side. We need them

CHAPTER TWENTY-TWO

to bend the ears of the local politicians." She grabs my forearm. "I know you hate this dog and pony show, but it's the only way. Daddy can crawl the backs of his friends, but then it's more his baby than it is yours. You deserve the accolades, Owen. I want to help you get them."

My back stiffens at her direct offer of help. Her deal makes sense, and I think it will work. It will require a ton of effort, but what price do you put on saving lives? I can muddle through a dozen meetings, presentations and banquets, if it clears the way for the cath labs to open for the patients who need them. "Why are you doing this, Charlotte?"

She focuses her emerald gaze on a distant point, and for the first time, I see the hesitancy in her face. "Let's just call it my personal apology for the way I treated you. I'm not very good with emotions, but I'm an amazing businesswoman. Use me, use my connections. Let's get this done."

"You also said this would help Tally, but I see no connection."

The softness in Charlotte's face disappears as she rounds her shoulders. Back to business as usual. "She's in a very unstable financial predicament, as I'm sure you're aware. She pays thousands for her father and donates what little time and money she has to the women's shelter. She's broke, Owen."

I stare at the ground, feeling sick to my stomach. I knew it was bad, but I didn't know the details. She didn't offer, and I didn't push. Charlotte, apparently, has no such qualms. "I make plenty of money. I can take care of Tally."

There's that famous tongue click again. I know this discussion is difficult for Charlotte, but so is the fact that the woman I planned on proposing to is MIA, and I don't have the first clue where to look. "She doesn't seem the type to accept charity. With the training center open, there will be many positions available. Agree to this deal, and I'll see that Tally gets a suitable position, with all the perks."

"Here, in South Florida. You're not sending her to Kansas."

Charlotte chuckles. "I'll give her a choice of locations. Where she goes will be up to her, not you." She extends her hand. "Do we have a deal?"

I hesitate, realizing that my plan to have a one-and-done lunch with my ex has now turned into an extensive project. Still, it's for the greater good, and she's willing to help my Tally. "This is not a reconciliation," I reiterate.

"This is a business deal, Owen. That's all." She pulls her hand back, grabbing a stack of paperwork. "Here is the business plan for you to peruse at your leisure. Please make any adjustments. I'll be hosting a dinner in ten days, to introduce the concept of the training facility. I've invited all the bigwigs and their deep pockets. You're expected to attend."

"Can't wait," I mutter.

"Owen, I know that you're upset about your fight with Tally, but this is an enormous opportunity. It goes far beyond what you or I want. Besides, you need to realize that this isn't a cakewalk for me, either. I didn't expect to find you with someone new. We all need to be adults in this situation."

I nod in agreement, but I pray that Tally understands. It might be too far gone for her to even consider. Then I think about what Charlotte said, how Tally spends her few leftover dollars on the shelter. That's her baby, and this is mine.

If anyone can understand why I need to do this, it's my tiny vixen. She has the most giving heart I've ever known. Now I just have to convince her to give that heart back to me.

CHAPTER
TWENTY-THREE
TALLY

"How's your food?"

I smile at Stefani. The woman has been glued to my side since the whole Owen debacle. Yes, that's what I'm calling the shit storm that is my life. "It's hospital fare. We aren't setting the bar too high."

She leans back in her chair, gauging me. Oh crap, here it comes. "Are you going to speak to him?"

I shove my food around my plate, avoiding her insistent stare. "Nope."

"That's it? Just nope?"

"I think that's a perfectly acceptable answer."

Stefani leans forward, grasping my forearm. "Only two problems with that answer. One is that you desperately love him, and the second is that you're carrying his child."

"Both are facts that Dr. Stevens never needs to know."

She shakes her head, tapping her fingers on the table. Yes, she has gone over—several times—how Owen stopped by Wicked Chucks and how desperate he was to speak to me. She swears up and down that the man is crazy in love with me, and that Charlotte is not a threat.

The trouble with all that? She's not on the receiving end of a bucket of lies, and she also didn't see the woman who wore Owen's ring.

I know it's petty. I know looks don't mean everything. Or they shouldn't. But I also know that when you put me and Charlotte together on a menu—she's filet mignon and I'm swiss steak. In other words? No comparison.

"Lu, you know that's not fair."

I release a groan, shoving my plate to the side. "You act like he's going to care and want to be involved. He has an opportunity to go back to his former life. I can't imagine why anyone would ever leave a world like that."

"He was miserable, or so he claims."

"And he's happy here, dating a nurse, when he was engaged to a woman whose father owns half of San Francisco? Come on, Stefani, let's not buy into another of Owen's stories."

My friend grasps my hands, squeezing them tight. "Then how about one of my stories? Will you listen to it?"

I soften, realizing that I've been a terrible friend this past week. I've been so focused on my predicament that a nuclear bomb could have exploded in Stef's life, and I wouldn't notice. "Always. I'm sorry that I've been so distracted."

"It's understandable, but I need you to hear my story before you make any final decisions about keeping Owen out of the loop. Do you remember when my family friend passed away from leukemia four years ago?"

I tap my finger against my chin, searching my memory banks. "I believe so. You'd only come back into contact with him recently, right?"

Stefani nods, her eyes filling with tears. "He wasn't a family friend. He was my birth father."

I'm glad I'm sitting, because I was not ready for that news. I've

CHAPTER TWENTY-THREE • 231

met Stefani's father; she calls him Dad. Suddenly two and two isn't four. "He's...wait, what?"

"The man who raised me isn't my biological father, but I didn't learn that until five years ago, when my birth father appeared on my doorstep. At first, I thought he was an escaped lunatic, but then I realized that I look just like him. Spitting image. So, I called my mother, and she confirmed it."

"Where the hell had he been?"

"Prison for the first few years and then rebuilding his life. He tried to establish a connection with me, but my parents threw up every roadblock, even resorting to blackmail. My mother thought she was protecting me, but in truth, she robbed me of knowing my birth father."

"That explains why you were so devastated when he died."

Stefani nods, pulling a sip from her water. "I only got a year with him, and he was sick for most of it. It took another year for me to forgive my parents for keeping me in the dark."

"I don't want my child to hate me for my choices." Her story sends my mind spiraling. It casts an entirely new perspective on the situation, one my anger and jealousy wouldn't allow before.

"Owen deserves to know. What he does with that information is up to him. If he acts like an asshole, cut him loose and never look back. But Lu," she grabs my hand again, "he told me and Dan at the bar he loves you and will be there for every single moment. Sweetie, he knows."

I'm shaking my head before she finishes. "I'm sure he doesn't know, Stef. But I will give my decision some serious thought. Thank you for sharing that with me. I'm sorry you had to endure it."

She wipes her eyes, forcing a smile. "Exactly. Which is why I don't want my future godchild going through it."

I chuckle at her assumption, even though she's right. Who else would I pick? "It's hard. I thought I found the one with Owen, but now I see that we have nothing in common."

"That's not true. He's still the same guy."

"No, he's this ultra-wealthy cardiologist who was about to marry into a family of billionaires. He's partied on private islands and yachts. I can't afford a dinghy." I motion to myself, moving my hands along my sides. "And his ex-fiancée, she looks exactly like a doctor's wife should look." I hate saying those words, but it's true. After seeing her, I realize that Owen went slumming with me.

"I'll bet Charlotte isn't nearly as beautiful as you think."

I choke on my water. "Trust me, she puts catwalk models to shame."

"It's probably all plastic surgery."

"Does it matter? The woman is the definition of perfection. It's funny though, and maybe it's wishful thinking, but they don't fit together. Both are so beautiful, but they seem mismatched somehow."

Stefani perks up at my words. "You see? You and Owen were disgustingly cute. The way you looked at each other, and all those caresses and kisses on the down low—don't think I didn't see them. You two were made for each other."

I would argue, but we were adorable. The spark between me and Owen could light up the eastern seaboard. It doesn't help my bruised ego, though. "I know that I'm cute and cool, but I'm also clumsy and fun-sized and hide behind glasses."

"All things I love about you."

My head flies up and I narrow my eyes at Owen, standing right behind my chair. I should be used to the man's secondary talent as a ninja by now, but as usual, he took me by surprise. It's the first words he's said to me since the showdown at his condo. No notes this time, either. He must realize we're too far past that point.

"I see the glare is going strong today," Owen comments, resting his hand on the back of my chair, his thumb tracing across my back. The move is subtle, and to anyone else, it looks innocent. But for me, it's stoking an already simmering inferno.

I sit up, scooting toward the edge of the chair, ensuring his hand can't touch any part of my body. Ever again.

CHAPTER TWENTY-THREE • 233

"I guess that's as close to a hello as I'm going to get, isn't it, Tally? Hi, Stefani."

My best friend nods in his direction but says nothing. She's struggling not to get involved, and I know she's torn with whom to support in this battle.

"Can I get you ladies anything? A coffee refill, a piece of cake."

Hell, no, we are *not* exchanging pleasantries. "You have a doctor's lounge," I snap, half turning in my chair to send him a withering glare. "Why are you here?"

"I was checking up on you. I do that about a million times a day." He stalks off and I swivel back in my seat, meeting Stefani's surprised look.

"What?"

"Lu—"

"What?" I repeat, my frustration mounting. "What do you have to add to this already crappy situation?"

"Nothing. Just know that I love you and please consider what I told you. I'm heading back."

I nod, pulling out my e-reader. "I have another fifteen minutes before my next meeting. Going to catch up on some reading."

She buses my tray for me, so I can focus on the next chapter. I'm devouring pregnancy books. I'm scared to death at what this little nugget is going to do to my body. I may be a nurse, but I don't know nothing about birthing no babies.

"Can I talk to you?"

Oh shit, Owen is back. Without looking up, I mutter, "I'm on lunch. Can it wait?"

My snappy question is met with silence. I finally pull my gaze from the book and meet his stormy one. I can tell by the look in his eyes the answer to my question. "Not really." Then Owen glances at my e-reader.

I press the button in a vain attempt to close the screen, but the man is too fast. He grabs the reader, his eyes widening. "What to Expect When You're Expecting?"

"Give me that," I bark, reaching for my reader. Damn him and his long arms. I don't stand a chance.

"Tally, what's going on?"

Time to play dumb. I despise the concept of the ditzy woman, but I'm about to test my acting chops with that role. "No idea. You wanted to speak to me, remember?"

"Darlin, why won't you admit that you're pregnant?" Owen sinks into the chair across from me, but I can't read his expression. He isn't angry, just guarded.

I cross my fingers under the table. God needs to understand. This is about survival. The survival of my heart. "It's for a woman at the shelter. I know very little about obstetrics, so I'm helping her understand some nuances. Not that I owe you an explanation."

Then I feel it, his hand on my thigh, tightening ever so slightly. "You're a terrible liar, Tally."

"I guess I should take some pointers from you, huh?"

I couldn't have hit harder with a baseball bat. He swallows audibly, but his hand never leaves my leg. "If that's what it took to have that time with you, I'd lie all over again. Loving you is worth it to me." He slides back the chair, grabbing a pad of paper and a pen from his pocket. He scribbles something down before sliding it across the table to me. "This book is better. You deserve the best. I'll get you a list of the best obstetricians in the area...for the woman at the shelter."

He squeezes the paper into my hand before striding out of the cafeteria.

With trembling fingers, I unfold the note. It's the name of a different baby book and underneath it, four words.

I'll keep fighting, Darlin.

It's in moments like these that staying angry with Owen is exceedingly difficult. Couple that with Stefani's heartfelt plea to tell Owen the truth about the baby, and my heart and mind are as confused as a rat in a maze. My stubbornness may be legendary, but even it knows some boundaries.

CHAPTER TWENTY-THREE

∽

I SPEND THE NEXT COUPLE OF DAYS TRYING NOT TO ENVISION WHAT OWEN may or may not be doing with his ex-fiancée. I hate Charlotte's beauty, how she's the complete opposite of me. I hate that Owen gave her a ring and planned to spend his life at her side.

But the worst part? That they might reconcile and live out a perfect life in their ivory tower.

I get it. I do. Charlotte is worth more money than I can earn in ten lifetimes. Her family owns properties around the world, villas in Monaco and bungalows in Fiji. They have private jets and can finance a few third-world countries, should the desire arise.

How do I know this? In my downtime, I replaced my fedora with an inspector's cap. I've been digging, not that it's hard to find information on the Auerback family. Their lives are the stuff of legends.

With them, Owen is set. He'll live a jet-set lifestyle, hobnobbing with celebrities and royalty.

Why would he ever settle for a normal woman like me?

Granted, I guarantee I'm a hell of a lot more fun than Charlotte—in and out of the sack.

I groan aloud. I didn't want that visual. *Sorry, Nugget.*

"Are you okay?"

I shift in my seat, nodding at Owen's concerned expression. In his defense, I groaned audibly in the conference room at Memorial. But I need him to stop being so caring. I can't ever get over him if he continues to be nice to me. "Yeah, I forgot to do something for work."

"Is this seat taken?" he motions at the chair next to me. There are empty spots all around the table. Why must he take the one next to me?

My mind is furious with the man, but my body is hot as hell for him. Just hearing his voice makes me flush with desire. I shake my head, catching the faint whiff of his cologne as he settles into the chair.

Pulling my braid to one side, I fiddle with the end. It's a nervous habit, but I have to focus on something. Namely, because my mind wants to scream at him, and my body wants to rip his clothes off.

I need professional help.

Then I feel it. His fingers move along my neckline, stirring up every nerve ending.

"Your tag was sticking out," he murmurs, his hand lingering against my skin.

"Funny. The scrub top is tagless," I volley back, maintaining a focused gaze on my laptop.

Owen chuckles, but he doesn't move his hand. "Caught me. I needed to touch you, Darlin. Even for a second."

Damn these pregnancy hormones. My eyes fill with tears, which I blink back. *I will maintain focus and control. I will maintain focus and control.*

Then he speaks again, cutting into my internal mantra. "How are you feeling? How's your stomach?"

"Fine."

"No more stomach virus?"

I shrug, but I don't look at him. I can't. If I meet his gaze, it's all over. I'll cave. Again. "All better."

"Glad to hear it. We should grab a drink after work. Celebrate."

My stomach flips. "What are we celebrating?"

"You."

"Me?"

"Yes. You feeling better. Unless," his fingers are back on my nape again, "there's something else you'd like to share. Something exciting we can celebrate together."

The nerve of this man. Damn him for being so intuitive. I open my mouth to retort, throw out some zinger about celebrating the return of his illustrious fiancée, but Dr. Watts strolls in, signaling the start of the meeting.

CHAPTER TWENTY-THREE • 237

"Is that a yes?"

I finally meet his gaze, ready to cut him down for his brazen arrogance. But one look at his face silences me. I've never seen his eyes so searching before. It's a false bravado, his upbeat statements. I see it in his face. He's terrified. "I—I don't know, Dr. Stevens."

"It's not a no. I'll take it."

As the introductions start and the lights dim for the presentation, my mind remains on the man at my side.

You can't give him another chance, Tallulah. You have already given him enough.

Without thinking, I place my hand on my stomach, glancing down at where Nugget lives. I want this baby to have a father. A man who loves this child as much as I do. But how do I separate our involvement together into boxes? I don't think I'm that strong. Hell, I know I'm not.

Something touches my knee, and I look up. Owen's eyes are on me, vacillating between my face and my stomach, a small smile on his lips.

He knows.

Thankfully, Dr. Watts starts speaking, and I force my mind back to the present. She's singing Owen's praises, but they're all deserved. Under his tutelage, we are expanding the cardiac cath lab, a smart move considering our aged population.

In the short time that Owen has been a member of Memorial's medical team, he has put into flux a huge number of changes. The most impressive part? They're all for the betterment of the patients and staff.

Dr. Watts gives Owen the floor, and he discusses the training facility. I want to hate the idea, since it's what brought Owen and Charlotte together again. But the concept is brilliant. Furthermore, it's desperately needed to improve outcomes.

The facility will be state-of-the art, ensuring Memorial is regarded around the globe as a center of cardiac renown. Dr. Owen

Stevens is a genius, and I'm as engrossed as the rest of the folks by his pleasant manner and engaging presentation.

There's no pompousness there, Owen is truly excited by the idea of helping others. He's like a kid at Christmas, speaking about improved patient outcomes.

A kid at Christmas.

Our baby will be here next Christmas. If Owen is one iota as excited about our child as he is about the training facilities, he'll be most the wonderful father, even if there's nothing more between us.

I swallow back the overwhelming emotions flooding my body. Damn hormones. I cry at the drop of a hat these days, and my co-workers will think I've lost my last vestiges of sanity if I start bawling as Owen discusses training labs.

"I know we'll need Tally's expertise to get everything running smoothly."

I snap from my reverie at the mention of my name. Crap, what did I miss while I was ogling the gorgeous cardiologist? "Sorry, what will I be doing?" I inquire, adjusting my glasses with an embarrassed laugh.

"Dr. Stevens was singing your praises, Lu. Or is Tally? That's what he called you. Which do you prefer?" Dr. Watts inquires with a smile.

My face flushes as Owen slides back into his seat, his body brushing against mine. He had plenty of room. That was *not* accidental. "Only a select few people call me Tally."

I realize, one second too late, that I just announced that Owen isn't like most people. At least where I'm concerned. I pray it slips by unnoticed, but the medical director chuckles, moving on to the next topic.

Busted.

I look at Owen, sending an apologetic glance. "I was listening, but I zoned out at the end. Sorry."

"It's okay. I was singing your praises. Not all of them, of course," he adds with a wink. "Only a select few people know the real Tally.

I'm lucky to be one of them. I plan on spending my life with you, Darlin, whether or not you like it."

His statement damn near bowls me over, but I don't have time to react. Stefani pokes her head into the room, and my heart sinks to the floor when I see her expression. She's drawn, biting her lower lip as she motions for me.

Oh crap, I hope no one fell. That will make for a banner afternoon.

"Everything okay?" Owen questions, and I feel his hand brush my leg in a supportive gesture.

I shrug. That's the best I can offer at the moment.

As soon as I step out of the room, a cold fear floods every cell of my body. Standing next to Stefani is the chaplain. "Oh, no," I groan, slumping against the wall.

"Come on, Lu, let's get you somewhere private." Stefani wraps her arm around me, attempting to steer me out of the hallway.

I'm standing my ground. "When?"

"They found him this morning. They think he suffered a massive heart attack and died instantly. I'm so sorry, Lu."

My Dad, my champion, is gone. The man who gave me piggyback rides and told stories of caves with dragons and knights, is no more. I fall back against the wall, hugging myself as the dam of emotions threatens to break loose.

I pull off my glasses, wiping at my eyes to ebb the flow of tears. I rub my hand under my nose, and I'm sure anyone passing by will think I just lost my best friend.

They'd be right.

"What the hell's going on? Tally, Darlin, what happened?" Owen's hand grasps my shoulder.

I don't care who sees. I need Owen now. I grab him around the waist, burying my head into his chest. There's no hesitation on his part as he enfolds me in his embrace, his fingers stroking my hair.

"Her Dad died," Stefani whispers. "I know my friend is dealing with her own grief over my father's death. She knew Mr. Knowles before the demon that is dementia seized his soul.

"Oh, Christ. I'm so sorry, Darlin. I'm here."

That's all it takes for the levy to break. My body shakes with sobs, but for the first time since the discovery of Charlotte, I feel safe.

Owen is the only place I feel this way. How is it that the same man who breaks your heart is the only one who can heal it?

The sobs subside after a few minutes, giving way to sniffles. Not once did Owen loosen his grip. He tips my chin up, thumbing away my tears as I force a smile.

"I got your coat wet," I mumble, wiping at my leaky nose and eyes.

"It's fine. It's more than fine. Let's get you out of here, okay? I'll tell everyone that I'm taking you home. Stef, will you get Tally's things for me?" Just like that, Owen takes charge.

He disappears into the conference room, and I make a beeline for the bathroom. There are a ton more tears to cry, but I don't want to field questions from everyone as I walk out of the hospital. Just like my nickname, only a select few are privy to my grief. Owen is one of them.

"Lu, are you in here?" Stefani asks.

"Yeah. Come on in." I unlock the door, and my friend grabs me into another hug.

"I'll be over right after my shift. I've put some calls out to get someone from night shift to come in a few hours early—"

"It's okay. Really. Owen will take care of me."

"See? I told you, he's crazy about you."

I nod, but I'm not entirely certain. He's not an ogre, I'll give him that. When I needed him, he was there. Just like he said he would be.

Too bad that doesn't excuse the other situations, but I can't focus on those right now. I need to focus on breathing.

"Owen asked if you could give him a few minutes. He's talking to some woman."

It's an innocent statement. The woman could be anyone. But

CHAPTER TWENTY-THREE • 241

Charlotte is supposed to be present during the meeting today, and intrinsically, I know it's her. "Where are they?"

"I think they went to his office."

I nod, a flash of anger overtaking the sorrow. "Tall, thin, gorgeous?"

"I wasn't really paying attention…yeah," Stefani admits when I shoot her a scathing glare.

"That would be Charlotte."

"What the hell is she doing at the hospital?"

"She and Owen are working together. Her family is financing the training center. Beyond that, I don't know what's going on with them. Doesn't matter." I ball up the towel, tossing it in the bin. "You have my things?"

Stefani nods, handing me my purse.

"Thanks. I'm going to get out of here."

"What about Owen?"

"Owen's busy. He has a training facility to build. I have a funeral to plan."

"Lu, let him help you."

"He helped. He let me cry it out. This isn't his problem, Stef." I give my friend a kiss on the cheek, offering a sad smile. "I got this."

"Please Lu, I know you're strong but the man—"

"I'm not angry at Owen. There's no point. It's a terrific undertaking, building the training facility. It's going to help so many people, Stefani. Owen needs Charlotte. Sometimes you have to sleep with the enemy. Will you thank him for me?"

"He's going to be furious if you leave without telling him," Stefani warns.

"No, he won't. We both have jobs to do, people to take care of. I'll see you later."

I pull open the bathroom door, stopping short. Not ten feet in front of me stands Owen and Charlotte.

Just wonderful.

"Tally, I didn't know where you were." Owen rushes forward, wrapping his arm around my shoulders. "Are you ready?"

I look past him, to where Charlotte stands observing the scene. I don't pick up on any hostility from her, but then, I'm not picking up on *any* emotion from her. "I'm ready."

"Let's go."

I put my hand to his chest. "I know you're busy. I can handle this alone."

His eyes bulge, and he shakes his head. "No way in hell, Tally."

"But Charlotte needs you—"

"No, she doesn't. You do, even if you'd sooner die than admit it."

I open my mouth to protest, but one look at his steel-gray eyes tells me to drop the argument. I'm not winning this one. "I have to go to the funeral home and—" It's all I can manage, as Owen presses my head to his chest.

"We'll get it done, Darlin," he murmurs, guiding me down the hall.

"I'm sorry for your loss," Charlotte says as we walk past, but I can only mumble a garbled thanks.

I don't have the energy to fight anyone anymore.

CHAPTER
TWENTY-FOUR
OWEN

"I'll meet you at the apartment," Tally says, forcing a smile as she digs out her keys.

I snatch the keys from her hand, shoving them in my pocket. "Nice try. We're leaving your car here."

"But I need my car—"

"We'll use my car. This is not an argument you're going to win. Now, you can get into my car or you can go digging for your keys." I have to speak Tally's language. Namely, sarcasm with a challenge.

I see her weighing her options, before sliding into my passenger side seat.

I glance over at her, my heart breaking. She looks so small and lost. "Would you rather take care of the planning first or go home and rest?"

She shrugs as a fat tear rolls down her cheek, underneath her glasses. "Might as well get the planning done. It's not involved. My father didn't want a big funeral. Hated the idea of a bunch of strangers standing around and pretending they gave a crap."

"Sounds like my Dad. He didn't want a ceremony. Told me and

my mom to scatter his ashes in the North Carolina mountains he loved so much."

"Do you miss North Carolina?"

"I love the mountains, and the change of seasons. Plus, my family is there."

"So, that's a yes," she offers, her delicate fingers tracing along the dash, creating aimless designs.

"I'll take you to my home one day. You'll love it, Tally."

She doesn't respond. She doesn't have to. I see the doubt and uncertainty in her face. I may be less than six feet from her, but I'm miles away from the door to her heart.

We spend the next few hours making funeral arrangements and ensuring everything is just as Mr. Knowles would want it. In summary—little to no fanfare. But that's easy compared to what lies ahead.

My girl has to say goodbye to her father before his body heads to the crematorium.

She's shaking when I park at the funeral home, unable to stop the onslaught of tears dripping down her cheeks. "I don't think I can do this," she whispers, and my heart shatters under the weight of her pain.

I grasp her hand, running my thumb along hers. "You're the strongest woman I know. You can do this, Tallulah Knowles, and I'll be right there beside you the whole way."

Finally, she meets my gaze, forcing a small smile. "Promise?"

"I promise, Darlin." I'm a strong man. I pride myself on the ability to present a brave face to the world. But I'm scared shitless. This is not your normal, run-of-the-mill errand. The woman I love has to tell her last goodbye to the body that held her father, and I'm not sure how she's going to handle it. How either of us will handle it.

The funeral director leads us to a room, sliding the door closed behind us. There, in a simple coffin, lies the body of Mr. Knowles. Tally squeezes my hand and I press my lips to her fingers. She needs to know I'm here. I'm not going anywhere.

CHAPTER TWENTY-FOUR

With a deep breath, she releases my hand and walks to the casket, her fingers gripping the side as she gazes down at her Dad. Then I hear the impossible. A chuckle.

"You okay, Darlin?"

She holds up the bag of clothes she brought for his final journey. "My father never got over his love of plaid pants. The more ridiculous, the better. He and I used to argue that when he died, I would bury him in a sensible navy suit."

I join her at the coffin, trying to read her emotions. "I guess he didn't like that idea?"

"Hated it," she giggles. She opens the bag, pulling out a ridiculous pair of plaid pants in a mix of orange, green, and blue. "You won, Dad. Here's to going out in style."

And then she breaks. Thankfully, I'm there to catch her in my arms, pulling her tight against me as the cries wrack her tiny frame. If I could, I'd take on every ounce of her pain, but all I can do is hold her until the sobs ease and her body softens against mine.

Tally gazes up at me, wiping her face and nose. "I must look awful right now."

That's a lie. She's never been more beautiful, even with the puffy eyes and reddened face. She's so genuine, so tangible. She's everything I never knew existed in this world. "You're always gorgeous."

"Liar," she laughs, pushing off me. "Would you give me a few minutes?"

I nod, stepping outside the door. I hear her speaking to her father, but I can't make out the words. They're not for me to hear. I text my mother and let her know what's happened. It's ironic. In all my years with Charlotte, my mother never warmed to her. It took thirty seconds for her to adore Tally.

The door opens and Tally steps out, nodding at the funeral director. "I'm ready to go."

We arrive back at her apartment, and I pull the bottle of vodka from the freezer. I know it's a dick move, but maybe after the events of today, she'll talk.

I pour two shots, holding one out to her. "You've earned this."

Tally shakes her head, solidifying her pregnancy in my brain. "I've got a headache."

"Vodka cures everything, haven't you heard?"

"I'm going to take a shower."

I want to join her. Hell, I'm tempted to sneak in behind her and kiss away the pain. But I hold back. It's definitely not the right time.

Tally passes out in bed right after the shower, her last remnants of energy drained. I tuck her in, stealing a kiss for the first time in almost a week. Christ, I miss this woman.

But I have another problem to deal with—and her name is Charlotte. My phone has been blowing up, with calls and texts from my ex.

The woman can't be serious.

I step onto Tally's porch, noting how the one side sags with age. No way will I let her stay here much longer. Not happening.

I answer the incoming call on the first ring. Time to put Charlotte back in her place. "This is not a good time."

"How is she?"

"Do *not* tell me you called ten times and texted ten more to inquire how Tally is feeling."

"No, but it seemed the courteous thing to ask."

I release a groan, scrubbing my face with my hand. "What do you need, Charlotte?"

"I've sent out the invitations for the banquet, and we've already gotten quite the response."

"That's great." It is great. The more investors involved, the less the Auerback family needs to contribute, and I won't feel indebted to them again.

"I want you to accompany me to the dinner."

"As your date?"

CHAPTER TWENTY-FOUR • 247

"Don't sound so horrified. Not as a date, just an escort. We are the two people spearheading this facility, Owen. It would make sense."

"I disagree."

"Will you at least consider it?"

A headache brews behind my eyes. "Charlotte, please don't push this issue. Especially not today. I have to go. Do you need anything else?"

There's a few seconds pause before she sighs, letting me off the hook—and call. "No. We can discuss the details at another time. Goodnight."

"Is she angry?"

I whip around. Tally is standing in the doorway, biting her lower lip. Wonderful. This is all she needs. Part of me wants to pretend it wasn't Charlotte on the phone, but I've seen how well dishonesty has worked in the past. "She wanted to see how you were doing."

I see Tally chewing the words, tasting them for sincerity. "That's kind of her. I'm fine, if you need to go."

"I don't need to go." I close the distance between us, stiffening when her hands raise, blocking any additional forward movement.

"You've been a tremendous help, Owen, but Stefani will be here any minute. Go, take care of Charlotte."

"I told you earlier, Charlotte can take care of herself."

"So can I, Owen."

"I know you can, but dammit, Tally, I *want* to take care of you."

"Because you think I need the help?" Tears bubble in her eyes again, and I can only imagine what mental film reel is rolling in her brain, starring me and my ex-fiancée.

"No, because I love you. I love every single, sexy, saucy inch of you."

"Was she a model? She looks like one."

I hate where this conversation is headed. "Yes, she modeled a bit in Europe."

There goes that lip biting again. She motions to herself, then throws up her hands and shrugs. "I don't get it."

"Get what?"

"She's gorgeous, filthy rich, and connected. I'm none of those things—"

"You sure as hell are gorgeous. Don't let me hear you say that again."

"Or what?"

There she is. My sultry vixen coming out to play. Even if it's only for a minute, I'm so damn happy to see her. "I'll find all sorts of ways to pleasure—I mean punish you."

"Tell me why, Owen."

"Darlin, I don't know what you're asking."

"Why are you here?"

"I love you, Tally."

"You don't even know me."

"I know you. I've known you since before this lifetime." I send her a narrowed look. "Don't deny it, either. I know damn well that you feel the same way."

Her gaze drops to her t-shirt as she picks off imaginary lint. "You were a great friend today."

Oh Jesus, please don't tell me I've landed in the friend zone. "I'm much more than a friend."

"I can't handle anything beyond friendship right now."

Houston, we have a situation.

I stare at her beautiful, tear-stained face and trembling lips, realizing that she doesn't need additional stress. If Tally is setting boundaries because of my behavior, I need to respect them, even though I loathe them. "I'll be whatever you need, Darlin."

There, that should cover all the bases.

Her front door opens and Stefani walks in, preventing any further conversation. She smiles, giving me a peck on the cheek. "Thank you."

I force a smile, even though I feel like I took a knife to the gut. At least I'm in her life again. Now comes the hard part—convincing her to fall for me one last time.

I leave thirty minutes later. Tally is safe with her friend, and I'm in desperate need of a drink.

I've been sidelined by the woman I'm in love with, and I can't blame her. I failed to tell her the whole truth—twice—and now, my past has pushed its way into my present, mucking up everything in its path.

But today, when Tally's world fell apart, she clung to me. I was her lifeline.

I know there's hope and I'm like a tenacious bulldog, holding on to that glimmer at the end of a shit-laden tunnel.

THE DAYS BETWEEN MR. KNOWLES'S DEATH AND THE FUNERAL WERE RAINY and depressing. But on the day of his service, the sun is shining brightly.

I'm running a few minutes behind, adjusting my tie as I walk to the gravesite. Per her father's wishes, the service is simple. A group of about forty people stand around the grave, and I'm certain Tally is shocked by the turnout.

She didn't think anyone would show. But it turns out Mr. Knowles is as beloved as his daughter. I catch sight of Tally, her head resting on Stefani's shoulder. She's lucky to have a friend like that. Hell, they're both lucky. Genuine friendships are rare in this world.

Dan stands at her elbow, nodding in my direction when he catches sight of me. I'm not sure if he approves of my continued quest to win back Tally's love or if he's acting as a sentry to protect her from me—either way, I'm not caving until she's back in my arms.

The minister finishes, mentioning that Tally would like to say a few words. She takes the microphone and even from this distance I see her slight hands tremble. I close the space between us until only a few feet separate me from the woman I love.

"I'm overwhelmed that you all came to see my Dad off on his next journey. Adventure, as he'd like to say. Maybe it was the plaid pants that attracted you all." A hum of laughter carries through the group, and even my beautiful girl manages a tremulous smile. "I hate that he's gone, but I know he's whole again, and he's with my Mom. I can't imagine the parties they've been holding in heaven since his arrival. I'm serious, the man could drink us all under the table."

God, she's gorgeous. So raw and real. Loving her is the single most right thing I've ever done in my life.

"He would hate all this crying and sadness. He'd tell me to rub dirt on it and get on with it." Her hand rests on the tombstone, tears streaming down her face. "He said he would visit us, let us know he's okay. I'm holding you to that, Dad, because even though you're okay, I'm not sure I am. I'll love you forever." She breaks, her body trembling with sobs, and I'm at her side in a few long strides.

I pull her to me, hoping I can hold her tight enough to ease the pain. "It's okay, Darlin. Let it out." I stroke her dark hair, my lips pressed against her head as she collapses against me.

Mourners and well-intentioned friends break into the moment, paying their respects with a kind word or pat on the shoulder. I stand my ground, my Tally tucked into me, shielding her from the onslaught.

"I think you would have liked him," she mumbles against my chest.

"I did."

Her head jerks up, a look of confusion crossing her features. "What?"

"I met him, Wildflower."

Her hand flies to her mouth as a fresh supply of tears stream down her cheeks. "When?"

"Last week."

"He spoke to you?"

I nod, reaching into my pocket to grab the drawing, but Stefani's voice cuts into our privacy.

"Hi, Owen. Will you be joining us at the restaurant?"

Crap. "I want to, but I have a meeting—"

Tally shakes her hand, dispelling my worries. "You're fine."

"I'll cancel it," I blurt, pulling out my phone. If Tally needs me, screw the meeting. Yes, it's an important meet and greet, with a potential whale of an investor, but Tally is more important. She'll always come first. That's what I swore that night in my office. I plan on living up to that promise.

Tally stays my hand. "No need to cancel. I'm okay. Hungry and tired, but okay. Thank you for coming, Owen. You didn't have to."

"Yes, I did."

"You've been a wonderful friend through all of this."

I cringe at the use of the term friend. I get it, I do, but I still hate it. "I would do anything for you. I'm serious, say the word, and I'll cancel that meeting."

"Go on." Tally stands on tiptoe, brushing her lips against my cheek, before walking off with Stefani and Dan.

I watch her leave, sandwiched between her friends, her tiny frame supported by their love. I'm on the outside, looking in, and I'm not sure where to find the key to unlock her door again.

"WHAT ARE YOU DOING HERE?" DAN INQUIRES, LEANING AGAINST THE DOOR of Tally's apartment.

I could ask you the same question.

I can't put my finger on it, but the way Dan held Tally at the funeral is rubbing me wrong. Maybe I'm just a jealous fuck and *anyone* holding my girl drives me nuts.

"I wanted to check on Tally. I brought her dinner."

Dan waves me into the apartment. "I already brought her dinner, but hey, the more the merrier, right?"

No. Wrong, actually. I force a nod, my lips pursed. I know I have no right to say anything. At least, that's what I keep repeating in my head.

"Hey, you're a surprise." Tally walks out of the bedroom, wearing a baggy t-shirt and shorts. I know she's dressed down, but she looks good enough to eat, and that thought is enough to make my dick twitch. "How was your meeting?"

I know what she means. "It was fine. Productive." I meet her gaze and hate the next words that fall from my mouth. "Charlotte sends her regards."

If the statement flusters Tally, she doesn't let it show, save for a small, sad smile crossing those full lips.

Lips I want wrapped around my cock; my hand twisted in her hair as she drives me out of my ever-loving mind. *Holy shit, I'm worse than a dog in heat..*

"Tell her I said thank you, the next time you're together."

"I won't be seeing her," I argue, but Tally has already moved on in the conversation. She plops onto the couch, a carton of Chinese balancing on one knee as she fiddles with the chopsticks.

She's terrible with chopsticks, but she tries every time. And every time, more food hits her lap than her mouth. It's the cutest damn thing in the world.

True to form, a pea pod hits her thigh, but any cuteness factor flies out the window when Dan snags it off her leg, popping it into his mouth.

What. The. Fuck.

"Am I going to have to get you a bib?" Dan ribs, tossing her a roll of paper towels.

Tally smirks, holding up the roll. "Nah, this should do. Have a seat, Owen. There's plenty of food."

I have two choices—storm out and look like a total ass or sit here and brood, looking like a total ass.

I go with option two because Dan should leave shortly. He'll take the hint. Bros before hoes and all that shit.

Wrong.

"I brought a change of clothes, so I can stay. I don't want you alone." I force a smile at her from across the coffee table, hating Dan more and more for his proximity to her on the couch.

"No worries, man. I'm staying here tonight."

I repeat. What. The. Fuck. My brows raise and I can't hide my surprise. "You are?"

Dan nods, popping a dumpling into his mouth. "Yeah, Stefani has to work tomorrow and I'm off. Easy choice."

"Or you can go, and I'll stay with Tally." Just like that, a chill settles over the room. Dan's gaze holds mine as I dare him to look away. Or disagree.

Tally looks between the two of us, forcing a smile. "Dan and I are heading up to West Palm tomorrow."

Oh, now it's a sleepover *and* a date. "What for?" I know I'm scowling. Now ask me if I care.

"I'm working with a tattoo artist up there, finishing a piece. I asked Lu to tag along."

I tap my foot on the floor; the vibrations shaking everything on the coffee table. "Since you two are all cozy, I'll head on home. Call me if you need me, Tally."

I offer a stiff nod, before stalking to the door and throwing it open. I'm beyond livid. The worst part? I don't have a leg to stand on.

"Aren't you going to say goodbye?"

I turn and see Tally leaning against the door frame, a knowing smirk on her face.

"Didn't realize I was interrupting."

"You aren't. Well, you interrupted dinner, but we managed to eat with you here."

She's joking, but I'm not in the mood. "Right. I'll see you later, Tally."

I hear her laugh and whip around, glaring in her direction. "What's so funny?"

"Would this sudden frostiness have anything to do with Dan?" Her words mimic my own, used against her with Nicole. She closes the distance between us, pressing a kiss to my cheek. "Just admit that you're jealous, Owen."

"Is there something going on?"

Tally shakes her head. "Friends shouldn't be jealous of friends. Remember?"

I don't think so.

I crush her body to me, my mouth claiming what is rightfully mine. I dominate her, pushing my tongue into her mouth and swallowing any arguments. My hands twist in Tally's hair, locking her in the kiss until I'm damn ready to let her go. She yields against me, and I take it one step further, backing her against the outside wall. My hand slips past her waistband, and I slide a finger inside her, feeling her clench around me.

That's right. You're mine, Darlin. Don't you forget it.

I curve my fingers around, feeling her moan into my mouth as I push her over the edge, her hips arching toward me. I pull back, smiling at the flush crossing her pale skin.

My hand rests lightly around her throat, tipping her chin up, my forehead pressed to hers. "I'm not your damn friend, Tally. Remember? You belong to me."

CHAPTER
TWENTY-FIVE
TALLY

I'd be lying if I claimed to hate seeing Owen jealous. There is something deeply satisfying about his obvious angst over Dan spending the night. It's an innocent situation, but Owen didn't see it that way.

Instead, the man turned alpha on me, his mouth and fingers owning my body, before reminding me that I belong to him.

Any other situation, I would have dropped to my knees to show Owen who's *really* the boss.

But this isn't just any situation.

Dan really *is* only a friend, and Charlotte really *is* Owen's ex-fiancée. An ex-fiancée who is once again involved in Owen's life. It's a minefield I have no desire to tread.

I'm dealing with my own life issues. Namely, being a single mom to my Nugget. Yes, I plan on telling Owen—eventually. I know it's the right thing to do, and since I have no expectations of him, there's no chance of being disappointed, right?

It sounds terrible, but I'll now be flush with cash since I'm no longer spending thousands of dollars on Dad's care. Don't get me wrong, I'd spend every penny for one more day with that man, but not the shell he'd become. If I could have my old Dad back, I'd gladly go through life a pauper.

"Tallulah, dear, might I have a word?"

I turn to see my landlord, Mrs. Smalls, standing outside the screen door.

"Come on in."

She's such a dear woman, the closest thing I have to a relative, besides Stefani and Dan. But today, something is bothering her, as evidenced by her incessant hand wringing. "How are you doing, dear?"

"As good as can be expected. My father didn't have a quality of life anymore, so now he's free." I volley my gaze between her face and hands. *Okay, spill it, Mrs. Smalls.* "Is everything okay?"

"I hate doing this, considering everything you've been through. But my grandson...he lost his job, and he needs a place to live. I told him you've been a perfect tenant and friend, but he can't find a place with his budget and credit—"

I grasp her hands, worried she'll rub the skin off if she keeps at it. "You're not renewing the lease."

"I'm so sorry, dear." Her eyes well with tears, and I grab her into a hug.

"Don't fret. I understand. You need to take care of your family."

"But I consider you family, too."

"I love you for that, but Hecate and I will be fine. How long do I have?"

Mrs. Smalls doesn't respond, but her nervous, darting glances make her answer clear.

As soon as possible.

I offer her a reassuring smile. "I just need to find a place and pack. It shouldn't take long."

"Thank you for understanding."

What's to understand? She has a family and they need help. I know the feeling all too well. I stepped in to help my family when the need arose. That's what you do.

"It's perfect timing. Moving will keep my mind off things," I reply, but it isn't the truth. It only adds to my ever-growing pile of worries.

∼

MEMORIAL GRANTED ME A WEEK OF MOURNING, BUT I RETURN EARLY. I need to stay busy, and helping others will make me feel better, right?

So very, very wrong.

"Ouch," I moan, laying my head back against the pillow, pressing the ice pack to my face. "He might be almost eighty, but damn, that man can hit."

"He was fast as greased lightning," Janine, one of the unit nurses, adds, lifting the ice pack to check the swelling. "I'm sorry, Lu. I tried to catch his arm."

Her patient, fresh out of surgery and still halfway under the effects of anesthesia, did not wake up in a happy mood. It happens, albeit rarely, and most of the time, their aim is clumsy, and I have no issue evading their swings.

Not this time.

I blame my pregnancy brain. I'm serious. Since I found out I'm carrying Nugget, my brain cells have up and flitted away into the ether. It doesn't help that I've yet to figure out how to broach the topic to Owen.

I know. I sound like a terrible bitch for hiding the pregnancy. Once I got past being mad about Charlotte and yet another lie, I realized Stefani was right. Owen deserves to know he's going to be a father. I also can't hide the pregnancy from him forever. Hell, it's already noticeable when I'm naked—one of the many benefits of being short. There's nowhere for my Nugget to hide.

So, I planned on telling Owen, but then my dad died and then the apartment situation...it's an ongoing menagerie of crap.

And now, to top it all off, here I sit, in the ED, a bruise forming on my cheek and a banger of a headache brewing behind my eyes.

"Are you sure you're okay? We need to check." Janine motions to my belly, and I wave her off. Yes, Janine knows that I'm expecting. She wasn't *supposed* to know, but she overheard a discussion between Stefani and me. It wasn't hard for her to connect the dots. Thankfully, the woman is Fort Knox when it comes to keeping secrets.

"Hazard of the job. Besides, he hit my face, not my stomach," I add with a chuckle, the last word barely escaping my lips as the bay curtain slides open.

Owen.

I'm not sure who told him, but he made it down here in record time. Hell, I only stumbled in ten minutes ago. But it's the look on his face. If he's this distraught about a bruised cheek, I can only fathom what he'll be like in the delivery room. Then I recall what I just said to Janine and wonder if Owen overheard our conversation. Let's be honest, privacy curtains are hardly soundproof.

He rushes to my side, cupping the good side of my face and giving Janine a look. "Can you give us a minute?"

Janine nods, sending me a wink. "No problem, Dr. Stevens. When did you transfer to the ED?" She giggles at his glare, but abides his demand, ducking out of the enclosed bay. Memorial is a big hospital, but it's not that big. She guessed Nugget's father on the first try.

Any rigidity dissolves once it's just the two of us, as he gingerly lifts the ice pack.

"You should see the other guy," I smirk, wincing when his fingers gently palpate the area.

"I'll bet. You can take a punch, Darlin. I'm impressed."

"See? Everyone has a talent."

"You have tons of talents. Several of which I've missed desperately this last week."

My body flames at his words. Glad to know I'm not the only one.

CHAPTER TWENTY-FIVE • 259

I avoid his probing gaze, my eyes focused on the pilled blanket. "These blankets are like sandpaper."

Owen releases a huff. He knows I'm not going to address his earlier statement. "Did he get you anywhere else?"

"No. He didn't know what he was doing. It was the effects of anesthesia wearing off."

Apparently, Owen isn't taking my word for it, as his hands slide down my arms and over my stomach. I release a small gasp when his fingers trail over my belly, and his pupils dilate, his gaze fixed on mine. "Are you in pain?"

"No," I shout, a bit too fast. "I don't need anything."

He clears his throat, those stormy orbs searching my face for deception, his fingers still resting on my stomach. Coincidence, right? It has to be a coincidence. "I hate that this happened to you."

Does he mean the punch to the face or the baby? At this point, and with that glare, I can't tell. My only option is to play it off. "Hell, I'm thrilled. I'll blend right in at Wicked Chucks."

"You're going to the concert tomorrow?"

I nod, glad to be on a different conversation path.

"The dinner is tomorrow."

Crap. It's not that I forgot about the dinner. I just hoped *he* would forget they invited me, and I could discreetly decline the invitation. I'm a strong chick. Hell, I can take a punch to the face, but it will be a punch in the heart to spend an evening with Charlotte and Owen. Add in that I now have a nice bruise on my cheek, and it's fodder for a soap opera. "Yeah, I know."

Owen stares at his hands, idly playing with my fingers. "I really want you there, Tally."

Oh God, don't do this to me. Please don't make me feel guilty about evading this situation. Then his eyes meet mine, and I lose what little spine I have.

"Please, Tally."

"Why do you need me there?"

His hand squeezes mine. "Because I don't think I can survive this dinner without knowing you're in the room."

"But Owen, *she's* going to be there."

"I know, and I want to be with *you*."

I pull my hand from his grasp. I need to put some space between us. Fast. "I can't. Please don't ask me to do this."

"I know I'm asking a lot of you, but this is a big deal for me, and you're the most important person in my life. I want those things interconnected."

I hate him. Truly, I hate him. Okay, I love him, but I hate that I'm being guilted into attending a soiree of elegant people while I bumble about in ill-fitting heels and a smashed cheek. "You suck," I pout, grabbing my glasses off the bedside table.

Even worse? The smile crossing Owen's features almost makes the idea of tomorrow night tolerable. Almost. He moves closer to me, pushing my thighs apart to stand in between them. "I can."

"No, sir, there's no *can* about it. You suck. End of story."

"Does that mean you'll be there?"

"Yes," I huff, hating how good his fingers feel as they wrap around my ass and pull me against his erection.

He buries his face in my neck, nipping gently. "I'll make it up to you. Any way you want. Even better, any way *I* want."

I bite back a moan as he grinds himself against me. Holy hell, but I'm hot for this man. "I'll figure out a repayment schedule."

"Don't forget to tack on interest payments." Another nip as his hands knead my ass, my body buzzing from his touch.

"Rest assured, I'll demand repayment in full." I push my hands against his chest, feeling the muscles flex under my fingers. "But I'm leaving early. I'm not missing the entire concert."

"Deal."

"Lu! I just heard! Holy crap, are you okay? How's the ba—" Stefani barges into the bay, her eyes widening at the sight of me wrapped in Owen's arms. "—battery on your phone? I heard you dropped it."

I squeeze my eyes shut in horror because a five-year-old could see through that save. "Yep, my phone is fine."

Owen's hands grip me tighter, and I meet his gaze.

Poker face, cooperate. Just this once.

"I'll take you home."

"I'm heading back to work," I argue, but Owen waves me off.

"You're done for today. Let's go."

I want to fight him on the decision, but employee health will send me home, regardless. Might as well save them the trouble. With a grumble, I gather my belongings and shoot him a mock glare. "I can drive myself. You don't have to take me home."

Those gray eyes focus on me with laser intensity. "Oh, yes, I do. I have to ensure that you and your *battery* make it home safe."

Chapter
Twenty-Six
TALLY

"Forget it, I'm not going."

I hope that my firm statement will suffice, that Stefani will agree wholeheartedly, and we can spend the evening eating ice cream from the carton and watching Bridget Jones.

It doesn't.

"Lu, you have to go. You gave your word."

I run my hands through my hair, giving it a sharp yank. "I shouldn't be held accountable for anything I said yesterday. I was injured, out of my mind. It shouldn't count."

"Nice try. You're going." She pulls a tea-length dress from the back of my closet. "This is beautiful."

"It's a black-tie affair."

Stefani pushes the gown into my hands. "This is more than sufficient. Trust me. Try it on."

With a resigned sigh, I strip down and pull the dress on. My breasts are already bigger, pushing up out of the dress, and my flat stomach is a bit more rounded than before. "I can't wear this," I gripe, pivoting in front of the mirror.

"Why not? You look gorgeous." Stefani walks behind me, giving my shoulders a squeeze.

"My boobs don't fit, and Nugget is showing."

"That's the first time I've ever heard a woman complain about too much cleavage."

"I'm serious." I throw my hands up in the air, flopping onto the bed. "This is a nightmare. If I go like this, there's no way Owen will not know I'm pregnant."

"Lu, he already knows."

I know she's right, and I've made a deal with myself. Should Owen ask, I'll spill the beans. I just hope it isn't tonight, because this evening is already going to be fodder for one of Dante's plays.

"I don't want to go." Now I'm whining. Perhaps if I whine enough, even throwing in a tantrum for good measure, my friend will let me slide.

My friend is not a very nice person today. "Part of being an adult is doing things we don't want to do. I know you hate being around Charlotte, and I get that, Lu. But this is important for our unit. Our hospital. Our patients."

I gape at Stefani's statements. "You are the worst! Guilting me into attendance as if everything hinges on my presence at the dinner."

"Maybe I'll meet you at Wicked Chuck's later."

I smile, wagging my finger at her. "Someone has it bad for Dan."

"He went on a date the other night," Stefani grumbles, but I see the anxiety passing over her face.

Damn. She really *does* like Dan.

"Huh, he didn't mention that to me." I give her arm a reassuring squeeze. "I'll talk to Dan. But for now, let's see what bag I can carry to hold over my stomach the entire evening."

∼

CHAPTER TWENTY-SIX

Stop fiddling. That's the mantra repeating in my head since I entered the hotel ballroom. There's a sea of tuxedos and evening gowns, all wrapped around people who spend more on pedicures than I earn in a year. Completing their looks are coiffed hair, designer jewels, and shoes that definitely didn't come from the discount rack.

Oh yeah, I blend.

Stefani swears that my tiny bump isn't obvious. I can play it off as a food baby. A good idea if I'd been able to eat anything all day. I'm starving and nauseous—a winning combination.

I have to hand it to Charlotte; the woman knows how to hostess a party. Granted, if I had a bottomless bank account, I'd be able to pull off one hell of a shindig, too. I stop to grab my seat assignment. I bet money on the fact that Charlotte sat me on the opposite end of the room from Owen—another power play attempt to rein him back into her clutches.

I guess right.

"Hey Lu, how are you?" Thank God, Dr. Jessop is at my table. At least I won't have to force a polite conversation with him. He's not only a top-notch cardiologist, but he's also a blast to hang out with, and these events are a breeding ground for his dirty jokes. "You look wonderful."

"Thank you," I murmur, sliding into my seat. "My style doesn't tend toward tuxedos."

"Mine either. I hate this penguin shit, but the top-shelf alcohol is flowing. In fact, I'm going to fetch another glass. What can I get you?"

"Just water, thanks."

"Water? Dear girl, you don't come to abysmal soirees to drink water. You drink vodka and insult the guests behind your hand."

"I can still partake in the insults. But I've had a headache all day, don't want the alcohol to worsen it."

"That's right. You took a wallop yesterday." He examines my cheek, offering a grin. "Can hardly tell."

What a liar. There is no foundation thick enough to cover a

bruise, at least none in my price range. At least my eye isn't swollen shut. Yay for silver linings. As Dr. Jessop saunters to the bar, I glance around the ballroom, taking in all the frocked finery and tinkling laughter.

My stomach flips when my gaze lands on Owen, Charlotte by his side. I take back what I said about them not fitting together—they look fantastic. Talk about a case study in beauty.

Owen fills out a tux like nobody's business—his shirt stretched across his defined pecs, the tuxedo jacket showcasing his broad shoulders and back. He's smiling, but I see from here that it's forced. He's playing the role of show pony, as required.

By his side, looking like a Gatsby-esque goddess, is Charlotte. The woman's exotic beauty is exquisite—her caramel skin looks as if she brushed it with gold. Hell, knowing her, she likely did. Her dark hair is pulled into a French twist, her body flawless in a strapless cream-colored gown.

I don't belong here. It's not the first time in my life I've felt this way, but it's the first time I've felt it regarding Owen. This is his life, surrounded by riches and royalty without the titles. People with villas and private jets and island retreats.

My gaze drops to my lap as I wipe my palms along my legs. Sure, my dress is nice, but it came off a clearance rack. My shoes aren't designer, and I purchase my makeup in a drugstore. Then, there are the tattoos decorating my arms and legs—ink that I'm ordinarily proud of, but is now making me self-conscious.

I wish I'd worn pants. And long sleeves. Thankfully, I'm tucked into a far corner. Let's face it, we may be the medical team for Memorial, but we are secondary players. Tonight isn't about us; it's an elaborate show for the whales.

And Owen's chance to shine like the star he is.

Charlotte takes the microphone as the music fades out. It's showtime, folks.

"Good evening, ladies and gentlemen. I'm thrilled to see so many representing not only South Florida but the cardiac community. I

CHAPTER TWENTY-SIX • 267

played a small part in the initial roll-out of the robotics cath lab, but it was my father who deserves the real credit. He funded a genius interventionist, whose ideas can change the face of cardiology. Let's give a warm welcome to the man of the hour, Dr. Owen Stevens."

There is no shortage of accolades as applause breaks out around the room. Owen deserves every second, even if he looks uncomfortable with the attention.

"We have ourselves a celebrity, don't we?" Dr. Jessop states with a smile, downing the rest of his scotch. "I'd hate him, but he's an awfully agreeable human being."

"That he is," I concur, sending Owen a smile I know he can't see across the ballroom. "We're very lucky to have him at Memorial."

"I've heard a rumor that Charlotte is more than a business associate. You always have the lowdown, Lu. Any truth to that nonsense?"

Flip. There goes my stomach again. "She was his fiancée."

"Ah, that's the connection. Wait, was? They're awfully chummy to be exes. Lord knows I'd rather set myself on fire than speak to the former Mrs. Jessop."

I chuckle at the visual, but I've met Dr. Jessop's ex-wife, and I concur with his words. She's a harpy. But it's the first half of his statement that sticks in my craw. *They are awfully chummy to be exes.*

"There will be several positions opening up with this new training center." Dr. Jessop sends me a pointed glance. "Right up your alley, Lu."

"I know." I don't admit how desperately I'm coveting the coordinator position. I know I have the experience, but Charlotte is the gatekeeper, and I'm sure she isn't keen to give me a key to her city.

"You get on well with Dr. Stevens. Hell, I thought you two were dating."

It's a play for information, one I'm ignoring. "He's easy to get along with, Ken."

Dr. Jessop smirks. The man knows I don't give up my secrets. "I'm sure he'll put in a good word for you."

"I would never ask that of him."

"You should, Lu. You've earned that position in spades. Time to collect on all the good works you've done."

"You just want me out of the area so I can't give you shit about your half-assed order sets," I rib, winking in his direction.

"You've found me out," he returns with a laugh.

My mind wanders as I gaze around the room. Should I mention the position to Owen? I hate the concept of being in anyone's pocket, even if the pocket belongs to the man I love.

The band begins playing an old standard that my father used to sing, and I feel the tears backing up, but I blink them away. Not the time, not the place.

Several couples make their way to the floor, swaying to the gentle rhythm of the song. But it's one couple that catches my attention. Charlotte and Owen. Together.

I can't tear my gaze from them as they glide effortlessly around the dance floor. It's obvious they're comfortable together, instinctively sensing the other's next step.

God, but they're beautiful. They're like professional ballroom dancers, and there's no way the crowd misses their fluidity. Even Dr. Jessop sits riveted, rubbing his chin as his gaze remains locked on the pair.

The dance ends about a million minutes later, and the adoration aimed at the golden couple is clear. I can even feel it from my table in Siberia. When another one of my father's favorite songs plays, I seek a hasty retreat. That's enough torture for one hour.

I step onto an adjoining balcony, sucking in a lungful of sea air. A few stragglers smile in my direction, and I return the favor before focusing my gaze on the inky blackness of the ocean beyond.

I grip the railing, fighting a futile battle against the tears. I need to get it together. I'm stronger than this, but the events of the last couple of weeks have brought me to my knees.

I shiver, even though it's hardly cold, and jerk when a jacket slips over my shoulders. Without asking permission, Owen wraps his arms around me, his lips pressing against my hair. "There you are. I've been waiting for you."

"I didn't want to intrude. I know you and Charlotte are busy."

"I'm sorry about that. The dance wasn't my idea."

I sniffle and shake my head. "You two move so naturally together."

"It's called dance lessons. There's nothing natural about Charlotte and me."

"Tell that to your adoring public."

"I only care about one person adoring me, and I'm failing miserably there." His hands slide down, pressing against my abdomen. "I thought you decided not to come."

I turn in his arms, wanting to move his hands from my stomach. Another coincidence, I'm sure. You know how it is—when you look for signs, they're everywhere. *Everywhere.* "I've been here since the beginning."

"Why didn't you come to me?"

"I didn't want to interrupt. You have far more important people than me to speak with tonight."

"You're my most important person. I've been looking for you for the last hour. I don't know how I missed you."

"Charlotte seated Dr. Jessop and me in Siberia. Likely a smart move, since we are known for causing trouble."

"You're trouble, all right. The best kind."

He's too close, and his hands haven't left my body since he joined me on the balcony. "I told you I'd be here, Owen."

The familiar strains of another standard float out to the balcony and Owen holds up his hands, gesturing to me. "Dance with me."

"I can't dance. You know that."

"Just follow my lead. Come on."

"No, Owen. I'm not following that contest worthy number of yours."

"You're not following anything. I want to dance with you, Tally. Only you."

I take a step back. "Thank you, but no. I can't."

No is not a word in Owen's vocabulary. He grasps me around my waist, pulling me against him once again. "There's no one here but you and me."

I slide my hand onto his arm, acutely aware of the clumsiness of my steps. But if Owen notices, he says nothing. Hey, I did warn the man.

"How is it possible?"

"For me to be this bad a dancer? It takes a ton of talent."

"You get more beautiful every day, Tally. Every time I see you, you're more gorgeous than the last time."

I'm not sure why his words make me blush. Owen has told me I'm gorgeous more times than I can count—or fathom. "You need your eyes checked, then. I had nothing else to wear. This was the best I could do."

"I told you, you're beautiful. Although I'd much prefer you naked in my bed. Or naked right here. Just as long as you're naked."

Time to veer away from the sex talk. It's a dangerous place. My body has no defenses against Owen when his salacious words spark up every cell. "I don't fit in here, Owen."

He releases a harsh laugh. "Darlin, I don't fit in here, either."

"You look like you do. You and Charlotte fit so well together."

He shakes his head, those stormy orbs focusing on me with fierce intensity. "I don't fit well with her. I never did. I fit well with this tiny, amazing woman who is exquisitely beautiful, wickedly smart, and the most amazing lover I've ever known."

"I hate her," I banter, gifting Owen a smile.

"I love her, more than life itself."

I tear my gaze away. I want so much to say it back, but I can't. That's not our arrangement any longer.

"I sometimes wonder if she meant what she said when she told me she loved me. I haven't heard her say the words in weeks."

"Owen—"

He chuckles, but it lacks mirth. "Let's get out of here."

CHAPTER TWENTY-SIX

"You can't leave."

"Who says? Do you actually want to stay?"

"Not at all, but I didn't want to come, either."

"Then let's go."

I shake my head, although it's the best idea I've heard all night. "They won't miss me. But you're the golden boy. They'll send out a search party for you."

"I have an idea. We have dinner, I give my speech, and we jet before dessert. Then we get changed and head to Wicked Chucks. Come on, Tally, I have to repay my debt."

"Eh, I'll let you off the hook on this one."

"I don't want off the damn hook."

The truth is, I don't want to *let* him off the hook, but I'm not up to competing against American royalty. I step toward the door, motioning inside. "We'd better get back."

His hand snakes around my arm, pulling me back to him. "Don't you miss me at all, Darlin?" The words are lighthearted, but the tone of his voice gives it all away. The faint tremble, the slight crack. He's hurting way more than I presumed.

I want to throw myself at him, slide my tongue along his luscious mouth, and beg him to sink inside me. He'd likely go along with every step. But I've risked my heart with Owen—twice—and I'm not sure that three times is a charm. Still, I ache for him. "You can't sneak out early, but if you leave straight from here, you'll make the second set. I'll save you a seat."

"In our balcony?"

I press a kiss to his cheek, my body screaming for more than that chaste gesture. "Absolutely."

"Owen, there you are. I wondered where you went. Hello, Tallulah."

I turn, offering Charlotte a small smile. She towers over me in her stilettos, and I feel like a mouse being stalked by a cat. "Hello, Charlotte. This is a wonderful party."

"If I learned anything from my mother, it was how to throw a proper soiree." Her eyes travel the length of my body, but she's too polite to mention my second-class clothes. "Owen, we have some investors to speak with about the project. If you'll excuse us, Tallulah. Enjoy the food and drink. It's all top-shelf."

Owen catches my gaze, and I force a grin for him, squeezing his hand. "Go on dancing bear, time for the second half of your performance."

"You're funny."

I laugh in earnest, shooting him my best smile.

"I brought a change of clothes with me. I planned on shedding the tux at your apartment."

"But we're meeting at Wicked Chucks," I argue. There's no way I'll last the entire night here.

"You haven't heard my version of tonight yet, and I like it way better. I show up at your apartment. You're trying to change, but I won't let you. Instead, I push you down on the bed and slide my tongue inside your sweet pussy. Then I spend the next hour kissing every inch of you, because I crave you, Tally."

"Owen—" Much more of his illicit narrative and I'll strip down right here, party etiquette be damned.

"But, since you're departing early, I'll have to wait until I get to Wicked Chucks." His lips caress my ear, his tongue dancing along the rim. "Don't forget to save me a seat. I will be there, and I will make it worth your while."

CHAPTER
TWENTY-SEVEN
TALLY

I f I force one more smile, my face will crack.

I hate watching Owen stroll back into the party, Charlotte by his side. I hate how naturally they move together. I hate the history they share and the opportunities a woman like that can bring to a man like him.

I hate that I'm on the outside, looking in.

Enough of this damnable self-pity, Tallulah. You want to be a wildflower? Start acting like one.

With a shaky breath and a false bravado, I waltz back into the party, grabbing some delicious and mysterious hors d'oeuvre off a silver tray as I glide back to my table.

Time to suck it up and put on my big girl panties.

Did I mention how much I hate big girl panties?

The next hour sails by, as dinner and drinks flow into the whales with the same ease their money flows out. I know it's on the up and up, but I can't help but detest the circus. Just ask the wickedly wealthy for some of their money and call it a day. What's with the endless buttering up?

As I make my way to the bathroom for the millionth time, I catch sight of Owen, speaking to a local Congressman by the name of Jeff Daniels. I envy Owen's ease with people of this echelon; I break out in hives when I'm close to the uber-wealthy and important.

Owen looks up and catches my gaze, sending me a wink.

It's funny how that silly gesture renews my confidence, and I move closer to them, intent on letting the Congressman know about all of Dr. Steven's assets.

"I think it's a fabulous idea. God knows the population isn't getting healthier," the politician mutters, sipping his drink.

"Exactly my point," Owen concurs, his gray gaze intent on me as I edge closer.

"I must say that you and Charlotte are quite the power couple. When is the wedding?"

I stop short, my heart clenching in my chest. Jeff Daniels isn't yet aware of me, but Owen is, and his widened eyes speak volumes.

"Charlotte and I are no longer engaged."

Whew. I can resume a normal breathing pattern.

"She intimated that reconciliation is imminent," Mr. Daniels presses.

Heart, we have a problem.

"Did she?" I feel the unease flowing through Owen as palpably as the champagne flows through the Congressman.

Jeff Daniels leans in as if sharing a secret. "We both know that most marriages are of convenience. But Charlotte Auerback is gorgeous, and landing a spot on her father's will would give you the life of Riley. I'd switch spots with you in a minute, old boy."

I stand my ground, my heart on its proverbial last legs as I await Owen's reply. He has to say something. Reiterate that they're no longer together, mention that he's in love with someone else. Hell, I'm standing right *here*. I may not have the pedigree that Charlotte does, but the man proclaimed his adoration not sixty minutes ago.

"Mr. Daniels, I'd like you to meet Tallulah Knowles. She's the cardiac nurse manager at Memorial."

Okay, this segue can work.

CHAPTER TWENTY-SEVEN

I extend my hand, offering the Congressman a smile. "How do you do?"

"Just fine. Are you enjoying the evening?" His eyes skitter over my tattoos, and once again, I feel sub-par.

"I am. I'm happy to help Dr. Stevens achieve his goal within the cardiac realm."

"Let's not forget Charlotte," Jeff Daniels reminds me. "They are the quintessential power couple."

Holy hell, but he loves that term.

I grit my teeth, my gaze swinging to Owen. "Are they? I wasn't aware they had reconciled."

"They haven't, but I know her family. He doesn't stand a chance." The poor politician has no idea of the melee he has wrought.

I raise my brows, my dark eyes flashing as I glare at Owen.

Say something, you bastard.

But Owen doesn't defend me, or our supposed love. Instead, the chicken shit changes the subject. "Speaking of Memorial, I wanted to introduce you to Dr. Jessop. He will be assisting me with the facility."

Just like that, the conversation stream winds away into seemingly innocuous waters, but there's not enough water in the world to calm the inferno raging in me.

"If you'll excuse me," I mutter.

"Tally, you don't have to leave."

"Actually, I do. I have a prior engagement. A very important one."

Perhaps I'm behaving like a child as I storm back to my seat to gather my things. But I've tried to be an adult where Owen is concerned, and I'm done taking the high road. The only road I want is one leading out of here.

I'm still fuming, but at least now I'm doing it on my turf. I swing the barstool back and forth, wishing to God that vodka was healthy for my Nugget.

Dan knows that something is up, but he sees the set of my jaw and opts not to push the issue.

Smart man.

"I'm so glad to be out of there." I jump at Owen's voice in my ear. The man definitely minored in ninjutsu. The tux is long gone, replaced by a body-hugging shirt and jeans. I hate how good he looks.

I need a vaccine against this man. Something to make me immune.

"Hey Darlin," Owen leans in to kiss me, but I turn my head before he gets the chance. "What's wrong?"

"I think you know."

"Congressman Daniels? The guy is a prick, Tally. Don't listen to a word he says."

I swivel on my stool, facing him, glare at the ready. "I didn't. What I listened to was the silence from your end, negating his statements."

"I didn't think it mattered."

"It did. It mattered to me."

Silence. I sip my drink, my gaze intent on the water ring. I don't want to argue or fight. It's not worth the energy at this point.

His hands clench the edge of the bar, and I see from the corner of my eye he has focused his gaze downward. "I fucked up."

I raise my brows but don't offer any retort. At this point, I'm not sure what Owen considers a fuck up.

"I should have corrected him. I didn't think. I beg you to attend this stupid dinner, and then subject you to that crap from some pompous twit who wouldn't know love if it smacked him in the face." Finally, that stormy gaze meets mine. "I'm sorry, Tally."

I can't lie; I'm shocked by his earnest apology. "You think you can stop hurting my feelings? I know I'm a tough cookie, but even I have limits, Owen."

"You're the last person I want to hurt."

"Yet somehow, you keep managing it." I release a resigned huff as I take in his distraught expression. "I don't think you get to share my balcony tonight. Your punishment is being relegated to the heathens down here."

I know that sarcasm isn't the right answer, but I'm tired. My heart and head are beyond weary. I just want to kick back and listen to a band rage about anarchy.

"I'll do anything to make it right."

"Well, that's a tempting offer."

He grasps my hand. "I'll drop to one knee right now."

My heart leaps at his statement, but I remain calm and collected on the outside. "What are you planning on doing while you're down there?" It's a joke. I know it, and I think he knows it, too.

"Ask me to show you."

Bastard is baiting me. I tap my chin before shaking my head. "While it piques my curiosity as to the legitimacy of your statement, I'll let you slide this time. This time," I reiterate.

He grabs my hand, pressing a kiss to my palm. "What if I don't want you to let me slide?"

"Behave, or I won't let you sit in my balcony. I'm not kidding, mister." I pop off the stool, heading for the upstairs stairwell. I push open the heavy door and settle onto the worn velvet couch. Home sweet home.

"Are you serious?"

I turn to see Owen, his eyes flashing in the low light. "What?"

"I mention proposing, Tally, and you get up and walk away."

"I knew you were joking, Owen."

"What makes you so sure?"

My eyes widen as my mouth goes dry. "You can't be serious."

"I know it's the least romantic place in the world to propose Tally, and I don't have the ring, but—"

"You were serious?" I'm not sure how I want him to respond. If he says he was, I'll feel like a total ass and totally confused. If he says he wasn't, I'll be relieved but disappointed.

What is wrong with me?

He offers a strained smile. "Bad timing. I just wanted you to know how I felt."

"Really? You know how you do that? Take my feelings into consideration. Don't ask me to fraternize with your ex-fiancée again. I know you say nothing is going on—"

"There isn't."

"But after tonight, that claim isn't entirely clear. That douchebag wasn't the only one. Tongues were wagging all around the room about you and Charlotte."

"I didn't tell anyone anything."

"Exactly. You failed to mention me once."

Owen throws his hands up. "Wait, just a damn minute. You wanted us to be friends, remember?"

"You're right, I said that."

"Did you mean it?"

"The truth is, I don't have the stamina to go toe to toe with Charlotte, or your former lifestyle."

"Who's asking you to? I love you for you, Tally."

"But you don't love me enough to negate Congressman Daniels's blasé statement. You don't love me enough to risk his deep pockets."

"That's bullshit. I never said I was with Charlotte."

"You never denied the possibility of reconciliation, either. You had a chance. I was right there, but you changed the subject."

"Tally, you need to understand—"

That does it. "No, *you* need to understand. I've been understanding for the last two months! I had to understand when I discovered that you lied about being a doctor. I had to understand when I came face to face with a fiancée I didn't know you had. I had to understand when you ask me to attend a party where you deny that

I'm anything beyond your nurse manager. I'm all out of understanding, Owen. You've reached your quota."

I storm out of the balcony. I need a drink, but since Nugget won't allow me alcohol, fresh air will have to do. I push open the exit door, throwing my head back and willing my temper back into its cave.

I wish our situation was cut and dried, but it's the exact opposite. It's messy and sticky, and I'm not entirely sure how much more either of us can stand.

"Hey," Owen slips his arm around my shoulder, and I hate how good it feels. How *right* it feels. "I'm sorry I hurt you."

"I've had a shitty couple of weeks, Owen."

"I know, and instead of helping, I've made it worse."

He takes the hat from my head and puts it on his own. It looks goofy as hell, perched on the top of his noggin.

I don't want to smile, but the visual is too much. "You look ridiculous."

"What? I think I look fab." He glances up at the smokers nearby. "Come on, Darlin, let's move over here."

"Why?"

He nods toward the group of people. "They're smoking. It's bad for you."

Shit. He said it was bad for *me*, not us. "Smoking is bad for everyone."

That stormy gaze meets mine, searching my face for answers I'm not willing to divulge. "I have a better idea. Let me buy you a beer. No, let's go do a shot."

Double shit. "I'm sticking with water."

"Are you driving?"

"No."

"Still have that incredibly rare stomach virus?"

"Are you prying?"

"Yes."

I guffaw at his brashness. "No, the stomach virus is gone."

"But you're not drinking?"

"Some might think that's a good thing."

Owen's phone rings and I know the second he glances at it, who's on the other end.

"Don't you have to take that?" I wonder now if it was Charlotte calling on our first date. At this point, everything is muddy and unclear.

"I can speak to her later."

My anger returns with a vengeance. Later is reserved for Charlotte. How much more of Owen's time will be usurped by this woman he claims is part of his past?

"By all means, don't let me stop you." I stalk back inside, pulling up a barstool and shooting Dan a warning look. *Don't even ask.*

"What are you mad about now?" Owen demands, swinging around the barstool so I'm facing him. "I can't stop Charlotte from calling me."

"Actually, you can. You can kick her out of your life, but you won't. Instead, you expect me to understand your situation. To understand your needs." The anger that simmered in the back of my brain surges to the front. "How many more lies do you plan on spinning, Owen?"

His fist hits the bar, making the glasses jump and earning a warning glare from Dan. "I never lied about my situation with Charlotte."

"You never told the full truth, either."

"You want to talk about the truth? Let's talk about truth."

Oh, crap.

"Anything you want to tell me, Tally?"

He knows. He knows. "Not right now, no." It's true. This is not the time nor place to discuss Nugget.

"Which means you are keeping something from me."

Now we're in a standoff. One of us has to back down first, and it's not going to be me.

I'm done for the evening.

CHAPTER TWENTY-SEVEN

I slide off the stool, throwing a ten on the bar and giving Dan a nod. Then, without a second glance at Owen, I walk away.

He's at my side within seconds. "You're just going to leave?"

"Yep. Hey, this makes it easier for you. Now, you don't have to choose between Charlotte and me."

"This is ridiculous, Tally," Owen grits out, his grip tightening on my elbow.

"You're right. This is ridiculous. This entire situation is ridiculous, Owen."

"So, let's stop fighting."

"I have a better idea. Let's just stop." I hold up my hand. "Don't follow me, Owen. Just let me go."

CHAPTER TWENTY-EIGHT

TALLY

Am I validated in storming out of Wicked Chuck's last night? Yes.

Do I regret stomping out of the bar like a juvenile? Also, yes.

I strive to keep my emotions on lockdown. It's a necessity in the medical field, and after the kicks that life has dealt me, I wouldn't be standing if I let every little thing bother me. That being said, the situation with Owen and Charlotte isn't a little thing. It's gargantuan, with a life of its own.

What really bothers me? That, for all intents and purposes, Owen belongs to Charlotte. He belonged to her long before he engaged in a tryst with me. They had plans for the future—plans that he up and left.

I realize that Owen never envisaged me, and he certainly didn't intend on knocking me up.

The selfish side of me wants to call Owen and demand that he put a ring on it, just like he promised. The magnanimous side knows that with Charlotte by his side, he can change the world of medicine.

I haven't decided which way I'm leaning yet.

I slept hard last night, but I'm still tired. Glancing at my phone, I see a few missed calls from Beth. One of the new residents has a medical situation, but she's too terrified to go to the doctor.

I pull on a flowing sundress, tie my hair back, and jump into my jalopy. Screw makeup, the women at the shelter do not care if I'm wearing mascara.

"Beth," I call out, walking from room to room as I search for the director. "Where are you?"

"In here, Lu."

I enter the kitchen and stop short. Owen sits at the table with the new resident, giving her an examination. Once again, I'm caught by how *good* he is at his work. He's a natural healer, and the women seem to trust him. That, in itself, is a rarity.

But it is also painful to see him after our row last night, more so in a place I assumed he would never return.

"Dr. Stevens was kind enough to come down and speak with Sophie." Beth stands, giving me a quick hug and motioning to the coffeepot. "Cup of coffee, love?"

I shake my head, strolling to the front porch. I'm weighing my options. Should I leave or stay? The decision is taken out of my hands when the screen door slams and Owen settles into a chair next to me.

"Hey." His tone is guarded, noticeable from just that single word.

"Thank you for helping them."

"I told them whenever they needed something to call me. Beth said she couldn't reach you. Are you okay?"

I nod, maintaining my gaze on the street. "I didn't hear the phone. I was exhausted."

"You needed to rest. I'm happy to help the women here."

"I appreciate that, but it's not your problem to handle. I should have turned my ringer on." I stare at my hands, idly pulling at my skirt. "I was so afraid it would go off during your speech last night."

"The one you didn't stay for?" Owen grunts, his gaze on the ceiling. "My only problem is being away from the woman I love."

I stand up, my heart shredding at his words. "I can't do this."

"Tally—"

There they are again. Damn teardrops. "I can maintain a professional distance at work, but this"—I gesture between the two of us—"is really hard for me."

"You think it isn't hard for me? I'm in love for the first time in my life, but the woman I adore won't let me near her. All because she's convinced that I want the woman I moved 3,100 miles away from!" Owen scrubs his face with his hand, his foot tapping erratically on the porch. "I get that this is hard, Tally. It sucks, and it's stupid, but I keep hoping one day you'll realize who I want."

I wipe my hand over my brow, feeling woozy. Yet another fun-filled symptom of pregnancy.

"Easy there. Are you okay?" Owen grabs my arm and pulls me to him, not waiting for verification. "You're pale, Tally."

"I'm always pale, Owen."

He tips my chin up, brushing my hair back from my face. His touch soothes me, and I lean into it. He's not mine any longer, but for the moment, I can pretend. "When was the last time you ate?"

"I had breakfast about an hour ago."

"Maybe you need something else. Why don't we go grab some lunch?"

"Have you seen how much I eat? I'm hardly underfed."

"You do have an impressive appetite lately. Almost like you're eating for two." He quirks his brow at me while I struggle to maintain a neutral expression. "But that couldn't be the case because I've asked you, and you've denied it, time and again." His hand slides down over my stomach—my ever so slightly protruded stomach—and stops there. "I always said you were a terrible liar, Tally."

I hear my dad's voice in my head, beckoning me to come clean. *Sink or swim, Wildflower.*

"Lu—oh, I didn't know you were still here, Dr. Stevens. I didn't mean to interrupt." Beth stands at the screen door, a knowing smile on her face.

I'd jump out of Owen's embrace, but the big, mean, handsome doctor isn't letting me. To be fair, it's also my favorite place in the world, and I've no desire for the moment to end.

"You're fine, Beth. Dr. Stevens was just leaving. I'll be right in."

"Take your time, dear." A low chuckle escapes Beth's lips as she steps back into the house. Oh boy, I'll have some explaining to do.

"I've got to go. Beth needs me."

Our gazes hold for a few beats more, before Owen presses a kiss to my forehead. "So beautiful, and so damn stubborn." He pulls back, nodding in the direction of the door. "Go ahead, don't want to keep Beth waiting. Promise me you'll eat something soon."

"Yes, Dr. Stevens." I nod, offering a wave as I walk inside, tracking Beth down in her office. "You needed to see me?"

"You didn't need to rush back in. I certainly wouldn't have rushed out of that man's arms."

I chew my lower lip, focusing my gaze on the waste bin. "He had to leave."

"It was so nice of Dr. Stevens to stop by. The women here trust him, and that's a godsend."

"He's a wonderful doctor, with a fantastic bedside manner."

"He's a wonderful man, Tallulah."

I shrug, hoping for a change in the conversation. "I suppose."

She reaches across the desk, squeezing my arm. "You *know* he's a wonderful man. I had a little chat with Owen when he arrived."

I groan, sinking my head into my hands. "Beth, tell me you didn't."

"I did. I needed to know why he broke my dear friend's heart. But the story I heard was different from your take."

Wonderful. Now he's spinning *another* tale. What a tangled web this man weaves.

"His ex-fiancée followed him across the country in hopes of reconciliation. There are only so many ways to spin that story, Beth."

"He doesn't want her back."

"That's not what she says," I grumble as I fiddle with my hands. I'm a nervous wreck today.

"It's what Owen says. He loves you. You love him. And you're having a baby together."

My head shoots up, my eyes wide as saucers. "How did you know?"

"I'm a mother, and a mother always knows. Owen knows too, dear."

"He said that?"

Beth shakes her head, shooting me a soft smile. "He didn't have to, but he intimated the fact."

My heart sinks to my stomach, both flipping and flopping at the realization that the jig is up. "Ugh. I know that Owen knows, but I haven't been able to tell him. I have this ray of hope that exists until then. After he hears about the baby, it's just me and a lifetime of single motherhood."

"Or a lifetime with the man of your dreams. Why are you so certain he doesn't want this child?"

I throw my hands up. There are a million reasons. Where do I begin? "We barely know each other—"

"You knew each other well enough to have unprotected sex," Beth retorts, her brows raised.

I hate my friend sometimes.

"I'm aware of that fact, Beth," I grumble. "His ex-fiancée wants to reconcile, and she's beautiful and important. I have a healthy self-esteem, but it's like competing against the Queen of England when she wasn't ninety."

Beth chuckles, staying my hands that continue to fiddle with anything in their way. "You still haven't answered my question."

Tears back up in my eyes, spilling down my cheeks. The truth—the hard truth—is something I don't want to admit. "I know he'll do the right thing, Beth. That's what Owen does. But how am I supposed to have this man in my life forever, knowing he'll never be mine?"

Beth passes me a tissue, stroking my hair. She really is such a mom. "My dear girl, sometimes you have to give people the opportunity to screw up. Owen just might surprise you."

"Or he might break my heart."

"Then," she states, pushing herself to a standing position, "you'll be on even ground. You've already broken his heart by leaving."

CHAPTER TWENTY-NINE
OWEN

I hoist the five steaming-hot pizzas from the trunk of my car and head into the shelter. Things are tense between Tally and me at the moment, but I'm hoping a delicious hunk of bread and cheese might soothe her nerves.

I hate the distance between us, and I know it's because of Charlotte's reappearance in my life. Hell, I don't blame Tally for being angry. I know how bad it looks.

I also know that my tiny vixen has little to no faith in me or my motives.

In other words? I'm beyond screwed.

But I'm not giving up. Tally is the greatest woman I've ever known, and I'll fight until the end to bring her back to me.

"What are you doing back here?" I turn to see Tally leaning against Beth's office door, arms crossed over her chest, and a curious expression on her face.

"I brought pizza for everyone."

She nods, a small smile tugging at the corners of her mouth. My woman is sexy without trying. Actually, the less she tries, the sexier she becomes, and right now, she's so delectable that I'm having trouble containing myself.

"That's most awesome of you."

"It gets better." I hand Tally the smallest box. "One personal supreme pizza with extra supremeness."

"Are you plying me with pizza?" she questions, opening the box lid and letting out a moan of contentment.

"Absolutely. I'm no fool. I'm well aware that you have a distinct weakness for pizza."

"Among other things."

And just like that, my dick is hard as a rock. Damn these tight jeans.

I run my eyes along the length of her body in a blatant eye fuck. Pregnancy looks good as hell on this woman. "Don't start something, Darlin, you don't plan on finishing."

Tally winks at me, giving those luscious hips a shake. "Oh, I'll finish, alright. I'll eat this entire pizza."

I chuckle as she strolls back into Beth's office. Fire. Pure fire.

The pies aren't on the table two minutes before the residents peek into the kitchen, their eyes widening with glee at the surprise.

To be fair, I bought the pizzas because my gorgeous girl needs to eat. I know she's pregnant, or at least I'm 99.9% positive about that fact. She needs to take care of herself, and Tally sucks at self-care.

That's where I come in.

But the pizza purchase isn't just for Tally's benefit. The women and children living in the shelter treat the smallest kindness as if you'd handed them the keys to the kingdom.

They're far more used to abuse than kindness, and their smiles as they dig in are worth every penny.

I feel a bump to my right and glance down to see Tally giving me a hip check, a piece of pizza in one hand. "Thank you. You made their day."

"Am I still in the doghouse?"

"Yes, but at least you're not chained to it anymore. There's hope for everyone." She giggles as I swipe a bite off her pizza, throwing an arm around her shoulder.

"Where the fuck is she?" a male voice thunders through the house. Across the kitchen, one of the newer residents, Marla, drops her pizza to the floor.

"Oh my God, no," she whispers, pushing her young son behind her in a protective gesture. "How did he find me?"

"Stay there," Tally warns, tossing her pizza box onto the table. "I'll handle this."

"Like hell you will," I thunder, grasping her shoulders and forcing her to look at me. "*You* stay here, too. I'll go handle this. Call the cops."

Tally nods, grasping my hand. "Be careful, Owen."

I press a kiss to her palm, forcing a smile. "Always."

I'm no slouch in the boxing department, but I'm sure as hell hoping I can reason with this man, at least until the cops arrive.

As soon as he catches sight of me, I realize that a logical discussion is not an option.

He charges, and I barely manage to block his swing. "Where the fuck is she? Where is the little whore?"

I raise my hands, my voice belying the apprehension in my belly. I can tell from his dilated pupils and the stench of his breath that he's high on a menagerie of drugs and alcohol. "You need to calm down. This is a private residence, and you are trespassing."

"I don't need to do shit. You tell me where Marla is right now, or you're going to be sorry."

"You think taking a swing at me is going to help your cause? The cops are en route, so the best thing you can do is walk away. Right. Now."

I plant my feet, prepared for the drunkard's onslaught. His inebriated state throws him off balance, and when he lunges, he goes down. This only infuriates him further as he stumbles to his feet.

"Get out of my way, man," he bellows.

"Get out of this house," I repeat, stretching to my full height. I have him by at least four inches, but he's got forty pounds of fat on me. Then I hear the sirens in the distance. Thankfully, the cops set a new speed record today.

If the man hears the sirens, he doesn't let on. Instead, his glare fixes on something past me, and I know intrinsically that Tally has disobeyed my direct order to stay in the kitchen. "You! I should have known you were behind this."

I have to hand it to Tally. If she's afraid, she isn't letting on. She marches right past me; her finger only inches underneath the man's nose. "Get out, Earl. You know the rules. You want to go back to the slammer again?"

"Fucking bitch," he mutters, as I grab Tally, pushing her behind me.

"I told you to stay put," I hiss, turning just in time for Earl's fist to connect with my face.

Getting punched sucks, and trust me when I say that it doesn't get any easier the older you get. Getting punched because one petite punk princess opted not to stay put sucks even worse. Lucky for her luscious ass, I love her.

Twenty minutes later, the cops have come and gone, hauling off the piece of trash named Earl. Now, I'm in the kitchen, a bag of frozen peas on my face and a panic-stricken Tally flitting all around me.

I wonder how many sexual favors I can garner from taking a hit for her? I know I'm a dog, but seriously; I wonder. "Darlin, sit down. I'm okay."

"I'm so sorry," Tally pulls the bag from my face, pressing gingerly on my jaw. "He was aiming for me."

"I know, which is why I'm glad I got you out of harm's way."

She stands in front of me, wringing her hands, her gaze focused on the ground as she gnaws her lower lip. "This is all my fault."

"Think you might listen to me once in a while? Just every so often, for kicks?"

"I'll make it up to you. Promise."

I smile, despite the soreness in my face. I'm lucky Earl was so inebriated. He didn't throw with the full force of his body weight behind him. Otherwise, the fat bastard might have broken my jaw. As it stands, I'm walking away with a bruise and a hell of a story.

"Don't worry, I have a long list of favors I plan on calling in over the next week. All sexual in nature, of course."

"I can't believe you're joking at a time like this," she murmurs, but I see the blush skitter across her cheeks. It's almost worth the punch to see my old Tally again.

"Trust me, I'm not joking."

Tally giggles, placing a fresh bag of frozen vegetables against my face. If Tally is distraught, Marla is beside herself with worry.

"I'm so sorry, Dr. Stevens," Marla whispers, clutching my forearm.

The poor woman. She wears a multitude of scars from years of abuse. "Marla, I'm glad it was me who took that punch and not one of you. You've endured enough."

"I'm worried he'll come back," Marla states, her hands trembling. "That restraining order isn't worth the paper it's printed on."

Tally puts an arm around her, soothing her nerves. "Beth and I are working on finding you a new home. Somewhere far away, where he can't hurt you again."

"I don't think I can move far enough away to satisfy that man." Marla hangs her head, dejected.

That's when I realize why Marla seems familiar. She's the woman Tally examined in the emergency department—a sexual assault case. No wonder Earl seemed so hellbent to hurt both women; he views Tally as the reason Marla is no longer his personal punching bag. That realization settles one thing for me—Tally is moving in, and I don't care what argument she presents.

If Earl found Marla this easily, he can no doubt apply those sleuthing skills to the woman I love.

That's not a chance I'm willing to take.

I GROAN WHEN THE REMINDER POPS UP ON MY PHONE. IN ALL THE excitement of the day, I forgot about my meeting with Charlotte and yet another investor. I swear, I'm juggling more PR now than I did during the initial launch.

I'm fully aware that my ex-fiancée could field many of these meetings by herself, but I hope that if I play nice, this project will achieve a speedy liftoff, and Charlotte will be on a private jet back to San Francisco. Far away from my new life with Tally.

Hey, a man can dream.

I left the shelter about an hour after Earl, assuring both Beth and Marla—about a million times—that I was fine. I then reminded Tally with a nip to the earlobe that she owed me, and I planned to collect.

I hate how little I see my girl lately—a few moments at the hospital, or at some public event, where stripping her naked and licking every inch of her is frowned upon.

Not that I wouldn't do it. All Tally has to do is smile with that come-hither look, and I'd take her right then, no questions asked.

That's what the woman does to me. The best part? She really doesn't see it.

The doorbell rings, and I groan again. It better not be Charlotte. She's made it a habit of dropping by my condo, despite my repeated protests.

I swing open the door, a smile crossing my face.

It's not Charlotte.

Instead, my tiny vixen stands on the threshold, a bag of goodies in her arms. "Hi."

"Hi, yourself." I stand aside, letting her into our condo. Well, it will be ours when her stubborn ass finally moves in. "To what do I owe this pleasure?"

Tally sets the bag on the counter, pivoting toward me with a smile on her lips. "I wanted to see if you were okay."

"I'm fine," I reply, closing the distance between us, my hands running the length of her arms. "Is that the only reason you came by?"

She bites her lower lip, and I have to hold myself back from ripping off every stitch of her clothing. "I may have had an ulterior motive."

"Do tell."

"Well, besides the repayment plan, of which we are both in debt, I wanted to talk to you."

"Good talk or bad talk?"

"I think it's good, but I'll let you make that decision."

I smile, brushing my lips across her forehead as I will my heart to settle. She's finally going to tell me, so I can stop wondering and start preparing for our new arrival. Hey, I got three bedrooms for a reason. "Can I get you a drink? Water, I presume?" I fill up a glass and offer it to her, leaning against the counter with a smirk. "How long are you on the wagon for, Darlin?"

She giggles, sipping the water. "I guess that depends. How's your jaw?"

"Sore, but I figure I'll invent some crazy story for the guys at work about how I acquired it."

"Isn't the truth crazy enough?"

"Good point. So, what did you want to talk about?" Yes, I'm pushing. The sooner Tally tells me, the sooner I tell her I'm thrilled and then proceed to give her about a dozen long overdue orgasms. "Do you want to sit down or—"

The peal of the doorbell cuts through my words. Fuck.

This time, there's no doubt in my mind who's knocking. Charlotte.

No matter how innocent it is in reality, this doesn't look good.

Tally's gaze shutters, locking me out. She already knows who's on the other side of the door. "I should have realized you'd be busy. I'm interrupting."

"No, you're not. I have this stupid meeting with Charlotte and an investor. She was supposed to meet me at the restaurant. Just hold on for a moment."

"So, I'm definitely interrupting." Tally grabs her purse and phone, giving the bag of food a forlorn look. "You two...enjoy those. There are all kinds of goodies in there."

"I'm going to cancel the meeting. Charlotte can handle it herself."

Tally places her hand on my arm, stopping my forward movement. "Owen, I'm the one who dropped by unannounced. I'm the one intruding. Keep your plans."

Christ, I feel the chasm growing between us with every word that falls from her lips. "You wanted to talk to me."

"It's not important."

"It's not?" I want to scream that our child is the *most* important thing in this world, but I bite my tongue.

Tally strides over to the door, greeting my ex-fiancée. "Hello, Charlotte."

"Tallulah. I wasn't expecting to see you."

My darling girl manages a smile, but I see the tears brimming in her eyes from across the room. Every tear she sheds is a knife in my gut. "I didn't mean to interrupt. I was checking on Owen, making sure he was okay."

"Why? What happened?" Charlotte's gaze swings to me, her pupils dilating when she notices the bruise on my jaw. "What in the world? Was this from that punk bar you've been frequenting? I know you went there last night after the dinner."

Thanks for the sympathy, bitch.

"Owen protected a woman from her abusive ex at the shelter." Tally holds my gaze, sending me a half-hearted smile. "He's a hero once again. Anyway, I know you two have a busy evening, so I'll leave you to it. Good night."

It's ironic. Charlotte was raised with a team of nannies to ensure her manners were on point. Yet, it's Tally, raised by ordinary citizens, who's the real class act.

Yet another reason I'm so damn crazy about Tally, and why I hate how bad this entire situation feels. I know this training facility will save lives, but it's not worth losing the woman I love, and I feel her slipping through my fingers.

"Hold on a minute," I bark, chasing Tally down the hallway. I swing her around, cupping her face and claiming her mouth. I know that Charlotte is watching this entire scene play out, and I'm glad. Both women need to know where my loyalties—and heart—lie.

I only pray it works.

"I'll come over as soon as I'm done," I murmur against Tally's lips, willing her to understand one last time.

But she pushes away, her eyes scanning my face. "It will keep, Owen. I promise. Charlotte is waiting. You need those investors."

"I need you." I've never meant those words more in my life, but it's too little, too late.

The elevator opens, and Tally steps in, offering a mouthed 'good luck' and a thumbs up before the doors close. Seconds later, I'm left staring at my reflection in the polished metal.

For the first time, Tally didn't kiss me back.

I trudge back to the apartment, my anger escalating with every step. "What part of I'll meet you at the restaurant, didn't you understand?" I demand, slamming the door with a vehement swing.

"I assumed this would be easier."

"No, you hoped it would cause waves between me and Tally, which it did. Bravo, Charlotte."

"Is that what you think I'm doing?"

"Yes. Another stunt like this one tonight, and I'm off the deal. Training facility be damned."

Charlotte's eyes widen. "You can't mean that."

"Yes, I can. You and your Daddy are just wallets. I can find another one." I whirl on her, my eyes flashing. "Are you having me followed?"

"What are you talking about?"

"You knew I was at Wicked Chucks last night."

"You...you mentioned it at the dinner."

"No, I didn't, because my life isn't any of your business. Outside of these meetings, what I do, and who I do it with is none of your concern. So, tell me, are you having me followed?"

"You're a valuable commodity, Owen. Daddy wants to protect his investment."

"I'm a human being, not a goddamn stock option!"

"You think I don't know that," Charlotte bellows back, and it's almost frightening to see her show of emotion. "You think he treats me any differently? We're all chattel to him, Owen. But you have a chance to change the face of medicine. This couple we are meeting with tonight has the means to fund the training center single handedly. I know you're angry, I know you feel like a dancing bear, but this could secure your financial future."

"The money means nothing."

"But helping people does. The bruise on your jaw proves that. The way you look at Tallulah proves how much certain people mean to you. This would help them. All of them. Don't forget, cooperate now, and I'll help Tallulah later."

Christ, nothing like a good bribe to keep you on the straight and narrow. She's right though, on more than one count. This procedure *will* save countless lives, and the coordinator position would be a gigantic step up for my Tally. I'm happy to take care of her the rest of my life, but I know my girl, she's far too stubborn to allow that to happen.

At this point, I'll be lucky if she even considers dating me again.

With a resigned sigh, I grab my wallet and motion to the door. "One dancing bear at your service. We might as well get this over with."

CHAPTER THIRTY

TALLY

For about the millionth time in the last few weeks, I cry myself to sleep, images of Owen and Charlotte in compromising positions dancing through my head.

But this morning, my tears have dried, along with any notion that Owen will be involved in our baby's life. Correction—*my* baby's life.

I stare at the growing pile of boxes stacked in all corners of the apartment. Perhaps now is the time to look for a new position far away from Memorial. That way, Owen will never suspect a thing, and I won't be privy to his reconciliation with Charlotte. Hell, I'm no fool. I know it's a forgone conclusion. Even if he claims to want me, a life with Charlotte is the smart route. The safe route.

Love isn't part of the plan when you're a man like Owen. There's too much at stake to follow the whims of your heart.

"What do you think, Hecate? Shall we try some other part of the country? Would you like to move to the mountains, fight off coyotes and wildebeests?" I stroke her glossy fur, giving her tail a tickle as she stretches.

To live the life of a cat.

I've spent the last fifteen years in Florida, but the place never felt like home. I followed my father down here when he retired, and there was no way in hell I was leaving him after he got sick.

But now, my father is gone. Maybe it's time for me to hightail it to my next adventure. *Our* next adventure, I bemuse, running my hand along my slightly swollen abdomen. To the outside world, I look normal. But when I shed my clothes, the outline of my bump is evident. That, and my ever-enlarging boobs. I swear, they'll be the size of watermelons at the rate I'm going.

By the time I put my vehicle into drive, headed for Memorial, I've reached a decision. I'll start looking for a new nursing position tonight. A travel gig is easy enough to come by, and that can take me, Nugget, and Hecate anywhere in the country. We may need to camp in a hotel room for a couple of weeks, but that's not a tragedy.

I feel a sense of calm now that I've let go of the idea of Owen and me being anything more than a passing fancy. The anger and anxiety are gone, replaced with the pressing knowledge that I need to get my ducks in a row, and those ducks need to swim far from Fort Lauderdale.

"I'M SORRY, NO."

I bite back a smirk. Stefani is not in favor of any relocation plans. "Well, it isn't exactly your decision, but I haven't decided yet. I just think a fresh start is a good idea, considering."

"Lu, have you even told Owen about..." she inquires, offering a pointed glance at my stomach.

"No, and I don't plan on it."

"That's not right, and you know it."

I release a drawn-out sigh, slumping back in the chair. It's an unusually quiet day on the unit, and the staff is taking advantage of the downtime to catch up—on gossip, mostly. "He's got so much going on, and his situation changes daily. Not to mention that his ex isn't really his ex."

"They're back together?"

"Might as well be," I grumble, flipping aimlessly through one of the file drawers. What I'm looking for, God only knows. "They're always together—a fundraiser here, an investment dinner there. It's all bullshit. Just Charlotte's excuse for spending time with Owen. But he's going along with it. So, that's why I want a change of scenery. It will do me good."

I really need to scan my immediate proximity before I say anything about our illustrious doctor because he always seems to be within earshot. As Owen clears his throat behind me, I realize he's used his ninja techniques once again. However, if he heard anything, he isn't letting on, as he passes me a file with a smile.

"Good morning, Tally."

"Morning, Dr. Stevens."

"Tell her she can't leave," Stefani blurts out, and I swivel my chair around to face her, a look of abject horror crossing my features.

"Where are you going?" Owen asks.

"She doesn't know yet. Just far away from here."

I hate my friend. What a bitch. All that ride or die crap? The real motto is she'll run you over, and then you'll die. The woman just backed over me repeatedly, and I can tell from her narrowed stare that it was intentional.

Owen swings my chair back to face him. "Tally? Are you moving?"

"I've considered it. I could use a change of pace. I stayed in Florida because of my father—"

"And now there's nothing left here for you, right?" he bites out, his mouth a rigid line. "Good to know."

Is the man serious? He's been shacking up with his ex-fiancée every night of the week under the guise of investment dinners, but I'm the asshole?

Oh, hell, no.

I push myself out of the seat, offering a stiff nod of my head. "Glad you approve," I spit out, marching into my office. I'm getting smart. This time, I lock the damn thing.

But it doesn't matter, because Owen doesn't try to enter my office, and after fifteen minutes, I realize he's gone.

In more ways than one.

Even if I'm planning a life far from Memorial, they're still my employer. Time to focus. I'm elbows deep in reports when my phone rings, startling me from my self-imposed work stupor.

It's a nurse in the cath lab. They need my help, and it shouldn't take but a minute. Can I please come down immediately?

With a sigh and equally heavy heart, I stroll down to the cath lab suite, throwing on a mask and cap before poking my head into the room. "You rang?" I inquire, my gaze landing on the nurse to my left.

Her only response? A nod toward Owen, who's observing Dr. Jessop as he performs a procedure.

His gaze meets mine over the surgical mask. "Tallulah, fill in for Jackie. Get a vest."

What the hell? He wants me to fill in for a cath lab tech? I don't want to expose Nugget to the radiation. I don't have a film badge to monitor my levels, and that idea makes me sick.

I feel my stomach hit the floor. Interesting, since it's been in my throat the last few weeks. "I...I can't."

"Why?" His words are clipped, but his gaze never wavers.

"I haven't worked in the lab for over two years."

"But you worked in the cath lab for a decade. Human anatomy hasn't changed, and all you need to do is pass a few instruments. Come on. Just make sure to put on the lead vest. A ton of x-rays today."

"I have a...thing." I stumble over my words, my entire body breaking out in a sweat. God, I'm the worst liar.

Owen's brows raise. "It will only take a minute."

Tears prick my lids. There's no simple way out of this situation, at least not without spilling the beans. "Owen, please." In my haste, I use his first name, and I feel the eyes of our coworkers on me.

Owen straightens, his eyes stormy. "Take over for me, Ken. Have April fill in for Jackie." He strides over to me, his hand on my elbow as he turns me toward the door.

Wonderful. Now, I'm getting fired. Let's add that onto this already banner day.

We walk out of the operating suite, and Owen pulls off his mask and surgical cap, running his hand over his head. "Let's get you something to eat."

Without a word, I follow him to the doctor's lounge, sinking into a chair. He grabs two waters out of the fridge and places one in front of me before taking a seat next to me.

"So…"

I fiddle with the bottle cap, willing my stomach to settle.

His fingers grasp my chin, forcing me to look at him. "How far along are you?"

I want to turn my head away because any falsehood will show in my face, but his grip remains firm. "I don't know what you're talking about."

"Don't do that, Tallulah. Don't you dare do that."

I jerk my chin away before the tears bounce off his hand.

"Tally, look at me."

I maintain a staring contest with the water bottle. It's winning.

"I already knew."

I suck in a slow, shaky breath. "I know. Well, after Saturday, I was certain you knew."

"It's been a lot longer than Saturday. I've known for the last couple of weeks. I was just waiting for you to tell me." His hand rests on my back, rubbing lazy circles between my shoulder blades. "How far along are you?"

"Ten weeks," I sniffle.

"It was the first week, huh? I guess I've got some good swimmers."

The man is *not* making jokes. Not right now. "This isn't funny, Owen."

"Actually, it's fantastic, Tally. We're having a baby."

That did it. Between the hormones, my father's death, our chaotic relationship, and losing my apartment—I don't stand a chance against the tears. And it's not a few pretty tears slipping down my face; it's a full-on ugly cry. I open my mouth to speak, but all I can manage is gulping sobs.

Owen wraps his arms around me, pulling me against his chest. "It's going to be fine. Why didn't you tell me as soon as you found out?"

I pull my head from his chest, meeting his gaze. "How should I have broken the news? Guess what? Not only are you my boss, and your bombshell former fiancée has just relocated to be near you, but I'm also pregnant with your baby. Happy Monday."

A smile quirks his lips, and it's a smile that I can't resist. "That's exactly what you should have done."

I shake my head. The man is incorrigible. "Right. It would have gone over like a lead balloon." Grabbing a napkin, I wipe my eyes and nose. I must look a sight. "Are we done here?"

His eyes widen. "Excuse me?"

"I said, are we done here? You know the situation now. Not that it matters."

"Not that it matters?" His voice is low, growling out a warning about the path of this conversation.

"I'm not asking you for anything, Owen. I don't expect your involvement with my baby—"

"Our baby," he interjects.

I wave off his correction. "The point is, I don't expect you to be an active participant."

His fingers drum the table, the muscle in his jaw twitching. "Sorry to break it to you, but I plan on being very active in my child's life. And yours."

Whether it's the urgency in his voice or the fiery set of his gaze, I can't be sure. But the tears reappear for about the twentieth time today.

"Tally, talk to me."

I wipe my eyes, unsure where to begin. Unsure of everything at this point. "I'm a big bucket of emotions all the time. Damn hormones. But the truth is that I'm terrified."

He grasps my hand, giving it a reassuring squeeze. "Of what, Darlin? You're going to be the best mother in the world."

I know he means what he says, but that only opens the faucet on the tears. "I wish I had your confidence. I'm overwhelmed at the idea of doing this on my own."

"What do you mean?"

I offer a shrug, because I do not want to have this conversation—not here and certainly not now.

"Tally, I'm right here."

See? I knew he would say the right thing. If only it made the situation easier. "I won't do that to you, Owen."

"Do what?"

"Tie you down. You were engaged only a couple of months ago. The last thing you need is to have a child with some woman you barely know."

The grip on my hand tightens. "I know every inch of you—mind, body, and soul."

I snatch my hand back, wiping away the tears, yet again. Damn things just keep coming. "I'm reassuring you that I don't expect you to be involved. I'm letting you off the hook."

"Christ, you love that term. Two things—one is that I plan on being very involved in your life, and two, stop letting me off the hook. This is the most amazing news. You're going to be a mom. I'm going to be a dad. I plan on being knee-deep in everything. So, get used to it, Darlin."

"This situation is complicated enough, with your and Charlotte's relationship—"

Owen's fist pounds the table, making me jump. "Charlotte and I are not together." His hands wrap around my shoulders, his eyes daring me to look away. "There hasn't been anyone since you, no matter what you think. Charlotte knows how I feel about you. It's hardly a secret."

"Is that why you kissed me last night?"

Owen shakes his head, a smile breaking across his face. "I kissed you because I was going to lose my mind if I didn't. Charlotte knew how much I loved you the night of the dinner. She bitched about how I was only focused on finding you, and once I did, that I couldn't stop staring at you."

I don't know why, but the idea that Owen flaunted his desire for me in front of Charlotte restores a bit of my self-confidence. Hey, it's taken a hell of a beating lately. "I was looking at you, too. Not to state the obvious, but you are pinup calendar hot, Owen."

"Is that right? Tell me more about how hot I am." I know that look, complete with his sexy grin. That look tells me he's picturing me naked, riding him into oblivion.

A tempting idea, really.

"Nice try. I'm not stroking your ego."

The grin widens at my unintentional sexual innuendo.

"Don't even say it, Owen."

"I was just wondering if other body parts were admissible."

I try to hold back my smile, but it's an impossibility. "And yet, you said it."

He holds up his hands in surrender, chuckling his defeat. "Have you had your first ultrasound?"

I shake my head, dragging my mind—and hormones—out of the gutter. "It's tomorrow, actually."

"What time?"

"Five-thirty. You don't have to—"

Owen isn't hearing any arguments. "Like hell, I don't. It's my first child's first sonogram. I'm going to be there."

I study his face. I swear I don't remember ever seeing him this...giddy. "Huh."

"What, Darlin?"

"You seem happy."

His smile fades to a wince of dismay as he runs a hand over his beard. "I am. I've always wanted to be a dad. Are you not looking forward to our baby?"

In that instant, it hits me. "I am." His face brightens at my words, so I spill my guts. "Don't get me wrong, I'm scared, but I'm excited, too. I hate the morning sickness, but I won the mother lode with the father. You're gorgeous and brilliant and talented and…I'm lucky. Our baby is lucky."

"You forgot one."

"I didn't give you enough props just now?" I ask, cocking a brow at him.

His palm cups my cheek as his lips brush against mine. Total sneak attack on his part. Not that I'm complaining. "You give me more credit than I deserve."

"So, what trait did I fail to mention? Killer body? Sex god? Sense of humor?"

"Totally in love with you."

I'm so glad I'm sitting down. Otherwise, I would have collapsed to the floor. Owen has told me countless times over the last few months, but this is the first time I actually feel his words. "Wow."

"Tally, it's always been you."

"I was afraid you might be mad about the baby."

Owen chuckles, shaking his head at me. "No, Darlin, I'm the complete opposite of mad. Now, I have to convince you to marry me."

That's enough for today. The sheen I felt only moments before shatters to the ground. "Relax, Doc. You do not have to marry me because of the baby. I would never expect that of you."

He studies my face, that smile still flitting across his lips. "What about the fact that I want to marry you? I've never said those words to another woman."

Talk about a crash landing back to reality. I shake my head, angry that I almost fell for Owen's lines. Yet again. "You just ended an engagement. I need total honesty now. No more fluff. No more telling me what I want to hear."

"I'm being honest."

"So how is it you were engaged, but you never asked a woman to marry you? Hmm? Can you answer that one for me?"

Owen is unruffled by my questions. Either he's the best liar in the world, or he's telling the truth. "Charlotte asked me. Asked is too kind a term. Demanded. Cornered. Those are more appropriate."

"You didn't ask her?" Holy crap, is that a tiny ray of hope at the end of the tunnel?

"No. I bought her a ring after she demanded one. I was totally uninvolved in the planning. I was miserable, Tally. And it got worse every day. So, I got slamming drunk with a buddy of mine who was visiting, and he mentioned Fort Lauderdale. He had worked at Memorial for a few years and loved the staff. Said the beach wasn't bad either."

"Who is your friend?"

"Dr. Weinman. He's a—"

"Pediatric surgeon. Dr. We. Good guy."

Owen nods in agreement. "Anyway, I woke up with a ripping hangover and a decision. I put in a call to Memorial and spoke to Dr. Watts. Then I sat Charlotte down and told her my plan. I also informed her she wasn't part of it anymore."

I cringe at his words. He's so blasé about tossing his fiancée aside. "Ouch."

Owen strokes my forearm, offering me a reassuring smile. "Don't feel too bad for Charlotte. She was knocking boots with some guy named Marco. I walked in on them together. He was the first one I caught, but not the first one she slept with."

Maybe I'm a bitch, but knowing how poorly Charlotte treated Owen brings me great joy. Some of her glitter has rubbed off, too. "Double ouch."

"It was the catalyst I needed. I packed my things and shipped them to Florida. When I landed here, I had a momentary freak out. I realized that I uprooted my entire life, and there was nothing guaranteed on the other end. After a week here, I was in doubt about my spur-of-the-moment decision, so I...you're going to laugh."

I lean forward, cupping my head in my palm. "I won't. Promise."

"I asked for a sign. I wanted something concrete to know that this was where I was supposed to be, and I hadn't lost my damn mind."

"Did you get it? Your sign, I mean?"

His face changes, but his hand continues stroking along my arm. "That night, I went to an underground club that my friend told me about, and my life changed forever."

"Wicked Chucks."

"I saw you at the bar with Stefani. Wearing that silly pink wig."

I huff with fake annoyance. "I like my wig."

"I like you better without it. You looked in my direction, and I felt everything I'd never felt with Charlotte. That I'd never felt with anyone. Fucking terrified me. I was always so sure of myself with women, but I couldn't get up the nerve to speak to you."

"I'm hardly intimidating, Owen!" Although the butterflies in my stomach are swarming after hearing his story.

"You absolutely are, in the best way. You radiate this energy, and I knew that if you didn't feel it too—if you were married or uninterested—that I wouldn't know how to handle it. So, I snuck upstairs for a better view of you. Thankfully, I unwittingly sat in your balcony."

I can't stop the smile crossing my face. "I'm so glad you did. Look at us now."

"I want to see you tonight, Tally. I need to see you tonight."

My mind is a jumble of thoughts and emotions. I want nothing more than to spend time with Owen, but I also have a ton of packing to do and a short time to get it finished. "Don't you have some important dinner function?"

"Yes, with you, if you'll have dinner with me."

"I know you're busy, Owen."

"Never too busy for you. Better yet, why don't you just come home?"

"Home?"

"I bought that condo for us. It has the bedroom for the baby, and we can't forget the rooftop garden for Hecate." He pulls me forward, between his legs, his hands wrapped around the back of my thighs. "I want us back. I miss us."

"I don't think there's room for me in your life," I grumble. Yes, I'm being difficult. Sue me, I'm hormonal.

"Bullshit, Tally. I will make room." His fingers press into my skin, inching me ever closer. "Are you showing?"

I smirk, sending him a wink. "You can't tell, can you?"

"You're wearing scrubs. You could hide a soccer ball under there."

"Hardly."

"Didn't answer my question."

I'm not ready to admit how much my body has changed, even if it's only obvious when I'm naked and analyzing myself in the mirror. "A little."

His fingers slide around my hips and under my scrub top, tickling my skin. "I want to see."

I stay his hands. "No. I'm insecure enough, after comparing my body to Charlotte's."

Owen's eyes narrow. "Why the hell would you ever—don't do that. I tell you I fell for you the minute I saw you, and that's your response? Unacceptable."

"We can wait until later."

But Owen has other plans, sliding my top up a few more inches. The man couldn't care less that this is not a private lounge. Anyone can walk in at any moment. "Nope. Not waiting."

His mouth presses against my abdomen, and my knees buckle as he tongues from one side to the other, his hands holding me fast.

"I'm kissing every inch of you tonight, so you'd better be prepared."

I hear the keypad of the lounge only moments before the door swings open, and I scramble away from Owen, adjusting my shirt and praying that our esteemed leader, Dr. Watts, didn't see anything too untoward.

"Sorry," I bumble, smoothing my hair. "I—Dr. Stevens was helping me with a medical situation."

Dr. Watts smirks, walking over to the coffeemaker. "Would that medical situation be the baby you're carrying?"

"You know, too?" Damn, here I thought I was slick.

"No one has a stomach virus for that long, Lu. I had a feeling Dr. Stevens was the father. Congratulations, you two."

"He's not—"

"Thank you. We're excited," Owen proclaims.

And there it is. Our boss, the woman who, in theory, signs both of our checks, now knows I'm carrying the new cardiologist's baby.

Unemployment, here I come.

You know in cartoons when the character's eyes bug out of their skull? That's me right now.

"Don't look so stricken, Lu. You two are hardly the first doctor and nurse couple," Dr. Watts comments, sipping her coffee.

"Right," I mumble.

"How far along are you?"

"Ten weeks," Owen replies, and I drop my gaze to him. How the hell is he so calm? There he sits, a grin plastered across his face, and his hand somehow linked with mine. I don't even remember that happening. I know the feeling of his warm digits enveloping my fingers makes everything right with the world. At least for the moment.

Dr. Watts exits the break room, granting us a few more moments of privacy.

"You'd better get back," I remind him, my gaze focused on our intertwined digits.

"True. I'll see you later tonight. Be safe, Tally. You two are precious to me."

I bite back a smile as he opens the door. "Owen?"

"Yeah?"

I close the distance between us, shutting the door and claiming his mouth with my own. "I forgot to tell you something. I love you. Very much."

My admission is risky; it lays my heart bare. But the smile stretching across his face and the way he kisses me back reassures me it's the right choice.

"I love you, Darlin." His hands caress my stomach. "Both of you."

CHAPTER
THIRTY-ONE
TALLY

"Spill it, Lu." Stefani pushes a cup of tea under my nose, a wry smirk on her lips. "You were all smiles when you left here yesterday, but today, you're a scowly puss again."

I lift the lid off the tea and take a sip of the scalding liquid. It may remove the top layer of skin inside my mouth, but at least it buys me a few minutes to figure out how to explain the last twenty-four hours. "Shit, that's hot."

"It's supposed to be hot. Stop avoiding the question."

"I'm sure you know that Owen is aware of my hitchhiker. I'm also certain that you were behind his sudden need for me to fill in for a surgical tech in the cath lab."

"I didn't have to tell him. He knew." Stefani shrugs, offering a droll grin. "He had to force your hand when he heard that you were considering relocation. He looked distraught over the idea of you leaving Florida. See? It all worked out."

"But it didn't. Here's what you didn't see. He said all the right things and swore he would be there—knee deep in diapers and formula. He even promised me a wonderful, romantic evening."

Stefani rubs her hands with devilish glee. "Ooh, give me the details."

"Not much to tell. He never showed."

"What the hell?"

"I'll give you one guess, and her name begins with C, but I have my own C-word nickname for her. She called some last-minute meeting crap that he *had* to attend, and once again, I took a backseat."

My friend wraps her arm around my shoulder, giving it a reassuring hug. "He's been so busy lately, but I truly don't think there's anything between him and Charlotte. At least not from his end."

I shrug, remembering to blow on the tea before scorching my intestinal tract again. "They might not be riding the hobby horse, but there's definitely something there. For a man who has no time on his hands, he finds extra hours for Charlotte." I rub my hand over my eyes.

I will not cry. I will not cry. Tear ducts, I'll make you a deal. Let me reach the privacy of my office and then you can go nuts. Fair enough?

"I'm sorry, Lu."

"If discovering that you're going to be a Dad isn't enough to free up time in your schedule, I don't know what is." I clear my throat and push myself away from the counter. "I'll be in my office if you need me."

"I'll go with you to the sonogram today."

I reach over, squeezing her hand. "A little bird told me that someone is having dinner with Dan tonight."

"I can cancel."

"Don't you dare. I want all the dirty details tomorrow morning." I rest my hand on my stomach, feeling lonelier than I have in years. "I'll be fine on my own."

I make it to my office, leaning against the door and blinking away the tears. The truth? I'm far from fine, but I have limited choices. I know that Owen will kick in funds, should the need arise, but I would sooner walk over hot coals than ask him for a cent. Besides, since my Dad passed, I have enough money to eke out a life for me and the baby. It might not consist of private jets and Caribbean villas, but it will be a life of love.

I'm not in my chair five minutes when the door opens. I swear, I really need to keep the damn thing locked.

Owen pokes his head in, a rueful smile on his face. "Morning, beautiful."

"Good morning, Dr. Stevens," I manage with a forced brightness.

I expect him to linger in the doorway or settle into the chair opposite my desk. Wrong on both counts. I take brief notice of the flowers and coffee in his hands before he sets them down, closing the distance between us and pressing his mouth against mine.

What fresh hell is this nonsense?

I pull back, resting my hands against his chest to put some space between us. Hell, there are miles of emotional space already. "What are you doing?"

"Giving the woman I love a kiss good morning."

I shift my eyes to the floor, releasing a heavy sigh. "Can you give me some space, please?"

I'm not sure if it's the dead look in my gaze or the flat tone of my words, but he obliges my request without argument, settling into the corner chair. Granted, since my office is the size of a shoebox, he's still within petting distance. "I'm sorry. I just miss you, Tally."

Wrong thing to say, buddy. "You miss me? Hmm."

"What's that mean?"

I could play dumb, but I've been turning a blind eye long enough. "It means that I highly doubt the words coming out of your mouth." Even if it is the most kissable mouth on the damn planet.

Owen hands me the flowers, nodding at the coffee. "I feel terrible about last night."

"Do you?" I volley back, my hands not moving to accept his offering. "Is that what the flowers are for?"

Owen looks down, and for the first time, I see him struggle with what to say. "I know you love lilies."

"Most people love lilies, Owen. But a bouquet will not fix this situation."

"I know, which is why I wanted to speak with you first thing." He motions to the bouquet again. "Please, will you hear me out?"

I slump into the chair, clicking my tongue against my teeth. "I'm really tired of this episode, Owen. I've seen this rerun several times already. It's time to change the channel."

"I know you're angry and you have every right to be—"

"That's just it. I *was* angry. Now, I'm just over it."

The poor man looks positively stricken, but my sympathy meter is on empty. "I wanted to come over, more than anything."

"See, that's a lie. If you wanted to come over *more than anything*, you would have been there last night. But once again, you were with your glamorous and wildly important fiancée."

"Ex-fiancée," he bites out.

"Does it matter? It's semantics at this point. Besides your patients, she's the only one who ever sees you." I hold up my hands, my attitude in full force. "Far be it from little old me to make a play for your time."

"Tally." I know that look. He's become adept at the beseeching, come-hither stare over the last several weeks. Perhaps he was always talented in that arena and I'm just realizing it now.

"What, Owen?" I shrug, forcing a dry laugh. "What can I do for you?"

"I'm so sorry."

"It's okay."

"It's not."

I nod—at least we agree on something. "It's not, but it is you who missed out on mind blowing sex."

His jaw slackens. "You're joking."

I shrug, keeping my gaze on the computer screen. "Guess you'll never know."

"How about I make it up to you? Twice as long, twice as good?"

"Nah. One and done. Sorry."

CHAPTER THIRTY-ONE • 317

His fingers tap the desk. Apparently being turned down for sex is not something he's used to in his life. "We'll see about that."

I peer at him over the top of my glasses, sending him a scowl. "Check your ego, Dr. Stevens. You're not that irresistible."

His hand snakes across the desk, clasping mine. "No, I'm not. You are. I told you, you're the purest heroin."

"Could we find another analogy? I hate being compared to something that destroys lives."

Owen chuckles, lifting my fingers to his lips. "How about this, then? You're every dream I never knew I had. I didn't believe in soulmates until I met you. You're it for me, Tally."

God, I hate him. I hate when he says things so profound and moving, and he looks so damn earnest and yet manages to smash my heart into bits on the ground. I pull my hand back, massaging the palm with my thumb. "Only one problem with that, Owen. I don't believe you anymore."

"Then I'll prove it to you."

I laugh, not because it's funny but because it's such a well-worn line. "Sure, you will."

"Will you give me a chance?"

"Owen, I've given you nothing but chances. We may be having a baby together, but I think the idea of you and me as anything more than friends and co-parents is a bad idea. Mostly for me and my heart."

"Did you ever love me or was it just a line, something to say back to me? Did you feel obligated? Is that why you said it yesterday?"

He is *not* going there.

"I'm not discussing this with you."

His fist thumps the desk, making me jump. "I didn't mean to scare you, but I need to know. Please, Tally. Here's the thing—if you're putting up this wall because I was a dick and fucked up, then that's one thing. I'll bash through it and prove myself worthy of your love. But if you feel nothing beyond friendship, put me out of my misery."

"Release you back to Charlotte, is that it?" Ouch, that was sharp, even for me.

"I don't want Charlotte."

"I don't know what you want, Owen. I don't think *you* know what you want."

"I want you—"

"You say that, but actions speak louder than words." This argument has left me exhausted, mentally and physically. "I'm getting a headache. Can we not do this right now?"

He latches onto my hand again, giving it a squeeze. "Of course, I don't want you stressed."

"I've been stressed for weeks."

"That ends today. I'm taking over...even if you feel nothing beyond friendship."

I know this is where I'm supposed to reassure him I feel *everything* beyond friendship, that my entire body is lighting up like a damn carnival just being near him. But I can't do it. Not this time. This time, I need to protect myself first. I spilled my heart yesterday, opening the door once again. And once again, he never showed.

I avert my gaze and pray that someone interrupts us.

The air between us hangs thick with tension, like the summer air before a thunderstorm cools everything down. I worry that if we don't put some space between us, we'll say something we regret.

"Five-thirty, right?"

My gaze swings back to him, narrowing in confusion. "Sorry?"

"The sonogram. It's at five-thirty."

"It is, but I know you're busy."

Do I want him there? Yes, indeed.

Do I want him to say he'll be there, only to cancel and piss all over my hopes? Not a chance in hell.

Easier to play it off and expect nothing.

That's what friends do, right?

God, being friends sucks.

"I'll be at the sonogram."

I push myself to a standing position, moving toward the door in an effort to move the conversation out of the office. "I told you, I'm fine. Me and Nugget got this."

"Nugget?"

I laugh, despite the sadness in my heart. "That's my nickname for him—or her. I think it's a boy."

Before I can react, his hand settles over my stomach, a smile I've never seen before playing along his mouth. "A boy, huh?"

"Just a hunch. Anyway," I remove his hand, giving it an awkward squeeze, "You go do you."

"Tally, I *will* be there."

Trouble is, he's said that several times in recent weeks and the only certainty is that he'll disappoint me.

"You'd better go. You've got a case waiting for you in the cath lab."

∽

"ARE YOU LOST?" A CHEERY VOICE CARRIES ACROSS THE WAITING ROOM, and I look up to see Harriet, a former nurse turned midwife. She crosses the room in three long-legged strides, pulling me into a hard hug.

"Hi, Harriet," I coo, returning her embrace. I miss this woman. She was my ride or die before Stefani, but between school and marriage and babies—you get the picture. "You look good."

"You look pregnant. Holy shit, Tallulah! Come on back."

I peer over my shoulder to the waiting area. A few women wait for their turn with the doctor, but Owen is nowhere to be found.

Knew it.

I wish that when you prepared yourself for disappointment, that it lessened the feeling. That's how it *should* work, right?

So very, very wrong.

It's a sinking feeling, knowing that the only part of Owen I'll ever have is the child growing in my womb. But that will have to be enough.

Within five minutes, I'm gowned and waiting for Harriet to return, my eyes darting around the sterile exam room. I know the staff means the decor to be soothing, but it leaves me cold.

"There's someone out here looking for you," Harriet states, leaning in the door. She offers a wink and mouths 'good job' before pushing the door wide.

Owen.

He's here.

He's also a sweaty mess. Still hot, though. Maybe even more so. Damn my pregnancy hormones.

"Did you jog here?" I inquire, turning my face so his kiss lands on my cheek instead of its intended aim.

"I didn't know where it was. Thankfully, Jessop told me. I've been scouring the hospital grounds for the last twenty minutes. I was so afraid I'd miss it."

"You didn't miss anything." Harriet gives him a friendly clap on the shoulder. "So, *you* are the new talk of the town. Pleasure to meet you. Technically, I met you at that dinner, but there were so many important people flitting about that night."

"Talk of the town?" Owen inquires, accepting Harriet's offer of a water bottle and guzzling half of it down.

"Yes, brilliant renowned cardiologist come to roost in our little enclave. You're very fancy."

"She's a smart ass," I murmur, looking anywhere but at Owen.

"Don't you forget it," Harriet counters with a wink. "So...you two, huh? Isn't that fantastic? I like this girl here far better than your purported fiancée, even if she is a billionaire's daughter." She squeezes my shoulder in a sign of solidarity, but the damage is done.

See, Owen? Everyone thinks you and Charlotte are together, which makes me look like the mistress. Fabulous.

Owen's face pales under his tan. "Who told you I was engaged?"

Harriet chuckles. In true fashion, she doesn't hold back. "The billionaire's daughter. She made it quite clear to all of us in the immediate area that you were off limits."

A muscle ticks in Owen's jaw. "I'll deal with her. Thanks for the heads up."

"I assume that you're the—"

"He's a friend," I blurt out, ignoring the incredulous look crossing Owen's face. I know he's pissed, but I'll deal with him later. Right now, I'm trying not to burst into tears, as what should have been a beautiful moment is marred—once again—by Charlotte's pervading presence.

Harriet glances between the two of us before offering me a pat on the arm. "You can't have too many friends. Let's get started, shall we? Lu, you're going to be a mom! That's amazing."

"Thanks." I feel Owen's gaze on me, but I keep my focus on the ceiling. That's a safe spot.

"How's your Dad?"

I swallow against the tears. So much for this being a pleasant visit. "He passed away a couple of weeks ago."

Harriet pauses, her eyes glassy. She knows what the man meant to me. "I'm so sorry. I didn't know, or I would have been there."

I nod at her words, but it's the feel of Owen's hand enveloping mine that brings me back to the present. I glance at him and he offers a sad smile, his fingers tracing along my palm.

"Okay, here comes the fun part."

I slide up my gown, aware of Owen's laser stare. Harriet squirts the gel on my stomach, and I flinch. "Holy hell, that's cold."

Owen has yet to release my hand, his lips moving lightly across my fingers. "You are showing," he murmurs.

I blame the hormones as tears back up in my eyes again. "I'm so short that there's nowhere for Nugget to hide. I'll be a waddling mess soon," I retort, forcing a smile in his direction.

"You're beautiful."

"You have to say that," I volley back.

"I mean it. You've never been so beautiful."

I meet his gaze, all ready with a sarcastic barb, but it dies in my throat. There's a softness in his face, and I'm not willing to ruin it with words. Particularly not the wrong words.

Meanwhile, Harriet is busy pressing buttons and flipping knobs with one hand, the other wrapped around the probe as it maneuvers around my stomach. She looks like she's operating a spaceship, but I see the smile flit across her face at Owen's words.

"There's your baby." She turns on a switch and the sound of our baby's heartbeat fills the room.

In that moment, I forget everything beyond my baby and its fast-beating heart. I've seen hundreds of sonograms, but this is different. This time, Nugget is mine.

I lift a finger, tracing along the screen as the baby moves its arms. It's love at first sight.

Wiping away tears that I know are happy—finally—I steal a gaze at Owen. The look on his face is priceless, his own eyes bright with emotion.

Our gazes hold, and he presses a kiss to my forehead. I've never seen the smile that decorates his face before. I hope our baby has his beautiful eyes.

"It's nice to see the father so involved," Harriet states with a knowing smile. "You must be excited, Dr. Stevens."

"See, Tally? Everyone else sees it. Now, I just need you to see it," Owen whispers, his mouth against my skin.

Harriet stands, printing out a copy of our baby. "It's obvious. The way he's looking at you and your baby, there's no way he *isn't* the father. He's in love. With both of you."

CHAPTER
THIRTY-TWO
OWEN

"I have an entire evening planned," I blurt as we walk out of the office, my hand holding Tally firm. I feel like I'm hopped up on speed after seeing my baby for the first time, and I'm beyond desperate to get the woman I love home to prove how much I miss her.

"Do you?" Tally offers me a smile, but it's forced, like most of her smiles lately. In fact, the first real one I've seen since the whole Charlotte debacle was when she gazed at the monitor and saw our baby.

Our baby.

It's crazy, but it's so right. I always knew I wanted kids; I just didn't want them with Charlotte. But with Tally, there's no hesitancy. Only joy.

Along with the sneaking suspicion that my gorgeous girl is going to make me jump through an array of hoops to earn back a place in her heart.

"I called in a takeout order from the best Italian restaurant in town, and I'll have a bubble bath ready for you the moment you arrive. Or just leave your car here. Let me drive you." I don't know if

I'm speaking at the speed of light because of excitement or fear that she's going to say no to date night.

Her face scrunches in confusion. "Hold up a minute. Who are these plans with?"

"You, Darlin. I'm getting us back on track."

Tally laughs, but it's not her husky chuckle of excitement. No, it's as stilted as the rest of her responses today. "Thanks for the offer, but I can't tonight."

"Why not?"

Her eyes widen at my pointed question. Good, at least it's a genuine response. "Excuse me?"

"I asked why not?" I repeat, crossing my arms over my chest. "This is a big night, Tally. We just saw our baby. Don't you want to celebrate with me?"

She falters, but it's only for an instant before the mask slides back into place. "I have a prior engagement, Owen." She lifts onto tiptoe, offering me a bland kiss on the cheek. "Enjoy your dinner. I'm sure you can find company, should you require it."

"Who are your plans with? Let me guess—Dan?"

She rolls her dark eyes at me, her full lips pursed in annoyance. "I'm going to pretend you didn't ask me that question."

"Is there something going on? He's been very devoted." My questions are clipped and harsh, but I'm finding it hard to contain my rage.

"Screw you, Owen." Tally turns on her heel, yanking open the car door.

I have a ton of things I want to say in response to her blow off. Scream in response, at this point. But all I can manage is clenching and unclenching my fists as she drives off, with nary a backward glance.

I'm so screwed.

I'm halfway to my car, stomping like a furious toddler, when I catch sight of Stefani walking off the elevator banks across the

CHAPTER THIRTY-TWO • 325

garage. "Stefani!" I bellow, waving my hand as I jog over. If anyone knows what's going on in Tally's head, it's her best friend.

"Hi, Owen. What can I do for you?" Her brows raise. "Don't tell me you missed the sonogram appointment."

Jesus, what these women think of me. The worst part is knowing that I've earned their skepticism. "I didn't miss the appointment."

"Is everything okay with the baby?"

I smile, despite my frustration, as I lean against her car. "The baby is perfect. It was such a trip, seeing him on the screen."

"Him?"

I shrug, offering a dry laugh. "Too early to tell definitively, but Tally and I both think it's a boy."

Stefani leans next to me, giving me a nudge with her elbow. "That *is* a trip. But it's not why you ran across the parking garage, either."

I know that I should make small talk, but I don't have that kind of time.

I need answers.

Now.

"Is there something going on between Tally and Dan?"

Stefani wrinkles her nose at my direct question. That's not a good start. "Where in the world did that idea come from?"

"Things have been shit between me and Tally—"

"And you're blaming Dan?"

This is definitely *not* going as smoothly as I hoped. "Not exactly. I know that they're friends, but I wondered if he'd made a move on Tally."

Stefani stretches to her full height, only a few inches shorter than me. "First, Dan and Lu are just friends. Period. They've been friends for years. Second, Dan has been keeping Lu company because her life has been crap the last few weeks. Third, and most important, Lu is pregnant"—she pokes me in the chest with her finger—"with *your* baby. So perhaps the strain in your relationship is less about Dan and more about how busy you've been entertaining your *ex-fiancée*."

Tell me how you really feel, Stefani.

I do appreciate her candor. Now at least I know that Dan isn't a threat, and my girl hasn't moved on.

Yet.

I run a hand over my scalp, shooting Stefani a rueful glance. "You're right. This training center and business with Charlotte has hijacked all my free time. But I allowed it. I was the asshole who let her get away with it, while Tally paid the price."

Stefani fiddles with her keys, and I'm uncertain I want to hear what more she has to say. "Owen, is this some battle of wills? Lu is my best friend, and she deserves to be treated with care and courtesy."

"I agree—"

"That's the trouble," Stefani cuts me off, raising her hand when I open my mouth to retort. "You say that, but look at the situation. How would you feel if the roles were reversed, and Lu was hanging out with an old flame several nights per week? An old flame that wanted her back?"

I have to hand it to Stefani; she has a way of cutting to the quick. "I would have mopped the floor with his ass by now, set him straight."

"Exactly. I know this situation is different, with the success of the training center contingent on your participation, but that doesn't diminish the fact that Lu's heart is hurting. And you did it." Finally, she raises her gaze to meet mine. "I really hoped you would be different. You seemed different."

"I *am* different. I have a ring for Tally, remember?"

She taps my chest with her key, narrowing her gaze. "Then might I suggest you treat her like the woman you love, and less like the woman who you think will be waiting when your business with Charlotte is finished? I have to go. *Dan* and I have a date." Another pointed glance.

CHAPTER THIRTY-TWO

Message received. I'm way the hell off.

I open Stefani's door, forcing a smile. "Have a good time. You two make a good couple."

"Owen, you and Lu were relationship goals. Seriously. I've never seen two people so intoxicated with one another. But she will not be sloppy seconds, even for a man like you." She slides the car into reverse, pausing with her hand on the shifter. "To be fair, she really is busy. Packing up her apartment and discovering she's pregnant has usurped most of the real estate in her brain these last few weeks."

"Moving?" As I eke out the syllables, my heart sinks. Is Tally making good on her threat to relocate?

"She lost the lease on her apartment. The landlord needs the space for her grandson, so Lu is packing and trying to be out by this weekend. I'm going to help her tomorrow."

"No need. I'll hire movers." I offer a wave goodbye before making a beeline for my car.

My destination?

Tally's soon to be former apartment, and if my girl is lifting heavy boxes, I'm spanking every inch of her sweet ass.

I PUSH OPEN THE DOOR, MY IRE GROWING AS I WATCH TALLY FUMBLE TO hoist a box above her head.

"If you don't put that box down—" I order, marching across the room and grabbing it from her hands.

"Owen, what are you doing here?"

"These are your plans? Packing? Why didn't you ask me for help?"

Tally lifts herself to her full height, more than a foot below me, and I can't help but smile at the size difference between her and Stefani. "Maybe I don't need your help."

"Maybe it's not up for debate."

She throws up her hands, flopping onto the couch with a pout that I'm tempted to suck off her lips. "You can't just walk in here and order me around."

I bite back a grin. Tally may be ready for battle, but this time, I've got my armor on, too. She's not winning this fight. "Yes, I can." I punch in a number on my phone, my gaze resting on her perturbed expression.

The woman is too damn delectable when she's mad.

Within five minutes, I've hired a moving company. They're even handling the rest of the packing. Tally has enough stress. She doesn't need to spend her downtime wrapping plates. "All done. They'll be here on Saturday."

"Great, that solves part of my problem," Tally states, chewing her lower lip.

I sink next to her on the couch, close enough to feel the energy sparking between us. "What's the other part of your problem?"

"I haven't found a place to live yet."

Leaning back, I shoot her a smirk. "Why not, Tally? That seems so irresponsible of you." Yes, I'm screwing with her, but I need to stoke the emotion that she's holding at bay.

True to form, my girl's temper flares as she adjusts her glasses. "I want to hit you. Preferably with something heavy."

"Go ahead. Still doesn't answer my question."

"What can I say? I enjoy living on the edge."

With lightning reflexes, I pull Tally onto my lap, feeling her tense in my arms. "You have a place to live. You, Nugget and Hecate are moving into the condo. I bought it for us, and it's about damn time you started living there. See? Two problems solved in less than ten minutes. This is why you need me." My lips caress her neck as I bask in the scent that is intrinsically Tally.

Christ, this woman smells like heaven, even covered in a thin sheen of sweat. Especially covered in a thin sheen of sweat.

"How does that solve anything?" Tally counters, her slight hands trying to put space between us.

CHAPTER THIRTY-TWO

Not happening.

"I'm going to pretend I didn't hear that." I murmur my words against her neck, as I trace a path along her skin with my tongue. My hands circle her hips, pushing her down against my erection. I swear to God, if I don't get inside Tally soon, my dick is going to explode.

"I can say it louder." Despite my sexual ministrations, Tally isn't willing to cave that easily. She's going to make me work for every inch of her delicious body.

Mission accepted.

"As I see it, we have three options. I can kiss every inch of your body, right here, right now."

"What are the other options?" Tally may act tough, but I feel her pulse quicken as I tongue the hollow of her neck.

"We can continue arguing, because that's so much more productive. Or, we pick up our dinner, which is waiting for us, and then for dessert, I feast on you." I stand up, taking my tiny vixen with me, only setting her back down when she squirms in my arms. "You have ten minutes to pack some clothes while I coax Hecate into the carrier."

Tally stands her ground, her hands locked on her hips and jaw set, but she looks more like a Care Bear than a fierce warrior.

Better not mention that fact.

With a chuckle, I drop a kiss on the top of her head. "Come on blood goat queen, times a wasting."

That did it. The grimace fades, and Tally grins, shrugging in resignation. "Fine. But it's only temporary until I find a place."

"We'll see about that. The final decision lies with Hecate."

"She's my cat. She's going to side with me."

I offer Tally a wink as I stroke Hecate's fur, her back arching into my hand. "You sure about that? She seems really fond of me."

"No accounting for taste."

"You know I taste good," I volley back, watching my girl flush. "Not as good as you, but—"

"Go collect the cat," she mutters, ushering me out of the room as she opens a suitcase on her bed. "I'll be done in a minute."

As I coax—okay, shove—Hecate into the carrier and cart her to the car, I can't keep the smile from my face.

Finally, my girl is coming home.

CHAPTER THIRTY-THREE

TALLY

Must maintain a strong front. Must maintain a strong front.

Who the hell am I kidding? I'm a marshmallow where Dr. Owen Stevens is concerned.

I'll admit that some part of me prayed he would stride into my apartment and sweep me off my feet, promising me and Nugget a happier life. But after recent events, I had my doubts.

I've never been so glad to be wrong.

I zipper my suitcase closed, glancing over my shoulder at Owen leaning against the doorjamb. "You don't have to look so pleased with yourself, you know."

"I've earned this smirk, Darlin. You've been a stubborn pain in the ass the last couple of months."

I spin around, crossing my arms over my chest and sending him a haughty glare. "I am *not* a pain in the ass." At his raised brows, I concede, "if I was, it's your fault. Don't forget that."

Owen drops the fedora on my head, swooping in to steal a kiss. "How can I? You won't let me. Come on, Tally, let's go home. Hecate's patience is wearing thin."

"You're assuming she had any to begin with. That cat is the definition of spoiled."

One arm drops around my shoulder, his other hand grabbing my suitcase. "How spoiled is our kid going to be?"

"As spoiled as Hecate. Obviously," I declare, a smile resting on my lips. It's amazing how much easier everything seems now that the truth is out on the table.

And who knows? Maybe I'll get that back-bending sex, after all.

∼

MAYBE NOT.

I release an audible groan inside my vehicle when I spy Charlotte standing next to her white Mercedes in Owen's parking garage. I swear, the woman always looks immaculate. She must have a beauty team hidden in her trunk.

But her presence reminds me, once again, of my place. I may be carrying Owen's child, but she's not ready to release the claim on her man.

Her man.

Wow. That's the first time I've uttered those words, even to myself.

Am I jealous?

Abso-fucking-lutely. She's gorgeous and rich and important and I...wear a fedora. I'm owned by the wickedest cat in the world, so that ups my cool factor, but I'm also the woman relegated to accepting Owen's charity until I find a new place. Charlotte could buy the state of Florida on one credit card and still have money for designer shoes.

Let's not get me started on the difference in the looks department.

I push open my car door, as all my excitement deflates like a day-old balloon. Owen is already by my side, a strained expression on his

CHAPTER THIRTY-THREE · 333

face. I shoot him a glare from the driver's seat, because I'm in no mood today.

Or any day, for that matter.

"Should I go?" I mutter, watching Charlotte approach from the corner of my eye. Fabulous.

"Why would you ask that question?"

Usually, I'm subtle. I try not to make an ass of myself or anyone else. Well, subtlety can kiss my hormonal butt. Raising my hand in Charlotte's direction, I roll my eyes. "I can't imagine where that question would have come from."

"Tally, I'm going to get rid of her."

"Don't do it on my account," I grumble, offering his statuesque ex-fiancée a thin smile. "Hi there, Charlotte."

"Tallulah," she replies, her voice even and measured. "You're a surprise."

"Actually, you're a surprise," Owen barks, pulling Hecate's carrier and my suitcase from the backseat. "What are you doing here?"

Charlotte blanches at his pointed accusation. For a split second, I feel sorry for her. I can't blame her for loving the man. God knows I do, too.

She pulls a large envelope from her satchel. "I have the paperwork regarding the lease for the training center. We need to discuss—"

"Not tonight," Owen shakes his head at Charlotte before nudging me with the suitcase. "Come on, our dinner is waiting."

I wish I was better at being cold-hearted, but sarcasm is about as far as I go. With a sigh, I grab the handle of my suitcase. "You two go ahead, I'll take my stuff up."

"Are you visiting?" Charlotte inquires, and I realize I'm going to have to speak to her.

"I lost the lease on my apartment, so I'm staying here until I find another place."

"She's not finding another place. She's moving in," Owen interjects, those gray eyes flashing at me.

I shrug, pulling the suitcase toward me. "Seriously, take care of business. I have to unpack, anyway."

"I'll take your things upstairs," Owen grits out and I realize I'm not winning this battle.

It's amazing how long an elevator ride can be. In reality, it's only twenty seconds. But, standing in between Charlotte and Owen, with both of them towering over me, it feels like forever.

As soon as Owen swings open the door, I grab my suitcase, awaiting further instructions.

"Since you insist on carrying it yourself, you know where the bedroom is," Owen mutters, freeing Hecate from her plastic prison.

The cat looks at each of us in turn, hisses, and runs under the sofa.

I totally get you, Hecate. Come to think of it, can I join you?

No point in standing around, staring—I mean glaring—at each other. I turn and haul my suitcase down the hallway, ignoring Owen's silent plea for understanding.

Sorry, Doc, I'm fresh out of love and understanding.

WITHIN THE SPACE OF FIFTEEN MINUTES, I'VE UNPACKED MY ESSENTIALS. Now, I'm sprawled across the bed in the guest room, laptop open and mission clear.

Owen's place needs to be a temporary landing. *Very* temporary.

I hear the door open, but don't bother to look. Unless Hecate has developed opposable thumbs, I know who it is.

The mattress sinks next to me, as Owen's talented hands skate along my abdomen. "What are you doing back here?"

I grab his hand, shoving it off my body. "I'm looking for an apartment."

Owen rolls me over, resting his forearms on either side of my body. "Tally, you moved in less than an hour ago. You live here now."

CHAPTER THIRTY-THREE

"I appreciate the help, but I can't live with you."

"Why not?"

"I don't want to be the third wheel with you and your ex-fiancée. Fiancée. What the fuck ever."

I expect that my statement will rile Owen's anger. Instead, I watch that sexy as hell smirk travel across his face. What the hell is so damn amusing?

"You are hardly the third wheel." He presses a finger to my lips, keeping me quiet. "I informed Charlotte that these unscheduled visits had to stop. I told her you were stressed enough, and that you and the baby—"

I bolt upright. "You told Charlotte about the baby?"

"Why wouldn't I?"

My mind races. "There are so many reasons to *not* tell that woman. First, she wants you back. Second, she could tank your deal. Third,"—I hesitate, because that's really all I have to work with—"you're not supposed to say anything until twelve weeks. It's bad luck."

The smirk widens as his large hands ease me back onto the mattress. "First, I don't want her back. Second, it's not Charlotte's deal. It's her father's and trust me, he wants it completed. Third," he murmurs, his lips caressing my neck, "I'm excited about our baby and I want to tell everyone. Sue me."

"I might have to," I grumble, shoving at his iron chest. "Get off, Owen."

"That's what I'm trying to do, Darlin."

His words are playful, coaxing me to let him back in and forget everything before this moment. But my heart is not a cat toy—something to be batted about and then discarded when a newer toy appears. "It's not going to work like this."

Owen sighs, pulling himself to a seated position. "Is that why you're camped out in here?"

"Should I take the other bedroom?"

"Yes, your sweet ass should be in *our* bedroom, where I can strip you naked and adore every delectable inch of you."

I throw up my hands, jumping to my feet. "See? This is what I'm talking about. We can't do this,"—I motion between the two of us—"anymore. It's not healthy."

Owen runs his hand over his scalp. "Trust me, I get it, Darlin. It's been difficult for both of us. Charlotte has ruined far too many nights."

I shake my head. "That's just it, Owen. It's not *just* Charlotte. You're an active participant, too. She's been destroying things between us, and she will keep doing it. Worse, you'll keep allowing it. Something has to give, and that something is me." I wag my finger at him, daring him to cut into my diatribe. "I really appreciate you helping me out, giving me and Hecate a place to stay. But this is temporary, Owen. I won't be a third wheel. I won't be your roommate, and—"

"Let me guess. We can't be intimate anymore," Owen spits out, his foot tapping against the floor.

"Exactly. I'm glad you understand."

"Like hell I do. I'm not giving you up, and I'm not giving up on us. Now, I'll admit that this situation is beyond screwed, but I fixed it tonight. Don't believe me? Call Charlotte."

"I don't want to call your ex-fiancée. I'd rather go through a root canal without Novocain. How many people have to put up with the crap I'm dealing with, Owen?"

He grabs my wrists, pulling my ass back onto the bed. "You're right, and it ended tonight. I promise you."

"I don't believe you."

A grin splits Owen's face as his mouth closes around one of my fingers. Damn this man and his talented tongue. "I'm fully aware of that fact, which is why you can remain stubborn and angry. In the interim, I will continue to seduce the fuck out of you until you cave."

God, I hate how delicious that sounds. "You think I'll cave? Have we met?"

"Darlin, I think those pregnancy hormones are going to be raging soon—if they aren't already—and you'll be begging me to sink inside you." His lips nip my neck, and I hesitate one second too long before shooing him away.

He knows he has me.

"I also have you living under the same roof, now. So, if it makes you feel better to draw your line in the sand and stay back here, be my guest. But don't think for one second that you aren't going to be mine. Not happening, Tally."

"Let me get this straight. You're living with Owen but not sleeping with him, and that is entirely your decision?" Stefani pops a fry into her mouth, shooting me an exasperated scowl.

I nod, ignoring her incredulous stare. "He didn't give me much of a choice. He barged into my apartment, hired some movers, and whisked me off to his condo. It actually worked out, because Mrs. Smalls needed the space for her grandson."

"Way to ignore the question."

"We both know that Owen is gorgeous and sexy as hell. But, and this is *huge* but, he also sees his ex-fiancée almost every day."

"I thought you said he fixed that problem."

Damn Stefani and her elephant-like memory. "Okay, so I may be exaggerating. Since I moved in, Owen sees Charlotte once or twice a week. But that's still too many times. He's not supposed to be hanging out with his ex-fiancée at all. That's why she's his ex!"

"Thankfully, the rigamarole for the training center is almost completed, right? Then, your life can get back to happy sex times."

I grunt, shaking my head. "It's not that simple."

Stefani gives my shoulder a gentle rub. "You don't feel you measure up? Am I right?"

I hate how transparent I am, and I worry that Owen realizes the truth, too. "How can I not? I have a healthy self-confidence, but that woman is supermodel material. I look like I ate a beach ball."

"You do not. You're adorable."

"Yeah, an adorable person who ate a beach ball."

I don't mention my battle with the full-length bathroom mirror today. It's unnatural how much bigger I look than last week. I went from a three-months pregnant belly to six in the blink of an eye.

I'm exaggerating again, but these pregnancy hormones are not helping my cause. Neither is the six-foot statuesque beauty who is champing at the bit to bring Owen back into her clutches.

At this point, I'm not sure which of us looks more pathetic. Me, homeless and crashing in Owen's guest room or Charlotte plying him with million-dollar deals.

"Stop being so damn hard on yourself. You also need to stop focusing your energy on Charlotte. Owen doesn't want her, Lu. If he did, he would have reconciled with her already."

"Fine," I mutter, stealing a fry from her plate. Stefani definitely got the bigger serving. "Tell me about your dates with Dan."

The smile creeping across her face speaks volumes, and for a minute, I forget about the craziness called my life.

Hey, at least one of us is getting laid.

I arrive back at the condo an hour later, and pause to appreciate the view. It's a gorgeous location, but aren't most million-dollar pads? I wager his apartment with Charlotte resembled Buckingham Palace.

Speaking of the ice queen, at least her car is nowhere around. I hold my breath every time I pull into the parking garage, certain I'll see her waiting for Owen like some gorgeous, insane stalker.

I open the front door, greeted by the smell of cinnamon apples wafting through the air. I don't know how, but this place always smells like the inside of a bakery. Damn, now I'm hungry again.

"Hecate," I call out, climbing the steps to the rooftop garden. No sign of little miss priss, but it is a gray day. "Hecate, where are you?"

"We're in here," Owen calls from the bedroom.

CHAPTER THIRTY-THREE • 339

His bedroom.

I pause by the door, releasing a fake scoff of indignation. "Seriously?"

Owen offers a sleepy smile from his spot on the bed, my cat curled up next to him. "I told you that Hecate makes the final decision."

"Now, I know where she's been the last few nights. Traitorous animal. So much for loyalty."

Owen chuckles, stroking Hecate's head. "Jealous? Come here, I'll scratch your head, too."

I glare at him even though a warm flush passes through my body. "Pass."

"You know you want it."

"I know no such thing," I volley back.

"Stop being such a hardass, Tally."

"Why should I?"

"You're not very good at it. You're no more immune to me than I am to you. But you wanted your space, so I'm letting you have it."

"Thanks," I mutter, although I'm not sure how thankful I am. Owen was right, my pregnancy hormones are raging, and the sight of him half-naked in bed is mighty appealing.

"Yep, you'll have to make the first move."

"Noted." I'm horny as hell, no doubt about it, but I would sooner swallow fire than approach Owen after everything.

"How are you feeling?"

I shrug. "Tired. But I guess that's normal. The best part is that I look more tired than I feel."

His eyes wander over my face, a smile lighting up his mouth. "You're glowing."

"I'm probably sweating."

"Okay, Ms. 'I can't take a compliment'. I stand by my first observation." Owen chuckles, putting his arms behind his head and showing off that delectable chest full of muscles and ink. I have to hand it to him, the man knows what he has to work with, and he is shameless about flaunting it. In front of me, at least.

I fiddle with the door handle, looking for a reason to continue conversing while not throwing myself into his arms. "Thanks."

"You're welcome."

I pivot on my heel, feeling the food coma settling in. Time for a nap, and maybe a few minutes with my battery operated boyfriend. Hey, a woman has needs.

"Sure you don't want that head scratch? I give a mean butt scratch, too. Just ask Hecate."

I flip him the bird, sticking out my tongue at the same time. Yes, I'm mature. Leave me alone.

"Your loss, Darlin."

Something in Owen's flippant remark ignites my ire. He's right, I lost. But so did he. "No, *Darlin*, I believe it's your loss. I wouldn't hold your breath if you think I'll come to you, begging sexual favors. If you want me, you'd better get busy seducing me. Or was that all talk, too?"

Owen pushes himself to a seated position, those gray eyes flashing at me. "You just gave me a green light, Tally."

"No, you're still on yellow."

"Better than red."

The heat between us simmers. All I have to do is make one move toward him, and I'll be halfway to orgasm land in ten minutes.

But I'm not ready to make that step. Not yet. My hormones are kicking and screaming, but my ego is dragging its feet.

I finger the door frame, staring at the wood floor. Everything is top end here. The guest bathroom is bigger than my old bedroom, and I know that this place is a step down from where Owen lived in San Francisco.

Just like that, the reality of the situation shifts into sharp clarity. I much prefer it fuzzy and out of focus. Then I can pretend I belong here, that there's a place for me. "What are you cooking? It smells delicious."

CHAPTER THIRTY-THREE • 341

"I thought we'd have an early dinner, followed by an evening of movies. Lady's choice, of course."

"I get to pick the dinner or the movie?"

"Considering the dinner is already prepped, you're shit out of luck there. But you can pick the movie. Fair enough?"

I nod. "That's really nice of you. Thank you."

"Oh, you'll make it up to me. Don't you worry about that." He stifles a yawn behind his hand.

"How much sleep did you get last night?"

"I got the call at around three, got back around one."

"The case took that long?"

"No, but I figured I'd round on my patients, make some phone calls."

Visit with Charlotte? The snarky retort sits on the tip of my tongue, but I bite it back. No point poking the bear, especially when he's feeding me later. "We have a few hours before dinner. Go back to sleep."

"Come, lay with me." He holds out his hand and my entire body throbs to go to him. "Just lay with me. I'll keep my hands to myself... if you really want me to." He pats the mattress. "This bed is far more comfortable, which you would know if you ever slept in it. So come on, consider it partial payment for dinner."

I kick off my shoes before sliding under the covers. He's not kidding. This bed is ridiculously comfortable. "What's the remaining payment?"

"You'll find out, won't you?" Owen's hand snakes around my waist, his body spooning me.

I try to focus on my breathing, instead of his proximity, but when his hand settles on my belly, his lips sliding against my neck, I lose all vestiges of calm. "Maybe—"

"Shush, Tally."

"Or what?"

"I'll be forced to tie you up, strip you down, and neither of us will get any sleep."

He's laid it out there, what he wants. What he knows I want. All I have to do is give him the go ahead, the proverbial green light.

But my heart and ego? Still stuck on yellow. I snuggle closer to him, my hand stroking Hecate's glossy coat. "I'm shushed."

He's silent for a beat before I feel his lips press a gentle kiss to my nape. "I'm glad you're home, Darlin."

CHAPTER
THIRTY-FOUR
TALLY

"This is so far beyond delicious, it ought to be illegal," I state, scraping my plate clean. "Is there anything you can't do? Cook, save lives—"

"Ridiculously good in bed," Owen counters with a wink.

"Calm your tits, Doc. There's not enough room at the table if you invite your overly inflated ego."

He laughs, finishing his glass of wine. "It's not bragging if it's true."

I roll my eyes, but the man is correct. In the sack, Owen is a god. An absolute god. That, and he *is* joking—he's one of the humblest men I've ever met. "Tell me about your emergent case."

"Forty-five, no real medical history. He developed a left main coronary artery dissection."

"Crap."

"It all worked out. We stented the LAD and left main, then placed him on a ventricular assist device. The echocardiogram after the procedure showed normal left ventricular function. It was a good day. We got lucky."

"It is so much more than luck. You are the most talented interventionist that I've ever known. You need to take more credit." I can't help it. The man never ceases to amaze me. He's truly a miracle worker, but to him, it's just another day at the office.

"Per you, there wasn't enough room at the table for me and my ego already, remember? Now you want to bolster it?"

"That had nothing to do with your occupation. That was strictly about sex."

He leans forward, clasping my fingers. "Are you saying that I'm not as talented in that area?"

I ignore his pointed question, offering him a fist-pump instead. "What I'm saying is that was some damn fine work today, Dr. Stevens."

"Thank you. Can we go play doctor and nurse now? Time to improve on any skills that may be lacking." The words drip from his mouth, his fingers running the length of my forearm. But it's the heat, emanating from every part of him, that has my body near implosion point.

"As tempting as that sounds, I have to do dishes." I stand up, collecting the plates.

Owen stays my hands. "Dishes can wait. Come with me."

My heart pounds like a freight train. I know it's ridiculous. I'm hornier than ever before in my life, but our situation is so complex, so convoluted. That, and I look like I ate a beach ball. "But—"

"Relax, we aren't playing doctor and nurse. I have something else planned for you."

I trail him to the bedroom where he's spread out a few towels on the bed. "Take off your clothes and lay down."

"How is this not doctor and nurse?"

"I'm giving you a massage. I've seen you rubbing your shoulders the last few days. I know you're hurting."

"I'm fine," I lie, the words racing from my mouth with the speed of a bullet train. "But thanks for the offer."

"Will you stop fighting me on everything?" He purses his lips, offering a defeated shake of his head. "Go sit on the couch, then, and

I'll give you a massage *over* your clothes. You might even enjoy it. I'm damn good at it."

Of that, I've no doubt. "You don't have to—"

"I want to do this, Tally. I want to feel like I'm involved in the pregnancy."

How do you argue with that logic? Answer? You don't. You sit your ever-widening ass down in the living room and let this hot hunk of man touch you.

I know. It's the definition of tragedy.

Owen settles behind me on the couch, his hand pushing my long hair over one shoulder. "Why are you being such a pain in the ass?"

"I'm not," I groan as his fingers press into my sore muscles. "I'm a New Yorker. We have a strict rule about three feet of personal space."

What a complete load of horseshit, and Owen knows it.

"Where in New York is there three feet between people?"

His hands knead my aching shoulders, and I release a small moan. He isn't kidding about being talented in this department. I tilt my neck, giving him better access.

"What happened to your three feet of personal space rule?" Owen questions, pressing his body closer to mine.

"Be quiet and keep going," I grumble, smiling at his chuckle.

"See? I told you."

Yep. He told me all right. He spends the next twenty minutes working over every sore spot along my spine, and trust me, there are plenty.

Then, just when I'm about to melt into his body, demanding that his hands seek out the R-rated parts of my anatomy, he stops.

Without a word, he slips from behind me, flipping on the television and handing me the remote. He's playing by my rules, just as I requested. But he's also got my body all fired up and begging to break every single rule I've ever created.

"Thanks for the massage. If I was any good at it, I'd return the favor."

"Practice makes perfect, Darlin," he retorts, his gaze intent on the screen.

Then I see it—his foot tapping against the floor. Something has him agitated, and I think it goes beyond sexual frustration. I reach over, placing my hand on his knee and settling down the erratic rhythm of his foot. "I'll gladly try it, Owen. Just don't be surprised if it sucks."

He smiles, his fingers closing over my hand. "There's never been a time that you've touched me that doesn't feel amazing. But," he releases a long sigh, "that's not the issue."

"Oh crap, we have another issue? I was certain we'd reached quota on those."

Owen chuckles, but his grip on my hand remains firm. "I have something for you. I've had it for weeks now, but I wanted to find the right time to give it to you. I wanted the moment to be perfect, and it's been anything but recently. Which is totally my fault." Those stormy grays connect with mine. "I don't want to wait any longer, Darlin. I only hope you understand why I didn't give it to you sooner."

My head spins at his enigmatic statements. What in the world could he have had for weeks that required the right setting? The proper moment? I bite back a gasp.

Holy shit, is Owen referring to an engagement? He mentioned purchasing a ring and making me Mrs. Stevens that day in his office. Was he serious? Did he really buy one?

My mind reels. "You're not making any sense. What are you talking about?" I stutter out, my body trembling with anticipation.

Owen stands up and walks into the other room, giving me a few moments to contemplate my answer. This hardly qualifies as an ornate proposal, but it *is* a proposal. Or it will be...if that's what he has planned.

But when Owen returns, he's carrying a piece of paper instead of a jewelry box, and I fight hard to swallow the overwhelming disappointment.

He isn't proposing. He doesn't want to make me Mrs. Stevens.

But for that brief moment, when I believed that to be his intention, all seemed right with the world.

Put on a smiling face, Tallulah. It's not his fault you had china patterns picked out.

"What's that, a lease agreement?" I ask, forcing a cheery smile to cover the fact that I want to dissolve into a puddle of tears.

"No," Owen shakes his head, unfolding the paper. "When I visited your Dad, he gave me something."

"I still can't believe you went to see him. I really love that you did that."

"It was that night after you met Charlotte. I had this whole evening planned, and instead, I ended up driving all over town, looking for you. I stopped at his facility, hoping you might be with him."

The mention of that night dissipates any remaining glitter from my imagined high. "I made certain to avoid any place that I thought you might know. I didn't want you finding me."

"Fair enough, but it didn't stop me from looking." Owen clears his throat, and I see his hands tremble. "I told your Dad what an amazing job he'd done raising you, and I promised him I would take over from here. I told him how much I love you, and that he was going to be a grandpa."

Tears fill my eyes as I realize that Owen got to tell my father the news. It was my one regret—he died without knowing his legacy would live on. "I wanted to tell him, but I didn't get the chance. Wait, that was weeks ago. How did you—"

"I knew, Darlin, for a long time. That dinner with my Mom? I knew then. Anyway, he gave me this when I told him you were pregnant."

I take the paper with shaking hands, a tear falling onto the aged parchment. "I made this for him in kindergarten. I can't believe he kept it. I didn't think he still remembered."

"He remembered you. You were his wildflower. And now, you're mine."

I launch off the couch, throwing myself into Owen's arms.

It isn't a ring, but for my battered heart, it's just as good. That, and the feel of his arms encircling me, offering the protection I crave, sets my world back to right.

"Thank you so much for this." I pull back, wiping my eyes. "I really hope our child is more artistically inclined than I was," I remark with a laugh, my finger tracing my six-year-old interpretation of a horse and buggy.

"It's adorable. It's perfectly you. I'm sorry that I didn't give it to you sooner. Things have been so—"

"Shitty between us?" I finish his statement with a smirk.

Owen barks out a harsh laugh. "Exactly. It's not an excuse, though."

"You're forgiven. This time at least," I growl, adding in a wink for good measure. "Let me put this away, and then I have just the movie for us to watch. Who doesn't love a screwball comedy?"

Owen sighs, running a hand along his trimmed beard. "We're still watching a movie, huh?"

I pause, turning back to face him. "What else would you like to do?"

"I'll tell you what else." He frames my face, forcing my chin upwards. Those dark gray eyes thunder with feeling as he thumbs lazy circles on my cheeks. "I'm sick of this, Tallulah." His breath holds the faint scent of alcohol, his words brimming with intensity.

I want to back away from him, put some breathing room between us, but Owen isn't allowing it. I'm fairly certain I know to what he's referring, but let's be honest, I also thought he was going to propose not five minutes earlier. I will not read him wrong twice tonight.

"Sick of what?"

"Sick of pretending that I don't crave you every time you're within ten feet of me." His lips glide against my hair while his hands curve around my hips. "I want to be inside you. I want to kiss every inch of you."

At least my pregnancy brain was right on the money this time. "Do you?"

"You know I do. Now, the question is, do you want me, too?" His hands slide down my ass to cup my cheeks, pulling me hard against his erection.

He's kidding, right? I'm soaking wet just thinking about it. "Is this your great seduction?"

Owen winds his hand in my hair, forcing my head back. "It will be as soon as you give me the go-ahead."

"Doesn't that take the work out of the seduction?" I muse, willing my heart rate to remain at a normal pace.

"Why don't you find out? Tempt fate, sexy mama."

"What did you call me?"

"You heard me. You're a sexy mama."

"I feel like an Oompa Loompa."

Owen chuckles, his free hand holding me firm against him. "You don't look like one. You're adorable."

It's meant to entice me, but instead it reminds me of my ever-changing body. His words are ice water, pouring over my heated form. I throw up my hands, releasing a resigned huff. "That's the problem. I'm adorable. Charlotte is statuesque, gorgeous, exotic. Need I continue?"

A look of understanding passes over Owen's face.

About time you woke up and smelled the Chanel.

He takes a step back, his hands folded over his chest. "Wait a second. Is that why we're not"—Owen motions between us—"because of *Charlotte*?"

"Not entirely, no, but—"

He throws his hands up, shaking his head. In dismay? Aggravation? Agreement? I can't be sure. "That's bullshit."

"It's not," I protest, my hands planted on my hips. "It's a legitimate reason."

"Like hell it is."

"Owen—"

I don't have time to finish my statement. Owen grabs me into a fireman's hold and marches into the bedroom. He turns me over onto the mattress, straddling me, his hands locking my arms to the bed.

"Owen—" I begin again, but my words are lost when his mouth claims mine. His lips crush against me with a savage intensity. It's our first kiss all over again, when his body waged a carnal assault on my senses. His tongue slides against mine as he steals every moan, his hands acting as handcuffs, limiting my movement. There's no teasing in his kiss. This is pure demand, and I damn well better obey.

Pulling back, he catches my lower lip between his teeth, his eyes glowing with desire. "You stay. Don't move a muscle."

"What are you doing?" I ask, my eyes widening as he strides to his closet, pulling out two silk ties.

But Owen doesn't answer, his gaze intense as he secures my wrists to the bedposts.

"Owen," I repeat, my heart racing from a mixture of apprehension and anticipation. I know he won't hurt me, but I'm also not ready for him to see my body in all its naked glory.

Apparently, he's more than ready.

"Are you hiding this body from me?" Owen demands.

I open my mouth to speak, but his hand presses against my lips, silencing my words.

"The only correct answer is not anymore." With a yank, he tears off my tank top, and for once, I'm glad I don't buy designer duds. This one came off the three-dollar clearance rack. He pops open my bra with a flick of his fingers, and my breasts spill out into his hands. He pauses for a moment, his fingers teasing my nipples into hard peaks, and I bite back a moan.

But he's not done. Not by a long shot. He slides off my shorts and tosses them over his shoulder, leaving me wide open to his visual inspection.

"Holy fuck, Darlin," Owen murmurs, raking his bold gaze along every inch of my body.

His hands start at my shoulders, skimming along my breasts, now a cup size larger, down across my baby bump to my hips. His breath hitches as he palms my rounded abdomen.

It's the first time Owen has seen me naked since I've popped. I feel beautiful, carrying our child, but I'm uncertain if Owen shares that sentiment. "Am I still sexy?"

"You're so far beyond sexy. God, look at this body."

His words stoke the fire smoldering in my core, and I crave his hands all over me. How the hell did I even last this long? "Bit more of me now than there was before."

He sends me a sexy smirk as his tongue slides along the curve of my belly. "More to love, Darlin."

I pull at my restraints, arching my back against him when he takes my nipple between his teeth, teasing the tip. "Can you untie me?"

"Not yet," he murmurs, suckling my breast.

A shiver of delight courses through my body from the slick friction of his tongue. "Turn off the lights, Owen."

"No way in hell. I want to see every inch of you."

"But the ambiance," I argue, knowing damn well how he'll respond.

"Screw the ambiance. I'm going to watch your face as I make you come again and again." He hovers over me, and I see all the desire raging in his face. "You are exquisite, Tally. Never hide this body from me again. Do you understand?"

I nod, captivated by his intense stare. I have to admit that his displays of dominance make me hot as hell. "Are you ever going to kiss me?"

"Everywhere," Owen smiles, tangling one hand in my hair as his lips claim mine. His free hand drifts down my body, his fingers sliding inside me. I buck against his palm, moaning into his mouth. "Demanding, aren't you?"

"You're offering," I murmur against his lips as his fingers pump into me.

"Damn straight. And you're going to take everything I give you." Using his tongue as a guide, he skims along my body until his head is between my legs. "I'll give you one last warning," he murmurs, his teeth sinking into the flesh of my upper thigh. "If you think for one second that I'm not enjoying this, I will hold you down and lick you until your pussy is raw from orgasms."

"That's the hottest threat ever."

"I have no issue making good on that threat." His tongue circles my clit, and I arch off the bed.

"I swear, I'm even more sensitive now."

"You shouldn't have said that."

I meet his gaze, heady with lust. "Why not?"

"You've just given me free rein to torture your delicious body all the time now."

"You wouldn't really torture me, would you?" I counter with a grin.

Wrong. It's delicious torture, but it's torture, nonetheless. Owen teases me open, his tongue sliding along my folds, as I grasp at the ties holding me hostage. He is merciless, his hands cupping my ass, holding me fast as my entire body vibrates with pleasure.

With a jerk, I shatter, my climax ripping through every cell. Owen releases a heated groan, low in his throat, but he's far from finished. His tongue continues to work me over, coaxing me to the edge and wringing spasms of pleasure from my body.

"Please," I beg, my body throbbing with desire.

Owen drops a kiss on my thigh, before wiping his mouth on the sheet. The man is a god at oral sex, and he can worship me anytime. "Please what?"

"I need you inside me. Now," I breathe. "Don't make me wait any longer."

His fingers slide along my rib cage as I arch toward him,

desperate for his touch. But Owen isn't caving to my desires. He wants me to beg.

One hand slips between my heat, sliding along the slick skin, his fingers dipping deep inside me. He grips my thighs, hoisting my ass up and guiding my legs around him.

Those huge hands palm my ass, his thumb trailing down my crack, teasing my rim. I meet his gaze, further inflamed by the raw desire on his face. Anything this man wants, he can take.

"I plan on spending the rest of the night inside of you. But I'm not done playing with you, yet. All you can do is lie there while I make you come. Again and again."

Owen presses his thumb inside me, and I buck at the intensity. "Relax into it."

His free hand circles my clit, sliding through my wetness, as he continues to open me.

It's a fine line between pain and pleasure, and I'm riding the hell out of that wave.

A throaty purr breaks from my lips, wordlessly begging for more, wanting him to go further. His shaft teases my entrance, and I whimper, desperate to feel him inside of me. Then, with a feral growl, he surges into me.

My hands may be tied, but my hips meet every thrust, moaning out his name. We come hard, fueling each other's climax. Owen collapses onto his forearms, panting, his breath hot in my ear.

I turn my head, nudging his mouth to mine, my tongue licking the seam of his lips, begging entrance. With a low groan, he tangles his tongue with mine in a leisurely dance.

"How about you untie me now?" I murmur against his mouth. "Let me have a turn."

Owen nuzzles my nose, dropping feather-light kisses along my face. "That was only round one, Darlin. I'm nowhere near finished with you."

CHAPTER THIRTY-FIVE
OWEN

"I know that look," Dr. Jessop remarks as I stroll into his office. "That is the look of a man who got laid last night. Lucky dog."

I chuckle, but I'm not denying a damn thing. I got more than laid. I tortured Tally's exquisite body for hours until we both collapsed from exhaustion.

It's pure heaven between her thighs.

"I'm glad things are better between you and Lu. I worried that Charlotte was going to screw up everything for you."

You and me both, buddy.

"It's not from lack of trying on Charlotte's part." My statement is accurate, although my ex-fiancée's definition of rekindling a romance is colder than an iceberg in the Arctic. To her, love really is a series of business transactions.

"How is Lu feeling? How's the baby?"

"Fantastic."

I'm grateful to Jessop—in more ways than one. He's one of Tally's biggest fans, so he had no problem concocting a plan to make my tiny vixen spill the beans about our baby.

Yep, it was totally his idea to saddle her with a task in the cath lab that included about a million x-rays. It might not have been the most original concept, but hey, it worked.

And after last night, Tally and I are finally picking up the pieces of our relationship and getting back on track.

I sincerely hope Charlotte has learned the meaning of healthy boundaries, particularly where my relationship with Tally is concerned.

"Any last-minute details I need to know before we meet with Dragon Lady?"

Another reason I love Ken Jessop. He saw through Charlotte from the start. Oh, he admits that she's beautiful, but he can smell her variety of bullshit from a mile away.

"It's just another meet and greet, although this time, you'll see the big man himself." I cringe, knowing that I must spend time with Mr. Auerback. "I hate that we have to go away for a few days."

"How's Lu taking that news?"

I shrug, perching on the edge of the table. "Like a champ, as always, but I know it's an act. How would you like it if your wife ran off with her ex, even under the guise of business? It looks bad. I wanted Tally to go with us, but the unit is short-staffed right now. Plus, she might kill Charlotte before the end of the trip, if she has to deal with her for more than an hour."

"We all might kill Charlotte before the end of the trip. Here's to alcohol and the beasts it soothes," Jessop smirks, smiling over my shoulder. "Hey Lu, your ears must be burning. We were just talking about you."

I turn to see the woman I ravished less than twelve hours ago, my dick hardening at her proximity. I'm worse than a dog in heat, but I can't be held responsible. The woman's pussy is magical. Fucking magical. "Hey, Darlin." I pull her to me, tipping her chin back and claiming a leisurely kiss from that talented mouth.

I'm done pretending I'm anything but obsessed with this woman.

"Hey, yourself," Tally chuckles, but I see the blush bloom over her cheeks.

I hate that there's any hesitation on her part about our future, but like she's told me before, sex won't solve problems.

Even our amazing, mind-blowing sex.

Hopefully, today's news will ease any lingering uncertainty.

"What can I do for you boys?"

The possibilities are endless, Darlin. "We're just waiting on Charlotte."

Tally's face blanches. My ex-fiancée is still a sore subject, and one night of intensive lovemaking is not enough to heal the wound.

I grab her hand, giving it a squeeze. "It's good news. Promise."

She nods, but apprehension lines her face. She's dismantled most of the emotional wall, but the bricks are still there, waiting, in case I screw up again.

No way in hell am I letting that happen.

Another knock sounds on Dr. Jessop's door. The Dragon Lady has arrived.

Charlotte enters the room, a well-practiced smile decorating her mouth. Her eyes travel to mine and Tally's conjoined hands, but her face gives away nothing. "Good morning, gentlemen. Tallulah."

Tally jerks her hand from mine, but I'm not letting her put space between us. Not again, and certainly not for Charlotte.

I run my fingers along the length of Tally's spine, soothing her already frazzled nerves. My girl needs to know where my loyalties lie, plain and simple.

Besides, I'm done kowtowing to Charlotte's demands. Thankfully, we've secured almost all the funding needed for the training center. Once the last dollar is donated, my ex can hop on her jet and scurry back to her opulent lifestyle, leaving me to my future with Tally.

Charlotte settles into one of the plush side chairs, smoothing her suit before meeting my gaze. "The flight is all set for tomorrow morning. We will be in San Francisco for three days, flying back late

Thursday. The plan is to tour the existing facility and make final preparations for the grand opening of this training center. There will be dinners both nights, and a welcome party, so please pack accordingly."

As Charlotte reads down the list of high dollar events, I feel Tally tense beside me. This is out of her element. To be honest, it's out of mine.

"I hate to cut you off, but why did you need to see me?" Tally blurts, stopping Charlotte's spiel midstream. "I have a very busy day."

Code for she wants to get the hell out of there as soon as possible.

"I wasn't the one who wanted to see you. You're here at the behest of Dr. Stevens and Dr. Jessop," Charlotte replies, her tone dripping with ice.

Tally's gaze swings between me and Ken. "Well, you behested. What do you want?"

Jessop and I chuckle at Tally's zinger in Charlotte's direction. Charlotte, on the other hand, is less than amused. "There's a position that we think will be a great fit for your talents." I lean down, nuzzling her lobe with my nose. "Not all of them, of course."

Charlotte clears her throat, and I meet her emerald gaze. If looks could kill, Tally and I would be writhing on the floor. "We need someone dependable and knowledgeable to oversee the training facility. Both Dr. Stevens and Dr. Jessop had one candidate in mind. You."

"I'm sure you hate that idea." God bless Tally's brashness. Until now, she's been on her best behavior. Glad to see my cheeky girl is making an encore appearance.

Tally's direct statement flusters Charlotte, but only for a moment. "I don't think it's a good idea at all. You don't possess a master's degree, a requirement for the position in San Francisco. However, you are, per *their* accounts, knowledgeable in this field. I have another few candidates in mind, and for fairness, we need to interview them. But these two doctors have unequivocally voted for you."

Tally crosses her arms across her chest, her baby bump evident under the scrub top. Fuck, but that's hot. That's my woman, carrying my child.

It doesn't get any better than that.

"Does that mean I have the job or not?" Tally questions, her pupils dilating behind her glasses.

"You have the job," I whisper, giving her hand a squeeze. "The interviews are just a formality."

"Owen," Charlotte warns, "we have a process."

"Yes, Charlotte," I respond, giving her my famous eye roll. I stand up, my hand still grasping Tally. "If you don't need me, I'm going to head back to the unit, check on a few patients."

Tally is silent as we walk out the door, making it to the end of the hallway before tugging me to her. "Are you serious? I have the job?"

I smile, stealing a kiss when no one is looking. "You have the job."

"Owen, that's more money than I've ever made in my life. I can do so many things for Nugget—"

"I'm here too, Darlin. Taking care of you two is my biggest priority."

"I believe you. I think I always did, but there were so many times—"

"That I let you down. Never again, Tally."

She stands on tiptoe, stealing another kiss. "I forgot to tell you something."

"What's that?"

"I love you."

I don't give a damn who's watching. My girl finally took the wall down and I need her to know I feel the same way. I capture her face with my hands, my tongue sliding inside her mouth. But this time, it's not urgent or forceful. It's slow, delicious, and has my dick throbbing when we pull away.

"Does that mean you love me, too?" Tally murmurs, her breathing harried and shallow.

"I more than love you, Tally."

God, her smile. It doesn't hurt that I know how very talented that mouth is in other areas, either.

"I have to go, but I'll see you at home?"

Home.

She finally said it.

"Absolutely, darling girl."

∼

"You shouldn't have assured Tallulah about the coordinator position," Charlotte mutters, not bothering to glance up from her laptop.

"How nice of you to make yourself comfortable in my office." I roll my eyes, sliding off my lab coat and settling behind the desk. "How long do you plan on camping out here?"

Those dark green eyes meet mine, but I see uncertainty behind her steely expression. "Should I go to the cafeteria? Is this too much impedance on your turf? Am I upsetting your beloved Tallulah again?"

"She's not thrilled with the situation, but she's trying to make the best of it. She's been a hell of a lot more accommodating than I would have been in her situation."

"Goes to show which of you is more dedicated in the relationship, or whatever it is that you two are doing."

I crack my knuckles, a habit born of heightened aggravation, and one Charlotte knows well. "No, I'm just far more jealous. Another man comes into Tally's personal space, and I'm all over it."

"When did you become so possessive?"

"The moment I met Tally. It increased a thousand-fold when I learned that she is carrying my child."

CHAPTER THIRTY-FIVE

"She certainly *looks* pregnant."

There she is, the bitch I spent so many years of my life beside. "She looks beautiful."

"It all makes sense now."

"What does?"

"Your insistence on staying with Tallulah; it's your dedication to your *child*." She taps her nails against the desk, glaring in my direction. "Are you so certain that you're the father? You hardly know this woman."

Hell, no. She is *not* pulling that card. "I know Tally intimately, in every sense of the word. She's also not the type of woman to sleep around, unlike other people in my past."

I try to rise above insolent arguments, but Charlotte is pushing every one of my buttons. If she wants to get dirty, I have buckets of mud to sling in her direction. After all, she's the one who screwed at least one other person during our relationship, but I guarantee the list is far longer that she's willing to admit.

"I'm only looking out for your best interests."

What a load of garbage.

I push myself away from the desk. Much more of this discussion and I'll personally escort Charlotte off hospital property. "I'm going to Jessop's office. I have a few calls to make."

Charlotte sighs, leaning back in the chair. "I'll leave, Owen. But try to understand my side. Here we are, a few months separated, and you're having a child with someone else. How do you think that makes me feel?"

"I have no idea, Charlotte, but I'm sure you're about to tell me."

She picks at an imaginary thread on her skirt. "We never even discussed children in all our years together. I want a family, too."

I hit the desk with such force that I make the pens and papers dance.

Wow. I can't believe she's going there.

There are certain statements that people should never utter. Statements that open up wounds, often still festering beneath the layers of bandages applied to staunch the bleeding. Charlotte's statement about wanting a family rips apart the last purulent boil I have from our time together. "Then I guess you shouldn't have gotten an abortion, Charlotte."

She blanches as white as the side chair. She didn't realize that I knew, but I was friends with the doctor who performed the procedure. He let it slip one evening, after a few drinks and rounds of pool. He thought I was privy to the information.

He was wrong.

"Who told you?"

"It certainly wasn't you." I hold up my hand, halting her rebuttal. "It doesn't matter who told me. What matters is that you terminated the pregnancy and never said a word to me. So, don't sit there and proclaim your desire for us to have had a family. You passed on that opportunity when you aborted my child!"

A tear slip past her lids, but I feel no pity. Not for this act. Not for what she took from me without any discussion. "It...it..."

"What, Charlotte?" I snap, letting the months of anger flow from every pore.

She lifts her head, her eyes full of tears. "I didn't tell you because it wasn't your baby. It happened on my trip to Greece. The father—"

"It wasn't my baby?" It might sound twisted, but the relief flowing through my veins is palpable. Charlotte has admitted to another tryst, but I couldn't care less about her infidelities at this point. Now, I can move on from our relationship, leaving behind the intense anger that I carried with me from San Francisco.

"I wish it had been yours. I thought about keeping the baby, but I knew you'd leave when you discovered you weren't the father." She offers a mirthless chuckle. "But you left, anyway. So, I lost you both."

I shake my head, walking around the desk and leaning against it, my expression stern. "You lost me because you lied and cheated for years. I don't even want to know how many other men there were during our relationship. But I now know of two, one of which resulted in a pregnancy. That you failed to mention having unpro-

CHAPTER THIRTY-FIVE

tected sex with someone else also blows my mind. You could have picked up any number of diseases and passed them to me. But I'm sure that concept never crossed your mind as important. And you didn't lose your baby, you terminated the pregnancy. Stop looking for sympathy in this situation. You were the one in the wrong. Not me."

"I know, Owen! When you left, I did some soul searching. I knew my actions had caused the breakup, but I was so mixed up that I didn't know if you leaving was a blessing or a curse." She dabs at her eyes, in a futile attempt to keep her makeup from smearing down her face. "I realized how much I missed you, and made a beeline for Florida, intent on winning you back. Imagine my surprise when I discover that you'd already moved on. You want to talk about unprotected sex? Apparently you weren't practicing it, either."

I lean in closer, my anger near boiling point. "Don't you ever intimate that my relationship with Tally is even remotely similar to your affairs. My life with Tally is none of your damn business. I assure you we're both thrilled about this baby. I can't wait to spend my life with them."

"Are you trying to be cruel?"

"No, I'm trying to be honest." I watch the tears slide down her cheeks and finally take some pity on her. Maybe she has a heart, after all. "Charlotte, if I was the right guy, you wouldn't have cheated countless times. If you were the right woman, I wouldn't have left San Francisco. We finally woke up to the fact that we don't belong together. I found the woman I'm meant to be with, and I plan on keeping her happy for the rest of my life."

"So that's it, then?" Charlotte asks, blotting her eyes with the tissue I offer.

"You know the answer to that, Charlotte. There has been nothing real between us for a long time. Now, per your own words, it's strictly business."

CHAPTER THIRTY-SIX

TALLY

"Coming," I call out, my heart sinking when I open the condo door.

Charlotte stands in the vestibule, looking coolly glamorous as always in yet another designer suit. Meanwhile, I'm the definition of anti-chic in a tank top and sweats.

Thank God Owen loves me just as I am.

"What can I do for you, Charlotte?" I inquire, leaning against the door as I gaze up the length of her willowy frame.

"I have some paperwork for Owen. I thought he would want to familiarize himself with it before the trip."

What a load of garbage. "Nah, you would have stopped by his office, considering you were just there today. You want to speak to me. Am I right?"

"Are you always this direct?"

"Yes. I find bullshit pleasantries tiresome." I open the door, allowing her entrance. "What do you want?"

Charlotte gazes around the condo before setting her purse down on an end table. "Interesting decor."

"I prefer homey to institutional. But let's cut the crap. You're not here to discuss my interior design choices."

"Will you be submitting the paternity test before or after the birth?"

I don't know why I'm surprised by Charlotte's question, but it rams me like a punch in the gut. I huff out a breath, shocked at her direct inquiry. "How is that any of your business?"

"Owen is my business. Mine and my father's. We like to keep tabs on our commodities."

I throw up my hands, my eyes blazing in disbelief. "Do you hear yourself? You just referred to the man I love as a commodity."

"Will you answer the question, please? I'll gladly pay for the testing."

"Owen never mentioned me having a paternity test. He knows he's the father."

Her dark green eyes bore into me, making me feel like a caged rat. So much for false bravado. "He knows no such thing, which is why I'm here to deliver the paperwork for the test. You don't think Owen wants to give his last name to a child who may or may not be his, Tallulah. You're smarter than that."

I snatch the document from her fingers, tossing it on the table. "Is there anything else?"

"There is one thing. You don't really believe he's going to marry you, do you?"

"It hadn't occurred to me," I lie, praying Charlotte can't see through my falsehood.

"Yes, it has. You've thought about it constantly, especially now that you're in the family way. He would be quite the catch, especially with this second center opening. You could claim a seat at the head table, regardless of your upbringing."

That's it. She can insult me, but when she throws shade at my deceased parents, I see red. "Don't you ever mention my parents again. They were two of the most wonderful people to grace this planet and you," I hiss, coming right under her nose, "aren't fit to shine their shoes. Now *get out.*" I pull open the door, slamming it hard enough that the lamp shakes on the foyer table.

Leaning against the wall, I slow my breathing and will my heart rate down. I need to stay calm for Nugget, even if that bitch shredded my last bits of sanity.

I know she's jealous and vindictive, but her statement isn't totally off base. Owen and I aren't married. He told me that Charlotte was unfaithful during their relationship. It's not beyond the realm of possibility that he would want a paternity test.

It's a fair and logical request. But that isn't what bothers me the most.

'You don't really believe he's going to marry you, do you?'

Charlotte's pointed barb zips through my head like a dart, poisoning every thought. I rub my brow, the headache fast becoming a pounding disaster. The events of the last few weeks have taken their toll. I need some downtime.

I find Hecate curled up on the guest bed, and I lay beside her, stroking her fur as her noisy purrs calm my rattled nerves. I swear, this cat is the best form of therapy.

"Owen loves us, Hecate. I know he does. He's told me so many times, assured me I'm more than just his baby mama. I'm being stupid, right? Letting Charlotte get inside my head again."

Hecate continues her therapeutic purring, but a small, niggling voice breaks through any surface calm. What if Owen's declarations of love and devotion are as false as the other lines he spouted throughout our relationship?

What if he is only staying because of the baby? Hell, then I've trapped him in the same manner as Charlotte. The details may be different, but it's the same concept.

Owen is very good at telling me what I want to hear, omitting things as he sees fit. His profession and former fiancée are proof of that fact.

But he wouldn't lie about the baby, would he?

"Darlin, wake up. You're having a bad dream." Owen's voice jerks me from my nightmare, and I gasp as I jolt into reality, my body trembling and covered with sweat.

His arms encircle me, pulling me against his chest.

I glance out the window, noting the street lamps illuminating the beach. How long have I been asleep? "I was drowning…"

"Shh, I'm here, Tally. You're safe." He traces my spine with his hand, his lips pressing against my hair.

"Did I wake you?"

Owen shakes his head, planting kisses across my face. "I only got in a little while ago. I had some last-minute things to take care of before the trip tomorrow."

The trip. With Charlotte.

My earlier conversation with his ex-fiancée roars back into focus, along with my insecurities. I sit up, putting some space between us. "I'm sorry if I disturbed you."

"You didn't disturb me. You scared me." Owen glances around the room. "Why are you back here?"

"I fell asleep with Hecate earlier." I stretch, rolling my neck to relieve the kinks. "I feel better now. I should be able to fall asleep again." I tug at the blanket wedged under Owen. "Can I have my blanket back?"

Owen scoops me into his arms, carrying me into the master bedroom. "*This* is your room now. I don't care if you want to nap on the counter, but at night, you sleep with me. Besides, I'm not going to see you for a few days. I want to hold you tonight." He places me on the bed, sliding in beside me.

He's fresh from the shower, his skin tinged with the scent of our citrus soap. He always smells so good. He pulls me against his chest, glancing in my direction when I resist. "Everything okay?"

My head doesn't want to get into it. My heart has had enough.

"She stopped by here earlier," I mumble.

CHAPTER THIRTY-SIX

"Who?"

"Charlotte," I huff.

His grip tightens around me. "What the hell did she want?"

"She gave me paperwork for a paternity test."

That did it. The bedside lamp flicks on and I squint up into his handsome face. His perturbed, handsome face. "She did what?"

I wave a hand, trying to dispel the tension. "I told her you hadn't asked for one, but I have no issue with it. She claimed that you wouldn't want your name on the birth certificate until you were certain the baby was yours."

Even in this low light, I see Owen's anger raging. Those gray eyes are now a thundering storm. "That bitch. I hope you told her where she could shove her paternity test."

"Owen, I wanted to tell her she was wrong, that you loved me—"

"Damn straight."

I wipe my tears with the heel of my hand. I didn't realize I was crying. "Then she insulted my parents and said I was foolish to believe that you'd marry me."

"That's it, I'm canceling the whole damn deal. I'm not playing this game with her anymore." He bolts upright and I grab his arm.

"Stop. I know you're mad. I'm mad, too."

"I'm beyond mad, Tally. I'm fucking livid." He shakes his head, his lips a thin line. "I should have known after my chat with Charlotte today that she would pull something like this."

"Your chat?"

Please be honest, Owen. I can't handle anything more.

"She made a last-ditch attempt at reconciliation."

"Trying to convince you to leave me, right?"

He grabs my upper arms, forcing me to look at him. "Don't you believe a word she says. Promise me."

"That's just it. I don't know what place I hold in your life." There, I said it. Finally. "I can't be certain you're not just with me out of some sense of obligation."

Owen rolls me onto my back, his hulking frame positioned on

top of me. "Little lady, we need to get a few things straight. Charlotte is my past, and no amount of finagling on her part is going to change that." His long fingers lift the edge of my shirt, exposing my baby bump. "You are my present, Tally."

His hands stroke along the sides of my abdomen, cupping my stomach. "God, you're beautiful. Just look at you, carrying our baby. This baby is my future. You and Nugget are my future, Tally. Not Charlotte. Never Charlotte."

My fingers caress his scalp as he presses kisses to my belly. "I needed to hear that, but I will grant you a paternity test. Ouch!" I snap as his teeth sink into my breast.

"I don't need a paternity test. What I need is to put a ring on this finger and lock you down for life."

I chuckle, even as a wave of heat courses through my body. "I already told you I'm not expecting anything."

"Well, how about I give you everything and shock the hell out of you?" He nuzzles my neck, smiling when I release a soft squeal. "I have the ring. You want to see it?"

I push at his chest, my eyes wide with a mixture of disbelief and anticipation. "You do not."

"I do. I'll go get it." He pushes off me, but I wrap my arms around his neck, giggling as I pull his mouth to mine.

"That's the worst proposal ever."

"True. But I could show you the ring and then plan a kick-ass proposal. Does that work?"

"No deal. I want kick-ass, or you get no ass."

"Is that a fact?" His eyes darken as his hand slides down my back, delivering a firm smack across one cheek. "I'd like to negotiate the terms."

"Hmm," I purr, grinding my hips against him. "I suppose I can hear your side."

Owen's hands slip under my ass, lifting my hips against him as he teases my opening.

I whine, desperate for the feel of him inside me, but once again,

CHAPTER THIRTY-SIX • 371

the man gets off on hearing me beg.

"What do you want?"

My eyes narrow as a seductive smile flits across my mouth. Two can play his game. "You. On your back. Now."

I straddle Owen, easing myself down his length, my body stretching around him. I ride him with deep strokes, my nails ripping down his chest as I grind against him. His hands grip my ass so tightly that I know he'll leave bruises, but I need this. We need this.

Owen flips me over, hammering into my body, driving deeper with every thrust. I lock my legs around his waist, arching my hips up to meet him, my body tightening around him.

"Tally—"

I cut him off, seizing his mouth and tangling my tongue with his. His body jerks hard, every muscle tightening as he comes inside me.

"Woman, what you do to me," Owen groans, rolling onto his back and pulling me tight against him.

"You need another shower," I giggle, tracing the sheen of perspiration on his chest. "We both do."

"Later," he murmurs, his hand tangling in my hair. "Right now, I need you here. I don't want you any further than that."

I manage a sleepy, satiated goodbye to Owen at some ungodly hour the next morning, before he flies across the country in a jet owned by his ex-fiancée. The woman who wants him back.

But for the first time in this whole situation, I feel like I have the upper hand.

Tough titties, Charlotte. That man is mine.

"I MISS YOU."

I bite back a smile at Owen's words. "It's only been a few hours. You haven't had time to miss me."

"Want to make a bet?"

"Is Charlotte behaving?"

"She claims to be sorry for her tirade yesterday. I claim that she's full of shit. I warned her to stay away from you. Otherwise, she'll have to deal with me."

"I think that's what she wants, Owen."

"What I want is you naked, that sexy ass riding the hell out of my cock. Maybe we can engage in a little phone sex later. It's sure as hell not the same as you sitting on my face, but it'll have to do for now."

My man and his dirty talk. Hot damn, but he'd make a whore blush. I can't say that I don't love it, though. Besides, with my pregnancy hormones raging, it's all systems go, all the time. "Too bad you're across the country. I guess BOB will have to fill in until you return."

"Don't you dare. You save yourself, and I'll do the same. That way I can ravage you the second I walk in the door."

I hear voices in the background, and the hair on the back of my neck stands up.

Charlotte. I yearn for the day when we are finally rid of her, but a small sliver of me wonders if that day will ever come. "You need to go?"

"Stupid welcome party. Have to mingle and pretend to have fun."

"My dancing circus bear." I chew my lip, pondering if I should broach the next topic. "Promise me something?"

"Anything."

"This is it with Charlotte. After the training center opens, no more, right?"

"Absolutely no more. Thank you for sticking by me throughout all of this."

"Eh, I guess you're worth it," I chuckle.

"I'll be thinking about you."

"You better. Hey Owen, I forgot to tell you something. Me and Nugget love you, with a love that's bigger than love."

His deep chuckle resonates through the line. "I'll see you soon, Darlin. Call me if you need anything, and I mean *anything*."

CHAPTER THIRTY-SEVEN
OWEN

My former life comes flooding back the moment I enter the glitzy ballroom. I forgot how much I hate it. Sure, it's glamorous as hell to the outsider, but it's like a poorly fitted shoe—rubbing me in all the wrong places.

I glance at Ken, a fake smile plastered on his face and his hand encircling the whiskey glass in a death grip, and realize I'm not the only one out of his element. We're doctors, much more comfortable in hospital scrubs than some black-tie shindig.

But, to help people, you have to follow the money. So, here we are.

"This used to be your life?" Ken exclaims, his eyes widening as he glances around the room. The man is used to hanging with the wealthy, but billionaires are a class all to themselves. Just ask them.

"Yep, and I hated every minute."

"I can see why. Don't get me wrong, the Ferrari is plush as hell, but these people make me want to run screaming out a forty-story window."

I chuckle in agreement. "They're terrible, all of them miserable people hiding behind their money and status. But that same money opened the first training facility, and now, it will open the second."

"Makes me feel better to know that they need us as much as we need them," he surmises, grabbing another cocktail off a hand-passed tray.

"Even with all their money, they can't buy life. That's where we come in. So, let's play our part, grab the check, and get the hell out of here."

"I have to mention something, old chap." Jessop taps his glass, a thoughtful expression on his face. "I got a call from a Dr. Jackson at Regent Hospital, regarding you."

My jaw slackens. I didn't expect to have this conversation tonight. "Shit, he already contacted you? I'm sorry, I didn't expect him to call until next week."

"Are you leaving Memorial?"

"I'm considering it, but not because I don't love the staff. Ever since I found out I'm going to be a father, my priorities have shifted. I realize how many years I've spent away from my family. Regent is in North Carolina, where my mother lives."

"How does Lu feel about moving?"

"I haven't mentioned it because I didn't know if they had anything available."

"That's a load of garbage. Any hospital will make room for Dr. Owen Stevens." He swigs down his drink, grabbing another off a tray. "I gave you a glowing recommendation, although I hate to see you leave."

"It hasn't been decided yet. I still have to speak to Tally."

"What about the coordinator position? She was so excited about that role."

"Ken, I don't trust Charlotte."

"You think she'd be that ruthless?"

"In a word, yes. She thinks she can hurt me by hurting Tally."

"You have a lot to consider, old boy."

CHAPTER THIRTY-SEVEN

"Don't I know it." I grab a champagne flute, motioning toward Martin Auerback. "The big dog just entered the yard."

"Charlotte's father?"

I nod, my muscles tensing in apprehension of this meeting. I haven't spoken to Mr. Auerback since that last dinner with the family a week before I moved to Florida. The man barely tolerated me when I was engaged to his daughter; I know the gloves are off now.

"Mr. Auerback, you look well." I hold out my hand, grimacing at his fierce grip. Laying down the law, I see.

"Owen, almost didn't recognize you."

I run a hand over my shaved head, forcing a smile. "Changed things up a bit."

"In all aspects of your life." He turns to Ken, holding out his hand in greeting. "You must be Dr. Ken Jessop. Charlotte tells me great things about your work. I can't wait to get you up to speed on the lab."

What a load of garbage. As if Martin Auerback has anything to do with teaching Ken a damn thing in the cath lab.

"Owen has already shown me the procedure, so I'm sure I'll catch on with no trouble. He's a hell of an interventionist, we're lucky to have him at Memorial."

I bite back a laugh. Ken is overdoing it, piling on the compliments, all aimed in my direction. I must send him a bottle of scotch for the effort.

"Dr. Jessop is a tremendous asset to our team," I add, noting the change in Auerback's gaze when he looks back at me.

"Let's hope *you're* more loyal to this team than your last one."

Yet another fucked up thing about the Auerback family. I was a team member, not part of the family. My pedigree wasn't posh enough to earn me that distinction. In his eyes, I should be grateful for any access to his family name and money.

"My loyalty never faltered, but I can't the same for my *teammates*."

I earn a glare from the billionaire, but I'm done singing for my supper. "I'm sure I don't know what you mean."

"I'm sure you do," I hiss, our icy glares holding. I want to spew out a rail of obscenities all over his custom cut tuxedo, reminding Martin Auerback that he needs this deal more than I do, but I resist the urge. Instead, I employ another tactic learned during my years of medical schooling—the art of diplomacy. "But this training facility is about far more than you or me...or your daughter. Think of all the people we can save. I only wish we might have discovered it sooner."

Mr. Auerback's eyes glaze at my words. His second wife, the true love of his lonely life, died from heart failure. She was an otherwise healthy woman, but her condition went undiagnosed for too long. She couldn't survive the surgery. All his money, all his power, couldn't save the one person he loved most in the world.

"She would be happy that this procedure has the aptitude to save so many." He claps my shoulder, an unspoken truce passing between us. "Let's get on with it, shall we? To be honest, I hate these things as much as you do."

I smile, the first genuine one since I entered the ballroom. "Business is far better conducted on a golf course."

"Quite right." Mr. Auerback returns his attention to Dr. Jessop, nodding toward the cigar bar. "Shall we mingle?"

Sorry, bud, but I've played that role far too many times. It's your turn tonight.

I chuckle under my breath at Ken's face, as my former almost in-law drags him round to one of a hundred whales. Hey, he wanted to live the high life. Now is his chance, and while they're busy, I can reach out to the woman who has been on my mind all day.

Ducking into an alcove, I pull out my phone, dialing Tally. It's late in Florida, but I know the woman only sleeps when I'm holding her. Another reason I want to get this business deal sewn up.

"Do you know what time it is?" Tally asks, her voice thick.

"Time for me to be home," I respond, leaning against the wall as I fall into her husky laugh.

CHAPTER THIRTY-SEVEN

"I agree. How's it going in La La Land?"

"La La Land is several hours south, and likely less artificial than the crap I'm dealing with tonight."

"That bad?"

"It's not good."

"Oh, you got a few phone calls and some mail from a Regent Hospital in Asheville. The woman on the phone said she was returning your call. Something about a job?"

Regent isn't wasting any time. "I field calls like that constantly."

"I'm sure you do. Any place would be lucky to have you. I know I am."

Something in her voice, mixed with the thousands of miles between us, catches up to me. "I need to ask you something."

"Uh-oh."

"What's the uh-oh for?"

"You're calling at half past midnight to ask me something? You're getting calls from other hospitals? Owen, please don't break up with me over the phone. I will kick your ass if you do that." She's joking, but I hear the undercurrent of uncertainty in her tone. I know this is hard for her. It's no secret Charlotte wants me back, and although Tally seems secure in her place, sometimes the cracks show. "Seriously, I don't want to pack again."

"Will you be quiet? I am not breaking up with you."

"Oh, I get it," she mumbles, a throaty chuckle escaping her lips. "Are you hiding in the bathroom, hoping for a bit of that phone sex you promised earlier?"

I laugh, although she's not wrong. Her voice, combined with the mental image of her naked ass as I pound into her, gets me hard in seconds. "You've got me pegged."

"Knew it." She stifles a yawn. "Are you okay, Owen?"

"Marry me, Tally."

"What?" She's wide awake now.

I feel eyes on me and look up to see Charlotte approaching. The woman is like a hound dog, tracking me down. I can tell by her expression that she knows exactly who I'm speaking with, but she won't grant me the courtesy of a private conversation.

Too damn bad, Charlotte. I'm done pretending that Tally isn't everything to me.

Deal or no deal.

"Marry me, Tally."

It's as if time stops as soon as the words leave my mouth. Charlotte, hearing my request, halts dead in her tracks, and there's silence from the other end of the phone line.

Charlotte I can handle, it's my tiny vixen's response that worries the hell out of me. "Are you there, Darlin?"

"I'm—I'm here," Tally stutters. "I damn near fell off the bed. Way to shock the hell out of me, Owen."

"You still haven't answered me." I widen my eyes at Charlotte. It's a universal signal to back off and give me some privacy, neither of which my former fiancée is doing. "I promise, I'll give you the best damn proposal in the entire world as soon as I get back, but I couldn't wait any longer. I love you so much and I want—"

"Yes! Of course, I'll marry you, silly man!"

Tally's laughter is the second most beautiful sound in the world.

The first? Hearing her say yes.

"You will? You'll marry me? God, I wish I was there right now."

"I'll marry you. Whatever order it comes, Owen. Remember?"

"I want a ring on your finger before our baby is born."

Tally groans, but it's tinged with laughter. "I already look like an over-inflated beach ball! I don't want to be fat in my wedding photos!"

I'm laughing, she's laughing. It's one hell of a moment. "You're not fat. You're beautiful. And if you don't want to be any bigger, we'll have to get married as soon as I get back."

I send one last glare in Charlotte's direction. Seriously, the woman can't take a hint. "I have to get back to the bullshit extravaganza. They're looking for me. You need to get some sleep."

"Fat chance of that. I have a wedding to plan."

"I love you, Darlin. I'll be home soon." I hang up the phone, releasing a sigh of relief.

"Isn't that cute?" Charlotte hisses, leaning against the wall next to me. "How nice of you to propose to another woman at the party that I'm hosting."

"You wouldn't have heard the proposal, if you weren't snooping on me." I shake my head. I won't allow Charlotte to rile me up. I'm too excited that Tally is going to be my wife.

Mrs. Owen Stevens.

It's about damn time.

"You disappeared. I was worried."

I shoot her a sharp glance. "No, you weren't." I sip the whiskey in my glass, knowing there's a permanent smile on my face. "I don't expect you to understand, but I expect you to respect my decision, and my fiancée."

"Marrying Tallulah before you know if the child is yours? Brave choice."

"I know the baby is mine. And now, so is Tally."

"I thought you didn't believe in marriage."

Oh Christ, she's going to drag me down this conversation path. "With the right woman, I do. Otherwise, it's a recipe for disaster. Charlotte, we were a terrible fit from the beginning."

"I know," she replies, a bit too brightly to be authentic. "You certainly didn't fit the image that my family name needs to portray."

"Not even remotely. Remember your father's face when he saw my tattoos for the first time? I wasn't sure which of you was going to faint first." I'm trying to bring the conversation back to a lighter topic, while still driving home how awful we were together. "I really believe the right man is out there for you. I just hope you treat that relationship more conscientiously than you did ours."

"I loved you."

Another lie. Charlotte has never experienced love, at least none that I'm aware of, and for that, I pity her. I tried to love her, but emotionally, she was an island, unreachable by any means. "If you really loved me, you wouldn't have cheated, no matter what excuse you provide."

"I wanted to love you," she relents, releasing a sigh.

"But you didn't. You loved what you thought I could become, loved me when I donned a tux and played the part of the millionaire husband. But when I stripped down, and you saw the real me—tattoos, hardcore music—you turned away. Tally embraces every facet of me. The real me."

"She's punk, like you are."

"We're not punks, Charlotte. We listen to punk music. We have tattoos, but that doesn't make us anarchists. We're actually upstanding citizens, pay our taxes and everything."

"I don't hate Tallulah, even if she is rough around the edges."

"She's real, Charlotte, and she's going to be my wife."

Charlotte downs the liquid in her glass, before grabbing the whiskey from my hand and doing the same. "Congratulations on your second engagement. I think we should celebrate."

Oh crap, I know that look. My sex life with Charlotte was as cool and calculated as the rest of our relationship, although she could get a bit frisky after imbibing one too many cocktails. Those few times over the course of the last several years were the only moments where Charlotte felt human to me. "We should get you some coffee."

Without warning, she presses her body against mine, and I tense at the unwelcome advance.

I just proposed to Tally. Charlotte heard my proposal. Only problem? She doesn't care.

"What are you doing, Charlotte?" I inquire, pushing her away from me.

Her hand slides down the front of my trousers, cupping my cock, those green eyes glowing with purpose. "I told you. We're celebrating."

With a grimace, I remove her hand, but she's not willing to relent. Her free hand takes its place, lowering my zipper and sliding inside to grasp my shaft.

I huff out a breath. Never in our relationship was the woman this forward, this demanding. "You need to stop. Right now." I jerk her hands up, grasping them with my own as I fumble my zipper closed.

"Or what? If you expect me to play nice, you'll have to bring something to the table."

I whirl her around so her back is to the wall, my arms caging her in, my body raging with anger. "I am bringing something to the table. The robotics cath lab, remember? The reason we are all here. Did you think you'd come to Florida after cheating on me and getting knocked up by another man, snap your fingers and bring me back into the fold? I'm not your servant, Charlotte. I don't work for you."

"You work for my father."

"Correction. I work *with* your father. He's trying to help save lives, you're trying to ruin them."

Her lips crush against mine, but I fend her off easily, wiping my mouth. "Stop it. Have some self-respect."

"Why do you want her and not me?"

"I love her, Charlotte. I never loved you. You never loved me. It was a business arrangement, more than it was ever a relationship."

I see tears in her eyes, but I know better. This is just another act, a ploy for sympathy. Besides, emotions in public are not Charlotte's style.

What she will do is negotiate. And I can see by the set of her jaw, her terms are non negotiable. "You stand to lose an awful lot, Owen."

"Are you threatening me? I'll walk away from this deal right now. There are plenty of investors out there, Charlotte."

"I'm not threatening you. You have something I want; I have something you need."

"What is that? We are not reconciling," I remind her.

"I'm aware of that, particularly after you proposed over the phone. How provincial."

"What do you want?"

"I'm a businesswoman. I know a good deal when I see it. I only hope you're as talented in that arena. Daddy wants to give you a payout once the training center opens, as thanks for all your hard work. But I thought it was overly generous, all things considered."

"Get to the point," I hiss.

"There's many more training centers that need to be opened. The two of us know the ins and outs, we are the natural choice to open the remaining centers around the country."

"There is no way I'm opening those centers with you." I would lose my damn mind first.

"I figured you would say that, but I convinced Daddy to quadruple your payout...once all the centers are open. Will you really walk away from a ten-million-dollar payday?"

Jesus Christ, the rich really are an entirely different species. They bend the rules according to their whims and because of their deep pockets; they get away with it.

"Let me get this straight. If I don't agree to spend every waking moment with you for the foreseeable future, you'll have your father withhold my rightfully earned monies?"

"You're getting paid, Owen. As per the original agreement, $250,000 for your time. It's more than fair. The ten million is a gift, one that need not be given if the recipient is ungrateful. You do have a child on the way."

I hate her, and I hate that a ten-million-dollar payday would ensure my family is taken care of for the rest of their lives—Tally, our children, and my mother. I hit the wall next to her, making her jump. "You are fucking evil, Charlotte."

"No, I'm a businesswoman."

"Is there a difference in your world?" I run a hand over my scalp, willing my heart rate down. "What about Tally?"

Charlotte shrugs, staring at her manicure. "What about her?"

"You were never giving her the coordinator position, were you?"

"No, I told you not to guarantee it. You're the lovesick fool who's going to disappoint her. Oh, one other thing. The payday is contingent on you fulfilling my needs. All of them."

"I just told you we're not reconciling."

CHAPTER THIRTY-SEVEN

"I understand. The little woman can wear you ring, but when we're on the road, you're mine." She traces her manicured nail down my shirt front. "Tallulah never has to know. I can be discreet, Owen. You discovered that firsthand."

I grab her fingers, tempted in my rage to break them. "Not a chance in hell."

"You might come to regret that decision."

I hate Charlotte with a vengeance for throwing Tallulah into the middle of our squabble. But I know that she's basing decisions on her negative emotions of jealousy and anger. I need to speak with Mr. Auerback, get to the real grain of truth. Of course, the man has never denied his daughter anything before. I highly doubt he'll make an exception for the man who left her.

"You don't have to decide now, Owen. Just let me know your choice...before it's too late. Just remember, you're as expendable as we are. We also have far more powerful attorneys in our corner." With a last pat to her hair, she straightens to her full height, and glides back into the ballroom.

I know that the Auerback family has ruined more than a dozen people who didn't play by the rules. Unfortunately, the rules bend and sway to their whims. Charlotte has made it clear if she doesn't get what she wants, she'll ruin me, and all I've worked for.

I'm tempted to pick up one of the elaborate side chairs and break every window in the place. Show them what a hardcore punk I really am. But I refrain—not for Charlotte or her father, but for the lives that can be saved and the petite angel I have waiting for me in Florida.

Tally deserves better than this garbage. Once I get home, I'm calling Regent and getting my family away from the sin and debauchery of the ultra-elite.

I stare into the ballroom, my blood raging through my veins. It may be a party celebrating innovations in healthcare, but it instead resembles a tank of hungry great whites.

CHAPTER THIRTY-EIGHT
TALLY

"You're going to be late," I murmur, giving Owen a half-hearted shove.

"I don't care." He presses kisses along my neck, hitting the spot that makes me squirm. The man has been attached to me since he arrived home last night, not that I'm complaining.

I didn't even manage a hello before he swept me into his arms and carried me to the bedroom, but we managed our own variety of conversation in the ensuing hours.

"What will we tell the hospital when you don't arrive to round on your patients?"

Owen smiles down at me, dropping a kiss on the tip of my nose. "I'll blame Jessop."

"How good of you, throwing your friends under the bus in such a manner." I'm joking, but the grin slides from Owen's face and his features cloud. I've hit a sore spot. "Are you okay?"

After a few silent seconds, he smiles, shaking off the doldrums. "Just jet-lagged."

"Likely tired from all the fawning and adoration in San Francisco. How did it go?"

"As well as expected," he mumbles, pushing himself out of the bed. "Come and take a shower with me."

"No way. You always hog the hot water."

"You can have it all. I want you near me."

There's a strange vibe emanating from Owen, but I can't pinpoint the cause. He hasn't mentioned his spur-of-the-moment phone proposal, and I'm sure as hell not going to broach it before he does. To be fair, we haven't done much talking—unless moans of ecstasy count.

Then there are those persistent phone calls from Regent Hospital in Asheville. I'm sure Owen does field offers from around the country, but they seem to be *returning* his calls.

What does this man have planned?

I pad into the shower after him, basking in the attention he lavishes over my body. Thankfully, my second trimester is far easier than the first, except for my insatiable sexual appetite. Who am I kidding? I'm always voracious around Owen.

Owen's pager sounds, bouncing off the tiled walls. "Back to reality," he groans, pressing his mouth against mine before exiting the shower. "I'm needed for an emergent case."

I poke my head out of the shower. "Be safe."

"Always."

I RUN MY HANDS ALONG THE FRONT OF MY DRESS, MY BABY BUMP NOW obvious under the satin. Hey, when you're as short as I am, there's not much extra space for a baby to hitch a ride. At least this is the last time I'll have to pour myself into an evening gown. I've had enough mingling with millionaires to last me an eternity. But tonight is for Owen, and that man is worth any inconvenience. Forcing a smile, I wave at Jessop, before entering the private room at the country club.

Figures Charlotte would spare no expense. The ironic part is that

CHAPTER THIRTY-EIGHT

she could have funded the damn training center herself with all the monies spent on entertaining the absurdly wealthy.

Weaving my way to a back table, I settle in for the dog and pony show, glimpsing Owen across the room. I wish I fit in better with this world. Owen, despite his arguments otherwise, makes it look effortless. He's as comfortable sporting a tux as he is Dr. Martens, or at least that's the front he presents.

Meanwhile, I resemble a scullery maid who stole the lady of the house's dress, but no amount of satin will allow me to blend into the fold.

"Why are you hiding in the back?" Jessop inquires, dropping a kiss on my cheek. "You look stunning, Lu."

"I look fat, Ken," I retort.

"You look pregnant, but pregnant women are sexy. Just ask Owen. He can't take his eyes off you."

I blush, but when I glance up, I'm transfixed by Owen's gray gaze as he strolls in my direction.

"I was wondering when you were getting here," Owen murmurs, pressing a kiss to my mouth. "You are gorgeous."

"I am popping out of this dress," I respond with a laugh. Hey, my boobs are enormous at this point.

Owen's eyes trail down my cleavage before sending me a wink. "Yes, you are Darlin, in the sexiest way possible." He slides into the chair next to me, taking a glass of champagne offered by the server. "I'm so ready for this to be over."

That nervous energy flows off him, ever present since he flew back from San Francisco. I've tried to coax him into talking, but he's closed off lately, and as usual, my overactive imagination is concocting all variety of stories.

I know he didn't sleep with Charlotte, although I'm sure she tried to wile her way into his bed. But it's been over two weeks, and he still hasn't mentioned that phone proposal. Part of me wonders if I dreamed the whole thing.

Either way, I'm not giving him any more angina. He has plenty between settling into his new role, opening the training center and dealing with his ex-fiancée. Tonight is a well-deserved celebration.

"I don't think you're allowed to hide in the back," I grin, squeezing his hand before turning my gaze to Jessop. "Either of you. Now scoot."

"Not without you, Darlin." I glance between Owen's probing gaze and his outstretched hand. "It's going to be okay, Tally. I promise. You belong next to me."

I want to believe his words, but Charlotte's raised brow when I arrive at the head table reminds me I'm anything *but* welcome. "Tallulah, come to join us?"

"Wanted to see how the other half lives," I reply with a forced smile. As always, the woman is stunning, and I can't help but compare my roly-poly stature to her regal elegance.

"You're always welcome here." What a load of crap. If her scathing looks are anything to go by, Charlotte has throttled and buried my body a few times already this evening. "Time to start the festivities," she replies, rising from her seat to greet another tuxedo clad gentleman across the room.

Next to me, Owen's leg is tapping a mile a minute. I squeeze his thigh, offering what I hope is a reassuring grin. "You keep stomping your foot like that, and you'll leave a hole in the floor."

"I hate all this pomp and circumstance." His hand squeezes mine, a thoughtful smile tugging at the corners of his mouth. "Christ, you're beautiful, Darlin."

"Want to take me to the bathroom, have your way with me?"

He releases a grunt, shifting in his seat. "Don't start what you can't finish."

I lean in, pressing a kiss to his ear. "I always finish."

His body relaxes as a chuckle reverberates through him, and I settle back into my seat. Laughter really is the best medicine.

My gaze is drawn to an older gentleman across the room. He's mingling, like the rest of the guests, but he oozes an air of importance. "Who is that man?"

"Martin Auerback, Charlotte's father."

"King Midas himself?"

"Close," Owen replies, frowning into his glass.

"He makes you nervous, doesn't he? Don't worry, Owen, you've earned every accolade. Tonight, we celebrate you and all of your achievements. I'm so proud of you."

"I don't deserve you, Tally."

"I think it's the other way around."

Strains of music fill the air. It's 'The Way You Look Tonight'—another oldie but goodie. In fact, it was a favorite of my father, but this time there are no tears, only a happiness that the man existed in the first place.

"Owen, would you like to twirl me around the floor?" Charlotte asks over my shoulder, offering me a half-hearted smile. "For old times' sake."

"I reserved this song—and dance—for Tally." Owen jumps to his feet, offering me his hand. "Come on, Darlin."

I can't dance. Owen knows this—he has the bruised toes to prove it. I want to say no; I don't want the eyes on me, but his gaze is raw and unnerving. He needs me to agree to this.

"You know I'm a terrible dancer."

His brows raise, but his voice is tender. "Dance with me, Tally."

With a sigh, I accept his hand and let him lead me to the dance floor. As expected, I'm as graceful as a two-day-old colt. "I much prefer our private dances."

"Me too, but right now, I have a public announcement to make."

"By dancing?" I wrinkle my brow, his palms clammy against my skin.

"Not at all, but I had to get you out onto the floor." He pauses, grasping my hands, and I notice the music has stopped and everyone —and I mean *everyone*—is watching us.

"Owen, what's going on?"

Instead of answering, he sinks to one knee, while mine threaten to give out. He releases a sigh, offering me a shaky smile. "I'm terrified right now."

"Oh, my God," I whisper, my entire body trembling.

"I know tonight is celebrating the training center, but I want to celebrate something else. I didn't believe in true love. I thought it was a series of compromises, a business transaction. Then I met you, and I felt everything I never knew I could feel, all in a matter of minutes. I messed up a lot, but you stayed. Now," his hands cup my belly, "we're having a baby and I'm so excited for this chapter of sleepless nights and unconditional love. But I have one request."

He pulls out a small box, revealing a gigantic pink diamond nestled against the velvet. The tears stream down my face, there's no holding them back now.

"Will you marry me, Tallulah Knowles? Marry me tomorrow, or the next day, but be my wife. I want to spend my life loving you. What do you say?"

My makeup is a mess, but I don't give a damn. The man of my dreams asked me to marry him. I manage a nod, laughing as Owen slides the ring onto my finger and sweeps me into his arms.

Even I have to admit, for an upscale crowd, there is no shortage of catcalls and applause.

"I love you, Tally."

"I love you." I look at my hand, heavy under the weight of the enormous rock. "It's pink."

"You love pink."

"I thought when you didn't mention anything about the phone proposal, that you were drunk or regretting your words."

He thumbs away my tears, peppering my face with kisses. "I've wanted to spend my life with you since that first night."

"Now you can," I murmur, claiming his lips and forgetting that anything beyond the two of us exists.

Happy times are so often short-lived.

"I see congratulations are in order. Let's have another round of applause for Dr. Stevens and his future wife, Tallulah Knowles."

CHAPTER THIRTY-EIGHT

Charlotte's voice is even on the portable microphone, but I hear the undercurrent of emotion.

I feel a slight pang of regret that Owen proposed in front of her, but it can't come close to the euphoria skipping through my veins. Besides, if the woman really loved him, she wouldn't have cheated on him. She would have proven her love, instead of spreading it around the globe.

"As you all know," Charlotte continues, drawing attention back to the front of the room and her elegant ensemble, "the training center will open in January. Christmas throws a bit of a kink in the wheel, but it looks like Dr. Stevens has his hands full with nuptials and babies. So, we'll grant him a temporary reprieve. A round of applause for the illustrious doctor and all his hard work. Now, for the exciting news."

I catch Owen's gaze, my hands stilling at the look on his face. "What's wrong?"

"I can't believe she's doing it here," he mutters, the color draining from his face. "Just promise me you'll let me explain."

You know that feeling when you're about to get into a car accident? The second before impact, when you see everything in slow motion and a million thoughts flood your brain, but you can't cling to one?

I'm living that moment.

Right now.

The buzz from Owen's proposal nosedives onto the carpet, as I try to gauge what news is about to befall me.

"Promise me, Tally. I love you more than anything in the world."

I cup his cheek, pressing my lips against that delicious mouth. "I promise."

Charlotte clears her throat, pointing at a middle-aged gentleman seated to one side. "It is my pleasure to announce the new coordinator for our training facility. After much discussion, Dr. Stevens and I decided to install our current San Francisco coordinator into this role. He has an illustrious resume, with over twenty years in the device industry and a doctorate from Johns Hopkins."

I scoff as Charlotte gets the last laugh once again. Can't say I didn't see that one coming.

"I should have known she would never let me have that position." I squeeze Owen's hand, smiling up at him. "Let me guess. She propositioned you, but you turned her down?"

"I'm sorry, Tally." He radiates such sadness, knowing this caused me pain.

"I know it was all Charlotte, Owen. Don't worry. Besides, I've got a good job at Memorial."

Owen cups my face. "I don't deserve you."

"I know," I smirk.

"Sorry to interrupt, but I had to come over and congratulate the new couple." Charlotte extends her hand in greeting, and I have to wonder if she sloshed it around a toilet bowl first. "I hope you understand about the coordinator position, Tallulah. You simply don't have the pedigree required."

I see the gloves are off. Well, no worries, I love a good catfight.

I link my arm through Owen's, my engagement ring on full display. "I understand perfectly. I may not have the pedigree, but I do have the man."

"Well, when he's around," she snips, boldly meeting my gaze.

"Charlotte," Owen hisses. "That has not been decided."

"But Daddy said you spoke with him, not an hour ago. Right before your future wife walked in. The deal is set. Those were his exact words, and we both know the parameters of said deal." Charlotte turns to me, a wicked flash of glee in her eyes.

Buckle up, baby. This is more than a fender bender. This is a head-on collision.

I take a step back, facing them both. "What are you two talking about?"

"Owen's days with Memorial are numbered."

My heart lurches. Suddenly the phone calls from North Carolina, the random pieces of mail from Regent Hospital, make sense. Did Owen accept a position at another hospital?

Not once did he mention leaving Memorial. At least, he never mentioned it to me.

"I can tell by your face that your *fiancée* never discussed this with you."

I turn to Owen, clinging to a thread of hope that is rapidly disintegrating. "Are you taking a job at Regent? I know they were constantly calling."

Charlotte is only too eager to answer my query. "The hospital in Asheville? No, although it was quite the deal they offered him."

I'm going to punch the bitch. Seriously, the woman is walking out of here with a black eye.

Then it hits me—how does Charlotte know about the deal that Regent offered Owen, when I'm in the dark?

"I mean it, Charlotte. Shut the fuck up," Owen warns, but I raise my hand, silencing him.

"No, I want to hear what Charlotte has to say. She's apparently privy to information that's been withheld from me. I'd like to level the playing field."

Owen grips my hand, the muscles in his neck bulging. "Let's go outside, and I'll tell you everything. In private."

"Okay. Let's go," I concede. Hey, the man asked me to marry him. I'm sure he's got a perfectly logical explanation.

God, please let him have a perfectly logical explanation.

But Charlotte doesn't grant us the courtesy of a private conversation. "Come January, Owen will help to open training centers around the country, and I, as his new partner, will be there every step of the way."

My stomach threatens to lose my lunch as my gaze swings upward, but Owen averts his eyes. No matter, one look at the muscle ticking in his jaw and his fists clenching at his sides and I know her words are true. "You told me this was a onetime deal with her, Owen. You promised me."

Charlotte laughs, but it holds only malice. "It started out that way, but he and I had a heart-to-heart in San Francisco. Besides, money is a wonderful motivator, and Dr. Stevens is making a windfall off this new position. You, and your needs, fell down the ladder of importance. But don't worry, he'll put you up in a lovely home."

"He wouldn't do that, Charlotte." I hear the desperation in my voice, my gaze seeking out the man I love. "Would you, Owen?"

"I could kill you, Charlotte." His shoulders slump as a defeated breath exits his body. "It wasn't decided, but it's so much money, Tally. Money that could take care of us forever."

It's a one-two punch. Not only did he betray me—again—with yet another lie, but he followed the sound of money instead of his heart. Maybe he's more like the Auerback family than I thought.

I sway on my feet, my head spinning. I glance at my hand, the once shiny diamond now a mocking reminder of another carefully calculated lie.

The tears spill down my cheeks, but I make no move to wipe them away. "I don't want the money. I want *you*. You didn't even talk to me about this, Owen."

"You see where his loyalties lie, don't you?"

I shove my finger in Charlotte's face, so tempted to knock her block off. "You'd better shut the fuck up, Charlotte, before I impale you with your designer earrings."

"My, my—"

"Charlotte, get the hell away from us," Owen growls.

She huffs and walks away, but I notice a spring in her step. So glad I could make her night. My gaze flits back to Owen, praying for a miracle. Praying that I heard everything wrong. "We don't need their money, Owen. I don't care about some fancy house."

He grasps my arms, his eyes wild. "It's a *ton* of money, Darlin. So much more than you can imagine."

I yank my arms away, not believing what I'm hearing. "That's it, then? It's all about the money. Not what's best for us, or our child, but what's best for *you* and your wallet. Got it."

CHAPTER THIRTY-EIGHT

"I told you I hadn't decided, that I had to give it some thought."

"Owen, *you* didn't tell me anything. Once again, I find out from a third party. My opinion doesn't matter. I see that now. It never did."

"It's all that matters, Tally. I'll go call off the deal right now."

I shake my head, throwing up my hands. "You've already made your decision. I'm sure it's a ton of money, and you *were* going to marry a billionaire. You have a certain lifestyle planned, and my meager earnings don't fit that profile. But what good is a pile of cash if our child never sees his father? What kind of marriage will we have if you spend all your time with your ex-fiancée? You know that won't work, Owen."

"Tally."

"*It won't work.*" Then it hits me. He knew about the deal and yet proposed that same night. "Why did you ask me to marry you?"

His jaw slackens at my pointed question. "Because I love you, Tally. I want to spend the rest of my life with you."

"You won't ever *be* there, remember? Your darling Charlotte saw fit to that, and you fell for it—hook, line and sinker. You're a fool, Owen Stevens, but don't feel so bad. I'm a far bigger fool, because I believed in you."

"Tell me what to do, Darlin. Tell me what you want, and I'll do it."

I shrug, wiping my face with the back of my hand. "You should already know. All I've ever wanted is you."

His eyes are glassy, mirroring my own. "Then stop running, Tally. For once, trust me enough to give me a chance."

"You're all out of chances, Owen."

I whirl on the ball of my foot, scrambling to the closest exit. I stumble down the hallway, desperate for air, for peace. Neither of which is coming.

I want to go back in there and rail against Owen and his pack of lies. I want to smack the smirk off of Charlotte's model perfect face.

I do neither. Instead, I get my keys from the valet and leave. If it's peace I'm looking for, I won't find it there.

~

Has anyone ever mentioned how difficult it is to hop a fence in an evening gown? While pregnant?

Thankfully, my dress is another thrift store find, because now it's headed for the rag bag.

I use the light from my phone to walk amongst the headstones. I had to turn off my cellular service, because I've been barraged nonstop by Owen and Ken, both desperate to know my whereabouts.

I don't want anyone to find me right now.

Finally, I spy my parents' graves. I know they're not there. It's just a marker, but it's the closest thing I have to family. I spend the next few minutes rearranging the flowers and brushing specks of dirt from the stone, but I can hear my father's voice.

'I can't answer it if you don't ask it.'

Settling down on the grass, I let the tears spill down my cheeks. God, I miss them.

"Hey, folks. I don't know if you've been watching the latest episode, but my life took a sharp turn into complicated. For the umpteenth time this year."

I snuffle, wiping my nose on my arm. I'm the epitome of grace.

"Owen asked me to marry him. I said yes, and for a moment, I was so happy. Happier than I've ever been in my life." Pulling my hand forward, I wiggle my fingers, watching the stone sparkle in the moonlight. "But he made some big dollar deal with his ex-fiancée, and I won't ever see him. He won't ever see our baby. It's a *ton* of money, whatever that means, and he promised me a fancy house. I don't want the damn house. I want him, and I want him here with me."

Drawing in the cool night air, I toss my head back, gazing at the stars. "What should I do, Dad? Do I suck it up, knowing I'll be miserable? Do I let him go back to his old life with Charlotte? Or do I sit Owen down and tell him that those aren't the rules we're going to play by?"

Then it hits me. That's exactly what I'm going to do. If I'm going down, I'm doing it my way. In style.

Owen wants me to stop running? Fine, I'm planting my feet and I'll be damned if marriage or millions will change my mind. Most importantly, I'm done letting Charlotte rule my emotions, my thoughts, and my relationship.

Screw her. Owen is my man, and I'm keeping him.

Owen has begged me to toss out the rule book since we met. I'm starting a new one. Tonight. And these rules, he'd better abide.

On the way out, I find an open side exit. Glory be, that is *so* much easier than climbing the fence. I turn back on my cellular service, and within seconds, the phone buzzes. It's Ken again.

Better let him know I'm okay. After all, he did nothing to me.

"Hi, Ken."

"Jesus, Mary and Joseph, you scared the hell out of me," Ken chides, his voice frantic. "Where have you been? I've been calling for the last two hours."

"I went to see my folks." I fiddle with the skirt of my now tattered dress, wondering if it might double as a Halloween costume next year. "What's up?"

Ken clears his throat, his signal that a story is imminent. "You missed quite the show."

"There was more?"

"To say the least. Things got loud."

I unlock my car door, sliding into the driver's seat. "Surprising with that crowd. I doubted they were capable of any genuine emotions."

"Well, Owen had enough for everyone. He called off the deal in front of the entire room. That role that Charlotte mentioned? Owen told her to shove it up her bony ass, along with any payout."

I wrap my trembling hands around the steering wheel. "He didn't need to do that."

"That's the thing. He did. The payout was huge, Lu, and he thought it would make your lives easier. But when you walked away, he realized that he lost the only thing that matters to him. All the shit tonight? He hates it. Owen only does the dance because he knows that he can save lives. That's what he's good at. That and adoring the ever-loving fuck out of you."

"He doesn't adore me."

"Bullshit. Yes, he does. He asked you to be his wife, Lu."

"Right before he neglected to tell me he planned on working with his ex-fiancée for the rest of his life. Owen offered me a ring to appease me."

"Lu, he just passed on ten million dollars. He asked you because he loves you. I knew he was going to ask tonight. I was privy to the details. My job was to keep you there since you are well known for disappearing like Cinderella at the ball."

"I never wanted Owen to have to choose between love and money. But I can't live my life knowing he's flitting around the globe with Charlotte, while I sit at home waiting for when—and if—he comes back."

"He passed on the deal," Ken reiterates, each syllable enunciated to drive home his point. "Do me one favor. Please talk to him before you make any decisions."

"We'll see." I hear Ken's pager beep, an all too familiar sound in our world. "You'd better go."

"I'm on it. I swear, an emergent case is the most normal part of this evening. Now that's saying something."

It sure is, Ken. It sure is.

CHAPTER THIRTY-NINE
OWEN

Holy shit, what a night.

My head is thumping after driving around for hours, looking for Tally. I left the banquet fifteen minutes after her, desperate to explain the truth of the situation.

No such luck.

Now, after going to every place imaginable, I head into Memorial, responding to a page. I force a smile for the catcalls from the night staff as I hustle into the locker room to change from my tux.

"I thought I was on call tonight."

I jump, turning to see Ken standing there, tying on his surgical cap. "Yeah, I figured you might want a break."

Ken shakes his head, clapping me around the shoulders. He sees right through my lie. "Did you catch up to Lu?"

"No. Then I got the page and..." I trail off, uncertain what to say at this point.

"She's safe."

I sink to the bench, my knees giving out. "Thank God," I mutter. I wouldn't allow myself to believe that something bad happened to the woman I love, but Tally was so upset when she left.

The worst part is the knowledge that had anything happened, I'm the one responsible. As usual, my girl didn't let me explain the situation, but how can I blame her? Charlotte hit her like a locomotive, and it was all out of spite.

Once again, I look like a total prick.

"That will go down in history as the most exciting banquet dinner I've ever attended," Ken remarks. "Seriously, that was quite the show. Way to stick it to the man."

I smirk, although there's nothing funny about my actions. Even though it felt good as hell. "Charlotte had it coming. She messed with my life one too many times."

"Agreed. I don't think anyone has ever told the Auerback family to shove a deal up their asses before, though."

That's a definitive no. The Auerbacks are royalty, minus the title. I not only told them no, I did it in the most public fashion.

"I sent myself to the permanent blacklist, but I stand by my decision. I'm sorry if I screwed things up for you." The last thing I wanted was to ruin the deal for the training center, or my colleague. Ken is a good man, and he deserves the recognition.

"You didn't. I spoke to Mr. Auerback on your behalf after you left."

My jaw drops at Dr. Jessop's admission. Everyone treads lightly around the Auerback family. Hell, I should know. I tiptoed around their bullshit for years. "You must be a smoother talker than me, considering you're still in one piece. At least he didn't set the dogs on you."

"He was actually quite agreeable, once the confusion surrounding you and Charlotte cleared. He had no idea that Charlotte was causing such trouble in your life. Apparently, she told a far different version of events. Something about Lu trapping you into marriage and blackmailing you with the baby. Charlotte, of course, painted herself as the innocent party."

That explains Mr. Auerback's dirty glances in Tally's direction, and his hesitation to consider her for a role within the training facility. He blamed her for the dissolution of mine and Charlotte's relationship.

Just wait, Mr. Auerback, I'll tell you all the details of your darling daughter.

"That's why he didn't care to meet Tally. At least now I know the source of his rudeness. He's still a bastard, though."

"I'm not denying that he's an arrogant prick, but Charlotte's behavior shocked him. Owen, he realizes your worth. You're invaluable to the future of robotics in the cath lab. He will not let a spoiled woman come in the way of his legacy."

"He can have his legacy. I'm happy to continue doing my job. I don't need all the accolades."

"Screw that shit. You deserve both, and you're going to get it."

We stroll down to the cath lab, gowning up for the procedure. Another young, overweight individual. I swear, the numbers skyrocket around the holidays. Too much rich food and drink, with nary a treadmill in sight. I need to get my head in the game, but my curiosity wins out.

"So, what happened?"

Ken shrugs, his mouth hidden behind the surgical mask. But I see it in his eyes. He's smiling like a fool. "Oh, the deal is a go, son. Minus one beautiful but vengeful ex-fiancée."

I force a smile, but the word fiancée hits like a fist. I asked the love of my life to be my wife. I should be in bed next to Tally, loving every inch of her, but because of my lack of transparency—again—I have no clue if she still wants to marry me. If she wants anything to do with me.

"Cheer up, old boy. Things are going to be fine."

"I'm not so sure of that. I don't know if I can fix this situation with Tally. Here I was, trying to convince the woman that not all doctors are bad. Instead, I helped prove her point."

Ken clears his throat, tapping his gloved hands together. "You're not anything like the man who hurt her. You know that."

"No, but in her eyes, I might be worse."

~

I leave Memorial at five-thirty that morning. The case was supposed to be routine, but anyone in medicine can tell you that there's no textbook cardiac patient.

This was no exception.

Thankfully, the patient is alive and well, and judging by his jokes when I left, he will be chowing down on more holiday fare within the week.

You can't win them all.

My phone rings, and I grab it without looking. At this hour of the morning, it's work related. "Dr. Stevens."

"Owen, we need to talk."

My heart jumps at the familiar baritone. "What do we need to discuss, Mr. Auerback? I made my stance very clear last night."

"That you did, but I wasn't aware of the full breadth of the situation until I spoke with Ken. I want to apologize for my daughter's behavior. Charlotte had no right to meddle in your private affairs. She claims an altruistic stance, looking out for the greater good. But I wouldn't be where I am today if I believed every line of bullshit that I heard. Even when they're spouted by my flesh and blood."

I clench my jaw at his statement. What Mr. Auerback fails to realize is that his daughter did more than screw up a deal with billion-dollar earnings potential. She screwed up my life. "I appreciate the apology, but it hardly fixes the damage your daughter caused. Her crafty ideals might work in some boardrooms, but I won't abide them. I can't work with her any longer, under any circumstances."

"Understood. But I also don't want to abandon this ship, Owen. It isn't sinking, it's just off course."

"What are you saying?" Get to the damn point, man.

"I'll be staying in Florida for the duration of the deal, ensuring that everything is fair and legal. As for Charlotte, she will stay on to save face, but she no longer possesses any decision-making power."

"What about Tally?"

His sigh resonates over the phone line. "I feel awful that we treated her in such a manner, even worse that I believed the lies about her. I've researched Ms. Knowles, and her work history is impeccable. You're right, she is an excellent candidate for the national coordinator position. Do you think she will be interested in hearing the details?"

Running my hand over my brow, I release a huff. "Damned if I know." I should be elated that they're going to offer the woman I love the opportunity of a lifetime, making the money her brain and work ethic deserve.

The only trouble? She may decline, based on past treatment, and I can't blame her in the slightest.

"I'm assuming that her sudden disappearance last night was because of my daughter's announcement regarding your new and unwanted role within the company?"

"You assume correctly."

"I can't ask you to forgive my daughter, but I hope you know that she was acting from a place of jealousy and pain. I also realize that Charlotte brought this upon herself, and she's paying the price for her insolence."

What a load of crap. I bite my tongue, holding back the sharp retort. "We're all paying the price for Charlotte's insolence."

"Quite right, but I intend to rectify things—with both you and Tally. I've got a conference call in Tokyo. I'll speak with you later."

Mr. Auerback's words should soothe me, but the truth is that I don't care about the deal. Do I want to help people? Absolutely. It's what I do, and what I'm good at. But nothing is more important than Tally and our baby. *Nothing.*

But I'm no fool. How many more times can I leave Tally in the dark before she turns off the light in our relationship?

I need caffeine. I'm exhausted and running on fumes, but my

brain is spinning too fast to consider sleep. While I wait for my order, I verify my mother's arrival time with the airline. She's flying in for Christmas, and I know she'll have some choice words for me regarding my latest screw up. The woman adores Tally.

I pull into the parking garage, my head thumping despite the caffeine jolt. There's no easy fix for this kind of pain.

With a sigh, I push open my front door, and am immediately greeted by Hecate. I stroke her from tip to tail, smiling when she winds around my feet. Tally claims the cat doesn't warm to people, but Hecate and I have been buddies from the start.

Too bad the cat can't put in a good word for me.

I hear Tally's voice, but it's too low to make out anything but the occasional curse word. My momentary excitement is tempered by the knowledge that she's likely packing, searching for the quickest exit out of my life.

I follow the string of obscenities to the back bedroom and push open the door, my heart in my throat.

Tally sits on the floor, cleaning a gash on her leg. Her head flies up when I open the door, but there's no malice in her gaze. "You're here."

"So are you." I kneel next to her, inspecting the wound. "What happened?"

She shrugs, offering her trademark smirk. "Let's just say that being pregnant has *not* improved my grace."

I grab the gauze pad and antiseptic from her, pressing gingerly around the wound. "Does it hurt?"

"It doesn't feel good, if that's what you're asking. But what can I expect when I climb a cemetery gate in a ballgown?"

I settle back on my haunches, my eyes wide. "Is that where you went? I looked everywhere for you."

"Not everywhere. I wanted to spend some time with my folks." She chews her lip, regarding me thoughtfully. "Our dear friend, Dr. Jessop, called me last night. He informed me of your escapades after I left. Did you really call off the whole deal?"

"I sure did."

"Are you okay with that decision?"

I nod, my hand still tracing her leg. "I am."

"He also mentioned how you told Charlotte where she could shove her new position, along with the ridiculously large payout promised you."

"You missed one hell of a blowout."

"Why did you do it, Owen?"

"For you." I grasp her chin, moving my thumb along her lower lip. "You were right. It's just money. Life is so much more than that, but without you, it's meaningless."

I open my mouth to say more, but she shakes her head. "We need to talk."

I help her to a standing position, eager to pull her to me and beg her to forgive me one last time. "Let's talk."

"Correction. I need to talk. *You* need to sit down and be quiet," Tally states, pointing to the bed, and I waste no time abiding her demands. Hey, when a five-foot-tall woman tells you to jump, you ask how high while holding back the snicker.

"Yes, ma'am."

She paces in front of me, a scowl lining her face. "We're in a mess and a lot of it is my fault."

My jaw slackens in a dumbfounded gape. Talk about an unexpected statement. "It's both of our faults."

"I said be quiet."

I bite back a laugh. My tiny vixen has the floor.

She stares at me for a moment, before walking out of the room. Perhaps she's gone off her rocker. It can happen in pregnancy.

"Here." She returns with a glass of water and two pills. "I can tell you have a headache."

"Thanks."

"I told you to be quiet."

"Are you exploring a career as a dominatrix?"

"That might be fun. But don't make me lose my train of

thought." She stands in front of me, her hands planted on her hips. "I was furious with you last night. I considered everything—the lies, the omissions, your stunning ex-fiancée—and decided I would be better off without you."

Shit. This does not look promising.

"Then I realized something. You're damn lucky to have me, and I'm damn lucky to have you. We're amazing together. Charlotte may be gorgeous and wealthier than Midas, but I have a cool cat and I'm ridiculously good in bed."

I chuckle, laughter floating up from my chest. "You're superb in the sack."

"And?" she questions, her dark eyes widening behind her glasses.

I take a minute to figure out to what she's referring. "Hecate is the coolest cat on the planet, bar none."

"Exactly. But..."

I grimace at her use of the word but. I hate that word. It rates right up there with fine on my most detested expression list.

"You claim I keep running away from you, Owen. You're right."

Another shocking admission. I expected to get an earful about how horrible I am, while dodging projectile kitchenware.

This scenario never played out in my mind.

Please don't let it be a trick.

She's chewing her lip again, a sure sign that whatever topic she's about to broach won't be pleasant. "You know that the doctor I dated screwed with my life, but you don't know the extent."

"Then tell me, Darlin."

She crosses the small space between us, shaking her head in exasperation. "One more word out of you—"

"And you'll what?" I counter. This conversation is offbeat, but I'm also hopeful as to the outcome. Hey, at least she isn't hitting me. Yet.

Tally rolls her eyes, looking skyward. "You know, Dad, maybe this isn't a good idea. Maybe I should just kill him." She chuckles before the laughter falls from her face. "You asked about my scars.

They were no accident. My ex-boyfriend drank copious amounts of alcohol. He claimed it eased the stress. But he turned into a monster when he drank, and I never knew which version of him I might encounter. One night, I worked late, missing a medical dinner where he was speaking. It was unintentional, a patient and staffing emergency, but he felt slighted. For that, I had to pay. When he got home, high off booze and God knows what else, he didn't give me a chance to explain. I saw all four corners of the room that night. He threw me against a mirror, and the shattered glass lacerated my side."

"Jesus Christ," I gasp, my blood near its boiling point. "Where is this man now?"

Tally rests her hands on my shoulders, willing me down. But that won't happen until the piece of shit is dead in the ground. "Shh. Just listen. I woke up in the hospital, with only a vague recollection of what happened. Fifty stitches in my back, another forty-two along my side, a fractured jaw and a broken wrist." She wipes her eyes, and I see the pain living there. "Then, for kicks, because beating the shit out of me wasn't enough, he got me fired. He was a brilliant doctor, and he spun quite the story for upper management. He convinced them I had attacked him—apparent from my severe injuries and his total lack of any. He gave them an ultimatum—him or me. They chose him."

My heart breaks as she tells the story of her past. I finally understand why she was so adamantly against dating doctors. This man ruined her, body and soul.

"He turned many of my coworkers against me, and I knew as far as New York was concerned, I was finished. My father had retired and moved to Florida. It seemed as good a time as any to leave, particularly when the phone calls started again, and the good doctor threatened that this time he would finish what he started."

"That's fucking it," I roar, jumping to my feet. "I want his name. That piece of shit is going to rue the day he hurt you."

"Owen—"

I shake my head, my body trembling with rage. "No, Tally. I won't let this rest. He's going to pay."

"I'm not telling you this so you can beat the shit out of him."

"I'll do more than that. They'll never find his corpse."

"I appreciate that, I truly do. But I have the floor. Sit down and listen." She points at the bed, her lips pursed. "I'm not kidding."

I sink back onto the mattress, my foot tapping erratically against the floor. Tally wants me to remain calm? Is she kidding? That someone inflicted that level of harm on the woman I love is enough to make me lose my damn mind.

"My point is that he was a monster, Owen. You are anything but. That's why I didn't date doctors. I didn't date anyone. I established these rules because in my mind, they kept me safe. In reality, they kept alone." She sits beside me, grasping my hand. Just that slight touch makes me feel like I can breathe again. "I'm proud of you, of what you do for a living. You save lives, Owen. Hell, you saved mine."

Men aren't supposed to cry, right? All that macho, tough crap is bullshit, because when the woman you love tells you that you saved her life, I dare you not to get choked up. I run my hand along her cheek, smiling when she presses a kiss to my palm.

"I realize now that all my rules made it impossible for you to navigate this relationship, and I kept inventing new ones every day. All to keep my heart safe. But my heart has been with you ever since we met. I just made you work *really* hard for it. Granted, you're hardly innocent in this situation."

I nod, because this woman made me work my ass off to prove myself. Would I do it again? Every damn day, just for ten minutes with Tally.

"Even when we reconciled, I wanted to hide our relationship, then I got jealous when other women looked at you. Who does that? Who hides a relationship with the most eligible doctor in the hospital? I need to have my head examined."

"Good times, Darlin," I tease, tweaking her nose. "But I earned your misgivings. I should have told you the truth—the whole truth

—about everything, right from the start. I figured no woman would want to handle my messy situation, but you're not just any woman. You're the most perfect woman I've ever met, and I meant what I asked you last night."

She holds up her hand, my ring sparkling on her finger. "I wasn't letting you slide. Hell, no. But I have made some new rules."

"Oh, Christ," I groan, not entirely sure I want to know. "Do they involve sexual favors, because I'm completely on board with that scenario."

"No, no, no. I admitted my shortcomings, but the shit you've put me through the last couple of months is ridiculous. You have to be punished. Hence, my new rules." She straddles my lap, her baby bump resting between us. "You may be a world-class doctor, but everyone has to toe the line."

"Give it to me, then. What are your rules?" I inquire, my hands stroking along the sides of her stomach. "You really have popped."

"Are you calling me fat?"

"Not a chance. I think you're even sexier now."

The corners of Tally's mouth turn up as a blush colors her cheeks. "See? That's just it. You knocked me up, but you don't seem sorry about it."

I smile, stealing a kiss from her full lips.

"I think you're happy about it, actually."

"You think so?" I'm not happy about the baby. I'm thrilled.

"I know so, and your punishment, because of your equal involvement, is that you're stuck with us. Me, Nugget and Hecate."

"Oh, no. Anything but that."

"It gets worse. I want you around. None of this flying around the globe crap. Once in a while, fine. But not every week. I need you here."

"Deal." Easiest damn decision I've ever made.

Tally bites her lower lip, looking at me over her glasses. "And Charlotte—"

"—is gone," I finish her statement, all too happy to say the words. "Permanently."

"I may not like the woman, but saying it like that makes me think she's wearing cement shoes."

"She's very much alive, but she's out of *our* lives."

"I'm sorry if you lost the deal because of me. I didn't want it to come to that. I know what this means to you."

I chuckle, pushing a strand of hair behind Tally's ear. "I appreciate that, but I didn't lose the deal. Not at all, actually."

"Good. Also, I'm sick of this secret relationship crap."

"Thank God." I throw my head back, so damn grateful I don't have to maintain a facade around Tally anymore. She thinks I'm affectionate now? The woman has no idea.

"So, you're going to marry me, no way around it. But I want to be the one to tell Dr. Nicole Hedges the news."

"Evil girl. Let's go to the courthouse now."

"That's not how it works."

"Buzzkill. You don't let me go down on you at the pizzeria. You don't want to have sex in the bathroom at Wicked Chucks. You don't want to march down to the courthouse and get married. Way to live on the edge, Tally."

"We both agreed that the bathroom at Wicked Chucks is hazardous to our health."

"Anything else?" I question, wanting to wrap up this conversation so I can have her pussy wrapped around me instead.

"You're going to tell me I'm pretty even when I look like a beached whale and not say a word about my strange pickle, peanut butter, and ice cream combinations."

My face scrunches at the thought. "Is that what you were eating the other night?"

"Didn't I just say we aren't discussing it? So, do you agree to my terms?"

"I do." I can sit and argue with her about the details of our disagreements, but I'd rather spend this time loving her. For the first time since she discovered I'm a doctor, my Tally is back. Fully and 100% back.

I'm taking advantage of that fact.

"What time does your Mom land?" Tally asks, cocking her brow and sending me her saucy grin. I love that grin. It means something sexy as hell is about to go down.

"We have four hours."

"Plenty of time for your bonus prize."

"I'm always one for prizes," I murmur, my mouth straining to reach hers.

Tally wags her finger at me as her hands slide underneath my shirt, scratching along my abs. She pushes me down onto the bed, skating her tongue along the waistband of my sweats. "Far too many clothes," she whispers, yanking off my pants.

My dick is about to explode, and she hasn't even touched me yet. When her slender hand wraps around me, I groan, my hips bucking toward her. Tally's tongue flits across my head, swirling and teasing. I wind my hands in her hair, guiding her down as she takes all of me. A low moan rises from the back of her throat, as her tongue strokes the underside of my shaft.

Holy fuck, but this woman gives amazing head. I prop up on my hand, watching her mouth take me deeper. Her gaze meets mine, and it's clear that she knows the truth.

She owns me.

Tally loves driving me out of my mind, but this morning, she's extra dedicated in her task. Her hand cups my balls, and when she sucks one into her mouth, I damn near levitate.

I don't want to know how the woman got so damn good at sucking cock, so long as I'm the last man she touches. She's a master, dominating me, her hands and mouth working me into a frenzy.

"I want inside you, Darlin," I beg, her long hair tickling my thighs.

"Mmm-mmm," Tally moans, upping her oral acrobatics to the next level.

Within seconds, I explode, and my entire world goes dark. When I open my eyes, she's lying next to me, her fingernails scratching along my chest, a flirtatious smile on her lips.

"I hope you've learned your lesson," Tally states with a wink.

"You are too good at that."

"So glad to have a willing participant."

"I'm willing any damn time of the day or night." I roll her onto her back, yanking down her pajama pants. "Now it's my turn to return the favor."

Tally's mobile rings, startling us both. She glances at the caller ID before answering the phone. "Hi, Beth. How are you?" She climbs off the bed, walking into the kitchen. Meanwhile, I'm trying to keep my dick from breaking in two. It doesn't matter that I just got my rocks off two minutes earlier. I need inside Tally. Now.

"Everything okay?" I ask when Tally returns to the room.

Tally shrugs, chewing her bottom lip. "Earl stopped by the shelter earlier. Apparently, he wasn't aware that Marla no longer lives there."

Shit. Some people can't take no for an answer. "Did he get violent?"

She shakes her head. "He threatened to cause trouble, but the cops arrested him. *Again*. He was less than happy at the turn of events."

"I'll bet. I'm glad he's behind bars."

"For the interim, at least. Unfortunately, they never stay there long. But that's not all Beth told me."

I bite back the smile threatening to break across my face. "Oh, no?"

"You sneaky bastard."

I chuckle. Typical Tally response. "What did I do now?"

She pushes me back on the bed, straddling me. "Beth just got a visit from Santa, in the form of a check. A *huge* check for $50,000 from one Tally's Trust. Care to explain?"

"What is there to explain? Santa came for a visit. It is Christmas time."

Tally shoots me a mock glare. "Spill it, Owen."

"I'm in awe of you and your dedication to these women. Even more so, now that I know how you suffered. I knew the shelter needed money for repairs, and I knew that if you had the money, you would give it." I run my fingers along her arms. "So, I established a charity in your name, to help women like Beth and Marla."

Tears brim in her eyes, and she pulls off her glasses, wiping her face. "That's likely the third best gift I've ever gotten."

"What are the first two?" I question with a grin.

"You and Nugget."

I thumb away the tears from her cheeks, pulling her mouth down to mine. "You two are definitely my greatest gift."

"You didn't have to give them that money, Owen."

"Yes, I did. You help protect these women. I protect you."

CHAPTER FORTY

TALLY

TALLY

My soon to be mother-in-law left for Asheville this morning, with a promise that she'll be back within the month. My handsome soon to be husband is dropping her at the airport, before heading to Memorial to round on his patients.

I know it's the holiday season, but I don't think the hospital units are full because of an overconsumption of food and drink. I swear it's to catch a glimpse of Man Candy Stevens. Yes, that is an actual nickname, one I personally approved.

Hey, they can look. They just can't touch.

We had a beautiful Christmas, surprising considering the loss of my father earlier in the year. But Owen and his mother went above and beyond to make the holiday special for me. It didn't hurt that we had an engagement and baby to celebrate.

The best part? I was right—Nugget is a little boy.

Owen is beyond excited at the prospect of having a son. He's bought all manner of baby sporting attire, so the kid will have his choice of jerseys. Yep, that man's smile at our most recent sonogram was the best one yet, and I know they'll keep getting brighter.

But now, it's back to reality, aka Memorial Hospital.

I stand in front of the bathroom mirror, clad in only my panties, and realize I'm going to have to buy bigger bras soon. This will make the second time in four months. At the rate I'm going, Dolly Parton and I will have more than a nickname in common.

"Just look at these things," I mutter, hefting a breast in each hand.

"I plan to do more than that."

I spin around, catching sight of my man lounging against the doorframe. Looks like his should be illegal. "Did you forget something?"

"Yes." Owen takes advantage of my half naked state as he rips the underwear from my body, dropping to his knees in front of me. Without ceremony, he hoists one of my legs over his shoulder, as he buries his face between my thighs. His tongue circles my clit, drawing the bud into his mouth, and I buck my hips against him.

I forget about my ever-changing pregnant curves. Not that it's ever been a turnoff for Owen. Quite the opposite.

All I feel is Owen's raw and untethered desire, aimed at me. If the man was sexually ravenous before, he's downright insatiable now.

My hands grip his scalp, pushing his face against me. His low groan of approval serves as an extra layer of friction against my overly sensitized skin. "I love when you forget things."

"I love how wet you are," he murmurs as his tongue lashes my clit. It's the most exquisite agony.

"Totally your fault."

My hands skate along my breasts as my fingers twirl over my nipples. Who knew pregnancy would turn me into such a voracious nymphomaniac?

His fingers slide inside me, and now it's my turn to moan. "I need you."

Owen shucks his pants, flipping me back to face the sink as he buries himself in me. "Fuck me, Tally."

"I think that's my line."

CHAPTER FORTY • 417

His hand winds in my hair, pulling me against his chest as he thrusts deep, filling me completely. "You want to play, little girl?"

"Always. Don't stop, Owen. You feel incredible."

His grunting response assures me that the feeling is mutual. "You want more? I want to hear you beg for it, Tally."

God. This man. Sexiest human being on the face of the planet. I'll beg all damn day. "Make me scream your name."

His hands curl around my hips as he drives his cock into me, in a relentless pursuit of my passion. He's so deep. I'm so full. With a cry, I grab the edge of the counter and push my ass back, changing the angle. That's all it takes to turn my body into a quivering mess.

Owen's face contorts before he nuzzles the base of my neck, emptying himself into me. "So damn beautiful."

He palms the curve of my belly, meeting my gaze in the mirror. "This is mine. Every inch of you. Mine."

As his lips glide along my skin, I make a final decision about my professional future. I know that putting my guys front and center is exactly what I want for my life. The coordinator position seems so unimportant. I'm seeking a new position. "Do you think he'll be a doctor?"

"I know he will be loved. That's all that matters."

I smile, leaning back against his muscled chest, watching Owen tenderly caress my stomach only moments after screwing me senseless.

That's how it is with us. Together, we're fire. But underneath that fire is a whole lot of love.

"You're late," I remind him, running my hands along his thighs.

"You're worth it." He drops another kiss on my shoulder, our gazes meeting in the mirror. "I was thinking...I know you wanted to wait until the summer for the wedding."

"Your mom wants a big wedding, remember? I don't want to look like a beached orca for the occasion."

"I meant what I said the other day. Let's go to the courthouse— just you and me—and get married. Then, we can have the big wedding that Mom wants next summer." Before I can respond, his pager sounds. The man is in demand. "You don't have to answer now, but the sooner I make you Mrs. Stevens, the better. I'll see you at the hospital?"

I nod, giggling when his pager sounds again. "Do they think if they keep paging you, you'll get there faster?"

"Apparently." His lips press to mine as his tongue dances along the seam of my mouth. "I love you."

"Love you more."

~

"Aren't you chipper this morning?" Stefani remarks, sending me a wink.

"Life is good," I respond, grabbing the laptop from my office. "I'm headed to yet another fun-filled meeting."

"How many of those do you have per day?"

"Seems like a million, but likely closer to a hundred. But this meeting has some sexy as hell eye candy for my viewing pleasure."

"So unfair, keeping Dr. Stevens all to yourself." I know the woman is joking. Stefani is thrilled that Owen and I finally worked things out.

"Says the woman who's doing the horizontal mambo with Dan."

"I am not."

"Liar, liar." Hey, she is lying. I have it on good authority—namely, Dan's—that he and Stefani are exclusive. Judging by the looks they shoot each other, they're also in love.

"Hey, Lu, before you go, there was a call for you."

"Who was it?" I inquire, sucking down the last of my water.

"I don't know. Some guy. He wanted to speak with you and when I asked who was calling, he hung up. He sounded a bit creepy."

CHAPTER FORTY

"Everyone sounds creepy to you. He probably got disconnected. No big deal. He'll call back. I'll see you later today."

I'm so glad that the training center is opening next week. That means I won't have to see Charlotte's perfectly sculpted face again. Oh, she's been pleasant since the celebration dinner, but I can see it in her face that she would like nothing better than to claw my eyes out.

Some people are such sore losers.

Thankfully, Daddy has her on a short leash. Turns out, blood isn't always thicker than water. Dollar signs trump either, and Mr. Auerback knows that Owen is a top-notch investment.

Even though Charlotte handed the coordinator position to someone else, Owen and Ken have asked me to sit in on some meetings, as a consultant of sorts. I know they feel guilty about the situation, but the meetings aren't all bad. I have a hell of a good time torturing Charlotte.

Hey, the woman earned it in spades.

I glance at my buzzing phone. Another text from my man.

Owen: *Well? Can we get our marriage certificate this week?*

I shake my head, chuckling at his persistence. He may have said that I didn't have to answer him right away, but it's obvious he'd like one. In the affirmative, preferably.

Me: *I love it when you beg.*

Owen: *That is not an answer, Tally.*

Me: *Close enough.*

I turn the corner; the blood freezing in my veins. There, directly in my path, is Earl.

Now I realize who placed the earlier phone call to my unit, and I'm fairly certain the man doesn't want to wish me a belated Merry Christmas.

With trembling fingers, I reach into my scrub pocket for my phone, praying that I'll get a call off to security before he sees me.

Too late.

His head swings in my direction, his eyes narrowing when they catch sight of me. "There you are. I thought you'd be harder to track down, but it turns out your coworkers are more than willing to give you up."

I step back, my fingers fumbling as my nerves shoot into overdrive "Earl, you're not supposed to be here. You know the rules."

"I'm not in the mood to follow rules today. You took my wife and boy from me."

"No, I didn't. They left because you mistreated them."

"Ain't how I see it. How I see it," he sneers, moving closer, "is that you took something from me, and now, I'm going to take something from you."

Screw being nondescript. This man is out of his mind. "I need help here. Code gray, code gray!"

The words have no sooner left my mouth than his hand slides into his coat pocket, and I catch sight of the shiny muzzle of a gun. Time grinds to a halt as I stand, rooted to the spot, my flight mechanism disabled by the incomprehensible truth that this crazy son of a bitch is going to shoot me.

"Tally!" I hear Owen's voice to my right, but I'm unable to move or even turn my head.

I'm shoved to the ground as the loudest crack I've ever heard whips through the air.

For a moment, I'm not sure if I'm dead or alive. My head is ringing, my vision blurred.

With a groan, I push myself to a sitting position and catch sight of the security team tackling Earl. Then my gaze—and heart—drops to Owen on the ground, blood oozing from his chest.

"Oh my God, I need help here!" I scream, pressing my hands against the wound as I try to staunch the flow of blood. "Owen, hang on, baby. Just hang on."

His breathing turns ragged as the color drains from his face, while I frantically try to control the red life leeching from his body. "Tally..." he mumbles, his face contorted in pain.

"I'm here, Owen. I'm here. You're going to be okay."

CHAPTER FORTY

No sooner have the words left my mouth than I'm surrounded by a team of medical staff, pulling me away from the man I love.

No chance in hell of that happening. As soon as they load Owen onto the stretcher, I push to his side, clutching his hand in mine. He's so pale, his breathing so shallow.

And the blood. There's so much blood.

I have to dig deep. "I never answered you. I want to get married, Owen, as soon as we can. I want to be Mrs. Stevens. I don't want to wait another day. I love you." I press kisses to his hand and arm, feeling the slightest squeeze in response before I'm pulled back by a nurse.

"Sweetie, they have to get him into surgery. Let's get you looked at."

"I'm fine," I wail, watching the stretcher disappear into the operating suite, while I'm stuck on the other side of the glass. "I need to be with Owen."

"They're doing everything they can. You're pregnant. We have to make certain the baby is okay."

"But Owen—"

"Would want to know that you and the baby are safe."

She's right. As a nurse, I know she's right. But I'm not a nurse in this moment. I'm a terrified spouse, uncertain of my fiancée's outcome.

She leads me to a wheelchair, headed for the emergency department. I hate moving away from the operating suite door, but Owen would want me to ensure our baby is okay. I turn in the seat, grasping her hand. "I need to call his mother. Please."

"Let's get you to the ED and then I'll call her."

I'm not in the emergency bay for two minutes when Dr. Jessop bounds into the area, pulling me against him, seemingly indifferent about the blood now covering his designer shirt. "I just heard."

"I have to call his mother," I howl, as the nurse hands me a washbasin and a clean set of scrubs.

"She's on her way. Mr. Auerback sent a car to fetch her from the airport. Thankfully, she had just boarded."

"He's going to be okay, right? He needs to be okay, Ken. I can't survive without him."

He grasps my shoulders, his dark eyes solemn. "If any man has a reason to live, it's Owen. He's lost a lot of blood, but he's young and healthy. He's in excellent hands, Lu. We need to stay positive."

"I need to pray. I need to go pray." I repeat my mantra over and over, as I clean Owen's blood from my body. Part of me hesitates to remove it, as it's another link to the man I love. The man I pushed away repeatedly. How many nights did I spend alone, instead of wrapped in his arms, because of my stupid rules?

Now, I can't get that time back.

I'll tell you one thing, once Owen is well, I'm never letting him out of my sight.

When I arrive at the chapel, I sink to the floor in front of the statue of the Virgin Mary. I don't remember the last time I was in a church, or the last time I prayed. But I'm willing to give it everything I've got, if God grants Owen another chance.

"I know I haven't been here in a long time, but I'm not asking for me," I sob, my body heaving from the strength of my cries. "Owen is such a good man. He saves so many lives. He's going to be a dad. He deserves to see that; he deserves to meet our son. To hold him and watch him grow. Please don't take him away."

"Come on, dear, that's enough." Strong arms lift me from the marble floor, and I collapse against the man's chest as his hands stroke my hair. "Owen's mother just arrived. She wants to see you. Let's walk back to the waiting room."

I pull my head from my rescuer's chest and gaze into Mr. Auerback's face, lined with concern. "What are you doing here? How did you know where I was?"

"Charlotte and I were here for the meeting this morning. As for locating you, I know where I went when my wife fell ill." He regards the statue. "He hears you, even if you don't sit through mass. I

CHAPTER FORTY • 423

believe God judges our works, and if that's the case, Owen Stevens is as good a man as they come."

"I love him so much," I bawl, wiping the ceaseless stream of tears from my face.

"He loves you. There's no doubt about that, not after the way he defended you. I know it might not be the right time, but I want to apologize. You became a pawn in my daughter's game, and I hate that you got hurt."

Those issues, once insurmountable, now seem so minor. "I don't care about the job or if I'll only see him once a year. I just want Owen alive. I promised God that I would do anything to make him happy."

"Then love him. Come on, let's get you back."

I lean against the billionaire as he leads me to the waiting room. My sobs start anew when I see Mrs. Stevens collapsed in a chair, Charlotte at her side. They both stand when I enter the room, and I run to them, gathering them in a hug.

There's a lot of hurt in this room, but there's also a lot of love. Maybe, just maybe, that love will be enough to get Owen through this obstacle.

I'm putting a ton of stock in faith because it's all I have left to bargain.

Charlotte helps me to a chair, and I sit between the two women. Any other time, this would be laughable, wedged between Owen's mother and his ex-fiancée. But now, it provides a measure of comfort, something in short supply these last hours.

Mr. Auerback hands me a steaming cup of tea. "Decaf, for the baby."

I mumble my thanks, blowing on the liquid before managing a single sip down my throat. It's as though I've lost every drop of water from my body, all of it cried out in the hopes that God might hear me.

I feel a squeeze, and I gaze down to find Charlotte's hand wrapped around my fingers. Looking up, I force a smile, but only a cry emerges. "I know you love him, too. You loved him for a long time."

"I never knew how to love him. But you do, you always have." She blinks back tears, her gaze focused on the ceiling. "I thought I had dibs, you know? I knew him first. I loved him first. Who were you to come in and take what was mine? I was wrong. He was always yours."

"He loved you, Charlotte, and part of him will always love you. I'm glad you're here. We need all the positivity we can muster."

The surgeon, Dr. Empeso, aka Dr. Sleaze, walks into the waiting area, his eyes scanning the room. When they lock on mine, I pull myself to a standing position, meeting him halfway across the floor. "Hey, Lu." He nods at the rest of our sad group, before breaking into a smile. "He's one lucky son-of-a-bitch. It missed his subclavian by half an inch."

"He's going to be okay?" The tears are back again as I clutch at Dr. Empeso's forearms. "Please tell me he's going to be okay."

"He's going to be fine, Lu. They're moving him to recovery, and you can go in and see him soon." He sends me a smirk, but this time, there's only joy in his eyes. "I knew there was something between the two of you."

I join in the laughter, pointing at my belly. "Little bit."

He squeezes my hands, offering a chuckle. "Lucky bastard, all around."

I'll admit that before that moment, the idea of touching the surgeon repulsed me. But knowing that his technique and experience saved the love of my life, makes Dr. Empeso my new best friend. I throw my arms around him, pulling him into a fierce hug. "Thank you."

"He's one of us, Lu. We weren't letting him get away. If you'll excuse me, I'll be by later to check on him."

The weight of the air in the room dissipates as the surgeon exits stage right, leaving our small band to hug and release the breaths we had been collectively holding.

"How long until we can see him?" Mrs. Stevens asks, clutching my hand.

"About thirty minutes. They have to get him settled in his room."

"Is he on a ventilator?"

"He might be, but only for a short while." I pull her close, offering her my highest level of nursing comfort. "Your son is going to be okay."

"Well, since we know that Owen is going to make it, we better be on our way." Mr. Auerback motions to his daughter, extending his hand toward me. "Welcome aboard, Tallulah. It's a pleasure."

I nod, not sure what in the world the man means. "Thank you for earlier."

"Daddy, I'll be down in a minute." Charlotte turns, motioning for me to step away from the group. "Might I have a word?"

I join her in the far corner, my eyes glancing to the waiting room door every few seconds, hoping I'll see the recovery room nurse appear, letting me know I can see my Owen. "You don't have to leave. Stay, say hello."

"I'll call him in a few days. I wanted to discuss the meeting."

"Meeting?" She can't be serious right now.

"The meeting this morning. It was to offer you a new position."

I wave my hand, my gaze intent on the door. "I don't care about any position."

"I know, but it means something to Owen. There's a national position, overseeing all the accounts. It would allow you to travel and see the world. It also provides a handsome payday, more than triple the coordinator position."

Say what now?

My gaze returns to Charlotte, my jaw slack with surprise. "Owen knew about this?"

"It was one of his stipulations. He set it up with my father that night."

"That night?"

"The night Owen proposed, and I threw a tantrum. I apologize. It was such poor form, but I wanted to ruin your moment."

"You succeeded."

"I'm a class A bitch."

"Agreed. But so am I. In another life, we might have been friends."

She shrugs, a smile on her lips. "Who knows? There might still be hope for us. Take care of him, Tallulah."

"What was that about?" Mrs. Stevens inquires when I return to her side, nodding at Charlotte's retreating form.

"They offered me the nationwide coordinator position." I narrow my eyes at Owen's mother. "Did you know about this?"

"I might have heard something. Come on, dear, a mother knows. I knew you were pregnant at that dinner, too."

"Smarty pants. Now I know where your son gets it from."

"You'll have quite the life, Tally. You'll be living the jet set with that job."

I nod, but the glitter of hobnobbing around the world doesn't hold any appeal. Not anymore.

CHAPTER FORTY-ONE

TALLY

TALLY

Hospital chairs are not conducive to sleep, but I'm so weary from the day's events that I pass out with my hand wrapped around Owen's fingers. His mother sits on the opposite side of the bed, crocheting yet another baby blanket.

Hey, it soothes her nerves, and at the rate she's going, our son will have a fresh blanket for each day of the month.

"Tally..."

My eyes fly open at the sound of Owen's voice. He's looking at me, his fingers moving against mine. I know he's dopey from the pain medication, but his eyes are clear. Those gorgeous gray skies that live in my Owen.

"Hey, baby, you're awake." I lean over him, pressing a kiss to his forehead. "You scared us."

"Scared myself for a minute. I much prefer to be on the doctor end of the doctor patient relationship."

I giggle, my hand stroking his scalp. He's here. He's still here.

He turns his head, offering a smile to his mother. "Hey, Mom."

That's all it took for the levee to break. As soon as the words leave

Owen's mouth, Mrs. Steven's calm facade crumbles and she collapses at his bedside.

"I'm okay, Mom. I promise." Poor Owen, he's a gunshot victim and yet he's reassuring his mother.

"I'm sorry, it's just seeing you like this, hurts my heart." She takes the tissues I offer her, wiping her eyes. It doesn't matter that her son is thirty-eight. He's her baby boy, now and forever.

I rest my hand on my belly, smiling down at Nugget. I get her pain. I understand the desire to shield this angel from everything life tosses our way, and the helplessness you feel when you lose any semblance of control.

Owen reaches up his fingers, tracing along my belly. "Are you two okay?"

I nod, stepping closer to the bedrail to allow him easier access. "We're fine. Scared to death about you, but fine."

Owen clears his throat, a flash of pain crossing his features.

"I'll go speak with your nurse, see if I can get you some ice chips and pain medicine."

His mom needs a few minutes with her son, and I need to pee—for the millionth time today.

Ten minutes later, I return to the room, a smile lighting my face. Right on the money. Mrs. Stevens is busy fussing over her son, fluffing his pillow and tucking in the edges of his blanket like a burrito. Finally, she sighs and shakes her head, her gaze moving between the two of us. "I know, you want me out of here, so you two can canoodle."

"Owen is definitely not canoodling for a while," I chuckle, watching my man wince when laughter reverberates through his body.

"Still, you two need a minute. I'll be in the waiting room."

The door isn't even closed before I climb into the bed next to him, careful to avoid any lines or wires. Protocol? Bite me.

I burrow my head against his chest and sob.

CHAPTER FORTY-ONE

His arm wraps around my body, and despite the pain, he presses a kiss to my head. "It's okay, Darlin. I'm okay."

I meet his gaze, tears running down my face. "You took a bullet for me. You saved my life. Owen, you could have died."

He thumbs away my tears, shaking his head. "I'd do it again, every damn day, to keep you two safe. Let's hope it doesn't come to that, though."

I chuckle, pressing kisses through his gown. "Only you would joke right now."

"I damn near died. Can you think of a better time to laugh?"

"I prayed. I went to the chapel and begged for you to be okay. I promised God all sorts of things."

"Anything interesting?"

"I may have mentioned oral sex daily for the next decade."

"I am so collecting on that promise."

I kiss his chin, more than happy to give the man whatever he wants. "You better. Charlotte and Mr. Auerback just left. They said they'll call in a few days, but if you need anything to let them know."

"I hope they were good to you."

"They were. Both of them." I settle against his chest again, feeling like I can finally breathe. "Charlotte told me about the position."

"Your position?"

I nod, toying with the leads on his heart monitor. "That's quite the illustrious role. She said it was one of your demands. I'm sorry I doubted you."

"I know how it must have looked, but I always had your best interests at heart, Tally."

"I finally get that. Sorry it took me so long."

"It's okay."

"Good." Here comes the big announcement. "While I appreciate being offered such a job, I'm going to have to turn it down."

His eyes narrow in confusion. "Why?"

I bury my head in his chest, loving the smell that is intrinsically

Owen. My Owen. "I have a couple of positions I want to explore, outside of cardiac nursing."

"Tally, are you leaving Memorial?"

I meet his bewildered stare and nod.

"What positions? Another hospital?"

"No."

"Okay, mysterious Sphinx. Talk."

I trace along the planes of his face, hoping he can feel the emotion in every touch. "I love taking care of people. It's what I do. But I'd like to focus on two specific people."

"What are you saying?"

"I think you should take the position at Regent Hospital. Move back to Asheville and be close to your family."

He stiffens beneath me as he struggles to sit up. "Tally, I'm not leaving you."

I stroke his chest, calming him. "Who said anything about leaving me? I'm going with you, but not as a nurse. I want to spend the next few years as a wife and mother."

He grabs my hand, pressing it against his lips. "You don't want to see the world? Live the glamorous life?"

I shake my head. "Nah, I'm the punk chick, remember? Besides, I will see the world, with my husband, and our children." His expression is so unreadable, I only hope I haven't angered him with my decision. After all, he went through an enormous hassle to deliver that position on a silver platter. "Is that okay?"

A grin splits his face, and I have my answer. "Tally, that's perfect."

EPILOGUE

TALY

It took Owen a month to recover from the gunshot wound, although he was up and around our condo after only a few days.

When Dr. Stevens re-entered the halls of Memorial Hospital a month later, he was no longer a single man. Good to my word, we got our marriage certificate and were married ten days after the shooting. Now, he has a petite, sarcastic edged wife, who also waddles with the grace of a hippo.

My husband is a saint.

We've decided to stay in Florida until after our son is born, which pleases Stefani to no end. She claims to be throwing the biggest baby shower the world has ever seen.

I'm threatening to boycott the event.

I'm kidding. Kind of.

Although it will be hard leaving our friends, we know that Asheville is the place to raise our family. Hell, we haven't even had this baby, and Owen is already planning the next few. I told him that's fine, so long as *he* carries them this time.

Regent Hospital is thrilled to have a doctor of Owen's caliber joining their ranks; his Mom is thrilled her son is coming home.

Me? I'm ecstatic about my new family, and terrified at the idea that I have to give birth to this baby, and there is no hole large enough on my body. Owen finds the entire situation amusing, reassuring me I'll be my kick-ass self in the delivery room.

I assure him I'll be on drugs and have little to no memory of the event.

I'm fairly certain I'm not winning that battle either.

Life and work with Owen is now a thing of beauty. I just had to let it exist, as it was always meant to. I bask in our mutual admiration, chuckling at our co-worker's sarcastic comments about how sickening our loved-up displays are to the rest of the world. But I know better. They're thrilled by the turn of events.

Hell, even Charlotte sent us a wedding gift, and I'm almost positive it's not tainted with any form of poison. *Almost* positive.

The one person who did not like the news? Dr. Nicole Hedges, but she found herself a new love interest in the form of Ken Jessop. I guess it all worked out.

All you need is love. A plethora of love.

And a man who can deliver over the top orgasms, but that goes without saying.

Hello Lovelies,

I suppose at this point, you know that I adore big, angst-filled steamy romances. I believe that novels should be a rollercoaster event, winding and twisting throughout the plot. Owen and Tally certainly deliver on that promise.

God, I love Tally. She is such a marshmallow with a tough girl exterior. And the heat between these two? It was a delicious undertaking, telling their story.

Anyone up for an exclusive extended epilogue? Curious to know about the wedding, the baby, and any additional drama Owen and Tally kick up? I'm putting the finishing touches on this tasty morsel, which will only be available to my newsletter subscribers, so be sure to sign up and get in on *all* the goodies and giveaways.

Join my mailing list here!

I've also included an excerpt from another one of my standalone novels, **Make You Stay**. Slow burn friends to lovers with a gorgeous lumberjack type—yummy. Be sure to look for it at the end!

One last favor—if you loved **Forgot to Tell You Something**, don't forget to tell everyone! See what I did there? LOL. Seriously though, lovelies, reviews are greatly appreciated (I've included the links below). They're like gold to an author.

AMAZON

BOOKBUB

GOODREADS

Best wishes for a life well-lived. Until we meet again.

M.L. BROOME

Also by M.L. Broome

Make You Stay

Friends to Lovers / Opposites Attract / Single Dad

And Then Came You

Friends to Lovers / Slow Burn / Celebrity Romance

Alchemy Unfolding

Reverse Age Gap / Sexy Surfer / Medical Romance

Forgot to Tell You Something

High Angst / Surprise Pregnancy / Medical Romance

A Series of Moments Trilogy Box Set

High Angst / Celebrity Romance / Medical Romance

Baby Maker (Cocky Hero Club)

Young Widow / Forbidden Romance / Love After Loss

Hook Up (KB Worlds)

Brother's Best Friend / Reverse Age Gap / Racing Romance

A Sinner's Memory (Leave Me Breathless)

Rockstar Romance / Second Chance / Single Dad

Yuletide Acres

Yule Holiday Romance / Second Chance / Single Dad

It Must Have Been the Mistletoe

Christmas Romance / Second Chance / Sexy Drummer

CONNECT WITH M.L. BROOME

Sign up for my newsletter!
(Freebies, Giveaways & Subscriber Exclusives)

BookBub

GoodReads

Amazon Author Page

TikTok

Facebook

Instagram

About the Author

I'm a bohemian spirit with a New York edge. I adore dressing up and kicking back, a nice glass of wine with an equally stunning view, and experiences that make the soul--and mouth--water.

When I'm not writing or holding one-sided arguments with my characters (spoiler alert—they always win), I love losing myself in nature on my North Carolina farm, one of my rescue buddies at my side.

Life is beautiful...so are you. Don't forget to look up. Peace, love, & magic.

"You'll climb as high as you dare believe you are capable. The stars are only as far as we imagine them to be, and time is neither friend nor foe. Magic is everywhere. Life is a thing of beauty."

MAKE YOU STAY

The phone slips from my grip, smacking against the floorboards with a thud, but I make no move to retrieve it.

Instead, I shift my gaze to the suitcase yawning on my bed, empty save for a box of photos and trinkets. Items I planned to share during my visit now serve as a mocking reminder that my upcoming vacation to Asheville is no *longer* a vacation.

Some part of me isn't even surprised at this macabre turn of events. It is *my* life, after all, and the gods seem fit to use it as fodder for their twisted senses of humor.

Slinking into the living area, I glare at the lights twinkling around my window, right next to the four-foot artificial tree I insist on putting up every year in my shoebox-sized Manhattan apartment.

I'm fully aware it's only November, but I'm one of *those* people who set up for Christmas before Thanksgiving arrives. Despite the latent commercialism, I adore the holiday season—the festivities and chaotic excitement flowing through the city warms my soul even as the northeast winds threaten to freeze me whole.

At least I *did* enjoy the season until the phone call a few moments earlier, which upended my equilibrium.

For the first time in twenty-four years, I planned to spend the Thanksgiving holiday with my mother.

Instead, I'll be attending her funeral.

She never mentioned any upcoming surgery, but I'm hardly surprised. Betsey and I rarely said much to each other. That was the point of this trip—reconnecting and rekindling our relationship, which died out years ago.

No chance of that, now.

The tears threaten to overpower me, clogging any other emotion from reaching the surface as my mind tries to reconcile the unfairness of this situation.

Granted, fairness was never a cornerstone of my life, thanks in part to Betsey. My mother, according to those who knew her when, was an unforgettable spirit. I'll tell you one thing, she was good at forgetting me, but that's a conversation for another time.

A one-sided conversation now.

With a sigh, I drag myself back to the bedroom. No point in wasting time wondering about what might have been.

Might have been is a terrible term, reminding people of all their lost chances and wrong choices.

Better to focus on the present and the task at hand. Namely, rethinking my wardrobe for this trip.

Originally, I planned on staying a few weeks, but now, it's anyone's guess. Her lawyer informed me that Betsey left me everything, not that I know what *everything* entails. I have the task of sorting her estate and putting up for sale the home I now own in the mountains of North Carolina.

The only saving grace in this situation? Betsey pre-planned her funeral, down to the last detail. She also paid for everything in advance, not that money is a problem. I make plenty of green as a freelance writer and can more than afford her burial costs.

The bigger issue? I don't know Betsey, except on a superficial level. Things that a daughter should know—her favorite color, food, and song—are all mysteries to me. To be fair, she doesn't know mine either.

Didn't know mine.

This whole past tense, when referring to Betsey, is going to take some getting used to, although she never was a constant in my life. Now that chance has flown away like autumn leaves in a November breeze.

Per her lawyer, who claims to have known Betsey for decades, she was a spitfire, and her memorial service will reflect that vibrant energy. At least I don't have to bumble my way through a generic service, which is the best I can offer with my limited knowledge.

How do you plan a memorial for a woman who's noticeably absent from your memories?

Thankfully for me, I don't.

Now all I have to do is fly to Asheville a few days earlier than originally planned.

How hard can it be? I live in Manhattan. Our airports carry thousands of passengers all around the world, every day.

Two hours and a martini later, I have my answer. I also have a flight to Asheville, with a three-hour layover in Virginia. Simple enough, especially for someone who has traveled around the globe.

The caveat? Mother nature is behaving like an uncooperative bitch. The meteorologists are calling for an unseasonably early snowstorm in the Appalachians on the same day I'm scheduled to fly out.

Per the airline reservation attendant, they're hoping to beat the storm, but, and I'm quoting here, it's anyone's guess how it will turn out.

Not instilling great confidence with that statement, and judging by my recent run of luck, I don't stand a chance for things to go smoothly.

WANT TO READ MORE? TRUST ME, IF YOU LOVE SPICY BANTER AND

flirtations, you need to finish this baby. Grab Make You Stay today!

Made in the USA
Columbia, SC
08 July 2023